FLAMESEEKER

Also by Rachel Terry

<u>The Guardians Duology</u>

Lightbringer

Flameseeker

FLAMESEEKER

GUARDIANS DUOLOGY BOOK 2

RACHEL TERRY

PHARUS PRESS

For information, contact: https://www.rachel-terry.com

Cover art by Coco Merwild

www.cjmerwild.com

Cover design by Rena Violet

www.coversbyviolet.com

Map made with Inkarnate

ISBN: 978-1-960519-03-0

10 9 8 7 6 5 4 3 2 1

To Dad.

I am so glad you got to read this story at least once.

(Even though that draft was probably terrible.)

I hope you would be proud.

Wysteria
Water Gate
Grasslands
The Green Sea
Lightning Gate
The Necropolis
The Swamps of Malenwar
The Briarwood

Ice Gate
Arctic Bay
Iceland
Ice Palace
The Glowing Gate
Flame Gate
Enchanted Forest
The Great Desert
Khae
Wind Gate

COMMON ELEMENTS

FIRE

EARTH

WATER

AIR

UNCOMMON ELEMENTS

LIGHTNING

ICE

RARE ELEMENTS

LIGHT

DARKNESS*

*According to the chronicles of Lumyn, darkness is considered a corruption of one of the other elements, caused by the practice of dark magic, and not an element in and of itself. Due to the forbidden nature of dark magic, it is therefore a rare occurrence.

1

Screams echoed in the air as Damaris ran, the cobblestones clattering beneath her hooves. The impact jarred her legs, but she did not stop, did not slow. It might already be too late.

The citizens of Malenwar ran toward her, bumping into her, in their desperation to flee the city that had been their home for so long. They moved past in a blur, no time for Damaris to snatch more than a few details. Some clutched meager belongings, weighing them down. Others carried babies and dragged sobbing children behind them.

At such high speed, Damaris risked colliding with them. They were elves, their forms lithe, and she a unicorn, larger and faster than a horse. Her black hooves could easily trample them to death if she wasn't careful, but this was no time for caution.

The winding streets of Malenwar proved an additional hazard. She skidded, slowing, as a family suddenly appeared from a side street, stepping into her path. They cried out at the sight of her, cringing, but she twisted at the last moment and managed to avoid them.

And then they were gone, her hooves once again ringing on the stone. Everywhere she looked there was stone, the city made of it. Flags hung limp, waiting for a breeze, bearing the symbolic sword and tree of Malenwar.

Where were all these people going? What were they fleeing from?

Damaris knew that Lylla had received word early that day that Galatea and Jack had been spotted, holed up somewhere in the warren of mazes that was Malenwar. Cassius and Cyren had gone off together and no one had seen them since. It gave Damaris a bad feeling. God only knew what those fools had done.

Weeks of conflict had now finally led to this. She knew Galatea would not give Jack up. She was too stubborn—typical earth attribute—for that. But neither would Cassius and Cyren stand to have a human in Wysteria. It was not a world meant for them. Was that not why they had sealed themselves off from the humans centuries ago?

For her part, Damaris had no preference. But something needed to be done. This impasse was not sustainable. The combination of the stubborn siblings and a bull-headed Earth Guardian was one sure to end in blows.

But who else would be caught in the crossfire? That was what worried Damaris now.

The screaming intensified the further she ran into the city, nearing its center. She slowed to a halt, inhaling deeply, her lungs burning as she surveyed the scene laid out before her. What had they done?

The elves of Malenwar continued to flee all around her, terror written across their faces. "Go," she called to them. "Hurry!"

Jack had already been instructed to return to his own world, but he had refused, and Galatea had made it abundantly clear that she would do nothing to persuade him. Nor would she go with him, which she could have easily done, damn her pride.

What would Galatea do if the decision were taken away from her?

What would she do if *Jack* were taken from her? Whether intentionally or a mere accident…

The thought sent a chill through Damaris that had nothing to do with the sweat that had gathered on her coat. She raised her head at the sight of green light, flaring above the distant rooftops. The Earth Gate being opened?

Her eyes widened, heart painfully faltering, skipping a beat. In that moment she knew, sure as anything, what Galatea was about to do. Whatever Cassius and Cyren or anyone else had done, it was far worse than Damaris could have imagined.

"No," she murmured, taking a step toward the fading light. But even as she did so, she knew she would be too late. The Earth Gate was too far.

All at once, the light flared, blinding in its intensity. Damaris was forced to close her eyes, look away.

"No!" she screamed.

She had the foresight to shapeshift in the last moment available to her, taking on her human form to make herself a smaller target. The explosion was initially silent, the shockwave radiating outward and the sound only catching up later. The air was torn from Damaris's lungs as the force threw her back. She would have gasped as her back collided with the cobblestone street if she'd had any breath left.

Eyes narrowed in pain, she looked up in time to see the stone buildings blow outward, shattering into a million pieces. She covered her head as hunks of rock were sent plummeting back to earth, shaking the ground beneath her.

Only when the ground stopped trembling did Damaris open her eyes, uncurling herself from her defensive position.

The city, which had been ringing with screams and cries only moments before, was now deathly silent aside from the settling of rubble. Not all of the buildings had collapsed. A few remained frozen moments after the explosion had hit, their shattered pieces suspended in midair, motionless.

Damaris blinked. It didn't make any sense. It was unnatural. Wincing, she gingerly got to her feet, staring at the dust rising around her. And now the cries resumed, hundreds of voices taking up the call, merging into one protracted wail as people cried out in pain or grief.

Her eyes fell upon a pile of rubble not thirty feet from where she stood. The building had collapsed on itself and there, peeking out from beneath, was a pale forearm. Whether it was attached to anything, Damaris couldn't say.

For a long moment, it was all she could do to stand there, trying to process what had just happened. The Earth Gate had been destroyed, but what did that mean really? A Gate had never been destroyed before.

There was something about the sight of that pale, lifeless arm and the screams ringing in her ears, that jolted Damaris into motion. Whatever had occurred here, it was a disaster and they would have time to dwell on it later. Right now there were people who needed help. She was the Flame Guardian, damn it all. She had seen far worse than this.

Damaris stumbled over to the pile of rubble and spread her hands, lifting the heavy stones into the air. It was as she'd feared, the body beneath crushed and broken. Lowering her hands, she let the stones fall to the ground on either side. And then she staggered towards the nearest cries, praying that not every outcome would be the same.

Damaris blinked, the flashback fading, as she found herself once more in the swamps, amid the ruins of what had once been Malenwar. The city had been destroyed in a single instant of madness, over fifty years ago. Looking at the ruins now, it was difficult to believe more time hadn't passed. And yet that night felt like only yesterday.

Only yesterday she had run among the ruins of a once-proud city, searching for survivors and offering what comfort she could to those who had been left behind. It had been one of the longest nights of her life. Everything had changed in that moment and they were all still paying the price.

Damaris sighed. Even now, this place still exerted a powerful influence over her.

Avoiding the swamp water as best she could, Damaris continued further into the ruins. It had been only a handful of days since she had confronted Galatea and blown up the Professor's house. His loss, and the other losses they had suffered, still cut deep.

Let this be an end to it. Let it be over. But Damaris knew better than that. They had assumed Galatea dead last time, fifty years ago, after she had betrayed her oath and destroyed her own Gate. The very Gate she was sworn to protect.

Whether Galatea was at last dead or not, Damaris wasn't taking any chances. The bodies that lay scattered at her feet were certainly dead enough—or they had been, until Galatea had resurrected them as mindless thralls. Desecrating the dead of Malenwar was yet one more injustice, one more insult to injury that she had caused them.

Damaris paused, the nearest body mere inches from her hooves. Wordlessly, she called upon her fire and set it alight, burning so hot it was rendered ash in seconds.

It was taxing work, searching for all the undead Galatea had left behind and incinerating them so she could never again hope to raise them. But someone needed to do it.

Never again would they do her bidding.

The same fate had befallen Jack. And now the human that never should have set foot in Wysteria would never live again.

Damaris sighed and moved on to the next body.

2

Galatea stumbled as she stepped through the Wind Gate, back onto her own side once again. She placed a hand on the wall of the Golden Temple to steady herself, breathing heavily. After months trapped on Earth, biding her time, it had taken more out of her than she would have liked.

Her time spent on Earth had weakened her and constantly having to maintain a glamour did nothing to help that. There was no longer any chance she could go about undisguised. Not only would she risk being recognized, but her new appearance would draw unwanted attention. Damaris had seen to that. Galatea reached up with one hand, tracing the skin on the left side of her face.

In her last confrontation with the Flame Guardian, the skin had been seared away, leaving uneven pitted burn scars. They lanced up from her left shoulder all the way to her scalp, leaving half the hair burned away on that side. No longer was she beautiful the way an elf should be. The elf that Jack had known and fallen in love with was no longer recognizable.

Jack. The thought of him brought a familiar pain to her chest and she closed her eyes against it. Where once it had been a searing, stabbing wound, now it had faded to a dull ache, which was somehow even worse.

She had done everything for him, suffered so much, and look where it had gotten her. Even her appearance, her ruined beauty, had been one more sacrifice that in the end had meant nothing at all.

But that was then, and this was now and she was here now because of all of that. It wasn't over—not yet—but it was time to finish it. There would be an end to it, one way or another.

Galatea straightened up, feeling her heart rate start to slow as her magic began to return. Wysteria's magic was as vibrant as ever, flowing through her like a living, breathing thing.

She looked around at her surroundings, wishing that her faithful fire wolf, Venryk, could be there with her. At first, she had felt uncertain what her course of action should be. All of her soldiers had no doubt been destroyed in the interim—that's what she would have done in their place— and she was once again without an army. If she were going to take on Queen Lylla and the Guardians, she would need one.

But then, in the long dark nights she'd had to dwell on things, inspiration had struck from an old legend. Perhaps she was too weak to pull off such a lofty idea, but if she succeeded, perhaps she wouldn't even need an army after all.

She stood in a large room, the cavernous ceiling stretching high above her head. It was dark, no windows in the building. It was a shrine. The Gate was commonly referred to as the Golden Temple and it was appropriately named, for every surface seemed to glimmer. The air was slightly stale, heavy with dust or sand particles from the desert. One could almost believe that no one had ventured within in a long time.

Galatea strode forward, heading for the entrance at the far end. The doorway was always open, lacking a door of any kind, and this allowed sand to blow in. She could feel the grains beneath her bare feet, scattered along the floor. Through the open doorway, she could see little.

As she moved, what little light there was caught on the symbols and runes covering the walls, sending multi-colored hues flashing. The floor tiles, which may once have been white and blue, were now a dingy tan and cracked in places, worn with age and the passing of time.

The walls on either side of her were coated with artwork. She peered at it with mild interest as she walked. Most of the drawings included symbols of the seven main elements; she noticed with a flicker of annoyance that her element, darkness, was not included.

Her original element, earth, was represented, but that was long gone, replaced by something darker and more powerful. Something that most were simply too scared to pursue. Their cowardice held them back.

Other images depicted desert elves, recognizable by their dark skin tones and snow-white hair, along with four winged, serpent-like creatures. One was blue, one green, one white, and the final a golden yellow. Beneath each beast, symbols had been carved into the wall, faint and unreadable. But Galatea knew the stories and thus knew the meanings.

They had brought her here after all.

In one picture, a solitary desert elf stood before three of the writhing serpents, arms raised. In the next drawing, the creatures were gone, replaced by the fourth. The golden dragon.

Everyone knew the story, whether they believed or not.

Many centuries ago, the first elf ventured into the desert. His name was Rehan and he was one of the first of what would come to be known as the desert elves. He had come into the desert hoping to establish a place for his people to live, but he soon discovered his presence did not go unnoticed. For the desert was a wild land, ancient and unwilling to be tamed. For centuries, it had belonged to none but the elements and they were not willing to relinquish control.

Rehan was a powerful elementalist of his time. He had not embarked very far into the desert when he was confronted by the four desert winds: the four powerful serpents depicted on the walls. A wise elf may have turned back, but Rehan was stubborn and determined for his people to make the desert their home. One by one, he managed to subjugate each of the winds, bending them to his will.

He began by taming the most aggressive of the wind spirits. The sisters, North, with the coldest temperament and West, the most aggressive, were the first to fall. The first brother, South, the green dragon, was captured next.

South, West, and North.

But legend had it that one spirit resisted. Rehan captured three of the winds, but was unable to tame the fourth. The golden dragon remained. Rehan had left the Eastern Wind, Azuma, to capture last, because of all the winds, East was the most serene and Rehan believed his calmer personality would prove little challenge.

Rehan was mistaken.

Such was the wrath of the Eastern Wind at the capture of his siblings that Rehan was unable to subdue him and lost his life in the process. But the damage had been done. The three captured wind spirits had faded from the realm and only Azuma remained. The desert elves were able to settle in their new home, but the Eastern Wind never forgot what their forebearer had done. And to this day, the desert people claim that storms always came from the east.

Now, every year on the anniversary of the event, pilgrims came from all reaches of the desert to bring offerings to the Temple, in order to appease the restless spirit of the Eastern Wind.

Galatea had no way of knowing which day the pilgrimage and subsequent festival fell on, having lost track of the days while on Earth. The closer she crept to the entrance, she could hear the wind whipping outside, rising to a guttural howl. She smiled to herself.

The tapestries dangling high overhead flapped madly, threatening to tear free. She crouched behind the massive statue of Azuma himself and peered at the entrance. It was hard to make out anything through the swirling sand, but she didn't see any guards. Kadir, the Gate's former Guardian, would no longer pose a threat to her. She had sliced his head cleanly off his shoulders upon their last meeting. Her hand went instinctively to the Shadowblade at her side, but it would be of little use here.

She didn't see any offerings or gifts placed around the base of the statue or cascading across the floor. Either the festival hadn't happened yet or she had missed it entirely.

Nor could she see any guards at all and she wondered if the tempest had forced them to seek shelter elsewhere. *Or perhaps Azuma has already killed them.*

Rehan had died long before she had been born. Galatea had never known him, but she tried to think how he would have gone about the daunting task of subjugating the wind spirits. Rising from behind the statue, she began walking toward the entrance, head held high.

Whatever came of this night, she would not be afraid. She had already lost everything that mattered to her; there was nothing left to lose.

The wind tore at her hair and she flinched, blinking to keep sand out of her eyes. As soon as she was clear of the temple, she gasped, staggering as the full force of the gale struck her. The sand thrown up by the storm's rage lashed at the exposed skin on her neck, face, and forearms, the sharp grains cutting at her. The wind's wailing itself sounded to her like the shrieks of some great beast.

And in a way, it was.

The creature at the center of the tempest was not an icy white, cool blue, or malachite green, but golden amber. What she could see of the creature through the darkness and swirling sand was limited, but she managed to make out solid, glowing gold eyes. The beast seemed to hover above her, floating as though made of air itself, its yellow underbelly flashing.

Its four-fingered hands flexed and clenched, huge fangs bared, whiskers flowing. The wind spirits had always reminded Galatea of the eastern dragons of Earth, except these dragons had wings as well. She could see them now—large and white and feathered—beating the air powerfully.

Azuma. Spirit of the Eastern Wind and what she had come for.

Despite the wind lashing at her, she did not move, though Azuma continued to pump his wings, body undulating in the wind. Peering into his eyes was like staring into a pool of molten gold, alight as though a fire burned within.

She was daring to do what no one else but Rehan had done. Galatea had no way of knowing how he'd done it, but she did have one weapon at her disposal he'd never had.

Galatea had created her fire wolves, imbuing ordinary wolves with fire itself. She'd done something similar last year, when she'd resurrected the horses of Malenwar, imbuing them with darkness, and creating her Nightmares.

Why should a wind spirit be any different?

She reached out with her hand, toward the dragon, never once taking her gaze off of his or allowing herself to blink. She could feel the spirit's power, its consciousness and latched onto it.

Darkness sprang up around her, lashing itself around the wind spirit. Azuma reared back, letting out a shriek as the darkness enveloped him. The wind lessened, the dragon futilely beating his wings against the darkness. The light behind his eyes dimmed.

No longer was this a creature of air alone, but also darkness.

This was not a test of physical strength but of magic and of will.

Galatea felt the rage that was always with her, simmering just beneath the surface, begin to rise and she let it, adding fuel to her magic. She could feel the wind spirit's own rage, wild, untamed, and unending, but hers was stronger still. That was why she would triumph over the serpent. She had not endured all that she had, only to fail now.

She thought back to the events of a year ago, last summer. How she had obtained a tome of spells that would allow her to resurrect her dead lover, Jack. How she had succeeded, after overcoming numerous setbacks. She thought of how Jack had looked at her, not with joy, but in horror.

His words returned to her, echoing like a whisper in her ear, so close she would have believed he stood behind her shoulder and she nearly turned to see. *What have you done?*

What have you done? They were the words that echoed in her mind at night when sleep would not come. That haunted her just as much as Jack's dead face had.

And then Damaris, the Flame Guardian, had arrived and Jack was murdered once more. She had incinerated his body so that there were no remains left for her to resurrect ever again.

That was the image she saw when she closed her eyes, as though seared on the back of the lids, and seared forever in her mind. Jack, retreating not away from the flames, but toward them as his body was consumed.

Galatea let out a cry, pouring all of her pain and fury into the darkness. It had nearly broken her completely, the knowledge that he was truly gone now, forever beyond her reach.

Instead, it had brought her here and she would see that they paid for what each of them had done. All of them.

She remembered even further back. It was like purposely probing a wound to see if it still hurt, only instead of merely probing, she dug deep, channeling it all into her magic. Emotions could be a powerful thing if one knew how to use them.

Over fifty years ago she had met Jack on Earth. He'd been a soldier, wounded in the Vietnam War and recently discharged back home. At that time, he'd been willing to die, desperate to be healed, but finding no such result on Earth. Galatea had taken him with her to Wysteria and his paralyzed arm had been restored.

He had wanted to stay, enamored with the new world he found himself in, but the other Guardians insisted she take him back to Earth where he belonged. She had refused and they had murdered him for it.

Simply because he had been a human and not a Guardian like them. But oh, they were more than willing to accept a human if they were a Guardian. What difference did it make ultimately? They were nothing more than hypocrites, the lot of them.

And that was when she felt it: the dragon weakening.

The wind died completely, sand settling back to earth. The sudden drop in pressure made Galatea's ears pop. The connection Galatea had felt earlier was now solid as a chain, linking her to the wind spirit in much the same way as she shared a link with her wolves. The darkness was of her and now it was a part of the wind spirit, corrupting it and binding it to her will.

The dragon vanished, as if he had become air itself, but Galatea could still feel his presence with her and knew that at any moment, he could return, at her beck and call. His power was hers to call upon.

She let out a shaky breath, not realizing how much magic she had used until now. Her anger drained away, leaving her exhausted and scoured out. But she knew it was still there, below the surface, waiting as always.

Galatea stood there for a few moments, staring out at the desolate desert laid before her. With the storm having died down, she could make out the sky, no longer blocked by the swirling sand. It was clear, the stars twinkling coldly up above.

The city of Khae stood in the distance, lit with a golden glow even at this late hour. The people were going about their business, completely oblivious to what had just transpired beneath their very noses.

Galatea chuckled to herself, heading away from the temple and further out into the endless desert. She needed to be long gone by the time the guards returned now that the storm was over.

How long it would take them to realize what she had done was anyone's guess.

The spirit of the Eastern Wind came and went as he pleased and so his absence would not be noticed until it was too late.

I do not need an army, Galatea thought, staring out at the rolling dunes. She had the spirit of air itself at her disposal.

3

Sara let out a huff of frustration, blinking her eyes rapidly to try and get them to focus. She had been concentrating so hard, her vision had begun to swim. She lowered her hand, the muscles in her arm quivering slightly.

The training dummy at the end of the field bore only a small singe mark in the center of its chest, and that had only come after multiple attempts to burn it. Lylla stood off to one side, slightly behind Sara, her arms behind her back. Her posture was straight yet seemingly at ease, the picture of elegance. It was difficult to discern her expression, but Sara thought she looked concerned.

Lylla's long blue hair was tamed into three braids and the sunlight shimmered on her tan skin, little lights glimmering in her hair as though it were woven with jewels. Sara felt awkward, hot and dirty in comparison.

"I can't do it," she panted, pushing her own braid back over her shoulder. Her brown hair had turned dark with sweat. She could feel loose strands clinging to her temple, sweat rolling down her back.

What she wanted most right now, more than anything—even more than to burn the target like she was supposed to—was a bath and a nap. Where the summer sun could not beat down on her mercilessly.

"Try one more time," Lylla encouraged. She seemed to have more faith in Sara than she herself did.

Suppressing a sigh, Sara straightened back up. She had one more attempt left in her. She could do this.

Last summer, Wysteria had quite literally invaded Sara's life, interrupting her small-town existence. At first, she'd thought she didn't fit in, in this strange and beautiful world filled with magic, since she had none of her own. After all, humans didn't have magic unless they were Guardians, beings who could control more than one element and were tasked with protecting the Gates that led between the two worlds.

But she'd been wrong. She did have magic and it had revealed itself. Her element was light, the rarest of them all and because she was also a Guardian, she could look forward to training the other elements once she'd mastered her main attribute.

Or so she'd thought.

Sara's senior year of high school had come and gone. During her spare time, she had come to Wysteria to practice and now that summer was here, she had the entirety of each day free to hone her skills and become the Guardian she was meant to be.

Focusing on the dummy in front of her, Sara channeled her magic, willing the light to spring forth and burn her target. A faint glow rose to the surface of her palm, feebly trying to strengthen its intensity. But Sara had no energy left to channel the skill and the glow died out.

She had reached the end of her limit, at least for now, but the thought gave her little comfort. Even before expending herself, she'd had very little reaction from her magic whenever she called upon it.

She felt tears of frustration spring to her eyes. Surely by now, this should have gotten easier?

Lylla approached her. "That's enough for today. You did well."

"How can you say that?" Sara exclaimed, her exasperation getting the better of her. The last thing she wanted was to take out her frustration on her mentor—who had become far closer to being a friend over the months, to say nothing of the fact that Lylla was queen. "I haven't made any progress at all. Last year, I could blind my enemies and now I can barely find my way in a darkened room."

"It takes time," Lylla said gently. Her blue dress moved gently in the wind, a few strands of her turquoise hair escaping its braids. "You had the Echo Stone to help you before. Now that it's gone, your magic is going to resist you more. None of us achieved mastery over our skills overnight."

They'd had this discussion before. Sara knew that her magic would be harder to control without the aid of the Echo Stone, an amplifier which made it easier to perform more complicated magic while using less energy.

Lylla had told her once before that it had taken centuries for some of the other Guardians to evolve into the powerful warriors they now were. Since humans didn't age in Wysteria, theoretically, Sara had all the time in the world.

"But I need to improve faster," she murmured. "What if Galatea comes back tomorrow and I'm still not ready?"

Something darkened within Lylla's gaze. "She has yet to show her hand, if she's even alive at all."

But they all knew better than to assume otherwise. Galatea had been believed dead before, for fifty years, only for her to prove them devastatingly wrong.

"Go take a break," Lylla added, putting an end to the conversation. "You've earned it."

Sara turned and trudged through the grass toward the massive palace, wishing, not for the first time, that she could have half as much confidence in herself as Lylla seemed to have in her. *Some Guardian I am. Pathetic.*

As she rounded the corner of the building, she saw Felix heading toward the stairs to the main entrance. He stopped as he spotted her and waited for her to reach him. His crimson hair was damp like hers, pale skin glistening with sweat from his own training session.

"No luck?" he asked, taking in her expression, already familiar with her struggles.

She had vented to him when she felt overwhelmed and he had mostly listened without giving his opinion, simply letting her express her frustration. He'd offered encouragement at times, when she'd needed it, no stranger to setbacks of his own.

"No," Sara answered, hating how petulant her voice sounded to her own ears. "It's not getting any easier."

He knew why it mattered to her so much, what was at stake, and how she had come to choose this path for herself in the first place.

Both of the Wind Gate's Guardians were dead. Like the Lightning and Ice Gates, it had come out on the Earth side in Sara's small town, forever changing the way she viewed Mayfair. Professor Lawrence, who had guarded the Wind Gate on her side, had been killed at the conclusion of last summer, struck down by Galatea.

And it was all Sara's fault.

The sorceress had needed Sara's Echo Stone amplifier to bring her dead lover back to life. Foolishly believing Galatea would let the Professor go unharmed if Sara handed it over to her, Sara had done precisely that—only to lose both the amplifier and a family friend in the span of one night.

It was a foolish decision that haunted her to this day and a piercing pain twisted in her chest at the memory of it. And yet…as much as she blamed herself for it, Sara didn't see how the outcome could have been any different. With her magic as weak as it was, she certainly couldn't have stopped Galatea on her own.

What was done was done and couldn't be undone now. Believing otherwise was what had led them all to this mess in the first place.

So Sara had done the only thing she *could* do, the one thing she thought Professor Lawrence would have approved of and perhaps even been proud of her for. She had made the decision to train her magic and take his place as Guardian.

Which was never going to happen because she was too *weak*.

She hadn't truly realized or appreciated how much the Echo Stone had amplified her magic. Without it, she was now in a worse position than she had been when her magic first revealed itself.

The Professor certainly wouldn't be proud of her and it was hard at times not to think that he wouldn't be downright ashamed.

Felix was still looking at her, his lips pressed together, and then he seemed to come to a sudden conclusion. "Come with me."

Sara hurried to catch up with him as he began walking away. "Where are we going?"

Felix fetched his Friesian horse, Tempest, from the stables and helped her up into the saddle, climbing up after her. Without answering, he steered the horse toward the large Glowing Gate that marked the entrance to the palace grounds and led to the Enchanted Forest beyond.

Sara had ventured beyond the palace grounds a few times over the past year, but it was a rare occurrence. She knew that while the others viewed it as mostly safe, there were always hidden dangers.

The undead that Galatea had summoned had collapsed after she had fled Wysteria and Damaris had since destroyed them. But her fire wolves were still out there somewhere.

The guards at the Gate opened it for them and they headed deeper into the forest. The canopy closed over them, the thick leaves blocking out much of the sunlight. Sara felt a sense of calm steal over her, her previous frustration mostly fading away as she took in its beauty. Instantly, she felt cooler with the sun no longer beating down on her back.

Many of the trees were massive, towering over their heads, soft moss littering the pathways, muffling Tempest's steps. Small golden orbs of light floated through the air.

Sara leaned forward at the sound of a faint roaring, growing louder by the minute. Through the trees, she could just make out a waterfall ahead, the water cascading down from higher ground into a large pool that flowed into a stream, cutting through the forest.

Felix pulled Tempest to a halt beside the pool of water, the sides of the ground sloping around to where massive stones ringed the water. He dismounted and Sara slid down beside him. They were far enough from the waterfall itself that its roar wasn't deafening.

"What are we doing here?" Sara asked.

"Isn't it obvious?" Felix replied, pulling his boots off and tossing them onto the grass.

Sara could guess his intentions. "It's not too deep, is it?" The water was a rich bluish-green but she couldn't see the bottom.

"Not this part. You can stand up in it." He paused, seeing that she hadn't moved. "Don't tell me you're not boiling out here."

The air wasn't muggy like it would be this time of year back home, with its Midwest humidity, but Sara had to admit that it was rather warm. And she did fancy a swim. Years ago, she'd had a pool in her backyard, but it had gotten to be too much trouble to maintain and was taken down. Each summer, she had missed it and she was too uncomfortable with the idea of going to a public pool to bother.

"All right," she conceded, pulling her own boots and socks off, stuffing them in her shoes. Her feet became unbearably hot inside sometimes and she longed for a pair of flip flops.

Felix tugged his shirt over his head, dropping it by his boots. Sara glanced at him out of the corner of her eye, trying not to stare in spite of herself. She had rarely seen him without a shirt on before and her gaze roamed over his form, at the muscles honed from hours of rigorous training, the freckles splashed across his shoulders.

She looked away quickly, feeling herself flush, the heat spreading from her cheeks and down her neck, over her chest and back. Without waiting a moment more, she hurried down the slope and waded out into the water, hoping he hadn't noticed her reaction. To her relief, the water was cool and refreshing, shielded from the sun's heat by the forest canopy.

Felix followed after her, the water only reaching his stomach, where it reached up to Sara's chest. He ducked his head under and resurfaced, shaking hair out of his face.

"I'm surprised you didn't ask Colin to come," Sara remarked.

Felix didn't look at her. "He was busy."

Sara wasn't surprised by the news. Colin, like Felix, was one of the queen's Shadows, or personal guards. Perhaps Lylla had needed him for something. But then, why hadn't she also needed Felix?

Despite her new surroundings, which should have been more than enough to distract her, Sara found her thoughts drifting back toward her dismal performance earlier. As usual, her mind seemed to be her own worst enemy, trapped with her thoughts and misgivings.

"Hey."

Sara yelped in surprise as Felix splashed her with water, shaking her back to the present. "What was that for?" she demanded, not at all angry with him.

"I know that look. That far-away thing your eyes do when you're thinking too much."

"I do *not* think too much," Sara retorted, slapping the water and sending a wave back at him. For some reason, his remark made her flush again.

He quirked an eyebrow. "Oh, really?"

Felix retaliated back at her and the war was on, all thoughts of training temporarily forgotten. He was bigger than her, but Sara was determined to hold her ground, only admitting defeat when he used his attribute, air, to push the water into a large wave that nearly swept her off her feet. By now, both of them were soaking wet, but neither much cared.

They stayed in the water for a little while longer and then climbed out to sit on the rocks surrounding the pool to dry off.

Sara's shirt clung to her and she shivered as the breeze cooled her. The stone was smooth and warm beneath her bare toes.

Felix glanced over at her. "Did you tell him yet?"

The last time they had spoken, Sara had told him of her plan to inform her father that she didn't want to go to college—at least not right away. Truth be told, she didn't really know what she wanted, other than to take Professor Lawrence's place at the Gate and that wasn't going too well.

She hadn't told her father that. He knew where she went and spent most of her time, but not the reason behind it. That had been yet another surprise last summer, to learn that her father knew of Wysteria's existence. And more than that, her mother had been a Guardian, though she'd never been assigned to protect a Gate. She had died without telling Sara, just one more thing they'd never get the chance to talk about.

If her father ever found out the reason behind Sara's motivation, he likely wouldn't approve. And so she simply hadn't told him. She hadn't told him about Galatea and the danger she represented, knowing he would likely forbid her from going back to Wysteria.

He knew of the Professor's death, of course, along with everyone else in Mayfair. But like them, he believed Professor Lawrence had died as a result of a gas explosion, not that he had been murdered by Galatea.

But college? Sara couldn't even think of college right now. Her dad had been pressuring her more lately now that school was over, but she didn't know what answer to give him. At the very least, she wanted to take a year off to think about it.

There had been a time when going away to college had been all Sara had wanted, viewing it as a ticket out of her small town where nothing ever happened. But then something had happened—a Gate had been opened and now she was here.

"No," she sighed, answering Felix. "Not yet."

"You know you're going to have to tell him eventually."

"I know…"

She might have to rethink her plans entirely if training didn't improve soon. Patience had never been her strong suit and yet she thought she'd been more than patient…but it wasn't enough.

As if reading her thoughts or the emotions written across her face, Felix leaned forward to nudge her with his shoulder. "You'll get there."

"But what if I don't have time?" she asked.

She could have kicked herself. If anyone didn't have time, it was Felix, not her. Her eyes went to the jagged scars that raked down the left side of his face, given to him by the fire wolf Venryk. If he didn't find and kill that fire wolf before it was too late, he would eventually die, succumbing to the darkness that lurked within him like a cancerous poison.

She looked away, changing the subject, her eyes tracing the droplets of water as they ran down his forearm. "Have you found any sign of them?"

Each week, Felix led a patrol deep into the forest to search for any sign of the fire wolves. They had been missing since Galatea had fled and no one had heard or seen them since. Sara knew that if Galatea had died, there was a chance that the wolves would never return and Felix would be left to his fate.

He smiled sadly. "Not so far. But it's a lot of ground to cover."

Sara suddenly found herself hoping that Galatea had survived, for Felix's sake, and would return soon so they could finish this.

Even if it meant she herself wouldn't be ready.

4

Malek knew the moment he reached the temple that something was wrong. He saw no sign of the guards he was supposed to relieve. Glancing over his shoulder, he saw his partner had lagged behind him and was still trudging through the sand.

"Hurry, Aaban!" he called. "They're not here."

"What do you mean they're not there?" Aaban's mumbled voice reached him. "Check inside the temple. Maybe Tihomer got a little carried away with the wine and is sleeping it off inside."

Malek's lips pursed in annoyance. It wouldn't have been the first time Tihomer had been caught drinking on duty. He didn't look forward to having to reprimand the man and report him to Sheba.

He stepped up to the temple entrance and into the darkened interior, letting his eyes adjust. A quick scan of the room revealed no sign of Tihomer or his partner. Malek called for them just to be sure, in case they were further in, but there was no answer. His voice echoed off the gilded walls and he could sense no presence within.

Malek found himself wishing there had been more guards on duty to keep Tihomer in line, like there had been months ago, when the threat of Galatea still hung over them all. But it had been a quiet past year, without the slightest disturbance or cause for alarm, and slowly the guards had been reduced.

Had it only been a year? It felt at once as though it had been much longer and yet no time had passed at all.

But still, it didn't matter how much time had passed by. The Gate needed protection. Kadir, the desert elf chieftain, had been killed in a confrontation with Galatea and now they had no Guardian to take his place. The human girl, Sara, was still practicing for such a task, but the reports that had reached Malek's ears were not promising.

Aaban had reached him by the time he stepped back outside. "Nothing," Malek reported. "Should we report to the chieftess?"

Aaban frowned, clearly annoyed at the inconvenience of the missing guards. "Let's not alarm her just yet. They could have moved off slightly from the temple. Check the surrounding area."

There's nothing but sand for miles, Malek thought. But he searched anyway, walking as far away from the temple as he thought realistic. He couldn't see an elf like Tihomer going far.

The two of them met up at the temple entrance again after their search. They didn't have to say a word to know that neither one had been successful.

"I'll check further in," Aaban decided, walking inside the temple. "There was a bad storm last night. Maybe they had to seek shelter deeper in."

The room was large, but other than the sand piles on the floor, there was nowhere to hide. It was possible that if they had been drinking, they might have passed out and been buried beneath the sand, Malek conceded. Perhaps that's why no one had answered his calls. He followed

Aaban inside, their footsteps echoing, but Malek couldn't shake an overall feeling of wrongness.

He had sensed that the temple was empty earlier, not so much a certainty as instinct informing him that there was no one there. He and Aaban searched every corner of the room, but there was no sign of Tihomer and the other guard, nor any indication that they had ever been there at all.

"This is bad," Malek muttered, dread beginning to gnaw at him. "You don't suppose that Azuma…killed them, do you?"

He wanted Aaban to tell him that that was absurd, but they both knew better. The Eastern Wind had killed desert elves before, though his wrath was not as strong as it had been centuries past. He still had not forgotten what Rehan had done.

"If so, then there must be traces of them somewhere," Aaban replied. The dragon did not eat his victims. "Regardless, we have no choice but to inform the chieftess now."

"I'll go," Malek offered. "You stay here. Someone should remain with the Gate."

With a heavy heart, Malek made the trek back to the city of Khae, leaning heavily on his spear, into the city's center where the chieftess lived in the large home that once belonged to the former Wind Guardian.

Sheba was a young elf, with bronze skin and long white hair, that on this morning was braided. The bodice of her outfit was cropped, baring her midriff, the pants loose-fitting. Her clothing was a garishly bright combination of pink and green. Malek was shown into the living quarters by an attendant and Sheba gazed at him with her fuchsia-colored eyes.

He nodded his head to her. "Chieftess, I bring news from the Gate." He explained to her how the guards were nowhere to be found when he and Aaban had arrived and how they had searched for them in vain.

Sheba listened to his account, expressionless. She rose from her seat. "I would like to see for myself. We must launch a search for them immediately. If it is as your partner suggests and they died at the Eastern Wind's hand, then there will be some sign of them."

The chieftess and the elves she selected to form a search party rode out to the Gate on white steeds. Sheba made a cursory search of the temple grounds while the scouts searched elsewhere. She had selected wind attributes and they were using the wind to sift the sand, in case the guards had been buried.

It wasn't until midday that one of them found anything. It was a sword, a curved scimitar, clearly belonging to one of the missing guards. From the purple tassel dangling from the handle, Malek recognized it as Tihomer's.

Something terrible had clearly happened to him and Malek felt a stab of alarm at the sight. Tihomer might not have been as attentive as he should have, but that didn't mean he deserved to die.

But nothing else was found.

"Should we tell the queen?" Malek asked.

From the back of her horse, Sheba glared at him as if the suggestion were absurd. "Why would we bother the queen with such a matter? Nothing has happened worth her attention. This is a desert matter and we can handle it ourselves."

"But…" Malek protested, thinking back to what had happened little over a year ago. "What if Galatea is to blame?"

Sheba sneered at him. "Is Galatea to become some sort of evil spirit, a story you use to threaten children to get them to behave? She cannot be blamed for every little thing that happens, especially seeing as how she's dead." She turned to address the others, her long earrings swaying. "Keep searching and inform me if you find anything else. I have festival preparations to oversee."

And with that, she wheeled her horse around and galloped back toward the city.

***

You know you're going to have to tell him eventually.

Felix's words rang in Sara's head for the remainder of the day. She knew he was right. She couldn't keep putting off the inevitable conversation with her dad forever. But she was scared of what he would say. She wanted him to see things from her point of view and to do that, she'd have to convince him. Which would be no easy feat. He wanted her to go to college and he'd been set on that path for some time.

Some nights, she stayed over in Wysteria. Since her dad knew of its existence and knew precisely where she was, she didn't have to worry about lying and saying she was spending the night over at her friend Nadia's house.

Neither of her friends knew of Wysteria and so it was best not to involve them in an unnecessary lie.

Sara wanted nothing more than to stay in Wysteria that night and ignore her problems a little longer, but as evening fell, she forced herself to return home. She made her way out of the palace to the Lightning Gate, a path through the forest that was well-worn and familiar by now.

Wanderer, the Lightning Guardian, greeted her and then she was through, stepping out of the gas station restroom. Hank, a family friend and also a Lightning Guardian, glanced up from behind the counter and nodded wordlessly. He had no objection to her leaving her car parked in the gas station parking lot, allowing her to travel seamlessly between home and the Lightning Gate.

Her dad wasn't yet home when she arrived—probably fighting through rush hour traffic—and so she busied herself with making dinner. There were few jobs in and around Mayfair and even fewer that paid well, forcing her dad to endure a commute each day to the nearest city. It meant she didn't see as much of him as she would have liked.

Dinner was done by the time he arrived, which he appreciated. Sara hadn't done it to be manipulative, but neither did it hurt her cause.

Sara waited until after dinner to broach the subject, thinking it best if she were the one to bring it up. They had gathered in the living room, the TV on. She took a deep breath, waiting for the next commercial break.

At last the moment came and yet she wasted a good thirty seconds stalling. One commercial was already over.

"Dad."

His attention remained on the TV screen, as though he hadn't heard her.

"*Dad.*"

The emphasis did it. He turned to her. "Hmm?"

Sara fidgeted. If she wanted to back out, now was the time to do it. "I want to talk to you…about college."

That instantly got his attention. He reached over for the remote, muting the TV. The sound was gone, but Sara still found the moving images to be distracting.

"Have you thought about it?" he asked, a certain eagerness to him. "Have you made a decision?" Perhaps he viewed the fact that she had been the one to bring it up to be a good sign. She'd never broached the subject before, usually avoiding it altogether when she could.

"I have." Sara took another deep breath. This was it. She could feel her heart hammering, in her chest, her neck, and even in her fingers where they met the arm of the sofa. "I don't think college is for me, really."

Her dad's eager expression morphed into a frown. "Of course it is. High school is over. Now is the time to look to the future."

"About that…I've actually been training to take Professor Lawrence's place. At the Gate," Sara finished lamely.

He still looked confused so Sara hurried to explain, "You know Mom was a Guardian, but she was never assigned to a Gate because there were no openings. Now there are."

A flicker of annoyance crossed his features. "And the Wysterians are fobbing the responsibility off on you?"

"No! This is something that I want to do." Sara didn't bother adding that she was the only one who could possibly do it. Wysteria was currently woefully short on Guardians and those that remained already had Gates to protect.

"But why you?" her dad pressed. "Why does it have to be you? Can't someone else do it? You have a life here, after all."

Sara wanted to tell him the real reason, why it was so important that she do this because of the danger Galatea posed, but she couldn't. He was already no fan of the idea of her becoming the Wind Gate's Guardian and if he knew that, he wouldn't want her to go back at all.

In the end, she said nothing, eyes straying back to the TV. The commercial break had ended and the show they'd been watching was back on, but her dad took no notice of it.

"What about your friends?" he asked.

Her friends. They already had plans for their lives moving forward after high school. Plans that increasingly did not seem to involve her, though that was no fault of theirs. The path she had chosen was different than theirs—her entire life was now so much different than theirs—and she couldn't tell them any more than she could tell her dad about Galatea.

Nadia had already begun talking about which college she was going to. It was the same one Sara had eyed and she knew Nadia hoped she would join her. Though their majors would be different, it would be nice to go to college with one of her best friends.

Max, who wanted to be a coder, had already begun looking into the basics online.

"You have a life here, Sara, don't forget," her dad said gently. "This is the real world. This is important. You've lived here your entire life. You can't just abandon it. I know Wysteria is still new and exciting, but your family, your friends—your *life*—is here."

The implication was clear. She'd been living in some fantasy world—quite literally, in this case—but that was over and now it was time to grow up. To move on and make her way in the real world. The world she had been a part of the majority of her life.

Her friends didn't know about Wysteria and the fact that she couldn't tell them was a constant source of anxiety and guilt. They were already beginning to grow apart, life taking them on different paths that led away from each other. It made Sara sad to think about.

She'd assumed, like most people probably naively did, that they would stay close beyond high school, but she could feel them already beginning to slip away. If she chose Wysteria over her life here, as her dad put it, she would only be widening the distance even further, rather than trying to bridge the gap.

If only they understood! If they knew what was at stake, they'd know exactly why this was so important to her. But she could never tell them, and so they would never understand. It made her want to scream!

How many secrets and emotions could one person keep bottled up? And for how long?

And weren't Felix and Colin and the others her friends too? She might not have known them as long, but what difference did that make, given all that they'd been through together?

"Why can't you do what the Professor did?" her dad asked, breaking into her warring thoughts. "He taught at the college and was still Guardian of the Gate."

It made a certain kind of sense, Sara had to admit. But she didn't have time! Galatea could return at any moment and she'd need to be stronger if she had any hope of protecting a Gate, making a difference. She needed to train her magic. God knew it needed a lot of work. She'd need to devote all of her spare time to it in order to even stand a chance, time she simply wouldn't have if she were also pursuing a teaching degree.

These things took *years*. Maybe one day, years from now, she'd look back on this moment as such a short, small time in her life. But not now. Now, years were simply time she didn't have.

But then again… That familiar feeling of doubt crept in, worming its way into Sara's gut, an unwelcome presence making itself known. She'd already been training her magic for a year, giving all she had to it, and she had made no progress at all that she could see. Would pursuing it finally yield the results she so desperately wanted or would she only be wasting more of that precious time?

Sara hated the idea of giving up, calling it quits, and moving on. It felt like she was yet again disappointing the Professor. But he was also no longer here, just like her mom. Maybe at some point you had to stop living for the dead and live for yourself.

Perhaps she did need to think more about her future, beyond the immediate. Beyond Galatea. *Beyond Wysteria?* The idea was almost unthinkable.

You don't fit in there, the doubtful voice whispered. *You're a human. You'll always be an outsider, even if you are a Guardian. And a Guardian without magic. What use is that?*

That certainly didn't fit in.

Sara sighed, finally turning her attention back to her dad. "You might have a point. I'll think about it."

He rewarded her with a smile, clearly pleased with her response. It wasn't a yes or a no, but it was a better answer than she'd been able to give him in a long time.

He unmuted the TV, the room flooded with sound, which seemed deafening after the silence. With his attention no longer on her, Sara retreated back into her thoughts.

She'd begun the conversation firm in her beliefs, if not quite confident, and ended it full of doubt and anxiety, making concessions pre-conversation Sara never would have thought she'd make.

What would Felix have thought of the way the conversation had played out? She doubted he'd be impressed. And possibly not pleased either. The thought sent another spear of guilt through her. Would he be disappointed in her if she called it quits on becoming the next Guardian?

His opinion of her shouldn't have mattered so much to her. But it did. And Sara was only now realizing just how much.

5

Felix blinked, finding himself staring up at a cloudy, overcast sky. He was certain that he'd been standing upright a moment ago, but here he was now, sprawled on the ground with an ache in his ribs.

"Come on, Felix. Get up."

Wincing, he heaved himself upright again. Damaris stood before him, pacing impatiently, no doubt waiting for him to stand so she could knock him back down again.

She had taken advantage of her ability to shapeshift and assumed the form of a wolf. Her fur was white, as it was when she was a unicorn, but it was so utterly different from the image he was used to. If not for her beauty mark beneath her left eye, or her crimson irises and yellow sclera, he wouldn't have guessed it was her at all.

It had been Colin's idea, actually. The fact remained that, while the fire wolves had become reclusive and impossible to find, Felix still needed to end his feud with Venryk and kill the alpha. If he didn't, the darkness in his scars would slowly eat away at him like a poison and he would die.

In the past, on the rare occasions he had been given to confront Venryk, he'd had a pretty poor showing. There either hadn't been time or he'd wasted what time he did have, freezing in place, seized with terror. He hadn't seen the wolf since he'd been given the scars and was marked and so it had been more than a shock to see him again.

He couldn't afford to make such a mistake again. The next time he saw Venryk, he would have to make it count. And so in order to help him prepare, Damaris had agreed to transform into a wolf so that they could spar.

Felix had no trouble with archery; it would be simple to shoot the wolf from a distance, but if that somehow failed and they had to fight in close combat—which is what Venryk would want—he was at a distinct disadvantage.

Damaris had even offered to go the extra mile and glamour herself to appear as a fire wolf would, with deep red fur, but Felix had asked her not to. It was realistic enough as it was, and if he were honest with himself, he didn't want to see a fire wolf with Damaris's eyes.

But she was perfect for this session for another reason. Like fire wolves, she could self-combust into flames, adding another dimension of realism that he would need to face.

Without bothering to ask if he was ready, Damaris launched herself at him, lips peeled back.

Felix did have one advantage over Venryk and that was that he could use magic. Fire wolves had only enough magic to ignite and extinguish their flames, nothing more.

Tapping into his magic, Felix summoned a gust of wind and directed it at the oncoming wolf. It slammed into her, knocking her back away from him and out of the air. She hit the ground on her shoulder and before she could scramble to her feet, Felix had an arrow nocked and pulled back.

Damaris nodded with approval. "Good. If you can use your magic against him, there's little he can do."

If Venryk could reach him, the wolf would use his superior strength and weight against Felix. *I just have to make sure that doesn't happen.* But he also knew he couldn't rely on Venryk to play by the rules.

"All right, one last thing," Damaris added. She burst into flames, the fire licking over her fur. If she'd been a true fire wolf, the flames would have been an eerie, unnatural red. "Like any fire conjured by magic, Venryk's flames feed off his own energy, rather than some type of fuel. But they can still be snuffed out using air."

And air happened to be the only element Felix could wield. There had been times when he'd wished for a more useful element, but now he was grateful for what he'd been given.

He took a deep breath, Damaris's past words during training coming back to him. *Remember, fire is just an element, to be used or controlled. Your element, air, can both compliment it or extinguish it.*

"I'll make it as hard on you as possible," Damaris warned, "without making it impossible."

Felix knew that in a real fight, he wouldn't have much time to do this. Summoning his element, he commanded it to snuff the flames out, to suffocate them. The fire flickered, but continued to burn. He clenched his teeth, feeling sweat break out over his skin, but though the fire dimmed, it did not go out.

Frustrated, Felix channeled his anger at his own failures and weakness—and at Venryk himself—into his magic the way he had been taught. His vision began blackening at the edges, but he refused to stop.

Suddenly, the flames went out with a *woosh* and Felix released his hold on his magic, gasping. The darkness slowly crept back. He felt utterly spent. This was no use against Venryk. Even if he managed to extinguish the wolf's flames, he would then be too weakened to fight him.

Not for the first time, Felix wished he was simply a Guardian himself.

He looked up at Damaris, expecting to see disapproval or concern written across her features.

Instead, she nodded. "Good. If you can manage that, Venryk should be no problem."

With a surge of relief, Felix realized just how hard Damaris had been pushing him, far harder than Venryk ever could. For the first time, he allowed himself to feel some pride in what he had accomplished.

But more important than that was Damaris's confidence in him. He had always believed she doubted him, even though she had never said as much. It seemed only natural to assume, since she had always had the role of protector—only to have it taken away.

Finishing Venryk was something Felix had to do on his own. And now he was beginning to entertain the notion that perhaps he was ready after all.

"That's enough for now," Damaris said, shifting back into her true form. "We'll have to put the training on hold. I'll be going to the festival and so I won't be around for a few days."

It wasn't surprising. Damaris went to the desert festivals every year. Only this time it would be different. He studied her expression closely, but she gave nothing away.

This would be the first festival without Kadir. To her, he hadn't been just the Wind Guardian but also a dear friend. Felix knew his loss weighed on her heavily. The losses they had suffered weighed on them all.

It was on the tip of his tongue to ask if he could accompany her, thinking she might appreciate the company, but then another idea occurred to him.

Felix looked up at her. "When do you leave?"

***

"There you are."

Sara looked up to see Felix making his way between the bookshelves, approaching her window seat. He didn't sound surprised to find her here; the library was a room they both very much enjoyed and frequented at the palace.

She had retreated here after yet another failed training session. Her heart gave a painful twinge at the sight of him, thinking back to the conversation with her dad. Had that only been last night?

Instead of disappearing with the dawn, her doubts had only intensified and today's failure hadn't helped. Much as she loathed to admit it, life seemed to be taking her further and further from the path she'd thought she wanted.

To her relief, Felix didn't ask her how training had gone and he didn't bring up her dad either.

He stopped a few feet from her seat, leaning against the wall with his arms crossed. "Would you like to go to the festival with me?"

Sara stared at him. Whatever she'd expected him to say, this was not it. "The festival?"

"Yeah, you know. The one the desert elves put on every year to celebrate and remember what Rehan did."

Is that really the best idea? Sara thought, but he was smiling at her and she didn't have the heart to dampen his spirits. Instead, she asked, "Are you sure that's okay?"

Amusement glittered in his eyes. "If it's Galatea you're worried about, I'm sure we'll be fine."

Sara flushed. He knew her so well.

"One night of fun isn't going to hurt anything," he added. "And besides, we deserve it, don't you think? After everything that happened last year. It would be good to take your mind off of things."

Sara had never been to one of the festivals, though she'd heard about it from Colin, and had to admit that it sounded fun. Felix had asked *her* to go with him. Her first festival.

She knew better than to look too deeply into his motivations for doing so, but she was flattered all the same.

"You're right. Of course I'll go."

"Great. We can travel with Damaris, make things easier." He grinned at her, which did weird things to her stomach. "You'd better get packing."

Later that afternoon, Sara had all the spare clothes and necessities packed and was transferring them to her saddlebags. Though the festival was only one night, traveling on horse would take some time to get there.

She was glad she'd been given one of the horses from the palace stable to ride. In the past, she'd ridden on Tempest with Felix. Not that she would have minded—but the horse might. Damaris stood to one side, flicking her tail, impatient to be off.

"Where are you off to?"

Sara looked up to see Colin approach, dressed in his black Shadow uniform, his blond hair tussled.

"The festival," Sara replied.

"I'll come with you!" Colin exclaimed, already heading for the palace stairs. "I wouldn't miss it for the world and it will only take a moment to pack—"

And then he had gone, disappearing into the building.

Sara turned to Felix. "I'm surprised he didn't know."

Felix said nothing, staring after his friend. There was something about his expression that struck Sara as slightly annoyed. Maybe it was the pursed lips or his clenched jaw. Whatever it was, Sara couldn't be sure because the next moment he blinked and the expression was gone, so fast she wondered if she'd even see it at all.

A few moments later, Colin returned, carrying a satchel. A few paces behind him was Lylla, also carrying a bag. Her white sword, Pharus, hung at her waist.

"I ran into Colin in the hall," she explained. "He said he was going with you and I thought why not come along."

"Are you sure?" Damaris asked, eyeing her.

Lylla handed her bag and sword to Colin, who would carry them on his horse. Also having been gifted the ability to shapeshift, Lylla morphed into her unicorn form, her coat lavender while her mane, tail and horn were all turquoise blue. It would save her the trouble of having to bring along and look after a horse.

"It's been some time since I last attended a festival. It would do good to be seen."

There were no two more reassuring presences than the queen and the Flame Guardian and Sara knew the sight of them at the festival would help put people at ease. Things were still tense and had been ever since Galatea had returned last summer.

"All right, then," Damaris said. "Let's go before it gets dark."

In fact, they still had several hours before darkness fell and they made the most of it, the Flame Guardian setting a brisk pace along the forest trails. With Damaris in front, Lylla brought up the rear, her long turquoise mane and tail flowing, glimmering as the light caught. Felix, Sara, and Colin rode in the middle.

None of them spoke much as they traveled. The sky remained overcast, muting the colors of the forest. Sara hoped it wouldn't begin to rain. Damaris consented to stopping for brief periods of time, but when night fell, they decided to make camp where they were. By then, Sara felt quite sore, not being used to sitting in a saddle that long— or at all, really.

Lylla shifted back into her true, elven form. The horses were unsaddled and given long tethers so they could wander a bit. Sara helped Felix and Colin gather wood for a fire and Damaris obligingly lit it.

Sara caught the Flame Guardian staring off into the distance, in the direction they were traveling, as though she could see through the trees to the desert beyond. She wondered if Damaris yearned to race ahead, moving as fast as she wished in order to arrive quickly and wondered if she resented being tied down with so many traveling companions.

Food that had been packed was dug out of the saddlebags and eaten around the fire—bread, cheese and some fruit. Damaris, for her part, did not eat anything until Lylla coerced her with a block of cheese.

Sara looked around at their surroundings appreciatively. At night, the Enchanted Forest came alive. The large trees seemed to give off a faint, gentle green glow, as if bioluminescent, while golden wisps of light drifted lazily through the air. Crickets chirped and somewhere, far off, Sara thought she could hear the quiet sound of windchimes. The sky had cleared and silvery moonlight filtered down through the thick canopy.

"Just like camping, huh?" Colin remarked.

Somewhere out there, Galatea's fire wolves still roamed. But Sara did not feel the least bit scared, being outside of the safety of the palace. If anything, she felt content, a sense of peace hovering over their little campsite.

Nothing bad could happen to them, not with the Lightbringer and Flame Guardian standing guard.

"I'll take the first watch," Damaris offered and walked off a little way into the shadows. Her strange eyes seemed to glow slightly in the darkness.

"Get some rest," Lylla instructed. "We move out at dawn."

Colin let out a groan at that. Diligently, Sara settled down on her bedroll. The ground was uncomfortable and the crickets were beginning to get annoying. She focused on the crackling of the fire and tried her best to tune them out.

***

It was still dark when Felix snapped awake, unsure at first what had woken him. For a moment, he feared he'd been having a nightmare of some sort, though he couldn't remember it, and was worried he'd somehow disturbed the others. He propped himself up on one forearm and glanced around the campsite.

The fire had dwindled, but was still crackling softly, sparks flying up into the air. No one else seemed to have been disturbed. Colin was snoring slightly and Sara was asleep in her bedroll next to him. It was impossible to tell whether or not Damaris was actually asleep. She'd changed into her human form and laid down by the fire, but Felix doubted she was asleep. She was probably listening to the sounds around them.

He remembered suddenly what had woken him. He'd heard footsteps of something moving through the brush. Quickly, he scanned the darkened forest for any sign of the culprit, but he saw nothing. Whatever or whoever it was, they were long gone.

Out of the corner of his eye, he spotted Lylla, leaning against a nearby tree, standing guard. Even in the middle of the night, she seemed to give off a slight golden glow, though not enough to be distracting.

Her posture was relaxed, but she had Pharus in her hand, the white blade's light gently pulsing outward and dissipating. She met his gaze and shook her head silently. The message was clear.

It had been nothing to worry about and he should go back to sleep.

It was probably a stag or something like that, Felix told himself as he lay back down.

But the fear of nightmares still lingered and he knew it would be a very long time before sleep returned.

One singular thought kept nagging in the back of his mind.

Why had Lylla drawn her sword?

***

Lylla continued to watch the place where the fire wolf had appeared, but it did not return. It had approached the campsite and then stopped, standing there motionlessly. Without a sound, Lylla had drawn her sword, Pharus slipping silently from its sheath.

She held it loosely in one hand, the blade dipping toward the ground, in full view of the wolf. It was both a symbol and a threat, communicating more effectively than words.

Finally, the wolf had turned, retreating back into the woods as quietly as it had come. *A scout?* Its presence made Lylla uneasy. Why had it shown itself?

There had been no cause to alarm the others. If it had been Venryk, she would have alerted Felix instantly and perhaps even run the wolf down herself, pinning it in place so that Felix could finish it.

His pride might have stung at having such a level of assistance, but Lylla didn't care. She would do anything to help him, in a heartbeat. It tore at her heart to see him suffer, this boy she had helped raise since he was a child, orphaned by such fire wolves.

He tried to hide it, but she knew the strain he was under.

But there had been no reason to alert the others. Perhaps the wolf had merely been drawn to the fire, wanting to know who was there. Regardless, it wasn't stupid enough to try anything, knowing she was there and that she had seen it.

The wolf itself was not a threat, but what its presence meant very well could be.

It was the first time one had been seen in a year and that did not bode well.

6

Sara awoke the next morning even more stiff and sore than when she'd gone to bed. True to her word, Lylla had them all move out at dawn and they continued to trek through the Enchanted Forest. It was so large, Sara felt like it must go on forever and that they would never find their way out of it. In her time spent in Wysteria, she had heard tales of travelers who had gotten lost, taken the wrong winding pathways and were never seen again. She hadn't believed it, but now she could understand how it could be true.

Finally, the trees began to thin, becoming smaller shrubs. Sara could see a wide expanse of sand stretching out before them and eventually, even the hardy shrubs fell away, leaving nothing green.

The sun was high overhead when they entered the desert. She, Felix, and Colin donned long-sleeve tunics and wrapped scarves over their heads and faces to protect their skin from the fierce glare of the sun. The heat was stifling and soon Sara was sweating profusely beneath the layers.

In some places, the sand stretched on for miles in every direction, with no end in sight. Other times the ground became rocky and uneven, with large stone cliffs rising from the sand, scoured by the wind. They passed through ruins of ancient dwellings that had been abandoned, trekking up staircases that had been worn smooth by the centuries.

Sara wondered what such buildings might have looked like in all their glory. The paint had long since worn off, but she could catch glimpses of where it remained, sheltered in nooks from the wind. The colors must have been vibrant.

There was no wind, which she supposed was good because they didn't have to worry about sand being blown into their eyes, but it also did nothing to ease the oppressive heat. There was no humidity, which she was very grateful for. Having lived and grown up in the Midwest on Earth, she was used to humid, muggy summers, but the arid air of the desert was something else entirely. The heat made her skin ache and her eyes felt uncomfortably dry.

She glanced over at Felix and Colin. What little she could see of their faces were flushed red. The hours stretched on and the heat worsened. Sara struggled to breathe through the scarf covering her nose and mouth, convinced she would pass out from heat stroke.

They had made sure to fill their canteens with water from a stream before leaving the forest, but Sara's had run out. She supposed she hadn't been as careful with it as she should have been. Damaris knew of a nearby oasis and offered to take them there.

It seemed to materialize out of thin air, the heat waves making its image shimmer, but it was real enough. A medium-sized pool of water, surrounded by palm-like trees that cast blissful shade. The sudden appearance of something green was startling after being surrounded by nothing but tan and beige for hours. Sara dismounted with relief and refilled her canteen, splashing some of the cool water on her seared face and hands.

She looked up to see Damaris staring off into the distance. A slight wind had picked up, stirring her black mane gently. The unicorn closed her eyes, completely at home in the desert. She wasn't the least bit affected by the stifling heat.

They met no one else on their travels, other than a group of colorful caravans in the distance. When Sara asked about them, Damaris explained that they were a group of nomads, quite common in the desert, heading to the city of Khae for the festival.

Mercifully at last, the Wind Gate came into view. It was a large building, the exterior pillars reminding Sara of an ancient Greek temple, the roof domed. The sun glinted off its golden façade.

In the distance lay the massive city of Khae. The sun had begun to set as they entered the city through its southern gate, the hideous visage of a snarling dragon carved onto the double doors.

Sara gasped in spite of herself as they stepped into the city. She had never been so far from the palace before and Khae was another world entirely. It was large and sprawling, many of the buildings with golden domed roofs and warm earthy colored walls.

Immediately along the road upon entering was a bazaar. Many stalls lined up on either side of them, the sun kept off the owners by colorful cloths functioning as roofs. The peddlers shouted and called to them and other bystanders as they passed, selling all manner of things from jewelry to woven rugs and tapestries, elaborate vases, weapons, clothing and food.

The pungent smell of spices assaulted Sara's senses and somewhere she could smell something delicious cooking.

They passed fish, exotic fruits and dates. The aromas were heavenly and made Sara's stomach growl.

A stall with a purple cloth roof was selling turquoise, emerald, ruby, and sapphire jewelry, the necklaces, bracelets and earrings winking up at her, along with polished stones. It all looked incredibly expensive and Sara hadn't thought to bring along money for any of it. She hadn't anticipated being tempted to shop.

"The city bazaar," Damaris confirmed, glancing over her shoulder, having noticed Sara's interest. "You can find anything you want here, for the right price, of course."

The sights, sounds and smells of the bazaar faded behind them as Damaris led them deeper into the city, through the winding streets. There were people everywhere, dressed in bright clothing, coming and going in preparation for the festival or doing last minute errands before heading home.

Several of them paused and began murmuring to each other at the sight of not only the Flame Guardian but Lylla as well. Some of them even pointed to Sara and she looked away, feeling her cheeks heat.

A large stack of logs stood in the city square, likely for a bonfire later. Colorful banners and lanterns had been strung along the entire forum. A fountain bubbled somewhere, out of view. Sara guessed this would be where the main action took place tomorrow night.

At last, they came to a halt before a tall, impressive building. To call it a mansion would have been a stretch, but Sara took an instant liking to it. Damaris explained that this was an inn, of sorts, and would be their lodgings for the duration of the trip.

Inside, the walls were painted red, the floor hard beneath their feet. There was a sitting room they would all share in addition to the separate bedrooms. The ceiling of this central room was draped with red, gold and purple cloths. Pillows were scattered over the floor, with several cushioned stools and a low table. The overhead lamp cast a weak but warm light over everything.

"Make yourselves at home," Lylla said. She had turned back to her elven form upon reaching the inn and looked relieved. "The festival isn't until tomorrow night, so in the meantime, feel free to explore."

"But try not to get lost," Damaris added and Sara had a feeling the instruction was directed at her.

"I'm going for a walk," Lylla announced. "It will be good for the people to know I'm here and for me to speak to them."

Without another word, Damaris also headed for the door, reverting to her human form as she did so.

Sara turned to Felix and Colin. "What's this festival like?"

"It's great!" Colin exclaimed. "Lots of dancing and drinking and free food. What's not to like? Trust me, no one knows how to party like the desert elves."

"It's just an excuse to get drunk, if you ask me," Felix muttered.

He had seemed somewhat sullen and withdrawn ever since they'd left the palace, his earlier enthusiasm gone, and Sara wondered why he'd even wanted to come.

"Oh, come on, don't be like that."

Sara had always disliked parties. They were noisy and crowded and in her experience, everyone always seemed to act like they were having fun as if they were trying to convince themselves. She would have skipped prom her senior year if her friends hadn't persuaded her to go along.

In the end, she did end up having fun, but mostly because it was their last year together and Sara thought they should make the most of it. After all, no one really knew where life would take them after high school.

But it was different when you had someone to go with and Felix had asked her. More than simply accompanying her, he had *wanted* her to go.

"Come on," Colin said, breaking into her thoughts. "Let's give Sara a tour."

It wasn't yet dark and there was still plenty of light to see by. Colin did most of the talking and Sara was content enough just to follow. They had just entered the shopping district, which was beginning to close for the night, when Colin looked up and exclaimed, "Look, it's Wanderer!"

Sure enough, the Lightning Guardian was just coming out of one of the stores. She looked up as she heard her name, face lighting up, and came bounding over to them. "Hey! What are you three doing here?"

"We're here with Lylla and Damaris," Felix explained.

"Well, you're in for one hell of a party."

Sara didn't want to dampen the mood, but she couldn't help but wonder if it was a good idea for Wanderer to be here at all. Her being in Khae meant that she wasn't back at her Gate. And with Galatea possibly still out there… Last year it would have been unthinkable for any of the Guardians to leave their posts like that. But she supposed that Wanderer's Gate did still have both of its Guardians. Hank was still on the other side. It wasn't like the Gate was completely unprotected or anything.

In the end, she said nothing.

"Speaking of which," Wanderer added, "can I borrow Sara for a moment, boys?"

"Of course," Colin answered.

Before she could ask what was happening, Wanderer grabbed Sara's wrist and tugged her away, out of earshot. As usual, her black-and-white striped hair was unruly and she had two white wolf ears protruding from the top of her head. Her white, black-tipped wolf tail swished excitedly, even though it was all just a glamour. Nothing more than an illusion. Her usual kimono was gone, replaced by the same kind of garb Sara had seen the desert elves wearing earlier.

"What is it, Wanderer?" Sara asked. "Shouldn't you be at your Gate?" Now that the two of them were alone, her curiosity got the better of her.

Wanderer waved the question away. "Oh, I come to the festival every year. I even brought Hank with me one time. You should have seen him. The man had two left feet but we had fun anyway. Now enough about me! We need to find you a dress!"

"Wait," Sara exclaimed, trying to take it all in. Wanderer talked so fast. "What?"

"Did you bring one with you?"

"No—"

"Well you can't go to the festival looking like that!" She gestured to Sara.

She glanced down at her clothes. The tunic and scarf had been removed, leaving her with the black, tight-fitting clothing she always wore for training, not dissimilar to a Shadow uniform. "What's wrong with it?"

"Please, we need to get you something else if you wanna stand out."

"But I don't want to stand out."

"Of course you do! Who wants to blend in? That's boring. And anyway, when are you going to get the chance to attend another festival like this, huh? I know the desert elves have them all the time, but none are as big or as fun as this one."

"Okay, I believe you, but I don't really care what I'm wearing," Sara protested. She looked frantically over her shoulder. Where were Felix and Colin?

"There will be boys there," Wanderer pointed out.

Sara whipped back around. "So?"

"So we got to make you look good. Now, it's a little late to go shopping tonight, but I tell you what, I'll stop by and get you first thing tomorrow morning. Sound good? Great! Now I gotta go. See you then!"

And with that, the Lightning Guardian waltzed off down the street, jauntily swinging the bag that contained whatever she had purchased from the store she had exited.

"What was that all about?" Felix asked softly behind Sara, making her jump.

She turned. "Wanderer wants to take me shopping."

He looked mildly amused. "You have my sympathies. Whatever you do, do not take her fashion advice on anything."

Sara thought back to Wanderer's kimono, which had been lime green and hot pink. "Yeah, I think you're right."

It wasn't until they had returned to the inn that Sara remembered she didn't have any money.

Wanderer arrived abysmally early, before Sara even had a chance to eat breakfast. Their little group had gathered in the sitting room, seated around the table on cushions on the floor. An impressive spread had been prepared, with toast, boiled eggs, fish, dates, and figs.

Sara wanted to wait until the meal was over, but Wanderer insisted that they needed to get as early a head start as possible, since anyone who didn't yet have attire for the festival that night would be out shopping for one. With a resigned sigh, Sara hurriedly finished a piece of toast and accompanied Wanderer. The whole thing reminded her uncomfortably of Black Friday.

As they reached the door, she explained to the Guardian that she didn't have any money and that getting a dress for the festival didn't really matter to her, thinking that Wanderer would somehow relent.

Instead, she said, "Oh, don't worry about any of that. Now come on. I know the best place to go."

"I saw some nice ones in the bazaar yesterday," Sara ventured.

"Yeah, yeah, they're okay. If you wanna pay an exorbitant price. It's basically daylight robbery!" Wanderer pulled her into one of the stores.

Sara blinked, letting her eyes adjust, and glanced around at the racks of costumes. She could see masks and capes across the room and jewelry near the front.

Wanderer plucked a white dress from one of the racks and held it up. "What do you think?"

Keeping Felix's advice in the back of her mind, Sara replied, "I'm not sure…"

I feel like I'm shopping with Nadia.

"You're right," Wanderer said abruptly, putting it back. "White is *so* not your color." She resumed looking. "Don't get discouraged! I have an excellent eye for fashion. Hank tells me that all the time."

Sara did not feel reassured as she roamed around while the Guardian searched, wondering if she could manage to find something suitable before Wanderer did. Briefly, she considered accepting the next one Wanderer suggested just to end it all.

She jumped as Wanderer suddenly cried, "Aha!" The Guardian darted into Sara's aisle, thrusting a dress at her. "This is it! This is the one. It's so perfect for you."

Sara took it from her, holding it up for a moment before lowering it with a frown. "It's yellow…" She'd never thought she looked good in yellow.

"Just try it on," Wanderer begged. "Trust me, I have a feeling about this one. If you try it on and still hate it, then I'll find something else."

Sara sighed. "Fine." Wanderer steered her over to the store's equivalent of a dressing room.

She stepped inside, pulling the curtain closed behind her. The room was small, with a full-length mirror and nothing but the curtain behind her to serve as a door. She suppressed another sigh and stripped off her normal clothes.

The dress fit surprisingly well, rather snugly in fact, which was a rare thing to find. Sara had always been on the thin side and it was a struggle to find something that wouldn't be too short on her but also not too large in the bust area. Once she'd wriggled into it and the skirt fell to the floor, Sara stared into the mirror in astonishment.

The bust was a light orange, with the rest of the bodice a bright yellow. It was sleeveless and strapless, save for the golden loop that went around her neck. A band around her waist was the same orange, trimmed in golden yellow. The skirt fell to cover her feet completely, the front and back colored orange. The sides were the same yellow, but sheer, showing off her legs.

Though parts of the dress were golden and yellow, the very color Sara had never thought she looked good in, there was no denying that it was gorgeous. *I feel beautiful in this,* she realized with a start, despite the faint sunburn her cheeks had acquired. *Wanderer actually did it.*

"Hey!" Wanderer called from outside, making Sara jump and spin around to face the still-closed curtain. "Are you done yet? I wanna see!"

Speak of the devil. Sara pulled the curtain back, stepping out. The silk skirt brushed coolly against her legs as she walked, flowing as easily as if the material were a part of her.

Wanderer's eyes widened. "I knew it. See? Didn't I tell you? What do you think?"

Sara blushed. "I do like it," she admitted. "You were right." She reached up, tugging at one of her bra straps, which were visible. "Gonna have to do something about this, though."

"I got you covered, don't worry," Wanderer said, nudging her back in the dressing room. "Okay, get changed again so we can get it and get outta here."

The Guardian paid the shop owner for the golden dress and the two of them departed. Wanderer insisted that she keep the dress hidden until the festival so it would be a surprise for everyone else.

Back at the inn, the sitting room was empty aside from Felix, who stood as she entered.

"That didn't take too long. How did it go?"

"It went good," Sara replied, subtly moving the bag behind her so he couldn't see.

He nodded thoughtfully and then gestured to the table behind him. "I saved you some breakfast."

Sara's shoulders slumped in relief. "You're a lifesaver. Let me put this in my room real quick."

All that was left now was to wait.

***

Once night had fallen, the festivities were well underway. The revelers gathered in the huge city square, clustered around the pile of logs, which had been lit, creating a large bonfire. The orange flames crackled and danced with the music, occasionally changing colors with a hiss.

People gathered around it, twirling in pairs or some by themselves. The cobblestone streets were hidden beneath a sea of bright, swirling colors. Some stood clapping in time to the music, which was light, playful, and fast.

The cool night air smelled of smoke from the fire, delicious scents of food, and perfume. Those who weren't dancing gathered in groups to talk and laugh, usually with a drink in hand.

Wanderer, of course, had jumped right in, twirling and leaping around barefoot in her bright blue and white dress. For the most part, she danced alone, wolf tail flowing behind her.

Even Sara, in her golden dress, was convinced by Wanderer to join in. At first, she hung back from the crowd, obviously shy. But one by one, the male desert elves approached to speak to her.

From where he stood, Felix couldn't hear what was being said, but it was obvious that they were all asking her to dance. She blushed each time and gave them an answer, too shy to look them in the eye. The answer always appeared to be yes, because after each one approached her, she was off twirling and laughing with them.

Felix sighed, leaning against the wall of one of the many houses behind him, situated around the square. He knew he should be enjoying himself. That was the purpose of the festival and why he had wanted to come in the first place. To forget your cares and troubles for one night and just have fun. But he found he had no wish to join in, watching Sara instead. A painful twinge twisted in his chest, only adding to his gloomy mood.

Colin, for his part, had already disappeared into the fray. Felix had been happy to leave him to it.

In a sea of vibrant colors and smiling faces, there was at least one other person who seemed to share in his gloom.

Damaris stood a few feet from him, observing the partygoers but not participating. She was in her human form, dressed in a dark red halter top, a gold collar necklace around her neck, and light brown baggy pants, and sandals. She retained her signature twin braids rather than putting her hair down as was customary at the festival.

"May I have this dance?" a voice spoke at Felix's shoulder. "Or are you already spoken for?"

He turned to see Lylla behind him, wearing a knee-length dress of vibrant gold. It was the first time he had ever seen her wear something that didn't reach the ground. Her blue hair hung loose, shimmering with a faint golden light in the darkness.

He smiled in spite of himself. "Of course." How could he refuse? It had been Lylla that had taught him and Colin how to dance all those years ago, never taking it too seriously.

Felix took her hand and together they moved closer to the center. She'd always had a way of shaking him out of a bad mood. He emptied his mind of such thoughts and focused on the movement. Lylla laughed as he spun her around, the sound one of pure joy. Not for the first time, he marveled at how she could be so positive in light of circumstances that sometimes were anything but.

It was over too soon and she was on to dancing with someone else. Felix found himself wishing he could work up the courage to ask Sara to dance with him, but he was afraid she would refuse, even though he could think of no good reason why she would do so.

He'd suddenly had enough of the party. *I need some air...* He shoved off the wall and walked on, leaving the city square behind. Felix didn't know where he was going, just wandering. The streets of Khae were mostly unfamiliar to him and so he let his feet guide him, until the music and sounds of revelry faded behind him to a dull hum.

His footsteps had taken him to a wide alley, bathed in silvery blue from the light of the full moon. The golden glow of the fire and lanterns in the town square were far behind. He was tempted to return to the inn and go to bed when he spied steps going up the side of the building, leading to the roof.

It would be nice to view the city from up there, he supposed, and have a view of the night sky, unimpeded by having to look up through the tall buildings. Felix started up the stairs in no particular hurry, walking out to the edge of the roof and taking in the city laid out before him. He glanced up in time to see a shooting star streak across the sky and sink out of view.

"You're supposed to make a wish."

Felix whirled around. He hadn't heard her approach.

Sara stood a little way behind him, looking out of place in her gown. Like a ray of sunlight in the black of midnight, undimmed by the darkness.

He blinked in surprise, walking toward her. "What are you doing here? Shouldn't you be at the party?"

"I needed a break from all the excitement."

In spite of himself, his eyes roamed over her, taking her in. Her hair was no longer in a braid, her long lashes dark against her pale skin and there were golden bangles wrapped around her arm and wrist. He could see why that dress had been chosen. It represented her element perfectly and the color looked good on her, too. She almost seemed to glow with the radiance of it, the way Lylla sometimes did.

There was something about her that he found fascinating. Perhaps it was the simple fact that she was a human and he, always surrounded by elves, was unaccustomed even now to more ordinary features or slight flaws.

Even now, in the dark, he could see the slight blemishes on her skin, the way her nose tilted to one side, not perfectly straight.

God, she was beautiful.

Her imperfections only served to make her more attractive in his eyes. She was not perfect and neither was he, so neither could judge the other.

Realizing he was staring, Felix glanced away, clearing his throat. "You look gorgeous in that dress." He internally winced. "Err—not that you don't always—" He clamped his mouth shut, feeling heat creep down his neck. He was only making it worse. Why had he said anything to begin with?

To his relief, she didn't seem to take it that way. She smiled, looking away. "Thank you…"

Unlike the other partygoers, who had put a great deal of thought into what they were going to wear, Felix hadn't changed into anything else. He still wore his black leather royal guard uniform, with the silver trim that marked him as a personal guard to the queen, the dark pants and leather boots. He suddenly felt rather inadequate, standing next to Sara.

"I saw you leave the party," she said, breaking into his addled thoughts.

So she had followed him. "I needed some air."

She nodded, tilting her head up to gaze at the stars. "So what did you wish for? Or can you not tell me?"

He could have wished for many things, but he suddenly saw an opportunity.

Felix smiled, facing her. "What would you say if I told you that I wished that you would dance with me?"

There. He'd done it. Now she would either say yes or she'd say no.

Her eyes widened, cheeks flushing a flattering pink. "You want to dance with *me?*"

"Yes."

"I'm not a very good dancer. I don't really know how…"

"It doesn't matter to me." He offered her his hand. "Besides, there's no one around to see how terrible we are."

Sara laughed softly at that, placing her left hand on his shoulder. Felix put his right hand on her back, aware of how close they were. They had been close before—sharing the same window seat in the library or riding the same horse—but this was different.

He began to lead and she followed, her long skirts swirling against his legs as they twirled around the roof, her gold bracelets glinting in the moonlight.

"Am I doing okay?" she asked breathlessly.

"You're doing fine."

Her posture was tense and rigid at first, but she relaxed as they went on, perhaps reassured by the fact that no one but the moon could see them.

***

The dance started slowly at first, but quickly picked up in speed and intensity. Sara found herself holding her breath, letting Felix guide her, aware that it was just the two of them up here. She was hyper-aware of every inch of her body, the night air cool on her skin, and Felix's hand on the bare skin of her back. The way he smelled, always of leather, horses and something else that made her think of the forest.

She gasped in delight as Felix's hands went around her waist, lifting her into the air as if she weighed nothing, spinning her around, the stars swirling dizzyingly above her before she returned to earth.

As the dance came to an end, she clung to the rush of euphoria, her heart hammering in her chest. That brief moment had been better than the entirety of prom.

Felix released her. "Thank you for granting my wish."

"You're welcome," she breathed.

"Do you want me to take you back to the square?"

"No, not yet. I like the quiet," she confessed, going to sit on the edge of the roof, dangling her legs over.

"Me too." He came to join her, their shoulders brushing. "So, how are you finding your first festival?"

She brushed a loose strand of hair out of her face. "I'm enjoying it so far." Her sense of joy faded suddenly, as though snatched by a thief in the night. "But it feels…I don't know, wrong somehow, doesn't it?"

Throughout the night, she had felt an overall sense of wrongness, as if they had no business throwing caution to the wind and having a good time when so many had died last summer. They couldn't be here to enjoy the festival and since Galatea could very well still be out there somewhere, why should anyone else be able to enjoy it?

She had managed to ignore it and it had been easy in the city square with the loud music and people lining up to dance with her. But here, where it was quiet, away from the bustle, the feeling had crept back.

"I suppose," Felix acknowledged. "But let's not talk about that. This is a happy night. Whatever tomorrow brings, at least we have tonight."

Sara turned to look at him and found he was already watching her. His crimson hair appeared almost black in the darkness and his eyes held a sudden longing in their green depths.

The uncertainty of the future struck her. What would she tell her father when her year to decide was up? Would she even take the year off, as originally planned, or would she go to college with Nadia come the fall? If Galatea returned, would she even have a year? Would any of them? How much longer did Felix have, before the darkness in his scars finally claimed him?

The only thing that was certain was him sitting next to her, right now.

How could she have considered leaving him and all of Wysteria behind, even for a moment?

"Yes," she whispered. "We have tonight."

She reached out to touch him, this time not flinching at the vision of Venryk that appeared for a split second when she touched his scars. He ran his callused fingers through her loose hair and leaned close.

Sara closed her eyes, savoring the sensation of his fingers in her hair. She'd never been touched this way before and she found herself craving it, needing it. She could feel his breath, warm on her skin. Sara breathed in his scent, heart thrumming, and waited for the touch of his lips.

But it never came.

Felix pulled back suddenly, untangling his fingers from her hair. She looked at him in confusion. She'd been so sure he'd been about to kiss her. Had she misread his intentions?

He refused to meet her gaze. "I'm sorry," he said, throat working, voice pained. "We can't do this."

Felix stood and walked away from the roof's edge, heading toward the stairs without glancing back. She called to him, but it made no difference.

Sara was left on the roof alone, feeling empty and confused.

***

Damaris stood on the dock of Khae's harbor, staring out across the water. Torches flickered along the perimeter of the harbor, casting a faint orange glow, but otherwise it was dark aside from the moon. Much darker than the city square had been. Boats, large and small, bobbed gently in the blue-green water, moonlight reflecting off its surface. Palm trees swayed in the breeze.

The sky was clear, giving an unobscured view of the stars above. Very few people milled around the dock on this night, giving her privacy. She had tried to stay at the party for as long as she could, but she'd eventually had to seek isolation.

Damaris sighed, closing her eyes and listening to the sound of the water lapping at the dock. It led all the way to the Green Sea in the distance, visible even from here.

In the past, Damaris had loved coming to the annual festivals the desert elves hosted and this was the first she had failed to enjoy. She had debated joining in some of the dancing, knowing that he would have wanted her to, but in the end, she couldn't bring herself to do it.

Kadir should have been here. Her friend should have been the one preparing for the festival, watching the sun set with her as they always used to do and reminiscing about shared past experiences.

But he was gone, killed by Galatea the previous summer. And it had been such a waste.

Damaris knew better than to think such things, but she still found herself wondering if she could have made a difference if he had only confided in her. If he had come to her for help, could she have saved him? Would he still be here now?

A wave of emotion swept over her, violent and sudden. Damaris clenched her teeth against the pain and rage that blossomed in her chest—partly pain at the loss and anger at his betrayal. It threatened to overwhelm her and sweep her away, but she stood firm. There was no point trying to suppress it, she had long ago learned. The only thing to do was ride it out. It dulled and faded almost as quickly as it had come.

Dwelling on such things never helped anyone. It was over and done with. Kadir was well beyond her reach now. But she was a Guardian, the Flame Guardian, and while she had sworn an oath to protect her Gate, that also meant Wysteria and its people as a whole. She had failed to be there for her friend when he needed her the most.

No, logic reminded her. *He failed himself by refusing to tell you the truth.*

She couldn't save him from himself.

"Still," Damaris whispered to herself. This wasn't the first person she had failed to save and she hoped it would be the last. What good was having such power if one couldn't use it to save others?

She reached up, undoing her braids and letting her hair fall free. She opened her eyes and peered down at her reflection in the water's surface.

There was still one she had vowed to protect and she would fulfill that oath, to the last drop of her magic, to her dying breath, if that's what it took. Nothing else mattered.

***

Lylla excused herself from the festival early. It was late, but not so late that people would begin turning in. Luckily, the festival was still in full swing. Between the dancing and the drinking, no one paid any mind as she slipped down narrow side streets, not wanting to attract attention.

The streets here were mostly quiet and empty. Lylla encountered few people as she walked briskly. The city gate loomed ahead of her and she was grateful that it had been left open on the night of the festival. Ordinarily, they were closed after nightfall. The guards nodded to her as she passed, hardly inconspicuous with her blue hair, but if they thought anything of her presence, they made no mention of it.

The sand was still warm beneath her bare feet as she made her way toward the Golden Temple in the distance. There was no sign of the wind spirit, Azuma. The pilgrims had already left their offerings and gone, leaving the temple empty. The gifts were still piled inside where they'd been left, so the wind spirit hadn't come to partake of any, if he was even interested in such things.

Lylla paused at the threshold, glancing over her shoulder at the city, still bright in the darkness. Turning, she headed straight for the back wall where the Gate was housed. She raised a hand, lifting it toward the wall, and commanded the Gate to open.

There was a brief flash of light and then she was through, stepping out into the muggy night air of Mayfair. Onto Earth. Crickets chirped and frogs sang, but it was otherwise quiet, aside from the occasional car, its engine audible in the distance.

Lylla stepped away from the Gate, which on this side was an unassuming, rusting red metal gate opening out onto a cornfield. She walked along the edge of the field and slipped between the trees bordering it, onto the property that had once belonged to Professor Lawrence, the former Guardian of the Gate.

She left the cover of the trees, stepping out to where the house had once stood. The wreckage had mostly all been cleared away, nothing to suggest he had lived here at all aside from a few charred splinters and chunks of wood. The ground was still blackened, a scar seared into the earth.

She had not been here when the house had been destroyed, but Damaris had.

It had been her that caused the house to explode after Galatea killed Lawrence. Damaris had been unharmed by the flames, but Galatea's resurrected lover, Jack, had perished. They had all hoped that Galatea had died in the fire as well, but there had been no body.

The sorceress hadn't shown herself since, likely biding her time, and there had been no further disturbances.

Lylla knelt down, trailing her fingers over the burned, blackened ground, unsure of what had brought her here. A bit of light-hearted revelry was perfectly fine—necessary even. But glancing across the desert, one could see the Wind Gate from Khae and it was impossible to lay eyes on it and not remember what had occurred here last summer.

Coming here now…it felt a bit like paying one's respects.

She stood, the familiar weight of Pharus shifting at her side. She waited patiently, for how long she did not know, but nothing changed. Nothing revealed itself. She was about to go when she heard the faintest sound, as of someone stepping down onto blades of grass.

Lylla turned, staring into the darkness, as a silhouette stepped clear of the tree line, slowly coming into the light.

Lylla did not draw her sword, but she rested a hand on its hilt. "Hello, Galatea."

The two of them had not been face-to-face since before the Cataclysm, when Galatea had destroyed her own Gate, destroying the city of Malenwar along with it, and fled to Earth. She looked different now, less carefree or kind.

The shadow elf's skin was a sickly shade of gray. Two curved ears protruded from her long black hair. Her eyes, which had once been yellow, as all shadow elves' were, now were pitch black, a tell-tale sign that she'd given herself over to dark magic.

The skin on her left side was puckered and scarred, traveling from her shoulder all the way to her scalp. Evidence of the burns she had suffered—but survived.

Galatea held her Shadowblade loosely in one hand, down at her side, the blade glinting in the light. A sword imbued with darkness. One cut could prove fatal, the darkness acting like a poison. If not healed with light, it would eventually kill.

The sorceress appeared to be alone. There were no Nightmares, wolves or undead with her this time.

"I thought it must be you," Galatea said softly. "You always did glow in the dark."

Lylla stood there, surveying her former friend and Guardian, and despite all that Galatea had done, she felt a twinge of pity to look upon her now. To see how she had withered beneath her rage and hatred.

She held out one hand toward Galatea. "Come with me, Galatea. It doesn't have to be this way."

For a moment, Galatea seemed to consider, wrestling within herself. Then she shook her head. "It's too late."

And perhaps it was. After what she had done, there could never be peace. Things wouldn't simply go back to the way they were. Justice still had to be served.

Lylla let her hand drop. "It's over, Galatea. Jack is gone."

And he's not coming back. Not this time.

Rather than discouraging her, the remark garnered a flash of anger. "Yes. He is gone."

"I'm sorry for what happened. Truly. I never gave my authority or permission…"

"And yet you did nothing to stop it."

Lylla frowned. "I gave you permission to return to Earth with Jack. To be released from your Guardianship and your oath. If you had gone with him, he would still be alive."

"You could have let him stay," Galatea said, slashing her arm through the air. "On Earth, my magic would slowly fade away to nothing and he would still die. And then what? In Wysteria, we could have been together forever."

"Yes, you could have. And perhaps you should have," Lylla admitted. "But what's done is done. I can't change the past. And neither can you." More softly she added, "None of this will bring him back, Galatea."

Galatea drew herself up. "No. It won't. I had the chance to bring him back, for all of us to atone for our mistakes and have a second chance. But you couldn't allow that either."

"You were dabbling in something you never should have tampered with."

Galatea ignored her. "It's too late for Jack now. Too late for atonement. Too late for second chances."

Sensing the conversation was going nowhere, Lylla sighed. "What do you intend, Galatea?"

The sorceress didn't answer.

"You're here for the Gate, aren't you?" What else would she be there for?

Galatea considered her. "I suppose you're going to try and stop me."

"I'd rather not have to," Lylla answered, sliding Pharus free, its light flaring. "But yes, if it comes to that."

Galatea nodded, unsurprised. She raised her Shadowblade and Lylla readied herself for the attack. But it never came. Galatea summoned an orb of darkness to her palm and threw it at her feet. The darkness exploded like smoke, obscuring Lylla's vision.

She flung her arms wide, the illumination radiating outward, the golden light searing through the darkness and for a moment turning night to day.

The glow faded. Galatea was gone.

Lylla whirled around, searching for her, keeping Pharus raised, expecting an attack at any moment. But the grounds where Lawrence's house had once stood were quiet. There was no sign of the sorceress.

Lylla let out a breath, lowering her sword, shaking her head in disgust. *Playing in the shadows!*

She didn't have time for Galatea's games. Keeping Pharus firmly in one hand, she set off for the tree line that would lead her back to the Gate. Whatever had brought her here tonight, whether it be remembrance or a premonition, she had learned something valuable.

Galatea *was* still very much alive and she had seen the proof of it with her own eyes. She needed to cross back over and warn the others right away. And it was possible that the sorceress had already crossed over while Lylla had been fruitlessly searching for her.

The thought made her stop short.

The festival!

Panic surged through her, lending speed to her urgency. She charged forward, thankful her dress was only knee-length or else she'd be tripping over it in her haste.

"No!" she cried, as if Galatea could somehow hear her. As if she would listen. As if that would stop what was about to happen.

She could just see the Gate ahead in the moonlight. It stood alone. Galatea was nowhere to be seen.

Perhaps there was still time. Perhaps she wouldn't be too late.

Her foot landed on something hard and sharp, but she ignored it, kept on going. Almost there. Lylla reached out toward the Gate with one hand. *No…*

A flash of light, blinding in its intensity.

And then the world exploded.

7

Sara remained sitting on the edge of the roof for a time, vainly hoping that Felix would return and offer some explanation for his actions. She had no idea where he'd gone after he'd left.

She could still hear the music from the city square faintly but she had no intention of returning. The festival had lost its charm and all she wanted now was to go to bed and forget.

She climbed down from the roof, heading back toward the inn, wishing there was someone she could ask for an explanation if Felix refused to give her one. Not Lylla or Damaris. They were both too close to him and she couldn't risk that they would mention it to him. Colin might help her, she supposed, even though he was close friends with Felix, but he wasn't a girl and she couldn't rely on him to understand how she felt in this situation, could she?

"Sara!" Wanderer hurried toward her. "You're not leaving the party already, are you?"

"Have you seen Felix?" Sara asked, seizing the opening it gave her. She could ask Wanderer for advice.

The Guardian opened her mouth to answer when there was a deafening explosion, as if something had just blown up, though Sara couldn't see anything. Wanderer's face drained of all color and she grabbed Sara, throwing her to the ground.

"Get down!"

Before Sara could comprehend what was happening, she felt the ground begin to shake beneath her and around her came the sounds of muffled cracking and crashing as the world seemed to fall to pieces around them. Dust rose, clouding her vision, choking her, burning her eyes. Small pebbles rained down onto her bare arms, wrapped protectively around her head.

It seemed to last for an eternity, but it might have been only a few moments before it fell eerily silent. The music from the festival had quieted and as Sara listened, her ears ringing, it became a cacophony of screams.

She felt hands grabbing her arms, hauling her to her feet. Wanderer stood beside her, bleeding from a gash at her temple. Sara coughed, dust falling from her hair as she moved. It coated her arms and beautiful golden dress; it covered everything around her. She looked at Wanderer. The Guardian's skin had been bleached white by the dust as if she were a ghost.

As the clouds of dust began to settle, Sara turned slowly, taking in the destruction around her. Buildings had collapsed along the street around them. Some hadn't been leveled entirely, others were reduced to their foundations. The few that remained standing had cracks spiraling up their sides and threatened to fall at any moment.

Where once it had been impossible to see far in the city due to the winding streets and buildings cutting off one's line of sight, now Sara could see destruction stretching out as far as the eye could see. And still the screams continued.

"Are you hurt?" Wanderer yelled, louder than necessary, but perhaps her ears were still ringing.

"I don't think so," Sara shouted back. "Are you?"

The Guardian shook her head. "Nothing major."

"What happened?"

Wanderer never got the chance to reply. The slap of sandals on stone rang out and Sara turned to see Damaris rushing toward them, Felix and Colin behind her, stumbling over the debris littering the road. All three of them were covered in dust. Colin was limping slightly and Felix had a cut on his forehead, the blood running down his cheek.

"Where's Lylla?" Damaris demanded.

Wanderer glanced around. "She's not with you?"

"Would I be asking that if she was? We thought she was with you."

Wanderer shrugged. "Haven't seen her."

A chill ran through Sara but she didn't have time to dwell on it long before Damaris took charge.

"We need to help the survivors. Get them out of the city and see to their injuries. Find some healers, if there are any left. But don't go alone. It's not stable and some of these buildings could still come down. Go in pairs."

"I'll go with Wanderer," Sara offered. Ordinarily, she would have hoped to accompany Felix, but she wasn't in the mood to share his company at the moment.

Damaris nodded. "Felix, go with Colin."

"What about you?" Felix asked.

"I'll look for Lylla. Be careful and stay safe."

The boys nodded and set off in one direction without another word.

Wanderer touched Sara on the arm. "Come on. We'll go this way."

She followed, picking her way through the rubble. It was difficult to walk over the uneven stones in her sandals and a long dress.

"What happened?" she asked again. "Was it an earthquake?" She hadn't heard of any occurring in Wysteria but she supposed it was possible.

Wanderer looked uncharacteristically grim. "I wish. The Gate was destroyed."

"*What?*" Sara exclaimed. She'd heard the story of how Galatea had destroyed her own Gate and obliterated the city of Malenwar along with it. Now, where the city had once stood, there was nothing but ruins and a swamp. The land had been transformed, becoming inhospitable. And countless people had died.

Wanderer shook her head. "I don't know how. But it was."

But I could guess. The unspoken words hung heavily in the dusty air.

Numbly, Sara followed after her, too shocked to ask what it was they were supposed to do to help. She could see some desert elves, disoriented and injured, making their way through the ruins.

Wanderer stopped before a large pile of rubble. She took a deep breath. "There could be people trapped under here."

She raised her arms. Her attribute may have been lightning, but Guardians could control more than one element and that was what set them apart from ordinary elementalists. Using her control over earth, she shifted the stone, lifting them and setting them carefully aside.

There was no one trapped underneath, much to Sara's relief. But they were not so lucky elsewhere when they continued on. Looking at the debris, Sara found it more likely that if it had fallen on top of someone, they would have been crushed rather than trapped and she was right.

She looked down at the mangled, crushed bodies and covered her mouth with one dust-coated hand. They found some who were injured when chunks of buildings had fallen on their legs or their backs, preventing them from escaping.

Sara shook herself out of her shock. These people were hurt and they needed her help. She reached out to help an elf with a wounded leg, allowing him to lean on her. She could barely control her own attribute, light, much less summon a secondary element to help shift the rubble. Safely escorting the injured out of the city was the least she could do.

Even as she did so, her movements did not feel her own. Her body felt strangely weightless, as though she were disconnected from it.

Dawn was still several hours away and the city had been plunged into darkness when it collapsed. She couldn't risk tripping over the debris and injuring herself or further hurting her charge.

Pausing for a moment, Sara closed her eyes and tapped into her element, the way she had practiced during months of training. *Come on. They need me.* A weak glow flared to existence. It was pathetic in the grand scheme of things, compared to what someone like Lylla could do, but it was enough to light their path and Sara was grateful.

At least she hadn't failed utterly in an emergency.

"It's all right," she murmured to the elf she was supporting. "I've got you. What's your name?"

"Malek," he hissed between clenched teeth.

At least during training Sara had been forced to strengthen her body as well as her magic or else she never would have been able to support Malek's weight. Even so, she was beginning to tire. Khae had seemed a big city when they'd first arrived, but now it seemed impossibly large, the destruction spanning out endlessly before them.

Sara gritted her teeth, ignoring her own pain and fatigue. This wasn't about her. She wasn't injured and someone had to help these people. *This is part of what being a Guardian means,* she realized. She may not have taken an oath and been assigned to a Gate, but she still had a responsibility to help Wysterians.

At last, they broke clear of the city limits, sand stretching out before them. Sara searched for the Golden Temple in the distance and saw that the beautiful building had been reduced to rubble instead.

Malek let out a sob at her side, though whether from pain or the devastation of his city, or both, Sara did not know. When they reached the group of survivors and she saw the extent of their injuries, Sara felt like sobbing herself.

Some of them had limbs that were crushed or wrenched at odd angles and blood flowed freely from cuts, some minor and others gaping wounds. Some of the women clutched children or babies, who were shrieking. Another woman wept because she had lost her children when their home collapsed on top of them.

Sara stumbled away, swallowing down her own grief. This was a second home to her, in a way. She would feel the same if her town had been destroyed, but she could cry after it was over. Right now, there were still people trapped in the ruins that needed her help.

Having handed Malek off to a healer, a bald elf with white tattoos running over his scalp and down his arms, she hurried back to find Wanderer.

***

Felix wiped sweat from his brow, hand coming away stained with blood. Though the desert air had cooled after the sun had gone down, it didn't seem to matter. His attribute, air, was marginally useful in shifting rubble,

80

though not as helpful as earth might have been. At least he could lift the stones if they weren't too heavy.

Colin stood by, his element of ice less useful.

Felix had yet to see any sign of Lylla and the longer she took to appear, the more dread gnawed at him until he thought he might be physically ill. He hadn't seen her since she had danced with him and then he'd gone off by himself. He felt a prick of guilt over how he'd handled things with Sara, but he couldn't think about that now.

If Lylla had been caught by one of the falling buildings, she might have been crushed. Even now, she might be lying lifeless beneath the next pile they came to. The more rubble he shifted, he half-expected to catch a glimpse of familiar blue hair and whenever he didn't, he sent up a silent prayer of thanks.

She *couldn't* be dead. She just couldn't be.

Other than Damaris, she was the strongest person he knew. She had given him a home and a purpose after his parents had been killed. She had shown him kindness and offered wisdom and advice when it was most needed. She probably could have advised him on what to do about Sara, counselling him on how to fix his mistake.

She couldn't do any of that if she were dead. But she couldn't be dead.

Where is she, then?

"We'll find her."

Felix looked up to see Colin watching him, as if reading his mind. His friend knew how much Lylla meant to him—what she meant to both of them. What she meant to the entire island. Felix gave him a grateful smile and continued on in his search. Colin was right, after all.

Any moment now, she would come racing up to save them all, healing the wounded with her light magic. Perhaps she was out there already, doing just that.

***

Damaris had found no sign of Lylla, but she tried to reassure herself that the city of Khae was massive and that it was impossible for one person to search every inch of it. They could easily have missed each other in the chaos, one arriving a moment too late, the other having already moved on. Everyone she passed, or pulled from the rubble, she asked if they'd seen any sign of the queen, but they'd all said no.

Until she came across an elf who had been guarding the southern city gate. He had been outside of the city itself and thus mostly spared from the destruction. He claimed he remembered seeing Lylla leave the city and head out toward the Golden Temple.

"I thought nothing of it, really," he added.

If Lylla had been at the temple when the Gate was destroyed, she would have been too close for there to be any chance of survival. Damaris fervently hoped that wasn't what had happened. But the alternative was little better.

If she had crossed over, she would have faced whoever was responsible for the Gate's destruction and since only one person had ever destroyed a Gate, Damaris was quite certain she knew who was responsible.

Lylla wouldn't have stood idly by and let Galatea raze the Gate, so she had either been injured and unable to stop her, or Galatea had killed her and then destroyed the Gate. Either option wasn't good. It was likely the queen was dead, either by Galatea's hand directly or by the blast itself.

And I can't cross over to look for her.

With the Wind Gate destroyed, the nearest one was Damaris's own, on the Wysterian side, but it came out in Egypt and that was of little use to any of them.

The next closest was the Lightning Gate, which would come out in Hank's gas station, two miles from where the Wind Gate stood on Earth. Or where it *had* stood. If Lylla was still alive, she would head for Hank's Gate.

Damaris needed to tell Wanderer her suspicions. The Guardian had to return to her Gate immediately.

It may already be too late.

***

Lylla stared at the stars, cold and unfeeling far above. Every nerve ending felt as though it were on fire, pain lancing through her body. Leaves slowly drifted to the ground around her, having been ripped from their branches, small pieces of tree debris striking her cheeks.

Something poked her painfully in the back. This field had not been planted this year and the remnants of corn stalks stabbed into her.

She gripped something hard and lean in one hand. Pharus. Somehow she had managed to keep ahold of her faithful blade.

Lylla coughed, gingerly pushing herself up into a sitting position. She had been blown back several feet. Some of the trees that had stood around where Lawrence's house used to be were now toppled over.

Grimacing, she got to her feet. The nearby grass had died, rendered lifeless by the blast. *Just like Malenwar.*

Galatea emerged from the shadows of the ruined tree line, from the direction of where the red metal Gate had once stood. Lylla tensed. She'd expected the sorceress to have crossed over and destroyed the Gate from the Wysterian side. She hadn't seen her during her desperate flight for the Gate, but perhaps she hadn't paid enough attention.

Or perhaps Galatea had destroyed the Gate from a distance. That would be the smartest thing to do.

Lylla gritted her teeth, sudden anger gripping her at the sight of her enemy. The Gate might be lost and she momentarily trapped here—but so was Galatea. There was still a chance to finish this and she intended to make the most of it.

She reached up, wiping blood from the corner of her mouth, ignoring the pain in her leg. She must have landed on it wrong. It wouldn't matter. Galatea had just expended a large amount of energy destroying the Gate and she would be in poor shape to fight.

"This madness ends now, Galatea," she growled.

The sorceress gripped her Shadowblade. "If you insist."

A massive form rose up behind her, feathered wings unfurling and Lylla sucked in a painful breath, the tip of her sword wavering. *The Spirit of the Eastern Wind.* Galatea had managed to somehow subjugate the creature and was using its power for her own desires.

Even as it rose, Lylla could tell there was something wrong with it, darkness leaking from its eyes. Its presence changed things. Galatea had more magic at her disposal than Lylla had thought.

Galatea did not tap into the wind spirit's power at first, relying on her own. She summoned darkness, the wispy tendrils swirling around her fingers, and set it surging toward Lylla. The queen flared an illumination with one dismissive flick of the hand, the light searing the darkness away.

Summoning her fury at what Galatea had done, she channeled it into her magic, striking relentlessly, illumination after illumination. Galatea desperately fended off the onslaught, but it was clear she was tiring.

Suddenly, a strong wind rose, knocking Lylla to the ground. She gasped at the force of it and knew it was the wind spirit's doing. Sensing her chance, Galatea gripped her Shadowblade and strode forward, pointing it down at Lylla.

"This is only the beginning," the sorceress hissed, her voice somehow carrying above the wind. "Too bad you won't be around to see the rest of it."

She made as though to plunge the blade down and Lylla raised Pharus to parry the blow, but it never came.

Galatea cried out, staggering back as the wind spirit writhed behind her. Azuma roared, the wind howling mournfully. His massive white wings beat the air as if the creature pulled against invisible tethers. Lylla blinked; if she squinted, she could just make out the tendrils of darkness that tethered him to Galatea, pulling her back away from Lylla as he struggled. The wind, though still whipping, had lessened its hold on Lylla and no longer pressed her down.

She scrambled to her feet. Galatea's eyes widened. She couldn't fight both the Eastern Wind and the Lightbringer at the same time.

Darkness exploded at the elf's feet, plunging the world into night, air blasting outward. Lylla once again called upon her own magic and the world momentarily lit up white. When it faded, both sorceress and wind spirit were gone.

With a muffled cry, Lylla sank to one knee, pain lancing up her wounded leg. It hurt to put weight on it.

If the sorceress intended to cross back over into Wysteria, there was only one place she would go. *The Ice Gate.* But there was no chance Lylla could get there in time to stop her.

She used Pharus to push herself up with difficulty. Of course Galatea would run. She was still running from her problems, from her past, even now.

But Lylla had learned something interesting. She knew that Galatea had the wind spirit, and could use his power as her own, but that he was fighting her, resisting her hold over him. Useful information indeed.

More pressing, she needed to return to the desert. With the festival, there were even more people crowding into Khae than usual and Lylla shuddered to think what the city must look like now. How many people had died? How many had Galatea killed with just one action, just as she had in Malenwar? If she was willing to destroy a Gate to get what she wanted, there was no telling how dangerous she was. She would stop at nothing.

Perhaps that is *what she wanted.*

It was a chilling idea.

Lylla thought of Sara and Felix, Damaris and Colin. Wanderer had been there, too. Were any of them hurt? Had any of them died? There was only one way to know. Her people needed her and she couldn't do them any good trapped here on the other side.

She began limping south. She had to reach Hank's Gate.

8

Biting cold greeted Galatea as she crossed through the Ice Gate back into Wysteria. She could feel the flow of magic around her as if it were a living thing, beginning to replenish what she had used to destroy the Wind Gate. Snow-coated mountains rose around her. Beyond the Ice Gate, the frigid sea writhed. It was just as dark here as it had been on Earth, but the sky was overcast, the stars hidden.

Galatea turned to consider the Ice Gate behind her, her long hair whipping into her face.

The Gate appeared as though it had been wrought from icicles, all hard lines and spikes, perfectly representing the harsh environment around it. Both of its Guardians had perished last summer and there were no others to take their place. It would be so easy to destroy it, too. She would have been tempted to try it then and there if she hadn't already used too much energy.

With a sigh, Galatea trudged through the snow, shivering. She could not remain out in the elements for long and she hadn't come this far to freeze to death in

Iceland. The cottage of the former Guardian, Cyren, stood nearby, appearing more like a lodge than a house.

It was empty and would serve her purposes well enough.

The door opened without resistance and she stepped inside, shutting out the howling wind and biting chill. The furniture was carved from wood and had animal pelts draped over the backs. The hearth was unlit.

Galatea shuffled over to the armchair nearest the fireplace. Even the act of summoning a meager flame took more effort than it should have, but she managed to get the fire going. Warmth began to slowly suffuse the room.

The truth of it was that she had used far more energy than she should have needed to. It wasn't just the act of destroying the Gate that had depleted her magic—although she had expected that much, having done it once before—but she'd had to face Lylla as well.

Eventually, the two of them would have a proper duel. It was inevitable. Their elements, their very natures, clashed and opposed each other. And in the end, one would stand victorious and the other would be defeated.

As powerful as Lylla was, it shouldn't have been a problem. Not with the wind spirit under her command. But Galatea hadn't expected the creature to resist her. After she'd first claimed him, she had taken him out into the far reaches of the desert, where no one would notice them, and practiced tapping into his power and using it as her own.

Azuma had fought her out there. He had succumbed to her influence easily enough, but it seemed that now, at every opportunity, he would actively try to break free of her hold. If he succeeded, the consequences would be disastrous.

After she had managed to keep ahold of him in the desert, she had thought that the end of it and had crossed back over to Earth before anyone had realized what had happened. If she wanted to use the wind spirit to achieve her goals, she would have to get a firmer grip on him than she had now.

I will, she vowed. *I have to.* Everything hinged on being able to use his power.

Her army was destroyed and she had nothing else. Azuma was enough for what she had in mind, but only if she could control him.

Somewhere out there, her faithful wolves would sense her presence and come to her, but it wasn't likely to happen while she was here in Iceland.

The Ice Gate would have to wait. She had plenty of time to act, regardless. They were all probably reeling in the desert from what she had done. It would take them some time to recover, but she would still need to act before they could assemble and take steps to oppose her.

Galatea sank down onto one of the chairs, tucking her legs up beneath her, and pulling one of the animal pelts over herself. She was no longer shivering.

She had failed to kill Lylla when she'd had the chance, but perhaps that was better in the long run. She couldn't allow herself to doubt if all of this was worth it or not. Galatea couldn't go down that road; there was no telling where it ended. She owed it to Jack to do this.

But is that what he really would have wanted?

Galatea shook the thought away, but the doubt lingered. She remembered the way he had looked at her in that brief moment she had brought him back. Instead of being overjoyed that they could be together again, he had almost seemed horrified by the knowledge of what she'd had to do to get to that point.

It doesn't matter. Jack is dead, for good this time. I'll never get the chance to know what he would have wanted. I will never have a lot of things…

There was no point in wallowing in self-pity over the things she wouldn't have. She only wanted one thing now and she was certain she would have that.

I will have my vengeance. If I have nothing else, I will have that.

Galatea closed her eyes, the warmth of the fire comforting. She could afford a brief respite. There was no way to know if or when she would get another chance.

***

Lylla was panting with exertion by the time she reached Hank's house at the far edge of town. She'd had to pause several times and rest, the ache in her leg growing worse—and also take a far more circuitous route than she would have liked.

Unsurprisingly, the blast had attracted the notice of some of the townspeople. Knowing she would stick out like a sore thumb, she had avoided them at all costs.

All the while, the thought of Khae and all its people urged her to push on; she needed to reach them as soon as possible.

There were lights on in nearly every house in town—no doubt awoken by the explosion. Hank's house was also alight when she arrived, thudding her fist against the door. All she wanted was to sink into a chair and take the weight off her leg.

The door opened a second later and Hank, fully dressed, stared out at her. He was a man in his mid-forties, with a thatch of brown hair—usually hidden beneath a newsboy-style cap—green eyes, and a stubbly beard.

He swore softly at the sight of her, stepping aside. "I knew it was bad when I heard the explosion, but I didn't expect to see you here. You look terrible, lassie."

His informal way of speaking to her was one of the qualities she admired most about Hank. He treated people the same, no matter if they were a queen of another land or a high school student come to buy something from the gas station convenience store.

"I feel it, too," Lylla muttered, easing herself down onto the sofa. Her dress was torn and dirty from where she'd lain sprawled in the field, but it didn't seem to have any blood on it.

She could hear Hank moving about in the kitchen and a few minutes later, he appeared carrying a tray, which he set on the coffee table. He handed her a mug of something steaming. Lylla didn't bother asking what it was. Coffee, by the smell. She would have preferred tea, but the extra caffeine could be useful.

He sat across from her. "What happened?"

Between sips of coffee, Lylla relayed what had happened, from her crossing over and seeing Galatea, to the destruction of the Gate and final confrontation.

Hank looked haggard by the time she'd finished. "So it's true then. We've lost another Gate."

"I'm afraid so."

"You were lucky," he said, a warning in his tone. "If that wind spirit hadn't fought back, you'd be dead." He hesitated. "Are you sure that's what the creature was doing? Resisting Galatea?"

"That's what it looked like and I can't think of anything else that would have stopped her."

"Well, that's something positive, at least. Means she hasn't truly got ahold of it."

"Not yet." Lylla set her mug down. "I need to go. The desert elves were hosting their festival. There would have been more people in Khae than usual. I don't know what the Gate's destruction did, but it can't be good."

"You're not going anywhere on a leg like that. You'd never make it. And I can't heal you."

"I made it this far," Lylla said stubbornly. She didn't mention that she hadn't told anyone where she was going or what her intentions had been. No one on the other side likely knew where she was and possibly they feared she was dead, killed in the blast, especially if they suspected what had happened.

Hank shook his head. "You stay here. I'll cross over and find someone to help. Wanderer will be there."

"No. She was at the festival."

His eyes darkened with worry for his fellow Guardian and something else—disapproval? "Well, I'll do something even better then and fetch the healer."

"Be careful. That's an order."

They could guess, but none of them really knew where Galatea had gone after she disappeared.

He nodded. "I'll be back, quick as I can."

Lylla watched him leave, propping her leg up on the edge of the coffee table. It was probably broken or nearly so and would need to be healed magically if she was to be any use. Though she could heal others, she couldn't heal herself.

At least Damaris was in Khae. She could rely on the Flame Guardian to take charge of the situation, whatever it may be. *Unless something has happened to her.*

***

Wanderer had set out for her Gate as soon as Damaris spoke to her, taking one of the red dragons that the elves used for fast travel between the desert and the palace. It was as quick as possible, but still not fast enough.

Damaris wished she could have gone; she was useless here. Her attribute was fire, the very nature of her magic to burn and destroy, not heal and restore. But someone needed to take control and the others would listen to her, simply because they feared her if not respected her.

The search for survivors had continued throughout the night and now, as dawn broke, remained ongoing. The stream of wounded seemed never-ending, but the tide of the dead was more overwhelming still. They had no time to bury them properly—there were far too many—and it was the desert tradition to burn their dead because of the sand. It was fickle, never staying in one place like the earth did; the slightest wind would stir it up and expose graves.

The bodies had been identified as best as they could and were lined up outside the city ruins. In this at least, Damaris was not useless, would that her power could be used for something other than such a grim task. She had summoned the fire and once it caught, left it to burn on its own.

It still burned now. She could see the flaming hill in the distance.

Damaris had instructed the healers to heal those who were too injured to walk first. The sun would reach its highest peak soon and these people could not remain in the direct heat without food or water. They needed to be moved as quickly as possible, but it was a slow process. Some of them were refusing to move until their missing family members had been found. Others were elderly or had children.

Ordinarily, elves only aged until they reached adulthood, but others sometimes aged further, worn down by the passing of time and the burdens that came with life.

Sheba, the new desert elf chieftess, had survived and though the girl was inexperienced when it came to leadership, Damaris had to give her credit. She was no healer, but she moved from one person to the next, offering words of comfort or reassurance as a good leader would. She was no Kadir, but perhaps there was hope for her yet.

Damaris called the chieftess over to her. "We need to start moving these people. They can't stay out in the direct sunlight. We can move them into the forest. At least then they'll have shade and we can find food and water for them."

Eventually, they would have to be moved to the palace or somewhere similar where they could be given shelter, but the palace was on the other side of the island and a further journey you could not make.

Sheba nodded. "I will gather any horses or dragons we have left. Those who can't walk can ride on them."

It was better than nothing.

As the chieftess set about her task, Damaris shouted for Felix and Colin. The two Shadows made their way over to her. She explained the task she had given Sheba, adding, "I want the two of you to go with them. They'll need water, so find a stream; you know where they are. Felix, you know how to hunt and Colin, you know how to set snares. It will be difficult, but I'm entrusting this to you."

"We won't let you down," Colin assured her, saluting briefly, his fist over his heart.

"I know you won't," Damaris murmured, glancing at Felix. She could see the emotion in his green eyes and thought it was gratitude.

She could understand it. There had been a time when she'd sworn she would never again let him out of her sight or trust him to go off on his own. He had been foolhardy then, but she could trust him with this.

She nudged his shoulder with her muzzle. "Go on, both of you. I'll join you as soon as I can."

When the last of the injured have been found and seen to.

9

It felt like an eternity of waiting for Hank to return, but it was only early morning. The sun was beginning to rise, the town outside starting to stir. If Hank didn't open the convenience store, questions would be asked, but it couldn't be helped.

Lylla breathed a sigh of relief as he walked through the door, Serai, the head healer at the palace, behind him. She was a desert elf with very dark skin and the snow-white hair that all desert elves possessed. Her eyes were a bright green and white tattoos marking her as a healer ran up her arms and face.

"Hank already told me what happened," Serai said as she knelt in front of the couch, laying a hand on Lylla's injured leg. "There's no need to explain." *Ever efficient.*

Lylla felt her leg begin to heal beneath Serai's touch, the damaged tissues knitting themselves back together until they were whole again. The healer seemed hardly affected by the use of magic, having experience in healing far more serious and complicated wounds.

"Thank you," Lylla said and was about to insist that now she was healed she begin making her way to the desert, when someone pounded on the door.

Wordlessly Hank went to answer it and Lylla heard a familiar voice in the hall.

"Where is she? Is she here? What happened?"

A moment later, Wanderer rushed into the room, her hair in even more disarray than usual. She looked unusually careworn, as though she hadn't slept all night. She probably hadn't.

"You're alive!" Wanderer gasped. "Everyone will be so relieved. Some of them think you're dead."

Your own fault, Lylla told herself. "Yes, I would have returned sooner, but I was injured."

"It was Galatea, wasn't it?"

She nodded and once more explained what had happened on her side of the Gate, adding, "How bad is it?" She wouldn't truly understand the destruction until she saw it with her own eyes, but Wanderer would be able to give her an idea.

The Lightning Guardian sighed. "Pretty bad. Most of the city is gone and we lost a lot of people, most of them crushed by the rubble. A lot of injured, too, though. Damaris is in charge but she sent me to find you."

Lylla smiled to herself, in spite of the poor news. Even in the midst of a crisis, she could rely on the Flame Guardian. "Then we must go. We've lost too much time already."

"I'll come as well," Serai offered. "I have a feeling my skills will be needed."

"They will be," Wanderer agreed grimly. "I've got a dragon waiting on the other side of the Gate."

"Be careful," Hank warned them. "And let me know if you need anything."

Even on the back of a dragon, it would still take them half a day to arrive in the desert and Lylla hoped they could reach the injured before another disaster struck. Galatea was once more ahead of them, and until they got control of the situation, they could only play the game by her rules.

***

Noon had come to the desert, the sun directly overhead, searing heat blistering down upon the remaining refugees. Sara was exhausted, both physically and emotionally, having done things over the past twelve hours that she'd never imagined she would have to do.

To say nothing of the things she had seen...

She had never had the slightest interest in nursing, thinking herself not cut out for it. It took a certain strength of character to view and treat severe injuries without flinching and show great compassion at the same time.

And yet, she had found herself comforting those that had lost family members when the city fell and holding the hands of others as they died, finally succumbing to their injuries. There were simply too many people for the limited number of healers to reach in time.

Sara felt numb as she sank down into the sand, in the shade cast by the collapsed Golden Temple, finally allowing herself a rest. There had been no time to grieve. She had spent all night trudging back and forth from the ruins to where the survivors were gathered, first escorting those that were injured and later returning to search for anything that could be salvaged from the wreckage. She helped retrieve pillows and blankets for bedding, changes of clothing, and any food that had not been crushed, transporting it back to those waiting.

Felix and Colin were going to take those who were not too badly hurt into the forest where they could get water, food and shelter. She gave some of the items she had salvaged to them, silently relieved that Felix was being sent away. They hadn't spoken since being up on the roof and she refused to meet his eyes.

There was a part of her that hated herself for it. How could she be so petty as to hold a grudge in a time like this, when there were people who needed her help? Their differences seemed pointless by comparison but she couldn't help but feel hurt. His aloofness and mixed signals confused her and she knew better than to ask for a straight answer. If Felix didn't want to talk about something, then he wouldn't.

What difference does it make anyway?

But it did make a difference. Something had changed between them. It had been easy when they were just friends to each other, but for a moment, it had seemed that they were about to become something more.

And it was in that moment, up on the roof, that Sara realized that at some point, she herself had crossed that line and began to think of Felix as something more than a friend. When had it happened, exactly? She didn't know; it had been a gradual thing. And now there was no going back, no pretending that they were just friends.

What they'd had before had been perfect. And she'd had to go and ruin it. She'd allowed herself to be discontent with what they'd had and yearn for something more. *And look where that got you.*

Sara buried her face in her hands, trying to force down the sob she could feel rising in her throat. She was overtired, that was all. She'd had no sleep at all and the images of what she had seen this night would never leave.

The tears cut tracks through the dust on her cheeks. Her golden dress, once so radiant and lovely, was now torn, dirty and smeared with dried blood.

"Here."

Sara shook the thoughts away, looking up from where she sat. Damaris stood over her, in human form. In one hand she held a canteen of water, which she offered to her.

"Thank you," Sara murmured, her dry lips cracking, taking the water gratefully.

With nothing to protect her from the sun, her skin had begun to burn and it would be quite painful soon.

"The heat doesn't bother you," she remarked, suddenly feeling lonely and wanting someone to talk to.

"I was born in the desert," Damaris answered. "Though not this one." She smiled wryly. "And being a fire attribute does necessitate some immunity to heat."

Of course. How could she possibly self-combust if she wasn't immune to being burned?

Sara handed the canteen back. The Flame Guardian had been transporting water from the oasis to the refugees all morning, along with a few others, using buckets they had found, miraculously undamaged.

There had been no sign of Lylla. Her body hadn't been found among the ruins, though Sara knew it was still a possibility. She felt sick whenever she thought of it and the longer the queen failed to appear, the more worried she became.

A sudden thought occurred to Sara. Was her dad wondering where she was? Hopefully not. She had spent enough nights away from home by now that he shouldn't worry. *If he only knew what I was doing.* Or Nadia or Max for that matter.

Staring out at the ruins of what used to be Khae, another thought came to her, sending her pulse racing.

If this is what the destruction of the Gate had done here, what had it done to the land on the other side? Had anyone been hurt? Professor Lawrence's house was gone and so they didn't have to worry about that.

Damaris glanced down at her. "I should have sent you with the others into the forest."

"I'm more useful here." She wasn't going to mention what had happened with Felix. Not to the Flame Guardian.

Damaris's lips quirked. "Maybe. But you'll be red as a lobster by the time we're done."

***

The stifling heat would finally begin to relent once the sun sank toward the horizon, but there were still several more hours to go. The healers rested when they needed to, and once their strength had been restored, they set about healing those who were too injured to be moved. Soon, hopefully tomorrow morning, they could set out and meet up with the others in the forest, beginning the long trek to the palace where these people could be given proper shelter.

For now, all they could do was wait. Damaris wandered the rubble, still in her human form, looking for nothing in particular. She kept telling herself that Lylla would be here soon, at least, and that alone would give the people more hope than they'd had thus far.

After all, she'd know it if the queen were dead, surely.

The desert elves would one day rebuild their great city and make it grander than before. At least Damaris hoped so. The desert was already a harsh, desolate place and so she hoped the land itself wouldn't be as affected by the loss of the Gate as Malenwar had been. Only time would tell.

She may not have grown up in this particular desert, but it had become home. On Earth, the kingdom she had called home was long gone. And now Khae had been destroyed, taken from her too.

A trace of anger she had been holding at bay broke free, washing over her for a brief moment, searing her skin white-hot. All she could do was ride out the emotion and let it burn itself out or else she would succumb to it. And she knew all too well the consequences *that* would bring.

Save that for when you face Galatea, Damaris told herself, repeating one of her mentor's favorite sayings, *I am in control of my emotions, not the other way around.*

But when she surveyed the wanton destruction of the city she, and so many others, had loved, the fury always threatened to break free of the surface. How many lives had to be taken before Galatea was satisfied?

There was only one life that needed to be taken now and then this madness could be brought to an end.

***

Galatea's eyes snapped open, jerked out of sleep by the sound of something moving outside Cyren's lodge. The fire had dwindled to coals and the wind must have died down, for she could no longer hear it howling. She sat up, throwing off the animal pelt and reaching for her Shadowblade.

"Come out," a voice commanded. "Whoever you are, or we'll have no choice but to torch the place."

Galatea knew that voice. She smiled to herself, having counted on it. They would have seen the smoke, of course, and come to investigate. She rose and opened the door, stepping out onto the snow.

Five white-furred dragons stood before her, the largest in the lead. They had black feathered wings, curving black horns, and black spines running from their foreheads to their tails. And the largest wore a jeweled headdress, the crystals falling down the sides of her face, glowing blue.

"Hello, Empress."

Empress Icicle curled her lip. "You."

She lashed her tail through the snow. Standing at about fourteen feet tall, with long, curved teeth, the dragons were intimidating creatures, but Galatea had faced them before.

"You didn't really think I wouldn't come back, did you?"

"I know better," Icicle said bitterly. "But one could always hope that we'd seen the last of you."

"No such luck, I'm afraid."

"Let's not waste each other's time with urbane pleasantries," the dragon hissed. "I think I can guess why you're here and before you *suggest* that we ally ourselves with you again, I'll make myself perfectly clear when I say we are not involving ourselves in your petty squabbles. We want no part in any of it."

"That's a shame, but I think you'll change your mind when you hear what I have to say," Galatea replied.

Empress sat back on her haunches and gestured with one hand. "Out with it then."

"I've come to tell you that I've destroyed the Wind Gate in the desert and the city of Khae along with it." She did not know for certain that the city had been destroyed—having not crossed over there—but it was in close enough proximity to the Gate that she felt it safe to assume.

"Well," Empress murmured. "There will be no going back now." The dragon shook her head. "Why? Why not let them all believe that you are dead? Why come back at all? You could have lived a long and peaceful life on Earth without any of them the wiser and yet you decide to come back and declare war. Because that's exactly what you've done and I'm not sure you understand the gravity of your actions."

"I understand them perfectly—"

"I can understand why you came back the first time," Empress interrupted. "You wanted to bring Jack back to life and in that regard, I can sympathize with you. I, too, have lost people that I loved to the civil war my people fought. To a certain degree, I have you to thank for that conflict coming to an end. *But*, unlike you, I understand how the world works and that you can't just bring someone back from the dead simply because you miss them. Or perhaps it was done out of some misguided sense of guilt."

"*Don't,*" Galatea spat. *Don't you dare insinuate that I was to blame.*

Sensing she was pushing her luck, Empress returned to her original point. "But Jack is dead, whether you like it or not and this time, you can't bring him back. So what's the plan, Galatea? What now?"

Galatea gripped the hilt of her sword to keep her hand from shaking. "They took him from me when they murdered him in cold blood simply for being different. All I wanted was to get him back but they took that away from me, too. So now I'm going to take something from each of them."

"I see," Icicle said levelly. Her shrewd eyes went to the Ice Gate beside the lodge. "And do you intend to destroy that one as well?"

Galatea glanced at the Gate and said nothing.

Empress grinned her ghastly smile. "Come now, if we're going to be allies, don't you think you should trust me with your plans?" Her mirth faded as quickly as it had appeared. "You intend to destroy them, and Wysteria itself as well, don't you? But what you don't seem to understand is that all of this can only lead to your *own* destruction."

"We'll see about that," Galatea said softly.

What she didn't tell the dragon was that she no longer cared whether she survived what was to come or not. With Jack gone, she had nothing left to live for.

She was well aware of the fact that this could only end one way.

The air was still bitterly cold, even without the whipping wind, and she wanted to bring as swift an end to this conversation as possible. Slippery as Empress could be, she wasn't going to let the dragon get away without giving her an answer.

Preferably the answer she wanted.

"Before you decide whether you want to fight with me or against, you should know that I've also stolen the wind spirit."

Empress scoffed. "I don't believe you."

Galatea drew on her power, commanding the wind spirit to show himself. It would be brief and she wouldn't use any of his magic. All she needed was for the dragons to see him.

She felt Azuma rise up behind her, his massive wings blocking out the sky. Empress's blue eyes widened and she visibly shrank back for a moment. Galatea ordered the wind spirit to disperse, pleased it had had the intended effect.

Empress straightened up, hackles raised. "And you think that the knowledge that you have subjugated that creature would somehow make me want to take your side?"

"I think it could be very convincing," Galatea said evenly.

"I think you're right." The dragon snorted. "You won't allow us to remain neutral or else you never would have come here. Very well, if you want an answer, I'll give it to you. We will join you as allies."

Galatea, who usually schooled her features into a blank mask, could not hide her surprise. Convincing as the wind spirt was, she hadn't foreseen Empress's acquiescence, but that was the way she was: unpredictable. Galatea had learned that the hard way last year and even if the dragon agreed, she would have to keep a watchful eye on the deceitful serpents.

You frightened her. She's only trying to save her own neck.

"Oh, don't look so surprised," Empress jeered. "I fought against you last time and that didn't go very well, now did it? I may as well try my luck on the other side."

It was true that the mountain dragons had fought on Lylla's side—or at least some of them had. There had been division among them about who they should fight for and Galatea suspected there would be again.

But Empress was shrewd and more than anything, concerned with self-preservation. No doubt she worried that Galatea would punish them for agreeing to fight with her and then betraying her at the last moment. If it had been anyone else, the sorceress would have. But the mountain dragons could still be useful to her.

And if their only motivation was to save their own skins, so be it. They had no magic of their own and they knew it.

"I'm pleased to hear it," she said. "So if I was to, say, destroy that Gate," she turned and looked once more to the Ice Gate, "you wouldn't have any objections?"

Empress snorted again. "I wouldn't care under normal circumstances, much less now. We're not Guardians and we have no intention of returning to Earth, so why should we care?"

For once, Galatea felt certain the dragon was telling the truth.

"Now if that's all, I'll leave you to it," the dragon added, likely eager to be gone.

Galatea nodded. "For now.

She had no intention of destroying the Ice Gate yet; she wasn't sure she had recovered sufficiently. But the dragons didn't need to know that. She watched them walk away, the fingers on their hands splaying to distribute their weight so they didn't sink into the snow.

Can you trust her?

"Almost certainly not," Galatea whispered to herself, the words lost in the bitterly cold air.

***

It was late afternoon when Lylla arrived in the desert. She could see the destruction of Khae from the air, before the dragon even landed. The city had been almost entirely obliterated and she could well believe that many people had died.

As soon as the dragon landed, she dismounted along with Wanderer and Serai. The gathered refugees began murmuring among themselves and some had even let out cries of joy upon seeing that she was alive.

Sara began to hurry toward her, but stopped, hanging back. Damaris had no such hesitation and ran up to her before anyone else could reach her.

"What happened?" the Flame Guardian demanded, voice pitched low.

She listened silently as Lylla relayed her story, her crimson-and-amber eyes glittering with some barely suppressed emotion. From the look on her face, Lylla expected her to tell her how foolish it had been to cross over alone, but she didn't.

"I'd have gone with you," Damaris said softly.

"I know you would have, but I didn't know that Galatea would be there."

"You should have come and got me as soon as she ran off."

"I could have," Lylla acknowledged. "But I'm not sure I would have had time. By the time I fetched you and returned, Galatea would have been long gone and the Gate would have been destroyed regardless, since that's clearly what she was there to do. Only this time, there would have been no one there to confront her."

"Yes, I suppose," the Guardian admitted grudgingly.

"I saw an opportunity to end this," Lylla muttered. "I only wish I hadn't failed."

They both knew Damaris would have done the same, perhaps without hesitation at all, charging headlong at the enemy. Reckless. Fearless.

"Even if you'd caught up with her, there was nothing you could have done. If you'd been closer, the blast might have killed you and then where would we be?"

Lylla appreciated her friend's reassurance. In hindsight, she wasn't sure she had done the right thing, but it had seemed that way at the time. *As it always does.*

"Yes. And there's something else you should know. She has the wind spirit, Damaris. I saw it. She used it against me and nearly had the chance to kill me then, but he…resisted her influence at the last moment. He fought back and distracted her."

"That's bad. But at least she doesn't have full control over him yet, from what you say. Maybe she never will."

"It's only a matter of time so we need to be ready." Lylla turned toward the refugees. "Are these all the survivors?" *There are so few.*

"No, not all. I sent those that weren't too badly injured into the forest with Sheba, Felix, and Colin. At least there they'll have some shelter from the sun, water and food. As soon as we can move the rest, we'll catch up with them."

"Right. To that end, I'd better get started."

***

Felix sank to the ground, leaning his back against the trunk of a tree as night began to fall over the Enchanted Forest. It was never truly dark in the forest, with the golden orbs of light that seemed to float through the air, and in some places, the trees themselves gave off a slight glow.

They were camped beside a stream that cut through the forest, from one end of the island to the other, emptying into the Green Sea. Water had been the easy part. Food was another matter. Sara had retrieved some from the wreckage but it wasn't enough for all of them. Colin had set snares, but those took time. Felix had taken his bow and gone hunting, which was something he rarely did. Elves did eat meat, but not very often as a rule. Now they had little choice.

There were some fruit trees to be harvested, but the vast majority of food came from hunting. His muscles ached and his feet hurt horribly from being on them all day, despite the supple leather of his boots. It had been a never-ending trek: tracking down the animal he had shot—or if he was lucky, it had dropped dead where it had stood—dragging it back to camp, and then preparing it to be cooked over the fires that had been lit.

Now at last it was over. Felix wanted nothing more than to sleep but Damaris had tasked him with protecting the Khae refugees and so he felt obligated to stay awake, knowing he would regret it tomorrow. *You're no use to them dead on your feet.*

Despite his best efforts, his eyes kept drifting closed and eventually exhaustion overtook him. His bow remained in his lap, an arrow nocked on the string.

The next thing he knew, he woke with a jolt, disoriented. It was still dark. He must have fallen asleep, but what had woken him? Then he heard it again—a scream splitting the air. He'd thought he'd dreamt it.

Felix sprang to his feet as someone rushed past him, fleeing deeper into the forest. He could make out the silhouettes of elves running through the trees, trying to escape or seek cover. Those that couldn't run were huddled together where he had left them, cowering, and still the horrible shrieking split the air.

He scanned the darkness of the forest, desperately searching for the cause of their distress and then he saw the first wolf. A fire wolf was dragging a man into the trees by one leg as he cried for help.

Without hesitating, Felix raised his bow, pulled the string back to the corner of his mouth and released. He didn't have to manipulate the air for the arrow to fly true, striking the wolf in the forehead. Released from its hold, the man began to drag himself away.

The beasts were everywhere now, appearing out of the darkness and picking off the refugees one by one, knowing that most were too injured or unarmed to fight back. Magic would work as a defense, but fire was useless as an attribute. The wolves were immune to it and the refugees didn't have a Guardian to protect them.

Where was Colin? Felix desperately searched the trees for any sign of his fellow Shadow, but couldn't see him. The sky was overcast, blocking out the moon and making it harder to see.

Sheba came running toward him. "I cannot do anything!" she cried, twin flames busting to life in her palms. "My magic is useless." And most of the survivors did not have weapons. Though some had been salvaged, it wasn't enough.

Those that had the strength to conjure magic did so, but many were still too weak. Climbing a tree was also out of the question. Even if the refugees could manage it, the fire wolves would simply burn the trees down.

Felix yanked another arrow out of his quiver and nocked it, taking aim at the next wolf. His hands shook and the arrow missed, grazing the wolf's fur. He swore. His heart was pounding in his chest so hard, his body shook slightly with each beat and it was enough to make his aim ever so slightly off.

He summoned the wind instead, throwing the wolf against a tree trunk, the force breaking its spine. All around him the screams went on as people continued to die. He couldn't afford to think, not about the danger or how many people he had already failed to save or the fact that Venryk could be here, sneaking up behind him for the kill right now—although his scars weren't burning.

If he allowed himself to think, he would freeze again and then all would be lost.

Felix thought instead of what Damaris would do, the way she would face the problem and tried to conjure even a shred of her courage. This was just another battle, just another situation he'd gone through in training.

Emptying his mind of all emotion, he merely acted, firing arrow after arrow until there were none left in his quiver. At some point, he handed his sword and twin, curved daggers off to someone else to use, relying on his magic the way Damaris had shown him.

This time, she wasn't there to help him.

10

There were more bodies for Damaris to burn when Lylla escorted the second group of refugees to the first. The scene they came upon was one of chaos, lit unflinchingly by the sunlight filtering through the forest canopy. Bodies of both elves and fire wolves littered the forest floor. Felix reported to her, saying that they hadn't lost as many as they could have, but it was still too many.

He avoided her gaze, keeping it locked on the ground and she could tell that he felt he had failed. He had retrieved his arrows from the fallen wolves, but she knew from the bodies that he had slain many of them.

"You did well," she murmured. Given the circumstances, it would have been impossible for him to save every life.

Some of the casualties had been killed outright by wolves, others lingering and succumbing to their wounds later. With no time for a proper burial, they were burned as the other dead had been and the journey to the palace resumed. The fire wolves were left where they lay. Burning them would have been of no use anyway.

Felix walked beside Damaris, on foot, leading his horse Tempest, who was carrying some of the injured.

She glanced over at him. She didn't have to ask if he had killed Venryk. The answer was still written there, the angry scars slashing down the left side of his face. If he had been successful, they would have been gone.

"Did you see Venryk?" she asked instead.

He continued to look straight ahead. "I saw him. I didn't get a clear shot and there was no time to chase after him."

Damaris could imagine how much that had pained him. He had waited for a sign of the wolf ever since Galatea had left. Now, a year later, the wolf had come to him and he'd been robbed of a chance to finish this by the responsibility he had to protect the vulnerable. It would have been a hard decision to make, but she was proud he had made the right one.

And not a little bit frustrated herself. As hard as it was for him, she was aware as well as anyone that time was running out. And there was nothing she could do about it.

***

It took the rest of the day, pausing to rest at night, and half of the next for them to reach the palace. Thus far, there had been no further news of disaster and no other catastrophe had befallen them. It was only a matter of time, but Lylla was thankful for every moment they got.

She gave instructions to the staff to see that the survivors were fed and given rooms, where they could bathe and change into clean clothes. They were exhausted after the journey and disheartened. Some of them just wanted to rest.

But for others, there was no time for rest. Before reaching the palace, Lylla had instructed Damaris to fetch Cassius from his cottage at the Water Gate. He likely had no idea that anything was amiss and he not only needed to know, but now that they knew Galatea had returned and destroyed the Wind Gate, they needed to decide what was to be done about it.

The other two Guardians, Cyren and Kadir, were no longer able to be part of the discussion and so they were two members short. The empty spaces in the hall seemed glaringly obvious, the room too quiet without them. Ordinarily, new Guardians would have been appointed to take their place, but other than Sara, there were no other Guardians and she was nowhere near being assigned a Gate.

Cassius glanced at his sister, Cyren's, empty seat as he walked into the council chamber, taking his own. Each place had a banner hanging over it, with the color and symbol of each Guardian's element. The upper balcony, high above their heads, was ringed with stone statues of great heroes and leaders that had come before.

Cassius broke the silence first. "Damaris filled me in on the way."

He was a tall elf, as all shadow elves were, with long black hair and yellow eyes. He wore dark blue robes, the color of the element water.

Lylla nodded. "Galatea has returned, as we feared she would. She has stolen the wind spirit and destroyed the Wind Gate. We do not know what she intends, but if she has destroyed two Gates, what is to stop her from trying to do so again?"

"Why should we stop her?" Cassius demanded suddenly, his sharp tone reverberating throughout the chamber. "Why not do her job for her and destroy the remaining Gates?"

"That is madness," Damaris growled.

"It's not madness if we can trap her on the other side. Then we will be free of her forever. Let her live among the humans she loved so very much. We would be better off separated from them anyway. What good did they ever do us? They're the reason we're in this mess in the first place."

"You know why we can't," Lylla said gently. She knew Cassius still felt the loss of his sister keenly and looked for someone to blame. The fact that he and Cyren were responsible for Jack's original death likely didn't help matters.

"You will destroy half of Wysteria!" Damaris scoffed.

"Perhaps, but Galatea will do it regardless. And this time, we can evacuate everyone in the line of fire beforehand so no one will be hurt."

"They still will have no place to live," Wanderer pointed out.

"A small price to pay. Besides, in a place like the desert or Iceland, it's already so desolate, it will probably suffer little damage."

"No," Lylla said. "We cannot destroy the Gates. Such an idea has been suggested in the past and we all know why it's not possible. Besides, even if we do succeed in trapping Galatea on the other side, as you suggest, what then? We will have left our human Guardians and countless innocents to her mercy."

Callous as his plan was, she could understand why Cassius would feel the way he did. After Galatea had killed his sister, in the battle of Malenwar last summer, she had reanimated her dead body, nearly using it to kill him.

"We can bring the other Guardians into Wysteria. As for what happens to the rest of the humans, why should we care? They've done enough harm to us and they're precisely the reason why we should have sealed ourselves off from them long ago."

"Personally," Damaris interrupted, "I would much rather have a chance to pay Galatea back for all that she's done rather than trap her somewhere and leave her for someone else to deal with. And I have a feeling you would feel the same, Cassius."

He frowned, shifting in his seat, and looked away. He could not deny it. To do so would be a lie.

At last he sighed, the anger draining out of him. "So what do we do, then?"

"We can't send guards like the last time," Lylla answered. "They're not enough against a Guardian as skilled as Galatea, especially now that she has the wind spirit."

What she did not add was the simple truth that most soldiers, being limited to only one element, did not have the skill or the training to go up against a Guardian. There hadn't been a need to train for such a thing before—and there shouldn't have been a need even now.

Guardians were supposed to be the protectors of Wysteria, not its greatest threat. And in better times, all of them had been. The betrayal of one of their own, of one sworn to protect the land and all those in it, to lay down their life if necessary, cut deep. It had left people shaken and afraid.

Through her scouts, that kept her apprised of such things, Lylla had even heard whispers of another fear among the people—what if another Guardian turned against them? What if they became afraid, lost faith in the cause, and joined with Galatea, perhaps not believing her to be right, but worried that the others stood no chance against her?

"So how many were you thinking?" Damaris asked quietly. "Some of the Gates still have Guardians, but the ones that don't…"

Lylla sighed. "We simply don't have enough Guardians to cover them all."

"Well, one bright spot in all of this—if you can call it that—is that we no longer have to worry about the Wind Gate," Cassius pointed out. "So the only Gate that's left without a Guardian is the Ice Gate. Damaris's Gate is hidden; she's free to move around. Galatea doesn't know where it is, so we can assume it's safe. Why not send Damaris to the Ice Gate? Then they're all covered."

"Yes," Lylla agreed, "except the Ice Gate is the only one without Guardians on both sides. Galatea may not destroy it for that reason alone. If she meets no resistance, she may find it useful to cross back and forth. Regardless, Damaris's protection wouldn't do much good, since she can only be on one side of the Gate at a time. Galatea could simply avoid her altogether by destroying the Gate from the Earth side."

"So what do we do with it then?"

"Perhaps it's best to leave that Gate as it is and focus instead on protecting the ones we know we can, to ensure nothing happens to them. And then, with a Guardian at each of these Gates, regiments of guards can be sent to further help shore up their defenses."

"In other words, you're saying the Ice Gate is already a lost cause," Wanderer said softly.

"I hope not," Lylla sighed deeply, hoping the decision she was making was the correct one. They couldn't afford to be wrong. "But I worry that it may be true, yes. We can't afford to be cautious. Too little protection and we can lose another Gate or a Guardian this time. After all, we don't know what exactly it is that Galatea wants and that's part of the problem. She may have only destroyed that Gate because there *was* no Guardian there. Next time, she may target one of you."

She eyed each of them in turn, driving home the severity of the possibility.

"Let's not forget that she has a powerful motive for wanting you dead, Cassius, and you as well, Damaris."

When Galatea had first brought Jack to Wysteria all those years ago, and then refused to return to Earth with him, it had been Cassius and Cyren, acting in secret, who had killed him, naively believing it would put an end to the issue.

And after Galatea had brought Jack back to life, it had been Damaris who had killed him the second time, burning his body until nothing remained so that such a thing could never be done again.

Damaris curled her lip, revealing the fangs that she retained even in her human form. "I'd like to see her try."

Despite her bravado, Lylla knew that the Flame Guardian took the risk seriously. Of all the Guardians, she had the best chance at defeating Galatea—and the sorceress likely knew it. Galatea wasn't likely to make a move on Damaris, at least not at first.

She would need to gain complete control over Azuma before attempting such a thing.

Wanderer shook her head. "We can't take the risk of losing another Gate. Not even the Ice Gate."

"What would you have me do, Wanderer? We don't have enough Guardians."

They had always been rare, but now, in their most desperate hour, there seemed to be fewer of them than ever.

"I think Cassius made a good point earlier," Wanderer argued. "We can bring the other Guardians into Wysteria. The other Water and Flame Guardians. Their Gates are on the other side of the world. I doubt Galatea would travel all the way over there just to destroy them on the Earth side. She'd still be trapped on Earth if she did that, and have to travel all the way to the next Gate. No, if she's going to do this, I think she'll do it here, on the Wysterian side.

"Think about it. The other Guardians probably have no idea what's been going on. It's only the town of Mayfair that's been affected by the Gates' destruction so far. Their Gates haven't been targeted. So why not bring them here, where they can help us?"

Silence settled over the room, all eyes on the Lightning Guardian. It was an interesting idea, to be sure, and would instantly solve their Guardian shortage. With two extra Guardians, they could each protect the Ice Gate, currently the most vulnerable—one on each side. And since they were both humans, accustomed to living on Earth, it wouldn't be a problem to assign one of them to the Earth-side.

Wanderer was right; there was no point leaving them where they were. Not when their skills could be put to better use here.

"Very well," Lylla said at last. "It is the best option, given the circumstances. We don't have any other choice. Damaris, I leave this task up to you. With your Gate hidden, you're the only Guardian free to move about. Find the other Guardians and bring them here."

The fact that only Damaris, the other Flame Guardian, and Lylla herself knew the location of the Flame Gate made it the most secure of all and allowed its Guardian to leave it for long periods of time, carrying out other tasks in service to the kingdom.

Damaris nodded. "It will be done."

"The rest of you—mind your Gates and stay alert."

Dismissed, the Guardians began to file out.

Never in history had human Guardians been brought to Wysteria to serve in such a way. *These are dark times, indeed,* Lylla thought as she watched the others walk away, off to their respective duties.

Failure wasn't an option.

***

Damaris left with Cassius, traveling side by side to the Water Gate. That was where she would begin. He bid her good luck as they reached the Gate, him standing in the doorway to his cottage.

The Water Gate stood exposed on the edge of the cliff overlooking the sea. As Damaris stepped up to it, the wind blowing off the ocean hit her in the face, bringing with it a tang of salt in the air.

She had lived long enough that she had crossed through each of the Gates on occasion, though it was a rare occurrence.

Part of Damaris wanted to ask if it was truly wise, leaving one side of the Gate unprotected. It was unlikely that Galatea would cross over to Earth and destroy the Gates from that side, although the fact remained that there was less protection on the Earth side. It would be an easy way to avoid the other Guardians while also getting rid of them. They would be killed by the blast and none the wiser as to what had happened until it was too late.

But at the same time, staying in Wysteria gave Galatea easy access to all the Gates. It would take far too long for her to travel from one Gate to another on Earth. And even if bringing the other Guardians to Wysteria left one side of their Gates vulnerable, the Ice Gate was a far bigger concern. It had no one to protect it.

Damaris stepped through the Water Gate. One moment, she had been standing on the edge of the cliff,

119

overlooking the Green Sea, and the next she was surrounded by a Neolithic ring of stones.

It was dark on this side of the world, unlike in Wysteria where it was still daylight. Damaris blinked a few times, waiting for her eyes to adjust to the sudden change. This was the only time she could safely cross over, where Stonehenge was not crowded with people. She couldn't risk being seen.

She sighed, taking a moment to peer up at the stones, nearly as old as she. Humans had debated their purpose for centuries. Regardless of what the stones had been intended for, no one had guessed that they sat upon a gateway to another world. Best to keep it that way.

Setting out, she headed east toward Amesbury, where the Earth-side Guardian of the Water Gate lived. It had been many years since she had last been here and she nearly lost her way, but at last she came to the cottage where Samuel lived.

Unfortunately, owing to the public nature of the Gate's location, the Guardians could not live directly beside the Gate they protected. It was a risk, but the place being a tourist site gave it a sort of protection in a different way.

With night having fallen, she needed to hurry. She'd go to the Flame Gate next and its time zone on Earth was even further ahead. Pounding her fist on the door, she stepped back and waited, hoping that everything was as it should be.

The door opened and a bleary-eyed man peered out at her. She'd stepped through as a human, but hadn't bothered to glamour her eyes. Even if she had, he probably would have been able to see through it and know who she was.

Samuel blinked, all signs of weariness gone. "Damaris? What's wrong?" He stepped back to let her inside and shut the door.

"I know it's short notice, but I need you to come with me. I'll explain on the way, but we need to hurry."

He pursed his lips. He was a middle-aged man, with a thick thatch of curly brown hair and gray eyes. If it had been anyone else showing up to his door in the middle of the night and saying such things, he might have been disinclined to believe them.

"All right," he sighed, running a hand over his face. "Let me get dressed."

He disappeared deeper into the small cottage, reappearing a few moments later, dressed in a white button-up shirt, black trousers, boots, a gray waistcoat, and a flat cloth cap. "All right, let's go."

They made the two-mile journey back to Stonehenge on foot, Damaris setting a brisk pace as she explained everything that had happened over the past two years. The threat Galatea had posed had been contained on Earth within Mayfair, on the other side of the world, so Samuel and the human Guardian of the Flame Gate hadn't been informed. Damaris assured him that if there had been any danger, they would have been.

"But things are different now. Galatea is targeting the Gates themselves rather than individuals. Lylla tasked me with coming here to inform you and bring you to Wysteria."

Samuel looked at her in surprise, his thick eyebrows rising. "To Wysteria?" He'd likely only been there once or twice the entirety of his life, when he had taken over for the former Guardian and been established as the current one.

"Yes. Your aid will be invaluable in helping us defeat her." *If only we could have done this sooner. Then the Gates that had had no Guardian would have had at least one.*

Switching the Guardians positions like that was unheard of, but these were desperate times.

Samuel sighed. They were approaching Stonehenge, visible and growing rapidly nearer by the moment. "Of course I'll go."

He couldn't have expected this and had taken nothing with him but the clothes on his back, but he would be well provided for when he reached the palace. Damaris knew the news came as a shock to him, and they were asking quite a lot, but he had taken an oath as they all had. His responsibility was primarily to the Earth side, but if Wysteria was in danger, so was his home and protecting one meant coming to the defense of the other.

He knew that and was willing to make the necessary sacrifices. Damaris admired him for it.

"I'm glad to hear it. Can you find your own way to the palace? I'd escort you, of course, but I have to reach the Flame Gate as soon as possible."

To her immense relief, he replied, "I think I remember the way."

She nodded and crossed over with him, leaving him to make his own way. She turned back into a unicorn and raced across the grasslands and into the Enchanted Forest as night fell across the land.

Her Gate was hidden deep in a grove of trees, always shrouded by a thick mist. There was no time to observe the weathered gravestones of the ancient cemetery surrounding her Gate. She stepped up between the two statues of stone angels and commanded the Gate to open, stepping through onto sand.

The instant change of transitioning from one climate to the next never became less of a shock. She breathed deeply of the fresh desert air. She could see the Great Sphinx of Giza in the distance, sand stretching outward beneath the starry sky. Behind her was the Great Pyramid, towering high into the night.

It wasn't home, but it reminded her of it and she felt a tug of yearning.

There was no time to lose. Damaris ran toward where she knew the house would be, passed down from one Guardian to the next. She had even further to go than she had with Samuel, venturing into the city, but her memory served her well.

Not wanting to draw unwelcome attention, she rapped softly upon the door, beating harder when there was no answer. Time was running out.

At last it swung open. A young man glared out at her. "Keep it down! You'll wake the children—" He broke off as he realized who he was speaking to. "You."

Damaris found herself staring into the face of the other Flame Guardian. It felt strange to think of him that way, of there being another at all.

He was dressed as though he had just climbed out of bed, black hair tussled, standing out starkly against his brown skin.

"I'm sorry for disturbing you, Imhotep, but I need you to come with me. It's urgent."

"Come with you where?"

"To Wysteria. You're needed."

He shook his head. "I can't come with you. My family…"

"I'm sorry, Imhotep," Damaris said again. "But I'm not asking."

He had to come with her, whether he liked it or not. Unlike Samuel, who had never married and had no family to the best of her knowledge, Imhotep did. She couldn't blame him for not wanting to leave his wife and young children behind—and he would likely be even more reluctant when he learned what he was being dragged away for.

His nostrils flared, jaw clenching, and for a moment, Damaris thought he would refuse anyway.

"Wait here," he said, ducking back inside. He shut the door, not inviting her in. Damaris took no offense, waiting on the step, trying—and failing—not to be impatient.

The better part of half an hour later, he returned, fully dressed in loose cotton clothing, having packed a small bag.

"Now what is this all about?"

She jerked her head in the direction she'd come. "I'll fill you in on the way."

***

Sara had never imagined that a shower could feel so good, finally being able to scrub the dirt and blood from her skin and change out of the golden dress when she returned to the palace. She never wanted to see the dress again. The joy it had brought her was gone and looking at it now only brought to mind memories she would rather put behind her.

As soon as she had changed into clean clothes and re-braided her hair, she roamed the palace halls in search of Lylla.

She found her as she was leaving the meeting chamber and informed her that she was crossing back over onto Earth for a little while. She needed to see what, if any, damage had been done to her town and catch up with her

124

friends. Even if there had been no damage, the blast of the Gate exploding would be the talk of the town.

Lylla had no objection, but she warned her to be careful. Wanderer was just leaving the palace and so Sara accompanied her. This time of day, the gas station might still be open, but she would just have to risk it.

The Lightning Gate, while in the middle of the forest in Wysteria, came out in the gas station bathroom on Earth. There was only one and it was single occupancy. There was always the risk that when crossing over, one would accidentally encounter someone in a most awkward situation, and so crossing very early or late was best, barring an emergency.

Luckily, the gas station was empty when Sara crossed over. Having left her car in the parking lot, she climbed in and drove out of town, wanting to see where Professor Lawrence's house used to be before going home.

There was no house anymore; that much was the same. Sara slowed, coming to a complete stop in the middle of the road at the sight of what remained. The tree line that had separated the Professor's property from the field next door had been leveled. Tree trunks lay sprawled on top of each other, the leaves ripped from their branches. Even the grass had darkened and shriveled, the damage extending to the other side of the road, where it kept going.

Sara swallowed, pulling into what had once been the driveway, now overgrown with weeds, and turned around. On her drive through town, she hadn't noticed any collapsed buildings, which was both a relief and a surprise, considering nearly everything in Mayfair was so old. It wouldn't have taken much force to collapse some of the buildings in town.

Her dad's car was already in the garage when she pulled in, hands stiffening on the steering wheel. Had he wondered what took her so long? Had he been worried? What did he think of the explosion?

The conversation was inevitable and the anticipation was only adding further weight, making her palms sweat. Best to get it over with. That was the only way she would get answers to her questions.

She found her dad in the kitchen, heating up a microwave dinner. He'd never been much of a cook and neither had she. That had been her mother. That had been before.

He looked up apologetically as she came into the kitchen. "If I'd known you were coming, I would have cooked something."

"That's okay. I might get something later with Nadia and Max."

His brow furrowed as he stared at the timer counting down on the microwave. "Is that where you've been? With them or…?" He trailed off, but the implication was clear.

"No, I've been in Wysteria."

"You were gone so long. There was an earthquake here, did you know? Couple of nights ago."

Sara fidgeted, sitting down at the table. "An earthquake? Was anything damaged?"

"No, it doesn't seem so, from what I've heard," her dad replied as the microwave beeped. "Some trees toppled out at the Professor's old place and further down, a crack ran across the road. Split it right in half. When I first heard about it, I was worried something more might have happened. But that seems to be it."

Their house stood at the edge of town, closer to the blast than most. She could see how he would be concerned and felt guilty for it.

He didn't understand the half of it. It wasn't an earthquake. It was something much worse. The threat that

Galatea posed was no longer contained in Wysteria. It had crossed over and affected her world. The Wind Gate had been far enough out of town that Mayfair had been spared.

But if something should happen to the Lightning Gate…

The gas station was on the other side of town, not out in the country like Professor Lawrence's house had been. If that Gate were to be destroyed as the Wind Gate was, homes and businesses would be decimated along with it. Sara imagined the shockwave that had leveled Khae radiating outward across her small town and felt a chill spread through her core, as if ice had formed in her stomach.

She suddenly felt exhausted. The secret that she had been carrying for the past year had never seemed so heavy. She'd avoided telling her dad about Galatea, about why she wanted to take Professor Lawrence's place as Guardian, because she knew he wouldn't approve of the danger she was putting herself in. Although there had never been quite as much danger as there was now…

Now it wasn't just Wysterians that were at risk. Her entire town could be wiped out in the blink of an eye, just like Khae was. Khae had been far larger than Mayfair. There'd be nothing left of it. Every home would be destroyed. People would die, just as they had in Khae. The images of the injured she had helped and the dead she had seen that night floated to the surface of her mind and Sara suddenly felt sick.

This was a secret that was too deadly to keep. Galatea now posed a danger to Mayfair itself; everyone in town was at risk and they didn't even know. If she stayed silent about what she knew and something were to happen, would she be to blame for it? Was there even anything she could do to prevent it?

"Are you feeling okay? You look a little pale."

Sara looked up. Her dad had joined her across the table, steam rising from the chicken and macaroni he'd microwaved.

She closed her eyes. She'd have to tell him the truth. All of it. She didn't want to, but what choice was there? If Galatea posed a threat to Earth and the people in it, that included her dad.

She looked across at him again, realizing her hands were shaking. With her mom gone, he was the only parent she had left. What if, by failing to warn him, she lost him as well? Fear gripped her heart at the thought of it—fear stronger than what his reaction would be if she told him. It wasn't worth risking it.

"Actually, Dad, I have something to tell you…" Sara said heavily, clenching her hands together. "Promise you won't be mad."

"I promise," he said, frowning, tone wary.

Sara told him everything, from where it had all begun last summer, starting with accidentally getting caught up in Wysteria, finding out she was a Guardian herself, the truth behind Professor Lawrence's death and why she wanted to take his place, the past year of training, and now Galatea's return and the destruction of the Wind Gate.

"That's what happened," she finished. "It wasn't an earthquake."

He sat there, staring at her without a word. As she spoke, Sara watched various emotions chase each other across his face. The shock, hurt, and anger had nearly undone her, but she'd forced herself to keep talking. Once begun, she couldn't stop.

At last, it was all out there in the open between them. No more secrets. Her heart beat an erratic rhythm in her chest. Now that the story was over, there was nothing to focus on but her anxiety over how he would react.

"My God," he said softly. His meal remained untouched, growing cold, completely forgotten. "Why didn't you tell me?"

Why do you think? "You promised you wouldn't be mad!" she reminded him "I didn't want you to try to keep me from going back. I didn't want you to worry."

"Of course I would have stopped you!" he exclaimed. "I'm worried now." He swore softly, something he never did. "And of course I'm angry, Sara. You could have died! That night in the Professor's house. You nearly did!"

She flinched. Before tonight, he'd believed as most in town had—that the explosion had been the result of a gas leak, not that Damaris had done it. Not that she'd been in the house mere moments before it had gone up.

It wasn't the only time she'd found herself in danger since Wysteria had come into her life, but it was perhaps the closest she had come to dying. She had been lucky, but others hadn't.

"Well, maybe that's for the best, that the Gates be destroyed," he added. "That the worlds separate. I think it's certainly best if you separate yourself from all of this, Sara. It's not your affair."

She swallowed. She knew what he was suggesting, but she wanted to hear him say it. "So you're saying I shouldn't go back."

"I'm saying you *can't* go back. Understand? I don't want you going back there."

"But I have to!" Sara protested, leaning across the table. "I can't just leave them."

"It's none of your concern. Let the others fight this battle. It has nothing to do with you. They're the ones who started it anyway, from what you say."

"That's not true. I am involved, whether you like it or not. I'm a Guardian."

"You're my daughter, first and foremost." He shot her a glare. She knew that look, having seen it throughout her childhood whenever she'd wanted something and pushed too far. It said that the conversation was over as far as he was concerned. But Sara didn't agree.

"It's not as bad as you think," she said, wincing inwardly. After everything she'd told him, now was not the time to downplay the situation, but it was her only hope. Make him think he was overreacting, being overprotective. "I'm a Guardian, Dad. I can take care of myself." That hadn't been true lately, but she hadn't told him about her struggles with her magic. It somehow didn't seem relevant. It was one of the few cards she had left to play and she wasn't going to give it up by admitting just how helpless she really was.

"So was your mother," he countered, "but she didn't get involved in any of this stuff."

"Because there was no need then," Sara argued. "There is now! If Mom were here, you know she would want to help."

"She might've, but she wouldn't have."

"Why not? How do you know?"

"Because of you. She left all of that behind when she had you. You were more important than any of that. Family was more important."

Even so, there hadn't been a threat then like there was now. If Galatea had returned while her mother was still alive, would she have gone? Or would she have stayed for Sara?

"She wouldn't have given up everything for a world and a life that wasn't hers," her dad pressed. "If you had died,

Sara, what would I have done? I'm only trying to protect you. That's my job, as a parent."

If he was trying to guilt-trip her, it was working.

"What about my friends?" Sara said, the argument sounding weak. "I can't just leave them there. I have magic, I can help."

"I'm sure they're more than capable. And what about your friends *here*? Do they know about any of this? You don't spend as much time with them, the way you used to. Remember what I said about not being able to live in both worlds? You have a life here that comes before anything else. Your mother realized that and now it's time you do the same."

It was hopeless. She couldn't convince him to let her go back to Wysteria, knowingly putting her life in danger. And it was true that anything could happen. She might cross over one day and never come back.

She thought of Felix, her heart twisting treacherously. He put his life on the line every day—all of them did. How could she do anything less? She was a Light Guardian for heaven's sake! If she had the ability to help them, she had to.

Her dad glanced down at the meal before him, grimaced and pushed it aside. "I mean it, Sara," he said softly. "I know you don't like it, and I'm not asking you to like it, but I don't want you going back there again. Do you understand?"

She looked down at the tablecloth. "I understand." *But I do not agree.*

An hour later, Sara pulled up outside of Nadia's house. When the text had come through, asking her if she wanted to come over and watch a movie, Sara had immediately accepted. It would be good to see her friends again and it was a relief to be out of the house after how the conversation with her dad had gone. She wasn't sure whether he felt the same, but he made no objection to her going.

Popcorn was already in the microwave when Sara arrived, its pleasant aroma suffusing the house. Nadia and Max were sprawled out on the sectional, Nadia waving her over. Sara collected the popcorn, dumping it into a bowl, and went over to join them.

"At last, you're here!" Nadia exclaimed. "You can be the tie-breaker. Max and I have been arguing over what movie to watch ever since I texted you. *He* wants Star Wars, *I*—"

"Whatever you're going to say, Star Wars instantly beats it," Max interrupted.

"*I*," Nadia continued, "want to watch something Marvel. Not sure which one yet. So those are your choices, Star Wars or Marvel. What will it be?"

Sara didn't really have a preference either way and said as much.

Nadia sighed. "Maybe we should just watch a K-drama instead."

Max groaned, burying his face in one of the throw pillows.

"Oh, come on! Don't act like you don't secretly enjoy them!"

"Really," Sara said, passing around the popcorn. "Anything's fine with me."

Nadia picked up the remote, mindlessly scrolling through their list of options. Sara watched the colorful icons scroll past almost too fast for the eye to follow. She didn't know how Nadia managed.

"Did you feel that earthquake a few days ago?" Nadia asked, jerking her thoughts back to the one thing Sara hadn't really wanted to dwell on. "Happened out by the Professor's old place. Or where it used to be. You live closer than I do."

"Yeah, I felt it," Sara said softly. It wasn't a lie. She had felt it, just not on this side of the Gate. And she had done more than simply feel it—she had lived through it. The fact that her friends had no idea just how much danger she'd been in put a bad taste in her mouth.

"Crazy, isn't it?" Max remarked, talking with his mouth full of popcorn, mostly unintelligible. "First a gas explosion and then an earthquake. Something's majorly not right about that place."

You have no idea.

Sara took another handful of popcorn, but didn't eat it. Guilt flooded her, weighing her down with the knowledge that she knew but couldn't share. She wanted to tell them everything she had told her dad, but to say that had gone poorly would be an understatement.

Nadia had already changed the subject, but Sara was barely listening. Something about having to take an online class before starting college that fall. She was complaining about having to take a personality test and something that would reveal her strengths and weaknesses, ideally to help her discover which careers would be suited for her and which wouldn't.

"As if I need someone to tell me that," she added, rolling her eyes.

That only made Sara feel worse, in addition to her sense of guilt, as she thought about how her life had diverged so differently from that of her friends. And she'd thought it had taken a turn when her mom had died of cancer, an experience neither of them had had to deal with or understand—not that she would wish such an experience on anyone.

And yet it had only diverged further. College was the only thing that Nadia and Max had to worry about, and while stressful, it was nothing compared to being caught up in a war. So much had changed in so little time and their friendship was no longer what it had once been. How could it be?

She had changed, too.

Here she sat, with two different paths in front of her, stretching out in two very different directions, and she no closer to a decision.

"Sara."

She looked up to see Nadia staring at her. "Huh?"

"You were spacing out. Were you even listening?"

She sighed. Some company she was. "No. Sorry."

"Are you all right? You can tell us, you know."

"I'm fine."

"Don't think I haven't noticed," Nadia warned. "You keep running off and disappearing, sometimes for a whole day or more. You don't answer texts. Is something wrong? Is this about what happened to the Professor? Or—your mom?"

Sara grimaced. "No." *Well, sort of.*

Professor Lawrence had been a Guardian and had died by Galatea's hand. Her mother had also been a Guardian, though she'd never been assigned to a Gate. *Or told me about Wysteria,* a fact that had hurt when she'd learned the truth—even if she'd understood the reasoning behind it—and still did if she chose to dwell on it for too long.

Their deaths were entirely different, and yet it all came back to the same thing in the end, didn't it? Someone she cared about had died and she was powerless to do anything about it.

"Is it a guy?"

"No," Sara denied, her treacherous thoughts darting instantly to Felix and how he'd almost kissed her that night up on the roof. Gosh, it felt so long ago now. A line of demarcation between the before and after in her life, when the ground had felt solid beneath her feet and she knew where they both stood.

She felt her cheeks heat, betraying her.

"It is!"

"Why does it have to be a guy?" *Let her think that. You can't tell her the truth.*

Nadia gave her a look. "Sara, everything's always about a guy. Spill!"

Sara opened her mouth to say that there was nothing to tell, when she realized that she could ask Nadia about Felix. She might be able to help make sense of his conflicting behavior. But she didn't know Felix and so that wouldn't help matters.

Just keep it general. "There *is* this guy I like," she admitted, looking away in embarrassment. "And I thought he liked me, too."

"Thought? Have you kissed yet?"

"No. I thought we were about to, but then…he just broke it off and left. And I don't know why."

"Guys can be weird like that. So confusing. Always sending mixed signals."

"I think you've got that the other way around," Max remarked. "Sure you're not describing girls?"

Nadia waved a hand at him to shush. "Do I know this person?"

"No. You've never met him."

"How did you meet him?"

"He…knew the Professor. Former student, maybe, or something like that."

"Ooh, so he's older. Is he hot?"

"*Nadia!*"

Her friend held up her hands. "Well, since I don't know him, I can't really begin to guess. But I'd say, if he likes you, he'll let you know. And if he doesn't," Nadia shrugged. "Forget him. He's not worth it, no matter how hot he is."

Sara didn't feel reassured the way she'd hoped. She knew Felix, after all, and even she couldn't figure him out.

In the end, Nadia chose a K-drama and the conversation died as they all settled back to watch. Sara stared at the subtitles without really comprehending them. Her thoughts were a million miles away, thinking of a certain crimson-haired elf and wondering what he might be doing at that exact moment.

There was only one thing Sara found herself sure of. How could she leave him there, whatever his true feelings for her? Or her feelings for him, come to think of it. God, it was all so confusing.

How could she do as her dad wished and *never* go back?

And even if she did go back, to what end? What was her place there? She'd meant to take Professor Lawrence's place at the Gate and now…

Now there was no Gate.

But what she'd done at Khae, the sense of helping people… Could that be the answer?

***

Wanderer quickly crept around the gas station to the back where Hank's house stood and rapped on the door. The lights on within told her that he was home. She needed to see him tonight, before it was too late. She didn't know when she'd get another chance—or if.

As soon as he opened the door, she squeezed past him and he shut the door behind her.

"I was wondering when you'd come."

She felt unusually nervous and tried to hide it. He would sense it and know something was wrong. But this was too serious a situation to be flippant about.

"We need to talk," she said softly.

He frowned. "Uh-oh. The words every boyfriend fears." He sat down on the sofa and she joined him, tucking her legs up beneath her.

"It's about the Gate. Well, and us. Have you seen Galatea?"

He shook his head. "No. I haven't seen her." She cursed herself as he reached over and took one of her hands. "What is it?" He'd noticed.

"I—I just want you to be careful." Briefly, she told him of Lylla's plan to send soldiers to shore up the Gates, as well as bringing the other two Guardians into Wysteria so that no Gate was left unguarded. Hopefully it would be enough to deal with the sorceress this time.

"I just want you to be careful," she repeated when she'd finished. He wouldn't have anyone on this side helping him. Lylla couldn't very well send hundreds of soldiers into a small town on Earth and expect people not to notice. The entire town only had a few hundred people in it!

Hank squeezed her hand. His hand was large and rough, dwarfing hers. "You know I will be."

"I know, but we don't know what Galatea plans. She's already destroyed two Gates. She may attack more. If she comes for this one, or if there's any trouble, promise me you'll cross over."

"You want me to run?"

Wanderer was asking him to do just that, but she couldn't phrase it that way. It would offend him, both as a Guardian and a man, suggesting that he might not be able to handle whatever might come.

"I want you to be safe."

He let go of her hand. "I took an oath, Wanderer. So did you. I swore to protect this Gate. I can't just run off at the first sign of trouble and abandon it."

"This is different," Wanderer insisted. She had to make him understand. She *had* to. "Galatea is more powerful now than she's ever been. You heard what Lylla said. She has the wind spirit! How can one person stand up to that, Guardian or not?"

"I'm not leaving, Wanderer," Hank said firmly. "That would be letting her win."

You don't understand! she wanted to scream. She felt tears well up in her eyes, thinking of the destruction of Khae and how many of its citizens had been killed. He hadn't seen it for himself. If he had, perhaps he would understand why she was asking this of him. Under normal circumstances, she never would have dared. There would have been no need. But these circumstances were anything but normal.

Wanderer had taken the same oath he had and took it just as seriously. Why couldn't he see that she didn't ask this lightly?

"It's just a Gate!" Wanderer snapped, her frustration getting the best of her. She brushed her tears away angrily. "We can lose the Gate. I can't lose you."

"You're not going to lose me, lassie." Hank put his arms around her, drawing her close. "I'm right here."

Don't make promises you can't keep. Wanderer gulped in air, trying to keep from sobbing. She breathed in his scent, of grease from the garage and woodsmoke.

If he wouldn't cross over, she would just have to protect him then. If Damaris could do it, so could she. She would fight beside him, if it came to that. Together, nothing could stop them, not even Galatea and Azuma. They were the Lightning Guardians, after all.

This was one Gate that was not going to lose either of its Guardians.

11

The next morning, as soon as her dad left for work, Sara crossed back over to Wysteria. It felt like a betrayal, guilt settling in her stomach like a stone as she imagined what he would have to say if he should find out.

But even so, he'd been wrong to forbid her to return. She knew he was only trying to protect her, in his own way, but it was misguided all the same. He hadn't seen what she had seen, lived through what she had. Otherwise things would be different. He would understand she couldn't just abandon her friends.

Yes, she had a life on Earth. That would always be true. But she had responsibilities to people other than just herself or the people she knew from her life on Earth.

And she was only going to the palace anyway, she reassured herself. That was the safest place to be on the whole island. Nothing would happen. If she wasn't safe there, she wasn't safe anywhere.

With the refugees delivered safely to the palace, her duty was done in that regard and business began to return to normal. She accompanied Lylla to the grounds behind the palace for another training session, though by this point, she didn't expect the results to be any different—and with the Gate gone, she wasn't sure what she was training for anyway.

She wanted to confide in Lylla what her dad had said, share the dilemma she now found herself in, but wasn't sure how to broach the subject. Perhaps seeking out the opinions of others would only make the choice that much harder. This was something she had to do on her own, after all. The choice had to be hers, and really, she didn't have much of a choice in the first place. She wasn't going to leave them, plain and simple.

"I thought we'd go over some of the defensive maneuvers again today," Lylla explained. It was no secret that Sara struggled with the offensive applications of her magic, but defensive could be even harder and it didn't instill her with confidence.

They'd already been through it once before, but Lylla demonstrated again for Sara's benefit. One moment she was standing before her and the next, she had disappeared, as if she'd turned invisible. By now, Sara knew better. It was difficult to see, but there was a faint outline of Lylla where she had been standing, that shimmered slightly, distorting the air around it if she moved.

The queen had explained it by saying that if things could only be seen because of the light reflecting off of them, then it stood to reason that if one could control the light so that it no longer reflected off of themselves, but instead reflected as it would had they not been standing there at all, they could make themselves invisible. Or nearly so.

It took a great deal of knowledge about light and how it reflected off of objects to master such an ability. Sara had thus far managed to turn one of her arms invisible—one of her prouder moments—which Lylla said was impressive with so little training. But it wouldn't be of much use in a fight.

Sara focused on the way the light hit her skin, but it was even harder today than usual. The sun was hidden behind thick clouds and there was no one direction the light seemed to be coming from. Try as she might, her magic wouldn't cooperate.

She sighed, tired of struggling with light and wishing she could try one of the other elements, though she knew it was pointless. If she couldn't control her own attribute, which would always be the element she resonated with best, she didn't have a chance with any of the others.

Now she was certain she'd been right. She had thought long and hard about her decision last night, ever since returning from Nadia's house—proving to her dad that she hadn't, in fact, gone somewhere she wasn't supposed to. She'd lain awake pondering various things and now she was sure.

If there had been some sign of improvement today, she might have reconsidered, but today was even worse than usual, as if only confirming her misgivings.

Sara let her arms drop to her sides. "I've been thinking about something and I want your opinion."

Lylla turned to her, eyebrows raised in interest. "Of course. What is it?"

"Ever since the Echo Stone was lost, my magic just won't respond the way it used to. I've been trying and trying, but I haven't gotten any better at controlling it, at least not in this way. I'm useless in a fight. I'd like to try healing instead."

There, she'd said it. If she had the Echo Stone, it wouldn't be a problem, but it was gone and she had no one to blame for that but herself. She'd asked Lylla once if there were other amplifiers she could use, but there weren't. Or if there were, they had been long lost and their location no longer known.

"Healing?" Lylla didn't seem at all surprised by her request.

"It's just…after what happened to Khae and all those people…I wanted to help, but I didn't know how. I think healing would suit me better than fighting anyway."

Fighting implied having to kill. The only people she would ever be fighting were enemies—Galatea or her creatures—and in a real battle, it was kill or be killed. Evil as Galatea undoubtedly was, Sara didn't think she had it in her to kill someone, though Damaris would have her believe otherwise.

"I think it would," Lylla agreed. "Light especially is well suited to healing. But that won't be easy to learn either. The more serious and complicated a wound is, the harder it is to heal."

"I know, but I have to try. I'd make more of a difference that way, I think. And you can be skilled at both healing and combat." Lylla herself was proof enough of that.

"Yes, you can, but it will take longer to master both. But I see no reason why not. You'll have to speak to Serai about it."

We don't have a lot of time, Sara reminded herself. But she was getting nowhere with her other training and if she was going to help, it would have to be in some other way than fighting on the front lines. Other more experienced warriors could do that, but they would need someone to heal them and you could never have too many healers. The destruction of Khae had proven that.

Sara nodded to her. "Thank you. I'll try my best."

"That's all anyone can ask."

She left Lylla to find Serai. While she had lain awake in bed, mind already made up, Sara had wondered if

Professor Lawrence would have approved of her decision. He was the reason she had decided to train so that she could take his place and one day be assigned a Gate.

His Gate was now destroyed and just because she chose to become a healer didn't mean she wasn't a Guardian anymore. Her own mother had been a Guardian but had never been assigned a Gate because there was no need at the time. There was a need now, but Sara was too inexperienced. Galatea would laugh if she could see her.

As a Light Guardian, she should be quite powerful, with access to another element that others did not have. Light could only be wielded as an attribute, so unless you were a light attribute, you couldn't use the element at all. Ordinary Guardians, if any of them could be considered ordinary, had access to only five elements, where Sara had the potential to learn and command six. And yet she was the weakest of them all.

Even an opponent wielding a physical weapon, like a sword, would be able to defeat her. Her magic was too weak to defend her.

Serai's chambers were in the far west wing of the palace. The desert elf was sorting through stalks of herbs when Sara entered, stripping off the leaves and setting them aside. The room smelled heavily of plants, the scent earthy and cloying. Various dried herbs hung from the ceiling, forcing Sara to duck in places. Cots sat in a row along the far wall, separated by partitions.

The head healer looked up. "What do you need?"

"Um," Sara said, suddenly nervous. She needed this woman's approval. "I was hoping you could teach me how to be a healer." Serai glanced at her sharply and Sara hastily added, "Lylla thought it was a good idea." The queen's opinion held more weight than her own and surely Serai would not refuse if Lylla approved?

The elf sighed. "I don't think you realize what you're getting into."

"Please. I'm no good at combat and I want to help."

Serai's bright green eyes softened and she snapped her fingers, gesturing for Sara to come closer. "How much do you know about anatomy?"

"I—took biology class, but—"

It was clear from Serai's expression that this meant nothing to her.

"Not much," Sara admitted.

She knew about muscles and bones, but not the names of the individual ones. At least she knew about the various organ systems and what they consisted of. Because nursing had never been a career path she had considered, she'd never delved deeper than the cursory knowledge taught in high school.

"All right, well, before we get to any real healing, we need to start there." Serai bent down to retrieve a thick tome from a lower shelf and plopped it down onto the counter. She opened it to reveal anatomical diagrams. "Elves are just like humans in terms of anatomy, with the exception of the ear. Your magic can knit tissue together. Skin, muscle, bones, even organs, but you need to understand how those tissues work and fit together *before* they get torn apart. Or else you won't be able to make them go back to the way they're supposed to be. Understand?"

"Makes sense," Sara replied, even though she was disappointed.

Somehow, she'd thought you just willed your magic to heal someone who was injured and that's how it happened. She hadn't anticipated having to learn in-depth anatomy. Was that what Lylla had meant when she'd warned her that it would be difficult?

Why do I always do this? She was always going into something new, with the mindset that while she didn't expect herself to be perfect at it, she always expected to be better at it than she inevitably was. Or that it would be easier than it turned out to be.

"You're not squeamish, are you?" Serai asked suddenly. "You may not have to open someone up and operate on them like you would on Earth, but you're still going to see some nasty things."

Sara thought back to the injured, broken bodies she had seen in Khae. That was the very reason she had decided to pursue this undertaking. Those people couldn't heal themselves and so someone had to do it.

"No, I'm not." She didn't enjoy the sight of blood, but as long as it wasn't her own, she'd be fine. Probably.

Although, seeing someone you knew and cared about wounded and in obvious pain would likely be harder than a complete stranger.

Serai nodded at the tome. "Get to work on that and then we can move on to herbs."

***

Felix tucked the last of his supplies into Tempest's saddlebags. He would need to bring everything necessary with him for his posting at the Lightning Gate as one of its many guards. Camps would be set up around it for the soldiers to stay in, but he didn't know when he would next be at the palace.

It spoke volumes of how serious the threat Galatea posed was if Lylla was willing to send her personal Shadows to the Lightning Gate. Of course, he knew better than anyone that Lylla didn't need guards. It was more a formality than anything.

He glanced back at the palace behind him and knew he would miss it, if only for the convenience it provided. He would certainly miss his own bed at night.

He frowned as he saw Sara walking toward him. She wore a black t-shirt and long pants, tucked into black boots as all soldiers in training did, although the shirt would ordinarily be a tunic of some kind. The color suited her; it made her look dangerous, like the Guardian she was, even if she did struggle with her magic.

Her brows were drawn close together, her lips tight, eyes piercing. Striding toward him, with her fists clenched, she looked every bit the deadly, vengeful Guardian.

Felix swore, bracing himself for the confrontation that was about to erupt. He'd known she would seek him out sooner or later, angry and hurt, demanding an explanation, but he couldn't give her one. It was for her own good, but pointing that out to her wouldn't make her understand. She would only push back and argue and that was precisely why he couldn't tell her.

He wished her ire wasn't directed at him. And then he thought he would rather her be happy and not angry at all. Anger was not an attractive emotion—he knew that well enough. He wanted her to smile, to laugh. He wanted to be the reason she laughed. He wanted her to look as happy as she had on the roof, while they danced together. He wanted to know how her lips felt against his, his hands tangled in her hair—

Felix squeezed his eyes shut, chiding himself. He was fantasizing about his friend and that's what she was. A friend. The moment he'd allowed himself to think of her as something more was what had doomed him and led to this moment.

You're a fool.

"Are you avoiding me?"

He opened his eyes to see her standing before him, arms crossed.

"Yes. No. I don't know," he replied, flustered. This was off to a great start. "Look, I'm on my way to the Lightning Gate. Because that's where I've been posted, not because I'm avoiding you."

"Could have fooled me."

"I'm sorry." He could tell her that much. He was sorry for ever letting his feelings get the best of him. He should have kept her at a distance before it got to this point, but what was done was done and he'd have to keep her at arm's length from now on. Even if it wasn't what he wanted.

"It's a bit late for that now, isn't it?" she demanded, turning and stalking away.

Her shoulders were taut and Felix knew, watching her, that his apology had done nothing to remedy the situation. He had hurt her and she wanted an explanation. When it was clear that he wasn't going to give her one, she had left rather than be disappointed again.

Felix felt frustration surge through him. Why did she have to be like this? He had made a mistake and apologized for it, but he was doing the right thing. Why couldn't she see that? They could never be together and that fact tore at him just as much as it must do to her.

He turned away, putting one foot in the stirrup and swinging up onto Tempest's back. They would be moving out any minute. At least he wouldn't have to worry about seeing her when he was out in the forest. It was for the best, after all.

He put her out of his mind and succeeded for a time, helping the others pitch tents around the Gate. But once the camp had been set up and everyone assigned a tent—some would hold only two soldiers, but the larger ones would hold dozens—his thoughts returned to Sara.

Night had fallen over the forest, the flags atop the tents flapping gently in the breeze. He had laid out his bedroll in the tent he would be sharing with Colin and was standing just outside it, scanning the darkened forest, but everything was quiet.

He reached up, absentmindedly running his fingers over the scars that raked across the left side of his face. Sara had done the same that night in the desert. She wasn't afraid to look at him and touch him as others had been.

If not for the curse, they could be together.

A howl split the air, deeper than a normal wolf's, and Felix tensed, reaching for his bow. He and the others waited, tense and anxious, for something to reveal itself, but nothing did and the sound did not come again.

He sighed, nerves on edge. *I have to finish this.*

12

The swamp was exactly as Galatea had remembered it. The stone ruins of what had once been the city of Malenwar protruded amidst green swamp water, the algae giving it a slight glow and foul odor. The trees were dead, black trunks gnarled, bare branches twisting toward a green sky. It was as if a sickness hung over this part of the forest. Nothing grew or lived here and never would again. This was what a Gate's destruction was capable of.

The torches that had been lit with an eerie blue flame were lifeless now. Nothing stirred, but there was evidence of the battle that had been fought here. Chunks of stone lay scattered, cracks in the stone path and holes where it had opened up entirely.

There were no dead bodies lying in the water, perfectly preserved, or scattered in the ruins. Galatea followed the main path through the ruins to the Necropolis, where the people of Malenwar had buried their dead for centuries. The entryway still yawned open, a chasm in the ground, leading deep into the earth.

Summoning a flame in her palm, Galatea descended the steps, mindful that they could collapse at any moment and send her plummeting to her death. *What an inglorious end that would be.* Occasionally, the stairs connected to various levels that had housed catacombs, continuing ever deeper down.

She checked on each of the levels. The coffins were still there, but the lids were either broken or had slumped aside, revealing an empty interior. She continued downward but did not hold out much hope.

Galatea had not found a single corpse by the time she reached the bottom. She could not see the entrance high above, blocked from view as it was by the levels spiraling above her. It was utterly dark aside from her meager flame.

She wasn't surprised. Of course her enemies had destroyed the bodies. They wouldn't take the risk of leaving them there for her to reanimate again and use against them. Rather than rebury them, they had been burned, destroyed outright, leaving her with nothing.

Terribly clever of them and inconvenient for her.

She made the long trek upward again. The swamp would offer a temporary shelter, but she couldn't stay here long. Someone would find her sooner or later. She only needed to regain enough strength to make her next move. It was frustrating being forced to wait when she wanted to act before someone could stop her.

Movement ahead caught her eye but she wasn't concerned. Her wolves had found her, just as she knew they would. There were fewer of them than before. They were the size of lions and built closer to them than wolves, with thick, shaggy fur. Dark red for males and orange for females.

Venryk was in the lead, unmistakable with his ice blue eyes. "Mistress," he greeted her. "What's the plan?"

Ah, yes, the plan. She was quite proud of what she'd come up with. It was too vague to say she wanted to kill them all, and there were some who were completely innocent that she had no quarrel with.

No, she didn't want to simply kill them, those that had betrayed her. She wanted to make them suffer as they had made her suffer. To know the pain and be helpless to do anything about it or bring back the person they had loved and lost.

"They took Jack from me," Galatea murmured. "So I will take something from each of them."

She cast an eye around the swamp once more. A wind spirit and the few wolves that remained. Hardly an army. She wasn't sure if she needed one or not, but one could never be too careful...

They may have destroyed the bodies she'd had here in the swamp, but no matter. She knew where she could get some more.

***

The Ice Gate still stood. Damaris had been visibly relieved to see it when she'd escorted Imhotep and Samuel there. A full regiment of guards went with them, but they would be staying on the Wysterian side. Samuel had been assigned to the Earth side and so he crossed over, leaving the two Flame Guardians shivering in the cold. Imhotep had been given a snow stag fur coat at the palace, but it wasn't enough. He found himself thinking fondly of Egypt. What he wouldn't give to feel the sun, searing on his skin.

Whatever he'd expected when Damaris had fetched him, this wasn't it. Of course she'd explained the situation after they had crossed back over through the Flame Gate and the queen had explained further at the palace—why they had been brought here and what they were being asked to do.

Asked. Imhotep snorted at that. The idea was laughable. As if he could refuse.

Guarding the vulnerable Ice Gate was one thing, but having to do so on this side was another kind of hell entirely. Why should Samuel get the better end of the stick? *Lucky bastard.* In the meantime, Imhotep stood outside the cottage, shivering in his ugly fur coat, waiting for a threat that may never come.

Damaris had left him there alone, going about her own duties, with nothing but the guards and the howling wind for company. At one point, it began to sound eerily like a voice crying out. Imhotep desperately wanted to retreat inside the cottage, but he couldn't very well do that with all the guards watching. They couldn't all fit inside and the last thing he needed was to stir up jealousy among them.

The only consolation was that they looked as miserable as he felt.

His thoughts drifted back to his family. What were they doing at that very moment? When would he get to see them again? *Would* he get to see them again? If this Galatea was as dangerous as everyone claimed, he very well might not.

That thought only soured his mood further. The idea that he would be expected to die in defense of a country and Gate that weren't even his, should it come to it, was unacceptable. He wouldn't do it.

Even so, despite the threat to his safety, he almost wished something would happen, if only to get the dreadful waiting over with. If not for his family, Imhotep would have said that death was preferable to the mind-numbing, soul-sapping cold.

Perhaps the best thing would be to kill Galatea and get it over with. Then he could return home. But who was he fooling? Imhotep knew better than to think he could best a seasoned Guardian and a wind spirit. Even Damaris would have a hard time with that and she was far more powerful than he was.

Bitterness blossomed at the thought, leaving a bad taste in his mouth. What did they even need him for? What need was there for an Earth-side Flame Guardian when you had her? Still, she wasn't all that great. Not if she couldn't handle Galatea on her own.

Galatea. Perhaps he should direct his anger at her. She was the reason he was in this mess, after all. And yet, he couldn't completely blame her. There was a small part of him—not that he'd ever admit it—that admired what she'd done. She was a Guardian, like him, who had dared break convention. She'd rejected the pre-determined life set out for her as a Guardian. There was a lot to envy in that.

Imhotep had often wished that for himself, but he didn't have the courage. He wanted the rewards but didn't want the risks that came with it.

Many people looked upon Guardians with jealousy, wanting such power for themselves. Imhotep could have told them it wasn't worth it. What good was so much power when you lived a life devoid of freedom? He would much rather have been born an ordinary, magic-less human, lived a boring, normal life. He could have died happily never having heard of Wysteria.

Sighing, he turned his attention back to the matter at hand, searching the distance for any sign of life.

Where are you? he thought, blinking as the swirling snowflakes caught on his eyelashes. *What are you waiting for?* He shifted, stamping his feet in a futile attempt to keep warm.

He wouldn't have to wait much longer.

***

Venryk's fire kept Galatea warm on the return to Iceland and she commanded Azuma to create a swirling tunnel of wind that wrapped around them, shielding them from the cold, whipping air beyond.

The two of them slowed, her hand moving to her Shadowblade as they approached the Ice Gate. No longer was it abandoned. Sprawling in front of the Gate were legions of soldiers, blocking her path. The whipping snow prevented them from spotting her straight away, but she knew she had only moments to make her decision.

A shout went up. Fingers were pointed, eyes pinning her.

Galatea clenched her teeth. She had come here for a reason and would not be deterred. Too late to run now anyway.

Magic burst to life in some of the guards' hands. Weapons were drawn. Venryk growled, low and deep. Above it all, the wind rose to a shriek as the wind spirit coiled up behind her, wings unfurling.

Muffled screams. More pointed fingers. Some of the guards stepped back involuntarily. A few even broke ranks and ran, but there was nowhere to go. Nothing but the cliffs and a steep drop into the sea, which would kill surely as the serpent rising behind Galatea. The cold was enough to shock a heart, the waves choppy.

With one beat of his wings, Azuma sent the nearest soldiers flying through the air. They looked like dolls, weightless and small. It was over in seconds. Any soldier who approached was sent hurling through the air. The first few went over the cliff's edge, but Galatea ordered Azuma to drop them back to the ground. She could use them.

He obeyed, lifting the elves high and slamming them back down, bodies broken and twisted. The wind suddenly quieted, the screams dying as quickly as they had come. The path to the Ice Gate now lay clear, mingled with the bodies of the fallen.

Galatea stepped over them and approached. Only a single guard remained, though he didn't look like the others. He wore a thick fur coat, for one thing, instead of armor like the guards had, a sword at his side, still in its sheath. He was young, with brown skin and black hair. She had no idea who he was, but no pointed ears protruded from beneath that black hair.

A brief gust of wind revealed that they weren't pointed at all. *Human.* That could only mean one thing. No ordinary human would be sent here.

Most tellingly of all—he hadn't made a move to stop her. He'd remained motionless in the doorway of Cyren's old cottage as his allies were slaughtered around him.

Curious, Galatea drew near. "Hello. I don't believe we've met."

"You're Galatea." He said it with conviction, his voice deep.

"That's right." Still he made no move toward her. "And you are?"

He straightened himself up. "Imhotep. The Flame Guardian."

The Flame Guardian, not the *other* Flame Guardian. *Interesting.* So this was Damaris's counterpart that Galatea had never heard of or given any thought to. Of course, being a human, she could accurately guess his age. He wouldn't have been born when all of this mess began.

"Well, Imhotep, what brings you to the Ice Gate?"

"You," he said at once.

Galatea found herself smiling at his bluntness. No one else would have spoken to her in such a way, but he didn't appear the least bit concerned.

"Ah," she said softly. "Then you know what I've come for. And I can guess why you're here. This doesn't have to end in unpleasantness."

Imhotep shifted his weight. "Doesn't it?"

She gestured to him. "You've made no move to stop me. You've seen what I can do. But it's your choice. Try, if you must, but we both know how this ends."

Galatea waited, but he said nothing.

"Dying for a Gate that's not even your own. I doubt any of the others would even do such a thing and yet they've asked it of you anyway. They must hold you in high esteem to place such trust in you."

Imhotep snorted. "Hardly. I guarantee from the moment I was appointed to the Flame Gate, none of them have spared me a second thought."

It was not exactly the reaction she had been expecting, but she was pleased nonetheless. Resentment, now that was something she could work with.

Galatea had no doubt that with Azuma at her beck and call, she could kill Imhotep easily should he prove a problem. But why waste that which could be useful? It was the very reason she hadn't destroyed the Ice Gate yet.

"Really? But you're the Flame Guardian."

"The *other* Flame Guardian, you mean. As far as I'm concerned, I may be a Guardian of the Flame Gate, but I've basically been resigned to outer darkness."

"Is that why you've been given this post?" Galatea asked. "I can't imagine anyone volunteering."

"Downright criminal to post anyone here other than an Ice Guardian."

Galatea nodded. "Seems especially cruel for a Flame Guardian as well. I suppose that was intentional. Still, being a Guardian must be worth something."

"It doesn't mean much. I'm not allowed to stay in Wysteria, am I? Where me and my family can live forever and not die."

That was something Galatea understood in a way none of the others ever would and he likely knew it. She frowned, not having to feign sympathy. "Yes. Instead, you'll age and die like any other human, never having reached your full potential. And then you'll just be replaced by the next Guardian that comes along. Not much of a life, is it? They ask so much of us in return for so little."

Imhotep shrugged. "It's the way it's always been. It's the way it always will be."

"Unless something changes. If there are no Gates, there won't be a need for Guardians anymore. No one else need live a life of servitude."

"So you mean to destroy all the Gates?"

"Maybe not all," Galatea said carelessly. "But some, yes."

"You'll never make it. There's too much against you."

"You've seen what I can do. But perhaps you're right. Perhaps I can't do it alone. But with the help of a Guardian like you, Imhotep…think of the possibilities."

"Why would I help you? I heard what happened to Kadir."

Galatea made a rueful sound between her teeth. "Kadir was…misguided. He lost faith. He understood what it was to love a human, but not to *be* human, as you are, Imhotep." *Keep saying his name. Stroke his ego, play to his wounded pride, make him feel important.*

"You didn't succeed last time."

"Look around you." Galatea gestured to the dead soldiers, felled by Azuma. "Things are different now. Not even Rehan could do what I have done."

He sighed, jaw tightening but resolve weakening. "What did you have in mind?"

"If you help me destroy the Gates, but leave one or two at the end, we can control who comes and goes. You and your family can come and go as you like. You can bring over whomever you wish. There's no limit to what we can do. No more gatekeeping that which should be given freely. You and your family can live forever and as far as I'm concerned, after we're done, you won't be the *other* Flame Guardian. You'll be *the* Flame Guardian."

He frowned. "So I'll still be bound to a Gate."

"Not at all! You can even stay at the palace if that's what you want. After all, you know deep down that the others only asked you to come to Wysteria now because they need something from you, not because they truly want you here. When it's all over and done with, they'll send you back and you'll be expected to stay there, same as always. I mean, it's hypocritical of them, really, after what they've done."

Imhotep narrowed his eyes. "What are you talking about?"

"Oh, so they didn't tell you about Sara? Convenient."

"Sara?" Clearly, it wasn't a name he knew.

"Of course. The young teenage girl they brought here last summer. She's an untested Guardian with no Gate to protect, but she can come and go as she likes. And she gets to stay at the palace! She's weaker than most elementalists, much less a Guardian. But I suppose all that's to be expected, seeing as she's a Lightbringer, like our dear queen."

"Must be nice, being a favorite."

"Your life doesn't have to be predestined just because you're a Guardian. I'm living proof of that. You can forge your own path. The others are too small-minded to realize that and take it for themselves. They always did look down on the human Guardians, you know. You may be a Guardian, but you're still a human. Lesser in every way. You have the chance to break the cycle, to make life better for all human Guardians, Imhotep. But the choice must be yours. Prove they were wrong to overlook you."

The sorceress, fire wolf, and wind spirit all waited silently to see what the other Flame Guardian's answer would be.

"You're not going to destroy it?" Imhotep asked, after she told him her plan.

Galatea tilted her head, considering the Ice Gate. "No. Not yet."

"You should know, then, that there's another Guardian on the other side. Samuel, the Water Guardian. I doubt you'll be able to sway him."

"Very well. Come with me."

He hesitated. Was he having second thoughts even now?

"There's no one here to see that you've gone," she pointed out. "It will only take a moment."

"What about Samuel?"

Galatea said nothing, approaching the Ice Gate. She tried not to smirk as Imhotep followed. The Gate opened without resistance and she stepped through. The icy chill of Iceland vanished, replaced by a chill of a different kind. The deep, slightly damp chill of stone.

They were inside a mausoleum at the far end of the cemetery in Mayfair. Galatea opened the door and stepped out onto the grass. It was dusk, night rapidly approaching. The fading light gave everything a strange look, as if not quite real. Row upon row of headstones stretched out before them. It had been from one of these graves that she had raised Jack last summer.

Galatea shook her head. Best not to think about that now. Stay focused, do what needed to be done. Though it was hard not to think of him. His loss colored her every move, even now.

Beyond the graves stood a wire fence, separating the cemetery from the small church that stood empty, abandoned. There was no Reverend to preach here now. Behind the church, nestled in the shadow of the tree line, was a house.

Galatea cast a furtive look around, but there was no sign of the other Guardian. The house should have been empty like the church, but she could just make out a dim golden glow from within. Of course, he couldn't be expected to stay in the mausoleum, nor would he remain outside, and so Samuel had retreated into the house.

No doubt he'd been informed of its empty nature and so couldn't turn the lights on fully. A candle or two, a flashlight. It was enough to see by. No one from the street would notice and the trees should shield him from any prying eyes.

"Would you look at that," she murmured to Imhotep and Venryk beside her. "Looks like he has the place all to himself."

She saw Imhotep's jaw clench. He'd been left to stand out in the cold and here Samuel had been provided with all the comforts of someone else's home.

"What should we do?" Imhotep hissed. "We could kill him now. He has no idea we're here."

"We could," Galatea agreed. "But I have a different idea."

The last thing she wanted at the moment was to tangle with another Guardian. Confident as she was in her own power as well as that of the wind spirit, it would waste valuable time and she couldn't risk wearing herself down to the point where she could no longer do what she had come for in the first place.

No, she needed to avoid the Water Guardian altogether and hope that his negligence would be his undoing. Also, she wasn't entirely convinced that Imhotep wouldn't make some move to stop her if it came to actually destroying the Gate or attacking his fellow Guardian.

"Keep an eye out," she said, as much to Venryk as Imhotep.

Galatea took a few more steps forward until she stood among the first headstones. Looking out the window, Samuel wouldn't be likely to see her. The grimoire she had stolen the previous summer, the book of spells, was gone, having been destroyed in the fire that had taken Jack from her. But she no longer needed it for what was to come.

The spell was one she had memorized and doubted she could forget it even if she wanted to. It was seared into her memory as surely as Jack's parting words to her.

What have you done?

Galatea ignored it, pushing the voice away. She began to recite the spell under her breath, each grave lighting up a pale green. Imhotep cast an anxious glance toward the house, but nothing stirred within.

When the spell finished, the green light faded.

"That's it?" Imhotep demanded.

So impatient.

Suddenly, moving at once, the ground shifted beneath each of the stones, churning and crumbling. Skeletal hands, in various states of decay, broke free as the undead clawed their way to the surface.

Imhotep took an involuntary step backward at the sight of the revenants, their eyes glowing green, their hair hanging limp, desiccated skin tight over the bones.

Every grave in the cemetery was emptied. Galatea smiled at the sight, as her new soldiers came to stand before her, awaiting instruction. It didn't matter that all her previous thralls had been burned. How easy it was to create more.

She turned toward the mausoleum that housed the Ice Gate. "Come on."

Grimacing, Imhotep followed.

"You don't approve?" Galatea asked, even though she'd told him what she intended.

"It sounds so simple on paper, but I have to admit, the morality of it—"

She gave him a withering look. "You choose now to grow a conscience, Imhotep? You needn't worry. It's the most moral solution of all, really."

"How do you mean?"

"They're already dead. I'm not risking anyone else's life. I'm not some all-powerful ruler who holds the lives of my pawns in my hands, sending them off to die. You can't kill what's already dead. No one else needs to die."

"I suppose you have a point. But the smell!"

"Oh, you get used to it."

They crossed back over, waiting for the last of the undead to shuffle through.

"Where are you taking them?" Imhotep asked.

"Back to the swamp. But first there's one more thing." She turned to the Ice Gate. "The time has come. Any second thoughts, Imhotep? Now's the time."

"I've already given you my answer."

She nodded. Once this was done, it would be too late to turn back. But he'd made his decision and she didn't think he would deviate from that path.

"Best get clear, then," she warned him.

He moved back with the undead. Galatea stepped back slightly as well, but she wasn't concerned for her own safety. The wind spirit would protect her now as he had at the Wind Gate.

Wind had protected her when Lawrence's house exploded around her last summer, both flame and debris rushing toward her. Inspired by the final fight with Kadir, the Wind Guardian, she had summoned a gale to protect her, pushing back against the blast and managing to keep the projectiles and the worst of the flames from striking her.

The heat had been another matter. She hadn't entirely escaped unscathed in that regard. Galatea ran an absent hand over her left shoulder, feeling the puckered flesh. No longer was she beautiful the way an elf should be, but she knew she'd been lucky.

A quick cover of darkness and she'd been able to make her escape, waiting until Damaris had left, unharmed by the flames, before returning to sift through the ash. Somehow, her Shadowblade had survived, but not much else. She had lived but the damage had been done.

Her magic was fully restored from the previous Gate's destruction. Raising the dead had taken a little out of her, but not enough to make a difference. There was no one to resist her this time, no Lylla or Damaris to come charging in and save the day, no Guardian to protect the Gate aside from traitorous Imhotep and oblivious Samuel.

The only other witnesses were the stars.

Galatea summoned the wind spirt and he rose behind her. Not even he resisted her as she tapped into his power as well as her own. A sharp wind rose, buffeting the Gate mercilessly. The icicles cracked beneath the onslaught until they finally shattered.

Snow flew up into the air as the blast radiated outward. Cyren's cottage exploded as if a twister had struck it, the logs that had made up its walls flying away.

Galatea summoned the wind again now, amplified by Azuma's mastery over it. It acted like a shield, a force field around her that the blast could not penetrate. She remained on her feet, neither struck nor thrown by the force of the magic radiating out from the Gate. Not even a strand of hair seemed to move.

When it had dissipated, Galatea commanded the wind to die. She once again felt exhausted by the effort of what she had done, but not as much as she had before. Azuma hadn't fought her this time, almost as if he sensed that it was pointless to do so.

This was a Gate out in the middle of nowhere and Iceland was already so inhospitable that it seemed unlikely the landscape could become any more desolate than it already was. Whether it would suffer as Malenwar had, only time would tell.

She glanced up to see snow dislodge itself from the top of one of the mountains, cascading down its slope, but they were well out of its way and the avalanche posed no danger.

Imhotep stared at the shattered remains of the cottage, dark eyes wide. If he were going to make a stand, now would be the time to do it, while she was weakened.

"Samuel," he muttered.

She realized he must be thinking of the other Guardian, believing himself safe inside the small house, less than fifty yards from the Ice Gate. The explosion would have radiated outward and slammed into the house before he had time to react or even realize what was happening.

The Water Guardian was almost certainly dead, without ever having the chance to lift a finger.

Galatea turned away. It was time to leave this place. She would go somewhere more familiar and comfortable, though not by much, back to the place where it had all begun.

There, surrounded by her wolves and new allies, she could begin setting into motion the next part of her plan.

But she wouldn't be going alone. Galatea gazed around at the bodies of the fallen guards, some of them already covered in snow. She commanded them to rise, as she had in the cemetery. One by one, they joined the others she had brought.

After all, it would be a shame to waste them.

13

After checking on the Water and Lightning Gates, which were both still fine, soldiers and Guardians alike in place, Damaris began the journey to Iceland, to check on the most remote Gate of all. By now, Imhotep, Samuel, and the guards should have had sufficient time to settle in.

The journey was tiring, her progress slow due to the heavy snow. Even as a unicorn it was difficult. More difficult than it should have been. In some places, she found her path blocked completely by snow. A recent avalanche, some of the locals said—the elves who braved such a climate, usually ice attributes. Damaris stopped briefly at one of their lodges, but they had nothing more to say.

She burned the snow away, steam rising into the air, clearing a path, which only ate up more energy. Some pathways were impassible, blocked not just by snow but also huge chunks of stone, as if part of the mountainside had sheared away in the avalanche.

It was late—much later than she would have liked—when she finally reached the Ice Gate. To say she was in a foul mood, her patience worn away by constantly having to backtrack, would be an understatement. But it would all be worth it to find the Ice Gate safe and everything as it should be.

Damaris froze, the fire she had wrapped around herself sputtering and vanishing. She stared at the ruins of Cyren's cottage. No one had occupied it since the Ice Guardian's death, but it shouldn't have been destroyed. The lodge had weathered the harshest blizzards Iceland could throw at it and had stood for many years. That it had fallen now was not the result of a storm.

Her eyes flicked to where the Gate had once stood, just beyond. There was simply nothing there. Part of the cliffside had fallen away, plunging into the icy sea below. Beyond that, nothing as far as the eye could see.

Damaris blinked through the swirling snow, the cold air stinging her eyes, breath smoking in front of her. She felt her mane stir in the wind as she stood there, so still she could have been made of ice herself.

Something wasn't right.

She turned and then it struck her. There were no bodies lying strewn in the snow. No soldiers or any sign of a Guardian. Surely they were dead. No one could survive such a close blast on their own. So where were they? Buried beneath the snow?

What must the destruction look like on the other side? Heaviness settled over her.

"Another one gone, then?" a voice spoke from behind. "I was wondering when someone would find out."

Damaris turned. Empress stood behind her, looking completely unfazed by the cold. "Did you see it happen?"

"I did. Quite a spectacle to behold."

The Flame Guardian bared her teeth. "And you did nothing to stop it?"

Empress snorted. "And what could I do, I ask you? Against two Guardians, a horde of undead, and a wind spirit? I was alone as it was and watched them from one of the ledges." She jerked her head upward, toward one of the mountains that towered over them. "I'm lucky they didn't know I was there."

"*Two* Guardians?" Damaris demanded.

"At least that's what I assumed he was. Human, young, tall."

"Imhotep. The other Flame Guardian. He was supposed to be here. He was stationed here to protect the Gate."

"Well I'd say he wasn't doing a very good job of it."

If possible, Damaris felt even colder. "What do you mean?"

"I mean, he didn't lift a finger against Galatea the entire time. I thought it rather odd and I admit that's part of the reason I stayed and watched."

"You're lying," Damaris growled. "Or mistaken."

Empress shook her head. "I know what I saw. The two of them left together."

Imhotep, a traitor? Why would he help Galatea? They didn't even know each other.

"Why would he do such a thing?"

"Search me," the dragon retorted. "He's your counterpart. You'd know him better than I would."

No mountain dragon had been back to Earth since the Exodus. Empress and Imhotep would have never crossed paths.

He's your counterpart. Guilt and shame speared red-hot through Damaris. She knew what had happened was in no way her fault, but it somehow felt as though it was all the same. Her counterpart had helped Galatea.

And yet, for all Empress's assurance that Damaris would know Imhotep's motivations better, she found she did not. She had no idea what could have possessed him to do such a thing.

"I didn't really know him," she admitted, feeling as though this was yet another failing on her part. She'd never given much thought to him before.

"Well, there you go. Why should it be so surprising?" Empress remarked. "You didn't even know him."

Damaris began to turn away, as though in a daze. "I need to warn the others."

"Before you go, there's something else you should know. This isn't the first time Galatea's come to that Gate. She'd stayed in Cyren's lodge and wanted to know if we would join her again or not."

"What did you tell her?"

"I agreed. She asked me if I would try and stop her from destroying that Gate and I told her I would not. And before you start bristling—" Empress had noticed Damaris's ears flatten. "—I ask you again what exactly we could have done? We can't stop her."

"You could have at least died a noble death instead of hiding like cowards. Is no one loyal around here? Why the hell are you even telling me this?"

"You know as well as I do that I want no part whatsoever in your war," Empress growled. "But she wasn't going to accept that. I had to choose. What good are my soldiers if they're all dead? Look at it this way: we survived so that we can be of use to you in the future."

"How can I trust you?"

"You can't," Icicle said simply. "I fought with Lylla before, hoping that by doing so, it would rid us all of Galatea for good. That didn't happen and now look where we are. I want to make sure I'm on the winning side, Flame

Guardian. Consider this a warning. I don't know how all of this is going to go, but I'm going to make the decision that is best for my kind. If you want me to join you, prove to me that you can win."

Damaris exhaled heavily. She couldn't prove to Empress that they could win. "Do you know where she's gone?"

"Not a clue. She didn't exactly confide in me, despite the fact that I swore allegiance to her. It's almost like she doesn't trust me, though I can't imagine why not." Empress flicked her tail. "Though if I had to guess, I'd say she's returned to the swamp. Her old haunt. Old habits die hard, after all."

It was as good a guess as any. No one was likely to venture into the swamp and Galatea would be undisturbed there. But Malenwar held no Gate, not anymore, and so whatever her goal was, it was unlikely she could accomplish it there. Sooner or later, she would have to emerge and Damaris didn't intend to let her get the chance.

Sometimes you had to do something reckless.

But there were more pressing issues to see to before she could pursue Galatea. No one else knew about the Ice Gate's fate and it was her responsibility to warn them— and tell them of Imhotep's treachery.

First the Wind Gate, then the Ice. She'll be wanting the Lightning Gate next.

Empress had been as honest with her as she could without compromising her own best interests and that was the best Damaris knew she could hope for.

"If you learn anything more, let me know. Whether we meet on the battlefield as friend or foe matters not to me, Empress, but I know which I'd rather have if I were you."

The dragon smirked. "Is that a threat?"

"As you said, consider it a warning. Because despite your reluctance to pick a side—and believe me, I understand—you will have to sooner or later. We will end up on that battlefield, whether we like it or not. So I'd think long and hard about where my loyalty lies."

Empress said nothing and Damaris took her leave, moving with more urgency now. With no thought given to conserving energy, she summoned fire to melt away the snow that hindered her progress and ran until the snow became shallower and trees began to crop up. Eventually, the snow thinned and trees thickened until she was once more in the Enchanted Forest.

She went straight for the Lightning Gate. The encampment had already been set up, row after row of tents interspersed through the trees as far as she could see. Damaris weaved around them, avoiding the soldiers and firepits and portable smiths that had been set up, where weapons could be repaired or sharpened. Some of the guards sparred with each other, the ring of steel carrying through the air.

Damaris galloped into the center of the camp, which was the Gate itself. Wanderer was there, talking to some of the soldiers, but she broke off, glamoured ears perking as Damaris skidded to a halt, sides heaving.

"Listen up!" she called, voice carrying. It was a voice of command, of confidence and authority. Coupled with who she was and her reputation, the soldiers stopped what they were doing and gathered around to hear.

"The Ice Gate has fallen. Imhotep has betrayed us!" She didn't really want to mention that part. First Galatea, then Kadir, and now Imhotep. It wasn't good for morale. People would begin to lose confidence in the Guardians and might even begin to look at them with suspicion. But they needed to know in case they should face him. This was the best she could do to prepare them.

"It's very likely that Galatea will attempt to strike this Gate next. You and the two Guardians on either side are all that stand in her way. Be prepared for anything and stand firm. Duty unto death!"

"Duty unto death!" they echoed back at her, the chorus rising as one voice, and for a moment, she felt instilled with pride.

"Send someone to inform the queen," she instructed. "I am needed elsewhere."

Without a glance back, she shifted into her human form and approached the Gate. Wanderer reached out an arm to stop her, eyes wide. "Hank—"

"I'll check on him," Damaris promised.

She commanded the Gate to open and stepped through. There was no time to worry about the humans who may be on the other side. Fortunately, the bathroom was empty and Damaris stepped out, marching up to the counter where Hank stood.

For all the misfortune they had suffered, fate seemed to favor her this one time. The convenience store was empty for now, but she wished such luck had been used on something more useful.

Hank looked up sharply, knowing that she wouldn't have come unless something was wrong. "What's happened?"

"Wanderer's fine and she'll be glad to hear the same of you. The Ice Gate has fallen."

"I'd heard some customers talking this morning about another earthquake at the church outside of town and feared as much, but I haven't gotten the chance to see the damage for myself."

"I'll take a look and tell you what I find."

She had more she wanted to say to him but it could wait until she'd seen the destruction the Ice Gate had wrought. Hurrying outside, she ran—not caring who saw her—until she came to the edge of town, where it gave way to farm fields and woods. She resumed her true form and galloped through the trees until she reached the small church and cemetery that had housed the Ice Gate.

There were houses along the road, not too close by, but she didn't want to risk being seen so she assumed her human form again and approached the hill the cemetery rested on. She stopped short as she crested the rise, taking in the scene before her.

The trees that had ringed the graveyard had either fallen in the blast or had their branches stripped. The church and house where Reverend Pierce, the former Ice Guardian, had once lived were obliterated, nothing remaining but the foundations.

Of the mausoleum that housed the Gate itself, not even that remained.

The large oak tree that Damaris always thought would be good for hanging a swing from had toppled. That one fact saddened her more than the rest.

Caution tape ringed the fence separating the churchyard from the cemetery. Gravestones had been toppled, especially the older, taller ones. Others had been cracked and a few that had been nearest the Gate seemed to have exploded outright, chunks of stone scattered in the grass.

More alarming still were the graves themselves, the reason for the caution tape immediately apparent. The ground had been churned up, as if something had clawed itself free, leaving the plots and coffins empty.

The destruction of the Gate wouldn't do that. Galatea had come here to get more undead. *She's rebuilding her army.*

Damaris felt a chill, cold enough that for a moment, she could believe herself back in Iceland. She turned away, having seen enough.

There was no sign of Samuel's body. Whether he'd been taken along with the others, or been removed by authorities, it was impossible to say. The only thing she felt sure of was that he was dead. Empress hadn't mentioned another traitor with Galatea. Only Imhotep.

The Gate had been far enough outside of town that no one's homes had been destroyed, no innocent, ignorant humans killed. But if the Lightning Gate fell, that would be another story altogether.

She went back the way she'd come. Hank had had the foresight to put the closed sign up in the door, ensuring there were no customers when she returned.

"How bad is it?" he asked over the tinkling of the bell on the door as he let her in.

"Bad." She described what she'd seen and what Empress had told her. "But at least no occupied houses were hit. That could easily change." She fixed him with a steely look. "She's going to come for your Gate next. You have to know that."

"I know it's a possibility," Hank conceded. "But why me? Surely she has more of a beef with Cassius. And even though Galatea has destroyed two Gates, they were both without a Guardian. When she destroyed her own, *she* was the Guardian. She's yet to attack one with both Guardians."

"True," Damaris was forced to admit. "And the soldiers Lylla sent have arrived and set up camp. But the more time goes on, the more control Galatea will get over that wind spirit. Just bear that in mind."

Warning him was all she could do. She wished there were about three more of her, that she could send to guard each of the remaining Gates. But she couldn't be in multiple places at once. If she could, much would have been different.

I have to find her before it gets to that point.

***

"Sara?"

Sara glanced up to see who had called her. Lylla stood in the doorway to Serai's quarters.

"May I borrow you for a moment?"

Sara looked to Serai, who nodded her head in the direction of the door. She set down the herbs she'd been sorting and followed the queen out into the hall. The pungent smell of the plants lingered, clinging to her hair and clothing.

"How are you finding training to be a healer?" Lylla inquired.

"It's all right. I haven't actually done any healing yet. You were right. It's harder than I thought it would be."

"Much in life is, I think."

They fell silent, walking side by side through the corridors of the palace until they reached one of the outer doors and stepped into the courtyard. Cobblestone paths weaved between arrangements of flowers, fountains and statues. Sara spotted the statue of Cyren, the Ice Guardian, commissioned after her death last summer. It looked so lifelike, it was as if a living elf had been petrified, from the strands of hair to the folds of her clothing. The effect was both beautiful and unsettling.

"I didn't bring you out here to discuss healing," Lylla confessed, expression turning grave. "Something has happened. The Ice Gate has been destroyed."

"Was anyone hurt?" Sara asked, thinking her limited knowledge of healing might be needed.

"There's nothing that can be done about that now. There were no survivors. The church and cemetery on Earth were ruined. Samuel, the Water Guardian, was killed in the blast, along with many soldiers who were sent to protect it. Imhotep, the Flame Guardian, has betrayed us."

"Why would he do that?"

"I can only speculate, but I'm sure he has his reasons, in his own mind," Lylla said with a shrug. "The point is, Sara, that there is only one Gate remaining that links Wysteria to your town. If it is destroyed as well, you will be unable to cross back over easily. And if we lose all the Gates, you will be trapped here. I do not believe it will come to that, but it is something that needs to be considered."

Despite the sun on her skin, Sara felt suddenly cold as Lylla's words sank in. *Trapped.* She would be stuck here, unable to return to her father and friends. Not so long ago, she had wanted nothing more than to escape what she believed to be her boring little town, but the thought of never seeing it again was more painful than she ever could have expected.

This was different from her dad simply forbidding her to go. This would be removing the choice altogether, completely out of her hands.

"The other Gates…how far are they from home?"

"The Water Gate comes out in Great Britain and the Flame Gate is in Egypt. It's not impossible to get back to Mayfair from there by any means, but it is a much longer journey than a gas station two miles away from your house."

Sara had asked Lylla once, over the summer, why her little town contained three Gates when the other three had been scattered across the rest of the globe. Ley lines had been the simple answer. The Gates simply stood in places of power, where the lines intersected and the magic was strongest.

Sara was silent for several minutes. She began walking again, Lylla following, hardly taking note of the beautiful garden around her.

"What do I do?" she asked finally.

"I leave that decision up to you," Lylla replied. "I won't force you to be a part of our war. You have a family and friends on the other side and a responsibility to them as well. You are a Guardian; you are one of us and you will always have a place here. I don't know what the future holds, but I won't ask you to give up yours."

Sara had rarely seen the queen look so grave. "I—I don't know."

Professor Lawrence had been a Guardian and had given up his life in defense of Wysteria. Sara, who still felt partly responsible for his death, had vowed to train to become a Guardian as he was and take his place. Now his Gate had been destroyed, her magic refused to obey her commands, she had abandoned that path for one in healing, and there was the very real possibility she could be cut off from her home if she stayed.

On the one hand, how could she stay? She was useless in a fight and there was no telling whether she would be good enough at healing to make a difference. She hadn't actually done any healing yet and she hadn't been assigned a Gate. What difference would it make if she stayed or left? They didn't need her to help them defeat Galatea.

But how could she leave? It would be giving up, in a way, running like a coward. She had friends here, people that she had come to know and care about. She couldn't leave them to face Galatea alone.

Her dad would be furious if he knew she was even debating the issue. He would be furious if he knew she was there at all.

Her mouth felt dry when she next spoke. "Can I think about it?"

"Of course. Though I don't know how long you'll have to decide."

She could think and think about it, failing to come to a conclusion, as Galatea destroyed the Lightning Gate and made the decision for her.

One thing was for certain in her mind. Whether she stayed or left, Sara had to tell her friends the truth. The Ice and Wind Gates had been far enough outside of town that no one had been injured. No one had had their homes destroyed. If Hank's Gate fell, that would change. The entire town could be wiped off the face of the earth. People would be killed like they had in Khae. Nadia and Max could die if she didn't warn them.

But how? How could she make them see that she was telling the truth and convey the severity of the situation? They hadn't seen the ruins of Khae, the dead bodies or the horrific injuries. They didn't understand the danger.

Tonight. I have to tell them tonight.

If she put it off any longer, she would chicken out and never tell them. Whether they believed her or not, she had to at least try. She had to make them believe her.

***

Another day had come and gone without a disturbance, other than Damaris charging into the camp to announce the fall of the Ice Gate and to warn them that Galatea would likely come here next. It was alarming news, but Felix knew the danger that monotony posed.

The longer it took for Galatea to show herself, for anything to happen, the more likely they would be lulled

179

into a false sense of complacency, letting their guard down. When something did happen, they would be neither prepared nor alert.

And so he vowed to stay watchful, but the constant tension was beginning to take a toll. As night fell, he joined Colin at one of the many campfires dotting the forest, burning like beacons. No doubt Galatea would see them, or had already, and knew what they signified.

As they had with the refugees, the soldiers were forced to scavenge fruit or hunt, which was dangerous because it took them away from the main group. Fresh supplies were sent daily from the palace, but it was never enough.

Patrols still kept a watchful eye in the forest, even as the camp had begun settling down for the night. The fires dimmed, the murmur of low voices just audible among the breeze, tents flapping gently.

"You're doing it again," Colin said.

"What?" Felix hadn't been paying attention.

"You keep staring off into space, back in the direction of the palace."

He hadn't noticed, but he supposed it was true. He could just make out the lights of the palace windows through the trees if he squinted.

"What of it?"

"I noticed before we left that you and Sara didn't exactly have a cheerful parting. I don't know what happened with you two, but I can guess."

Of course he could. Colin appeared to see through him at times. He understood his motivations in this instance better than Sara would, having grown up with him.

"You need to tell her the truth. You owe her an explanation at least. Even if she won't like it or understand, you have to tell her."

Felix grunted noncommittally.

"You can't just leave it like this," Colin insisted. "You heard what Damaris said earlier. The Ice Gate is gone. We could be next. We could die, defending this Gate. All of us. And Sara will have no way to get home if we fail."

Felix hadn't thought of that. His only concern had been Venryk and making sure the Gate wasn't destroyed.

It would probably be best if Sara did leave. She had people on the other side that she cared about and that made her different from the others. Their homes and families were here, but hers weren't.

He wasn't going to try and convince her to leave—she would resent it. But he would offer advice if she asked. That meant reconciling with her or else she'd never speak to him. His previous reservations mattered little now. If she decided to return to Earth and they failed to defend the Lightning Gate, he would be cut off from her.

Although that also meant that he would most likely be dead.

What Colin said was true. He could die here, defending the Gate with the rest of them, and never have told her how he felt or why he'd acted the way he had. Felix didn't want that on his conscience.

No matter what happened, he had to make things right.

***

Sara crossed back over to Earth that evening, still unsure how she was going to make her friends understand. She sent them a text, asking them if they could meet, and Nadia's house was chosen, as it always seemed to be.

Sara had considered asking Hank to help her. The only way she could guarantee that they would believe her was if they crossed over and saw Wysteria with their own eyes. After all, she wasn't sure she would have believed it herself had she not seen the Gate opening, and the Professor, Felix, and Colin disappearing through the bathroom wall.

181

But while Hank might be willing, she couldn't risk it. No one would fail to miss the Gate suddenly opening from the other side and with the all the soldiers currently camped out at Wanderer's Gate, her friends would be spotted for sure.

This was the next best thing and Sara reminded herself that it was better than nothing.

"Made some tacos," Nadia said when she arrived. Max was already there, living just down the road. "Put whatever you want on them."

Sara joined them at the table and began assembling her own taco, but her fingers moved mechanically, her mind already trying to come up with the best way to broach the subject.

"There's something I have to tell you," she said, both sets of eyes swinging in her direction.

Sara thought she felt more nervous now than at any other point in her life. She looked from one of her friends to the other. She had known them since kindergarten. Nadia, with her blonde hair always in a ponytail, thin as a rod, and Max with his disheveled hair and glasses.

What if, despite her efforts, they said she was crazy? What if they didn't want to be friends with her anymore? Hard as it would be, she could take it as long as it meant they were safe—she thought—but she didn't want them to brush off the danger.

"Does this have something to do with the reason you keep sneaking off?" Nadia asked.

"Yes. It's the whole reason and it explains everything that's been going on."

"Well, let's hear it then."

Sara realized then how much she had been neglecting her friends and how much her silence and absence may have hurt them. This was a long time coming.

"What I'm going to say is gonna sound crazy, but I swear it's true." And then, before she could second-guess herself, she told them everything, just as she had with her dad.

What the Gates were, how there were three of them in Mayfair and how they kept the worlds of Earth and Wysteria separate. How each Gate had a Guardian, one in Wysteria and one on Earth. How Hank was the Guardian of the Lightning Gate. How Professor Lawrence and Reverence Pierce had been Guardians, too, and how their Gates had been destroyed.

She told them about her magic, how Guardians could control more than one element and each Gate had a corresponding element. She explained how Galatea had been Guardian of the Earth Gate and destroyed it, how she had fallen in love with Jack, a human, and brought him to Wysteria where he had been killed. How she had returned after over fifty years to resurrect him, only to fail. How the Professor hadn't died in a gas explosion, as they all believed, but that his house had exploded while fighting Galatea, who had killed him.

"We hoped that Galatea had died in the explosion but a body was never found. And recently, she's come back, this time bent on revenge by destroying the Gates one by one. That earthquake at Professor Lawrence's place wasn't an earthquake, but the Gate being destroyed and the one at the church, too. This Lightning Gate is the only one left in town and if it's destroyed, the town will likely go with it. I'm telling you all of this because you're in danger and it's not fair for you to have no idea what's happening on the other side." Sara took a deep breath, only to realize there was nothing more to say. "So now you know."

Her throat ached from talking for so long. She'd held nothing back, laying it all out there. Whether they believed her or not was out of her hands. She could only hope that she'd done enough. Certainly, she'd done all she could.

She'd been desperate not to leave out any important details and tell them before one of them could interrupt. To their credit, neither of them had. Their tacos lay on the table, untouched, having gone cold.

Sara waited for their response, but they just stared at her, saying nothing. "Well say something!" she cried, her face burning.

Max shrugged. "I believe you."

"You do?"

"Sure. Why would you lie?"

Leave it to Max, with his love of conspiracy theories, to believe her. Nadia had always criticized his willingness to believe anything but he believed her now, when it mattered most. Sara didn't think she would have believed him had the roles been reversed and she felt a sudden rush of warmth toward him.

"I don't know..." Nadia said slowly. "It really is crazy. I mean, Hank. You mean to tell me our Hank has magic? Look, Sara, I know you're probably under a lot of stress right now, dealing with your dad and trying to decide whether or not you want to go to college like he wants—"

"I'm telling you the truth," Sara insisted, a sudden thought occurring to her. "And I can prove it."

She might not be able to take them across with her, but there *was* something she could do. She squeezed her eyes shut briefly, praying this wouldn't be the one time her magic chose to abandon her completely.

She raised one hand, light flaring to life in her palm. It was nothing compared to what Lylla could do, but in the gathering dark and to someone who had never seen magic before, it was stunning.

Nadia gasped, jerking backward in her chair. "What is that?"

"I told you. My attribute is light."

She shook her head. "It's a trick of some kind. It has to be." She glanced around her own dining room. "Okay, Sara, where are the hidden cameras?"

But her voice lacked the conviction it had a moment ago and Sara knew the doubt had begun to creep in. Maybe this was real after all.

Sara pushed her magic harder, half-expecting nothing to happen at all. But to her utter relief, the light flared, growing brighter in her palm until it physically hurt to look at.

Nadia cried out and looked away.

Sara extinguished the light. "Still think it's a trick?"

Nadia held up her hands. "Okay, okay. Consider me suitably chastised." She stood, abandoning the tacos, and strode over to the freezer.

"What are you doing?" Max called.

"Getting ice cream," Nadia replied, withdrawing tubs of it. "We're going to need it. I have a lot more questions." She pointed the scoop at Sara. "We're not done, not by a long shot."

Sara let out a breath of relief. She would answer all the questions they threw at her. They believed her and that was what mattered. "Ask away."

It was going to be a long night.

14

Sara opened her eyes to see sunlight filtering through the far window and she sat up in the recliner she'd fallen asleep in. Nadia and Max were sprawled on the sectional, still asleep. They had stayed up nearly all night discussing Wysteria and though her friends believed her now, none of them had been able to decide what should be done about it.

They couldn't simply leave town until it was safe; not without bringing their parents with them. They couldn't leave them in danger, but trying to make them understand would be even more challenging.

When Sara had told them that her mom had been a Guardian, Nadia had asked if she'd told her dad about the danger yet. She admitted that she had and explained the dilemma he had placed her in.

"You're an adult now," Nadia had pointed out.

It was true, she was eighteen now. But she knew that her father would be disappointed if she went against his wishes and probably hurt as well. He only wanted to do what he thought was best for her. And after what had happened to her mom, he was likely terrified that he would lose her too. He would view returning to Wysteria as a callous disregard for her own safety.

Nadia had cocked her head to the side. "What do you *want* to do?"

"I want to go back." That part wasn't hard to figure out.

"Then you should go."

"Life isn't always about what you want to do. It's not that simple."

Nadia shrugged. "Sometimes it is."

Could it really be that simple? She had yet to come to a decision about whether she should stay in Wysteria or go, given the danger of being cut off, but she didn't want the choice made for her.

Sara rubbed the sleep from her eyes and got up. She needed to get back to Wysteria. For all she knew, Galatea could have struck in the night, though seeing as how the town was still here, she found that unlikely. She couldn't wait for her friends to wake up and didn't want to disturb them, so she left quietly, heading back to Hank's Gate. She could shower and change clothes once she got to her room in the palace.

As soon as she reported to Serai's quarters, the healer informed her that they needed to take inventory of all the remaining herbs.

"Is the stock running low?" Sara asked, wondering why the task seemed so urgent.

The elf pursed her lips. "Not low, but I need to make sure I have enough of everything. Because if I'm right about what's to come..."

She didn't finish the thought and Sara didn't ask what she meant. Without complaint, she fell into place beside the healer as she took out bundles of herbs, their fragrance perfuming the air, and began to sort through them.

"If we can use magic to heal instantly, why do we need herbs?" she asked, counting the silver rose petals, which she'd been told were good for pain when ground up.

"Not all wounds need magical healing and for some things, herbs just work better," Serai replied.

Sara glanced over at the healer's white tattoos, her long hair unbound. "What do you know about the wind spirit Galatea has?" she asked suddenly. "I can't remember the name."

She remembered Colin making a remark about the spirits last summer, but he hadn't been able to tell her much about them, saying to ask Serai instead since it was a part of her culture. Somehow, she'd never gotten around to it.

"Azuma," Serai supplied. "Spirit of the Eastern Wind."

"Yes. Colin mentioned him once, but told me I should ask you about it."

"Azuma is a wind spirit that takes the form of a dragon. There used to be four such spirits, one for each of the four directions, but now there is only one."

"What happened?" Sara asked. "To the other spirits?"

"Rehan, a powerful Guardian, and leader of the desert elves, wanted his people to settle in the desert, but the desert winds had other ideas. So he challenged them and, one by one, subjugated the spirits, banishing them from this world. He saved East for last, believing him to be the weakest, but Azuma was the strongest of the four and Rehan had spent too much energy battling the other three. Azuma killed him, but not before three of the four spirits had been dealt with. Or at least, such is the legend." Serai looked up with a wry smile. "My people took Rehan's bones and put them in the Golden Temple. Every year, they make a pilgrimage to the Temple and offer gifts to

Azuma in the hope of appeasing him, that we will have a peaceful year ahead."

"Does it work?"

Serai shrugged. "Sometimes, it would seem yes, sometimes it would seem no. Who can say? But every year, there is a festival to celebrate Rehan's memory and what he did for us. The desert elves love their festivals. You should know; you went to one."

The mention of that night brought Felix to mind. Sara shook the thought away. "Do you go?"

"I used to, but the desert is such a long way and I find I am more useful here." She frowned. "And now there may never be another festival again."

"I'm sorry," Sara told her and meant it.

Serai shook herself. "A healer's life is about service to others, not service to oneself. Now enough questions. We have work to do."

By noon, they had finished and Sara was relieved to be done, to leave the healer's quarters and the pungent smell of herbs behind. She was so caught up in her own thoughts as she made to leave that she didn't realize Felix was standing by the doorway until she nearly ran into him.

Immediately she considered ducking back inside, pretending to have forgotten something or inventing some excuse about Serai needing more help, but Felix straightened from where he'd been leaning against the wall. "I need to talk to you."

Instantly on guard, Sara crossed her arms, but she followed him outside into the rear garden where they could speak privately. Here, willow trees stirred in the gentle breeze, purple wisteria vines were interspersed between the fountains and stone trees that marked the edge of the garden. Windchimes tinkled above, from Lylla's quarters at the top of the palace.

Felix stopped and turned to face her. "I'm sorry. I should have explained things before now."

"Yes," Sara agreed, though not unkindly. "You should have." She kept her arms crossed, not knowing what else to do with them, but she felt some of the tension ease out of her shoulders. Whatever he was about to say, at least she would get some answers.

And she appreciated that he hadn't prevaricated.

He swallowed nervously. "The truth is, I care about you, very much. I'd even go so far as to say I think I'm in love with you. You're witty and brave and compassionate. You're not afraid to look at me, the way some people are. And when you do, I feel like you truly see me for who I am."

It was what she had wanted to know ever since that night on the roof. She hadn't imagined it, the look she had seen in his eyes. Her feelings weren't unrequited.

I think I'm in love with you. He'd said the word *love.*

Sara took a shaky breath. "Then why?" *Why did you make me think you were going to kiss me and then ran away, leaving me alone on the roof?*

Felix grimaced. "I didn't think we could be together. At first, I tried to tell myself it was because of what Galatea and Jack did. Aren't we doing the same thing? A human and an elf? But it's not the same and I know that. You're a Guardian; Jack wasn't. And I didn't go to Earth and bring you here like Galatea did with Jack."

"Actually, you did bring me here," Sara pointed out.

He smiled. "I suppose I did."

She found herself smiling in response, thinking back to how they had first met. Felix had been at Professor Lawrence's house when she had arrived. At that time, she had known nothing of Wysteria. And so when Galatea came to the house and the Professor insisted they hide in the wardrobe, she hadn't known what to think, cowering in the dark with Felix beside her.

Felix shook his head, staring off into space for a moment as if he too were remembering, before continuing, "You may not care about my scars, but neither of us can ignore what they mean. That's why I pushed you away. I have to kill Venryk or I'll eventually die. I may never get the chance to confront him and even if I do, there's no guarantee I'll win. It's not fair to you, playing with your feelings and giving you hope where there might be none. The truth is that I could die, that I may have to leave you, however unwillingly. It's not fair to you."

Especially after what you've been through. The words hung unspoken in the air between them.

Sara took a deep breath. So this was the reason. "I know the risks, Felix. I think it's my risk to take, if you'll let me."

She knew that if he lost his battle with Venryk, it would hurt her as much as he warned her it would, but if they were destined to have little time left, surely it was better to enjoy it together than apart?

"Why are you telling me this now?" she asked. "What made you change your mind?"

"Colin, funnily enough. He talked some sense into me. I realized last night that, if the Lightning Gate is destroyed, you'll be trapped here. If you decide to return to Earth instead, I'll very likely never seen you again, especially if I die defending the Gate. Whatever happens, I had to tell you the truth before it's too late." He reached out, gently taking one of her hands and she let him. He ran his thumb over her knuckles thoughtfully. "The fact is we could all die before this is over. Our disagreement seemed pointless once I realized that."

Sara had been thinking much the same thing lately. "I don't know what the future holds, but I want to spend it with you."

Felix smiled. "I'd like that." He hesitated. "Can I kiss you? I know I botched it the first time, but I'd like a second chance."

Not trusting herself to speak, Sara nodded. He was so tall, she had to stand on her tiptoes. His lips pressed gently against hers, the whiskers on his chin tickling her, as he leaned down, reaching up to gently cup her face. His thumb brushed across her cheek. Sara's hands rested against his chest, solid and real, breathing in his scent of leather and horses.

When they separated, his face was flushed and she could see every one of the freckles splashed across his cheeks and the bridge of his nose. She laughed nervously.

Felix glanced toward the palace. "Do you need to get back?"

"No," she said honestly, even more pleased now that her work was done.

His expression turned somber. "Have you thought about what you're going to do? About the Gate, I mean."

"Lylla came and talked to me about it yesterday. I'm staying." How could she leave any of them behind, much less him?

"I won't try to change your mind. I just want you to be safe. Venryk's vendetta may be against me, but he wouldn't hesitate to kill you."

She thought he was probably right. It was exactly the sort of thing the wolf would do in order to hurt him. It was the reason he'd given Felix the curse in the first place, so that Damaris would be helpless to aid him.

"I'll be careful."

"I know you will." He looked rueful. "I need to get back. I've probably been away too long as it is. But I had to see you."

Sara was disappointed to see him go, but he had a job to do, just as she did.

He gave her a lingering kiss, as if he too were loath to part with her, and then was gone, leaving her alone with her thoughts. Despite the obstacles in their way, Sara found her heart lighter than it had been in days.

***

Felix found that he was smiling to himself on the way back to the Lightning Gate. He felt as though a great burden had been lifted from him and now he could move on to better things.

His good mood evaporated when he returned and saw Colin's expression. His friend looked worried, lips pressed together, shoulders tight with tension, fists clenching.

"What's happened?" he called, sliding off Tempest's back and tethering the horse.

"Zanna's patrol hasn't returned," Colin answered. "They went out hunting and were expected back an hour ago, but there's been no sign of them."

"Maybe one of the hunters didn't make as good a shot as he thought and they had to track their quarry further than they anticipated," Felix suggested.

Colin wasn't convinced. "Maybe. But it doesn't feel right, does it?"

"Has anyone suggested a search party?"

"At first we were told that no one's to leave the camp to look for them. We couldn't be spared apparently. But they sent a second patrol out just a few minutes ago. We're waiting on both of them now."

Felix didn't say as much, but he knew that with fire wolves still roaming at large, the patrol could very well have run into trouble.

All they could do was wait and see.

***

Galatea stared down at the dozen bodies lying at her feet, Shadowblade held loosely in one hand. Its silver blade was stained crimson, as was the grass around her. She took care to keep her skirt from trailing in it.

Imhotep stood impassively off to the side, Venryk beside him. With the three of them, the hunting party had been easy enough to subdue, unaware that they were the ones being hunted and unprepared to mount a defense in the face of an ambush.

Their deaths served two purposes. Galatea did not delude herself by thinking that killing a few of the soldiers at the Gate would make a dent in their numbers—not one large enough to be significant anyway—but every one helped.

No, there was a far more useful purpose for them now. She recited the memorized spell, commanding those she had slain to rise again. Green light flared in their eyes and slowly, they rose to their feet, mindless thralls that would do her bidding.

She smiled. What did it matter if all the bodies in the Necropolis had been burned? She no longer needed them, when there was such a bounty to be had on Earth as well as those waiting for her in front of the Lightning Gate. It was as if they had been put there just for her.

And in a way, they had been.

***

An eerie silence enveloped Damaris as she entered the swamps of Malenwar. There was no sign of anything living, no evidence that anything had been disturbed since she'd last been here or that Galatea had returned. But she must have; the Flame Guardian was certain of it.

And it wasn't the living she had come for.

There was no point in searching for proof of Galatea's presence. Her existence was no longer something that needed to be proven. But the sight that had greeted Damaris in the cemetery had disturbed her. *All those empty graves.* If Galatea intended to rebuild her army, there was only one thing to be done about it.

She walked slowly, taking her time, eyes scanning every inch of the ruins, muscles tense, prepared for something to jump out at her. Nothing did, but she continued to walk quietly, making as little noise as possible.

Still, her hooves clopped on the stones, the sound seeming to ring out in the still air. The slightest noise was magnified in the silence. The air was heavy and close, smelling of rotten eggs and flesh from the foul swamp water. Damaris glanced at the shattered buildings, hanging in midair above her, frozen in time.

The path groaned beneath her, threatening to collapse, but it held and she continued onward. There was no sign of fire wolves or any other abominable creature that Galatea may have conjured, but she wouldn't take her army with her everywhere she went. They must be here somewhere.

Damaris flattened her ears, the sense of wrongness that pervaded the swamp growing stronger by the second. But she continued, unafraid of what she might find. Something had to be done and there was simply no one else to do it.

Especially not with Imhotep having turned traitor.

She was nearing the Necropolis. If she didn't find Galatea here, the sorceress wasn't to be found in the swamp. She drew up sharply as she spotted movement through the ruins—a flash of white. Her mind was trying to make sense of what it could have been when Empress climbed up over the remains of a crumbled building, her claws clacking on the stone, wings partially unfurled.

More dragons emerged from the ruins and trees, along with fire wolves, surrounding her.

"So good of you to join us," Empress said flatly.

"What is this about?" Damaris demanded, though she thought she already knew. It was a trap. Wherever Galatea was, it wasn't here.

"Galatea thought you might stop by," Empress replied, as one of the other dragons shot a bolt of blue flame into the air. It surged above the trees.

A signal of some sort? For what? Was Galatea on her way at this very moment?

Damaris found she suddenly didn't much care to meet the sorceress at the moment.

"I told you once what it would take for me to join you," Empress added, lifting one hand in a languid gesture. "So, Flame Guardian, prove to me you can win."

15

Damaris surveyed the enemies gathered around her. It amounted to a small army, but how many would dare risk their lives was another matter. She didn't care to assume. Before she had a chance to think of a retort, they had lunged, closing the distance fast.

She sighed, her crimson eyes beginning to glow a bright scarlet as she channeled her magic. A ring of fire encircled her, preventing those who were not immune from reaching her. One of the mountain dragons launched off the ruins and blasted a stream of blue flames down at her.

Damaris remained motionless, letting the flames wash harmlessly over her. She thought she saw Empress roll her eyes through the flickering ring of flame. The fire wolves began stalking toward her, stepping through the fire seamlessly, teeth bared. Damaris bared her own teeth in response, revealing her fangs, and let out a snarl. There was only one of them she could not kill and she didn't see Venryk among them. Likely he was with his mistress, wherever she was.

The nearest fire wolf sprang. Damaris reared up on her hind legs and lashed out at him, hooves striking the wolf and slamming it down against the stones. Behind her, a second wolf lunged for her ankle. She retaliated, kicking out and connecting with its eye. A sharp yelp rang out.

She wasn't fast enough for the next one. The wolf leapt onto her back, claws digging through her coat and into her skin. Damaris clenched her teeth against the pain as she felt teeth sink into the back of her neck. She reared, whipping her head around and sinking her own fangs into the wolf's shoulder. Whirling, she flung the creature off of her. It collided with the stone and did not move again.

Heart pounding, adrenaline rushing, Damaris spat blood out of her mouth and turned as one of the dragons rushed forward, claws outstretched. She waited until they were nearly upon her and then summoned more fire. The dragon had just enough time to let out a shriek as the flames caught, reducing it to ashes in moments.

She extinguished the flames then, allowing the rest of the dragons to get close. Without stopping to think, she raced around the ruins, narrowly avoiding slashing claws, summoning fire beneath the dragons and lightning crashing down upon the remaining wolves. The ruins were lit with flickering red and flashing blue light.

The Flame Guardian felt one of the dragon's talons rake down her side, but she ignored the pain, hardly noticing. The rage of battle was upon her now and she wouldn't stop until all her enemies lay dead at her feet.

The swamp around her became a blur as she focused only on her target in a frenzy of bloodlust. Screams rang out as her flames found their mark. It was the only sound she could hear above the blood pounding in her ears.

And then, suddenly, there was silence.

Damaris skidded to a halt in the center of the ruins where she had begun, panting from exhilaration rather than exhaustion. Slowly, she turned, surveying the carnage around her. The broken bodies of fire wolves lay scattered among the ruins, mingled with the scorched corpses of mountain dragons, laid low despite their superior size. Some of them had been destroyed outright, reduced to ash, which slowly drifted down through the air.

She turned to face Empress, who still perched on her ruin. She hadn't joined the fray herself. There were more dragons gathered behind her, but they made no move to attack.

The glow faded from Damaris's eyes though the adrenaline remained. "Are you satisfied?" she growled, taking one step forward.

Empress looked down at the Guardian, at her unsettling crimson and amber eyes, the fangs that were bared, the blood dripping down her white coat, unable to know how much of it was really hers.

Damaris thought the dragon looked afraid. It was not something in her posture but rather her eyes.

Wordlessly, Empress nodded.

***

The missing hunting party had still not returned by the time dusk approached and neither had the search party sent after it. Several other patrols had gone out in search of food and they had not returned either. Despite the assurances he'd given Colin, Felix was finding it less and less likely that they had merely gone off chasing a deer. The dread that had been gnawing at him ever since Colin told him the news had only grown worse as time went on.

It had been breezy all day but the wind picked up sharply as the sun began to sink below the horizon. If Galatea was going to strike, after dark would be the time to do it. Felix stood rigidly, an arrow nocked on his bow, waiting, but nothing stirred.

"Hey," Colin said suddenly. "Isn't that Zanna?"

199

Felix looked up sharply and saw that Colin was right. He could just make out Zanna, moving through the trees, heading in their direction. The sight should have come as a relief, but the feeling that something was wrong refused to leave him. Why was she alone? What had happened to the rest of her patrol?

"Zanna!" Colin called out, waving to get her attention.

She did not reply, as if she had never heard him.

"Colin—" Felix warned, raising his bow.

He pulled the string back and fired, the arrow whistling through the air. It struck Zanna squarely in the forehead, snapping her head back.

Colin whirled on him. "What—"

He didn't see what Felix saw, who had never taken his eyes off Zanna. She didn't fall. Her head lolled forward again, the arrow still sticking out of it, her eyes flaring a bright, unnatural green.

Felix had seen it before, during the Battle of Malenwar last summer and he knew arrows would be of no use. He cried out a warning.

No sooner had he done so than more elves came rushing out of the shadows, their eyes strangely unfocused and glowing with necromantic light. Colin, blanching, turned, drawing his sword as Zanna reached him. He cleaved her in two, but the severed body continued to try and make its way to him, the hands clawing and grasping. The only way to stop them entirely was to incinerate them.

Felix's attribute was air and Colin's ice. Neither one was particularly useful against the undead.

Suddenly, the wind turned into a gale, whipping through the trees with enough force to topple some of them. Felix was forced to his knees, hair whipping into his eyes. Behind him, some of the soldiers cried out as they were thrown into the air and then left to plummet back down. He cringed and looked away. It was too high for anyone to survive the impact.

He wasn't the target of the direct onslaught; his life had been promised to another. He struggled to get to his feet, but it was impossible, fighting against an invisible weight that pressed upon him. The wind was so powerful it seemed to suck the air from his lungs and he struggled to draw breath. It howled all around them like the keening of some great beast.

Because it is. Felix looked up through the trees and saw the form of Azuma towering over them, his massive white wings beating the air. It was then he looked down and saw Galatea stalking toward the Gate. She met little resistance; the soldiers being kept mostly at bay by the wind spirit. Any that did manage to reach her were swiftly cut down by her Shadowblade or the advancing undead.

Felix's heart constricted in his chest. *Sara!* If the Gate were destroyed, she would be cut off—

"Where is the Lightning Guardian?" someone cried above the wind.

Felix glanced around desperately but could see no sign of Wanderer. Where had she gone? If Galatea reached the Gate, she would destroy it and everyone would be killed.

Another figure was moving through the crowd, fire in his hands. Felix watched as soldiers ignited, searing away to ash as the newcomer burned a path to the Gate. Though Felix had never seen him, he recognized Imhotep, the other Flame Guardian.

Clenching his teeth, he forced himself to stand, staggering slightly from the force of the wind. Firing an arrow at Galatea was out of the question. It would never fly straight in this wind and even if he used his own magic to try and control its path, Azuma's mastery over the element was far greater than his own.

He drew the sword at his side and followed after Galatea. It was like trudging through molasses, the wind fighting him at every step.

Colin must have had the same idea because he, too, approached Galatea, sword drawn. He was much closer than Felix was. The sorceress had nearly reached the Gate. Colin slashed at her, Felix watching as the blade seemed to move in slow motion. The tip neared her arm and then stopped as if it had struck a solid wall.

Colin jerked at the blade, but it refused to move forward. He staggered back from her as she turned, her cold black eyes raking over him. He lunged at her, then, bringing his sword up once more.

Felix's breath caught. For a split second, he thought his friend had her, that his aim was true and the sword would find its mark.

A massive hand reached down, slamming Colin to the ground and pinning him at Galatea's feet. *Azuma*. One of the dragon's long, silver talons had pierced Colin's breastplate. The wind spirit released him but Colin did not move.

Felix screamed Colin's name, but the wind tore the sound away. From where he stood, he could just see the gaping wound in Colin's chest, his blue eyes staring sightlessly up at the forest canopy above.

He was gone, in the blink of an eye, just like that. Quick and callous.

A white-hot rage speared through Felix, consuming every thought until his only desire was to destroy Galatea for what she had done. Venryk emerged from the trees to stand beside his mistress, ice blue eyes fixed on Felix.

Galatea turned to her wolf and glanced over her shoulder. "Kill him."

Felix had read her lips, unable to hear the words. Venryk lunged at him and Felix swung his sword down to meet the wolf, slicing into the beast's shoulder. He was rewarded with a yelp, but that didn't stop the wolf from barreling into him, knocking him to the ground.

Venryk scrambled up, his dark red fur hardly showing the blood from the wound Felix had dealt him. The wind cut out suddenly, the pressure dropping. Felix's ears popped. He reached for his daggers, the fire wolf still standing over him, trying to remember what Damaris had told him during their training session.

And then a white form loomed over him, crashing into Venryk and throwing the wolf off. Dazed, Felix caught a glimpse of Damaris, appearing as though his thoughts had conjured her. Her white coat was bloody from multiple gashes and lacerations, her eyes alight.

The Lightning Gate still stood, but it hung open. *Galatea must have crossed over, taking the wind spirit with her.* Damaris charged through the opening without sparing him a second glance and vanished from view.

Felix sat up, glancing around him, but Venryk had gone, leaving him with the injured and the dead.

***

Damaris was met with chaos as she stepped through the Gate to the other side. The wind was whipping, which seemed impossible inside the convenience store. She didn't see Azuma, but his presence filled the room. Smaller racks of goods had toppled over. The refrigerator doors were pulled open and slammed back, knocking the glass out. Light flashed dizzyingly as both Hank and Wanderer summoned lightning, trying to keep Galatea at bay.

The sorceress stood in the center of the store, cloaked in a swirling mass of darkness that absorbed the lightning and prevented it from reaching her. Damaris hadn't seen

Wanderer on the Wysterian side when she'd arrived at the Gate and figured she must have crossed over to help Hank. It was hardly surprising.

No sooner had Damaris taken all this in when Galatea thrust out a hand. Some of the darkness snaked off from the main group around her, surging toward Wanderer. She cried out as it enveloped her, blinding. The wind redoubled, tossing her backward into one of the racks.

Galatea hefted her Shadowblade and threw it, the blade arcing through the air, guided flawlessly by the wind. There was no time to react. It sank, nearly hilt-deep, into Hank's chest, pinning him to the wall behind.

Wanderer let out a wail, reaching out toward him. Galatea strode forward and yanked the sword out, leaving him to slump to the floor. Damaris could just hear his ragged breathing over the howling wind.

With a cry of rage, Wanderer scrambled to her feet, lightning completely enveloping her and flashing randomly around the store. Damaris had never seen the Lightning Guardian lose control, but she knew what an emotional spill-over looked like.

She lunged forward, summoning her flames. The wind tried to snatch them away, but she was stronger and they held fast.

A groaning noise rang out as part of the roof tore away, ripped by the gale as if it weighed nothing. Side by side, Damaris and Wanderer simultaneously assaulted Galatea with bolts of lightning and fire, forcing the sorceress back away from the Gate.

Each attack was absorbed by the all-consuming darkness, but it began to falter, dwindling before their eyes. Soon, there would be nothing left standing between Galatea and their magic.

The sorceress seemed to realize the danger she was in, eyes widening. She had likely already used up too much magic fighting three Guardians at once to destroy the Gate now. The wind swirled around her feet, spiraling up around her. Before their eyes, she seemed to turn into darkness itself, and then she was rushing forward, past them and through the Gate, closing it behind her.

Wanderer stumbled as the wind abruptly cut out. She straightened and ran across the room to where Hank lay.

"Wanderer, the Gate!" Damaris called. Galatea could be working to destroy it at that very moment and they were far too close. The blast would instantly kill them both.

The Lightning Guardian ignored her. "We have to help him! Damaris, please." She looked up, blue eyes wide and pleading. "You would do the same for Felix."

Damaris suppressed a sigh, hoping she wasn't committing a fatal mistake. Carefully picking her way through the fallen debris, she came over to join the two of them.

Hank was still breathing, just. Wanderer knelt beside him, her hands hovering uselessly above the gaping wound in his chest. She pressed them down then, trying to staunch the bleeding, but it quickly seeped through her fingers.

"Hank," she gasped, trying to stave off hysteria. "You're going to be okay. Just hang on." She turned to face Damaris. "Can't you do something?"

Damaris looked down on her friend with pity. They both knew that what Wanderer had told Hank was a lie. He'd been stabbed with a Shadowblade. Even if the injury itself wouldn't prove fatal on its own, darkness was in the wound, spreading through him even now, acting like a poison.

Only light could heal it and there were only two people who could wield the element. And they were on the other side of the Gate. Even if they could move Hank, they would never reach the palace in time. Such an extensive wound would only cause the darkness to act more quickly.

"I'm sorry," Damaris said softly.

I'm a warrior, not a healer. Her magic was only good for taking lives, not saving them. Even if she could have somehow cauterized the wound to stop the bleeding, it would do nothing for the darkness within.

The only way her magic could have saved Hank was if she had arrived sooner—and she would have, if Empress hadn't delayed her in the swamp. Now she knew what the signal had likely meant—she would be held up in the swamp, giving Galatea time.

The only other thing Damaris could offer Hank was a quicker death and she couldn't bring herself to use her flames on one of her own.

"Do something!" Wanderer screamed at her.

There was nothing either of them could do but stand by a fallen comrade so that they didn't die alone. And wait.

They didn't have to wait much longer. Wanderer muttered incoherently to Hank, who stared up at the ceiling, gaze distant, as she touched his cheek. His rasping gasps suddenly ceased and the room fell silent. Wanderer stared at his lifeless body for a moment, as though not quite believing he was gone, and then let out a sob, folding in on herself.

Damaris didn't want to leave her alone, but neither did she wish to stay. She cast a longing glance at the Gate, but it still stood. There had been no explosion, no sudden pain and then darkness. They were still alive and so she had to assume that whatever had happened on the other side after Galatea had crossed back over, they were safe for the time being.

Instead, she pushed aside her own desires and knelt beside Wanderer, shifting into her human form, offering what comfort she could.

***

Sara was utterly unprepared for the influx of wounded that flooded Serai's door. She had yet to actually heal anyone and so the most she could do was bustle about, fetching whatever Serai needed and more likely succeeding in only getting in the way. She was relieved when the other healers arrived to help.

What had happened? Why were there so many wounded and where had they come from? As they worked, she caught snippets of conversation that chilled her blood. *Galatea. Lightning Gate.*

The Lightning Gate had been attacked and these were the survivors. *Felix!*

She searched for his familiar crimson hair among the crowd, but couldn't see him. Had he escaped injury or was he lying out there even now, dead or dying? Without stopping to think, she left the healer's quarters and ran to the stables, fetching one of the horses there and racing toward the Lightning Gate.

Surely it still stood. There weren't likely to have been many survivors if it had been destroyed, but she had to know, had to see it with her own eyes. She couldn't have been cut off from home.

Her thoughts were a revolving whirl of Felix, Hank, her town, the Gate itself, Wanderer and Colin as well. They had all been at the Gate. The horse charged through the forest at nearly a gallop, likely far too dangerous a speed for an inexperienced rider such as herself, but to Sara, it didn't seem nearly fast enough.

And then she was suddenly upon it, the scene stretching out before her. Bodies lay between her and the Gate; from a glance, she couldn't tell if they were dead or merely injured. She let out a breath at the sight of the Gate, still standing.

She searched for Felix or Wanderer, but could not find either of them. The air was heavy with the tang of blood and something charred. Suddenly, Sara needed to know what had happened to her town, that she could still go home. The Gate still stood, so it was unlikely to have been destroyed, but if Galatea had crossed over, there was no telling what sort of destruction she had wrought.

The Gate opened at her command and she stepped through, blinking. Sunlight streamed down through a hole in the ceiling, where the roof of the gas station had been peeled back. In one corner, Wanderer knelt beside a motionless figure, sobbing quietly.

Nearly tripping over the rubble, Sara approached, stopping short. A gasp escaped her lips as she took in the sight of Hank, the gaping wound in his chest and the unnatural pallor of his skin. Wanderer looked up, her face streaked with tears.

Damaris, in human form, stood near the door. Sara spotted other people milling about—people she recognized from town, who appeared to be trying to clean things up or else standing in small groups, talking amongst themselves in hushed voices.

Her gaze stopped its roaming as she recognized one in particular—her dad.

"Sara?" he asked, stepping forward.

She shook her head, dazed. This couldn't be happening. This meeting of her two worlds couldn't be happening. Not here, not now. Not like this.

Her eyes flicked back to Hank.

"Sara."

She whirled. Felix had crossed over behind her, his eyes reflecting the numbness she felt. Her knees went weak at the sight of him, that he wasn't injured. Stumbling forward, she all but fell into his arms. She gripped his shoulders, solid beneath her, clinging to him as if he could somehow shield her from the horror that had happened here, turn back time and make none of it real.

"I was so worried," she whispered. She pulled back slightly, looking up at him. "What happened?"

"Colin's dead," he said, voice sounding flat.

She stared at him, taking in the pain in his expression. Her heart ached at the loss and knew he must feel it even more acutely. "I'm so sorry," she whispered, knowing how inadequate the words were, but powerless to do anything else.

"Sara."

She looked up again as her dad approached. His expression was thunderous as he looked from her to Felix and back. Whatever he had seen pass between them, he hadn't liked.

"Sara, what is going on here?" His gaze flicked to Hank and Wanderer, expression darkening further.

Her heart began to thrum. "Dad, I—"

"I believe I made my wishes clear, did I not?" he demanded, eyes glittering with anger. But beneath that, there was something else, something somehow worse. Disappointment.

From the moment she had promised not to return to Wysteria, Sara had imagined her dad discovering her broken promise a dozen different ways and his reaction. Somehow, the reality was even worse.

She swallowed, holding her tongue. She didn't know what to say and felt sure that anything she did say would only make it worse. In the doorway, Damaris glanced over her shoulder. As if sensing the growing tension and Sara's distress, she came over to stand beside her.

"I'm disappointed in you. I explicitly told you not to associate with the Wysterians." He glanced at Damaris, whose eyes were not glamoured, and Felix, hovering behind Sara, his scars clearly visible. "With these freaks."

"Dad!"

He looked directly at Felix. "Stay away from my daughter."

Felix took a menacing step forward and Sara sucked in a sharp breath, heart seizing in fear of what was to come next. Thankfully, she never had to find out.

Damaris reached out, pressing one armored hand against Felix's chest, pushing him back, glaring at Sara's dad all the while. The Flame Guardian struck an imposing figure, as tall as Sara's dad, eyes hard.

"You deliberately disobeyed my wishes," he said, addressing Sara once more. "You knowingly put yourself in danger. You promised me you wouldn't go back, but you lied. You didn't mean any of it, did you? You were going to get involved regardless."

"It's not that simple!" Sara cried.

"Your daughter was already involved," Damaris said softly.

"Why did you drag her into this? This is not her fight!"

"She made her own choices," the Flame Guardian said. "All of you are involved, whether you realize it or not. This is bigger than any of us."

"What difference can one person make?" her dad demanded. "Her skills are still new." He turned back to Sara. "You're all I have left. If something were to happen to you…I can't protect you over there."

"Whether you like it or not, your daughter is safer with us."

Sara looked away, hot tears stinging her eyes. She felt as though she were being talked about as if she weren't even there, her dad's words cutting straight to the heart of the matter.

"You can't guarantee her safety."

"No one can."

Her dad shook his head. "Enough. Let's go, Sara. We're done here."

Her head jerked up, panic shooting through her. He was reaching out to her with one hand and she thought that if Damaris hadn't been standing between the two of them, he would have reached out and grabbed her arm.

He wanted her to leave with him. Leave and never come back.

"Sara," Damaris said without turning around. "Go to the Gate."

Her pulse quickened. If she crossed back over, she would be directly defying her dad right in front of him. His disappointment and anger were already hard enough to bear. She'd already gone against his wishes once; she didn't know if she could do it again.

"Now, Sara," her dad insisted, tone impatient. But there was something else in his voice. Fear?

Why was he putting her in this position? Why didn't he understand? But she knew why. He'd said as much—she was all he had left and she had chosen Wysteria over him.

"The wounded need you," Damaris said, voice once again soft. "We must think of them now."

Sara met her dad's gaze and the conflicting emotions she saw there, wishing she didn't have to choose between two halves of herself.

"I'm sorry," she said, the tears she had been holding back finally slipping free.

Turning her back on her dad, the act feeling like a betrayal, she trudged through the debris toward the Gate.

16

Serai said nothing when Sara returned, about her previously having run off without explanation, which Sara was grateful for. She didn't think she could put her thoughts together if asked. The wounded were still streaming in and so she fell into place silently beside the head healer, helping where she could.

Some of those who had been injured at the Gate couldn't be saved and she stood by, once again holding hands and offering what comfort she could as they slipped away. She felt numb, which suited her just then.

Some wounded soldiers had suffered horrific burns and others appeared to have been mauled, likely by fire wolves. Sara's stomach clenched at the sight, but it helped keep other intrusive thoughts and memories at bay, while also providing a welcome distraction from the enormity of what she had just done.

She knew she wouldn't be able to put it off forever. She had turned her back on her dad, going against his wishes for a second time, and walked away. She'd walked through a Gate, back into Wysteria, the very place he did not want her to be.

Sara swallowed against the bitter taste that had risen in her mouth. Nadia was right; she was an adult and could now make decisions for herself. She didn't *have* to listen, but she worried what her dad would say or do when—if—she returned. Her return wasn't certain; she could still be cut off from home.

Would he even want to see her or would he want nothing to do with her? She didn't want to destroy their relationship. They'd grown closer than they'd been before her mom died and the bond would have no doubt been even stronger if he wasn't called away so often for work. What would she do if that bond was lost to her forever?

Would he disown her? Throw her out? Sara didn't know. She didn't think so, but the possibility alarmed her. The fact that the thought even occurred to her was frightening. She had little money and no place to live if he threw her out of the house.

Sara took a deep breath, realizing she was spiraling. The tide of wounded had finally stopped. No longer able to put off what had happened, she left the healer's quarters.

After some searching, she found Felix in the rear garden, sitting on the back palace steps. He held a small piece of wood in one hand and a knife in the other, slowly whittling away at it, but Sara couldn't tell what the piece of wood was meant to look like. He stared at it as if seeing right through it, carving at the same spot.

Hank. Colin.

She had liked Colin; he'd always been kind to her, cheerful and funny during the time she had gotten to know him. Only a year ago, she'd met him. She blinked at the realization. It seemed so much longer than that and yet as though no time had passed at all.

Felix, who had grown up with Colin since boyhood, would have taken the loss much harder. And after what had happened to his parents, the blow must have been all the more crushing. Little wonder he seemed to carry a sort of melancholy within him. Sometimes, Sara felt the same.

"What happened?" she asked as she reached him.

He didn't look up and didn't have to ask what she meant. "Azuma." His throat worked as he swallowed hard. "One talon…just ran him straight through."

"I'm sorry," she said again, joining him on the step.

He looked so miserable, she ached to comfort him, this boy who'd said he loved her, to take the pain away, but she knew that was impossible. A pain that deep couldn't be taken away. It could only be shared.

She wrapped her arms around him, his body warm and solid. He was too tall to lean his head on her shoulder, so she rested hers on his shoulder. For a moment, they remained there, silent and motionless.

Then Felix pulled away. "I need to change." He still wore the same clothing he'd had at the Gate.

Sara nodded, letting him go. He probably needed time alone and that, too, was something she understood.

***

Felix had crossed back over with Sara. Damaris and Wanderer followed moments later, taking Hank's body with them. Wanderer had protested, wanting him to be buried on Earth, in the town he had loved so much. And there had been some pushback from the townspeople who had gathered, drawn by the commotion at the gas station.

That was unfortunate, but not surprising. The police had been called, of course, even though Hank was beyond helping now. The coroner would come and take the body away and they needed to be gone before that.

Damaris ignored the townspeople, who were demanding to know what they thought they were doing and where they were taking him. It was also less than ideal that the townspeople had already seen people use the Gate, but at least they wouldn't understand what they had seen.

Lylla came out to meet them when they returned to the palace, her face a mask of pain. Damaris met her gaze and saw the unshed tears that a queen was not allowed.

"You should get those wounds seen to," Lylla murmured as they passed.

Damaris had glamoured her injuries for the benefit of Felix, Sara, and the townspeople, but the queen could see through her disguise. She'd nearly forgotten about the injuries she'd received fighting in the swamp. They had long since stopped bleeding.

"They don't hurt," she replied. And it was arguable that half the blood wasn't even hers.

It was nothing she couldn't deal with, having had far worse in the past. Somehow, it seemed wrong to get them healed when so many others hadn't been given the chance. But she did, heading to the healer's quarters after a hasty ceremony for Hank and the body had been burned to make sure it couldn't be used by Galatea—or anyone else.

Dawn had broken by the time they were called together in the meeting chamber. Cassius had been summoned away from his Gate to attend. Damaris and Wanderer needed to give an account of what had happened. Sara also found herself summoned this time, along with Felix, since he had been present at the Gate.

The good news, if there was any to be had in all of this, was that the Lightning Gate still stood, albeit at the cost of one of its Guardians.

"Hank was a true Guardian," Lylla murmured. "He upheld his oath without fear or hesitation, laying down his life for both of our worlds. His loyalty never wavered. He will be missed and his sacrifice remembered for generations to come." She looked up. "I am truly sorry, Wanderer."

"Is there nothing that could have been done?" the Lightning Guardian asked softly. Her eyes were fixed on the floor and her typical glamoured wolf ears and tail were gone. Somehow, she looked small without them. "Is there no other way to heal such a wound than light magic?"

"I'm afraid not," Cassius spoke up. His usual stoic expression was gone, replaced by one of sympathy. He'd always been fond of Wanderer and shared her pain now.

"Well," Lylla said, somewhat hesitantly. "There may be a way, but no one would ever attempt it."

"Why not?" Wanderer looked up, but without hope at the news. It was too late for such hope now.

"Because there's no guarantee that it would work," Lylla warned. "In truth, I do not even know if it is possible. I've never known anyone who has tried it. But there are stories that claim a Guardian could heal such a wound that would otherwise prove fatal by pouring out all of their magic in the effort of healing. It may not work at all or it could heal the wounded, but result in the Guardian's own death. It would depend on how powerful the Guardian is, whether they could overcome the darkness. Even if both survive, the Guardian will no longer have magic. They will have given it up in exchange for the other person's life. Or such is the legend."

Wanderer seemed to shrink into herself and Damaris wondered if she would have attempted such a thing to save Hank if she had known about it.

"I can see why no one would do it," Cassius muttered. "To a Guardian, their magic is everything. What Guardian would risk permanently forfeiting their power to save just one life?"

Beyond him, Damaris exchanged a silent glance with the queen.

***

After the meeting had adjourned, Sara helped Serai with cleaning up—the healer's quarters were a mess of strewn herbs and bandages that hadn't yet been cleared away—and then snatched a few precious hours of sleep.

There had been no time to speak to Felix during the meeting and afterward he had gone off on his own again. She found him later standing at one of the balconies of the palace, staring out at nothing. He didn't look as if he'd slept at all. She wasn't sure what to say or do and so she merely joined him, hoping her presence would be comforting in itself.

Finally, he broke the silence, voice rasping slightly. "He loved that wind spirit. Colin."

"I remember him telling me about it when I first came here." At the time, she hadn't had a clue what he was talking about. Now she knew all too well.

"He used to love flying kites when we were younger, but it was usually too windy or not windy enough. He used to talk to the wind spirit, as if it could hear him all the way from the desert." Felix smiled ruefully. "I thought he was crazy, talking to the empty air, but he would ask Azuma to send him the right breeze so he could fly his kite."

"Did it work?"

"Not always. And if it did, we couldn't prove that it wasn't just coincidence, but Colin was certain it had worked and there was no convincing him otherwise. When it did work, he was so happy and he always made sure to say thank you." Felix's gaze darkened. "He loved that wind spirit and it killed him."

Sara didn't bother pointing out that perhaps Azuma hadn't had a choice, if he was under Galatea's control. It would serve no purpose and she had to admit that she really didn't know whether the creature's actions had been willful or not.

His eyes filled with tears suddenly and he looked away. "I'm sorry. I—I need some time to myself."

Sara watched him go, feeling tears spring to her own eyes. The pain seemed to come out of nowhere, washing over her, so intense she thought she might burst from trying to keep it all in. She wanted to force it back down so she didn't have to feel this way, but knew from experience that it was no use.

For a split second, Colin's death had reminded her of what had happened to her mom, Professor Lawrence, and now Hank. The circumstances were different each time, but she had lost people she loved too.

And then there was the conflict with her dad that risked another kind of loss.

Her mom had died over a year ago and Sara had thought she'd gotten over the pain by now. She sank down onto the edge of the balcony, heat rushing over her skin, breath hitching as she tried to fight down the sobs that wouldn't stop.

She sucked in a gasp—and nearly choked—at the sound of footsteps behind her. What was she thinking, having a breakdown here where anyone could come upon her? She should have gone to her room—

Someone settled down on the balcony beside her. Through eyes blurred with tears, Sara saw a glimpse of blue hair and then a pair of arms were around her, pulling her close and she smelled a hint of lavender.

Lylla.

The queen said nothing, merely holding her—*the way a mother would*, Sara realized. For a moment, the realization made her cry harder. Ordinarily, she might have been embarrassed to be comforted in such a way at her age, but she had forgotten what it felt like to be held and how much she had missed it.

Slowly, her sobs quieted and then faded away altogether, leaving her exhausted, emotionally wrung-out.

"I'm sorry," she mumbled, pulling away, wiping at her face with her hands, knowing it was probably only making her eyes even more red. She must look a mess.

Lylla still sat beside her, long skirts spreading out on the stone. "I'm sorry about Colin and Hank. I know how much they meant to you."

"It reminded me of my mom," Sara confessed, the words tumbling out before she could think. "I don't know why. The pain just resurfaced, as strong as it's ever been, almost like it never really went away." And then she'd found herself drowning. As soon as she said it, she felt even more foolish, feeling her face heat.

"It never does," Lylla said gently. Sara looked up at her and saw tears reflected in the queen's eyes. "When you lose someone you love, it is not only their life that is lost, but also a part of your own. The pain never goes away. But in a way, I think that's a good thing. It only hurts so much because you care and the moment it no longer hurts would be the day that you no longer care. And I would never want that to happen."

Sara swallowed. "Me neither." She would never want to stop caring about the people she loved.

"That's the funny thing about grief. The way it sneaks up on you when you least expect it."

"I wish none of this had happened," Sara murmured. "I wish we could just go back to being a whole family."

In the back of her mind, she knew that by wishing such a thing, it would mean wishing away Wysteria. If none of that had ever happened, she likely would never have come here. But she was speaking out of pain, not reason.

Her friends had tried to help when it had happened, but they didn't understand what it was like and short of having to experience it themselves, likely never would.

"It's easy to look at someone else and think that they have the perfect life, that nothing bad ever happens to them, nothing ever goes wrong. But you're seeing only the outermost layer. You don't know how deep it goes or what may lie beneath. There is not a single person in life who has not been touched by tragedy of one sort or another."

Sara said nothing for a long while. She wondered if the queen expected her to say something or how long she would stay. Surely she had somewhere to be, something important to see to, but she didn't make a move to leave.

Together, they watched the sun rise higher in the sky, fighting with the clouds for dominance, the light washing over the courtyard below in waves. One moment it disappeared, the sudden shade leaving Sara chilled, only for it to return, warming her skin.

Sara took a deep breath. "I thought about what you said. About whether I should stay or go."

Her decision was more important now than ever, now that the Lightning Gate had been directly attacked as they had feared. It hadn't been destroyed, but there was no guarantee that Galatea wouldn't try again.

"And?"

"I'm staying. Whatever happens, I'm staying."

17

Storms rolled in overnight and it was still raining the next morning, suiting the somber mood that seemed to have fallen over much of Wysteria. Damaris left the safety of the palace, making her way through the courtyard toward where the Glowing Gate stood. The rain soon soaked into her mane and it hung limp.

Through the gloom, she almost didn't notice the forlorn figure sitting hunched on one of the stone benches. Wanderer was already soaked to the skin, with nothing to protect her from the downpour.

Damaris stopped. "Shouldn't you have returned to the Gate?" She spoke softly to remove the judgement such a remark would have ordinarily carried.

Wanderer did not reply.

Damaris sighed. She couldn't ever remember the Lightning Guardian being like this. "If there is no one to protect the Gate and Galatea destroys it, then Hank's death will have been for nothing."

At that, Wanderer did look up, but still she said nothing. Damaris made to brush past her—she did have somewhere to be—but Wanderer called after her. "How do you do it?"

She turned, questioning.

Wanderer motioned with her hands, futilely trying to convey what she meant. "Do you ever feel…old?"

"All the time." Though the sheer number of years she had lived did not weigh on her physically, mentally was another matter.

"I am immortal," Wanderer murmured. "I will live forever while Hank had only a short time given to him and even that was cut short. He didn't get to live it to the fullest extent and I don't understand why he was killed and not me."

There were things Damaris could think of to say, but none of them seemed particularly helpful. She could tell Wanderer that Hank had died and she had lived because Galatea had only intended to kill him that day—and that was precisely what she had done.

The Flame Guardian didn't think Galatea had intended to destroy the Gate at all. Killing Hank had been her only goal. She couldn't prove it, of course, but it seemed if destroying the Gate had been Galatea's intention, she would have gone through with it.

Perhaps though the sorceress hadn't gotten the chance. Maybe Damaris's arrival at the Gate had prevented its destruction, even though she couldn't prevent Hank's death.

"I have to go on," Wanderer added. "Living like this."

"Do you want to?" Damaris asked quietly. Part of her feared what Wanderer's answer would be, but it was important and so she had to ask. Had to know.

"Yes, but I don't know how." Wanderer was barely audible over the rain. "You've lived longer than anyone else I know, Damaris. You've seen so many things. How do you do it?"

"You find something you care about, something to protect, and that is what keeps you going. You find a why."

Wanderer nodded thoughtfully and then stood, shuffling off into the rain. Damaris hoped she was returning to her Gate. Perhaps that would be her why now that Hank was gone.

She continued on, toward the Glowing Gate. By now, her mane and tail had grown heavy, the rain taking out what little curl it naturally had. She scarcely noticed, lost in thought.

Before she had quite reached the Gate, someone spoke behind her. "Where are you going?"

Damaris knew without turning who would be standing there, but she turned anyway. *Her why.* Felix was dressed, as usual, in all black. He'd thrown a cloak over his clothes, the hood pulled up to shield him from the rain.

"To check on my Gate," she answered. "Why?"

"I want to know where my parents are buried."

His request surprised her. He had never asked such a thing before and she hadn't brought it up, always assuming that it was too painful for him and he preferred not to know. After all, what good would visiting graves do? It wouldn't change what had happened or magically bring them back.

And yet, something about recent events must have spurred on the request. Regardless of why he was asking, it was something she could grant, conveniently coinciding with her current trip.

"They have to be buried somewhere, right?" he added when she didn't reply. "They weren't burned back then. There was no need, really…"

She sighed softly. "Then you'd better come with me."

She waited as he fetched his horse. Wordlessly, he followed her as she led the way into the Enchanted Forest, walking in no particular hurry. She knew the way by heart, cutting through the pathways and heading deep into the forest, to a location known only to a select few.

Revealing the location of the Flame Gate to Felix would do no harm and Damaris had often wished she could share it with him if for no other reason than the one he'd requested.

The moss that covered most of the paths felt spongy underfoot and the dirt had turned to mud. The thick canopy of leaves kept most of the rain from reaching them and the only sound other than their footsteps was that of the droplets falling.

There was no way to know how much time had passed since they had set out and when they finally arrived. There was no sun to rely on. A thick mist had gathered, clinging to the forest floor, rising and becoming more dense the further they went on. Felix stayed close to her for fear he would lose sight of her white coat in the fog.

She stepped through a thick copse of trees and the mist fell away instantly, though it could still be seen on the other side of the trees. Felix followed her, glancing around.

"We're here," she said, breaking the silence.

A cemetery stretched ahead of them, the stones mingling with the trees. Most of them were ancient, weathered and crumbling—impossible to read. Damaris had no idea who was buried here. Silver roses bloomed at the foot of each grave. A set of stone steps rose out of the ground to form a small platform, two stone angels standing on either side of it. In the middle stood an iron gate. There was nothing physically remarkable about it.

Damaris approached anyway, even though she could see it was still intact. She'd expected as much but had to be sure. Surely if anything did happen to it while she was away, she'd know?

Felix dismounted, tethering his horse to one of the nearby trees. Slowly, he began walking around the graveyard. He took his time but Damaris knew what he was looking for. The two newer graves stood out from the others, less worn able to be read.

They were side by side and listed no date of birth or death, reading simply *William* and *Bella Archer*.

Felix stopped before them, running his fingers over the inscriptions and then stood back, sinking down onto a tree stump. "I'd always wondered where they were."

"I suggested that they should be buried here," Damaris said. "So I could still watch over them, in a way I failed to do in life."

"What happened wasn't your fault."

"Hm," was all she said, knowing the truth of his words and yet not convinced.

"What was my mother like?" Felix asked suddenly.

Damaris glanced at him. "You were nine when the attack happened." *You should remember something.*

He gave her a wry look as if he knew what she was thinking. "Old enough to remember some things and young enough to forget others."

Ah.

"She was kind," Damaris answered, remembering her friend. "Gentle. A good listener. She was one of the few people to see me as merely Damaris and not the Flame Guardian. She didn't try to befriend me for what I could give her. The only thing she wanted was friendship. I remember when she was worried about the instability Galatea had caused—thinking about the future and whether it was safe to bring a child into the world. And then when Jack was killed and Galatea fled Wysteria, it was a great load off her shoulders. Your parents were still living in Malenwar before all that. I managed to convince them to leave, when Galatea fled to the city with Jack, fearing it wasn't safe." She paused, voice dropping even lower. "Now I wonder if I didn't lead them to their deaths…"

"You saved them from dying in the Cataclysm," Felix pointed out. And, by extension, him as well. "If they'd still been there, they would have been killed when the city was destroyed."

"Yes, but had they chosen a different village to live in after that, much might have been different."

"They still *chose* to live there."

"On my suggestion."

Her despondency seemed to bother him because he changed the subject, wrapping his cloak more tightly around himself. "What about my father?"

"William? He was brave, strong. An archer, like you. There was so much he wanted to teach you." *And he never got the chance.* "He was so proud to have a son."

"I don't think he would be very proud if he could see me now."

"What makes you think he can't?" Damaris countered. "I happen to think he would be quite proud of who you are, how strong you've become. There are some people who would have laid down and given up, if faced with the same circumstances you've been given. But you are your father's son and he raised you better than to give up."

Felix looked up at her in surprise and with something else in his gaze. Gratitude? For her faith in him? She didn't give praise or encouragement very often. Not as much as she probably should.

He glanced away, eyes shining. "I couldn't save Colin."

"You can't save everyone." Despite her best efforts, she failed to keep all of the bitterness out of her voice.

All the magic in the world didn't make a difference. She herself had arrived too late to save Hank. Another name to add to the list of people she had failed. What good was being the most powerful Guardian to ever live—as she had once been told she had the potential to become—if you couldn't prevent such senseless death?

You can't save everyone.

The two newest graves in the cemetery were proof of that.

***

Galatea surveyed the undead soldiers arrayed before her. She had acquired quite a few more after her attack on the Lightning Gate. Of course, her efforts in destroying the Gate itself had been unsuccessful, which was disappointing. But she had killed one of its Guardians and obtained more soldiers in the process so it wasn't a total loss.

In fact, Hank's death made her quite pleased. She had intended to take something from each of them that they cared about and Wanderer was the first. She hadn't been personally responsible for Jack's death the way Cassius and Cyren had been, but she also had done nothing to stop it from happening.

And the wind spirit had put up less resistance than before. His power had flowed through her, perfectly at her command. It was as if they were one, precisely what she had hoped for, what she had envisioned when she had stepped through the Wind Gate and stolen Azuma.

Galatea turned to Imhotep, who stood a few feet away. It seemed that her investment in him had paid off.

She studied him now. Perhaps if he had been with her, she would have succeeded in destroying the Lightning Gate, but he'd had to stay on the other side, keeping the way clear for when she crossed back over.

"Where is the Flame Gate?" she demanded suddenly.

"I—the location is a secret and I was only ever on the Earth side of things."

"Oh, come now, you must have crossed over at some point. Surely you were curious…"

"It's in the Enchanted Forest somewhere, but I doubt I could find it again if my life depended on it. It's not like I stumbled upon it, I just crossed over and there it was."

"But you must know something," Galatea pressed. "You would have crossed through it when Damaris brought you here. Surely you can find it again."

"Yes, all right," he admitted, somewhat irritably. "I can take you there."

She would have preferred him to tell her exactly how to find it herself, but she would take what she was being given. "Very well. We'll go now."

***

Empress watched, glaring balefully from where she perched atop one of the swamp's ruined buildings, as Galatea left with the human Flame Guardian in tow. The fact that Empress had lost a good many soldiers, sending them to futilely fight the other Flame Guardian, didn't seem to bother Galatea.

The sorceress had merely cast the resurrection spell on the dead fire wolves and mountain dragons, reanimating them the same way she had the fallen elves. Their eyes now glowed an eerie, unsettling green.

It didn't sit well with Empress, but at the same time, she knew it was her own fault. She had been reluctant to pick a side, trying to outright refuse. In the end, she had chosen wrong and paid for it. It rankled, coming to terms with her own failure.

And she was more sure now than ever just how big of a mistake she had made. She'd heard that the Flame Guardian was powerful, but hadn't really witnessed such displays herself, aside from the brief appearance Damaris had made at the end of the Battle of Malenwar last year.

But what she had seen the Guardian do in the swamp was something else entirely. It was one thing to hear about the power someone supposedly possessed and another to see them put it to use right before your very eyes. Empress had seen fellow dragons rendered to ash in seconds. She had asked the Flame Guardian to prove that she could win and she'd done just that.

Empress had tried to tell herself that it didn't matter. As long as she was still alive, she could do something. When such an opportunity might present itself, she had no idea, but she'd vowed to be watchful.

She'd have liked to have gone straight to the palace after Damaris had left and declare her intention to switch sides. But she had done that one too many times and neither side was likely to trust her now. Besides, she had authorized an attack on one of the Guardians. Damaris wouldn't welcome her—she'd be more likely to kill her.

Only now Empress knew something the Flame Guardian would be most interested to hear. The traitorous human Guardian was leading Galatea to Damaris's own Gate at this very moment.

Empress waited until the two were out of sight and then set off. If she played this right, it might be just the thing to return her to Damaris's good graces.

There was not a moment to lose.

18

While Empress's wings carried her faster than Galatea and the human Imhotep could travel on foot, she had no idea where to find Damaris. Ordinarily, she would have begun her search at the Guardian's own Gate, but she didn't know the location of the Flame Gate. And if she followed Imhotep in order to find it, she would arrive too late.

She growled to herself in frustration. If she failed to do this, she would lose her one chance at redemption.

In the end, it was perhaps sheer luck that she saw what she was searching for. Her vision was quite good, able to pick out a stag trying to hide among the snow. After following Imhotep and then going ahead in the general direction he'd been traveling, she caught a flash of white beneath the leaves of the forest canopy and swopped down, landing in front of the Flame Guardian.

Felix was with her and his horse, Tempest, tossed his head nervously at her sudden arrival. Damaris stepped between Felix and Empress, her teeth bared. Empress had the feeling that if Felix hadn't been with her, the Flame Guardian wouldn't have hesitated to lunge first and ask questions later.

"What do you want, traitor?"

Empress made no effort to deny the accusation. Damaris wasn't exactly wrong. "A peace offering," she replied, knowing she needed to move quickly. She didn't know where the Flame Gate was, but it was possible that Galatea and Imhotep might have reached it already. "A show of good faith. I'm not the traitor you need to worry about right now."

"What is that supposed to mean?"

"Imhotep. He's leading Galatea to the Flame Gate as we speak. I don't think I need to spell out what she intends to do once she finds it."

The anger in Damaris's gaze faded, replaced with a look of horror. "I don't believe you."

Empress shrugged. "Believe me or not as you wish, but do you really think I'd have come to you if I were lying? Is it a risk you want to take?"

Damaris turned to Felix. "Go back to the Glowing Gate."

"But—" He started to protest.

"*Go!*"

Without waiting to see if he obeyed, the Flame Guardian whirled and began running back in the direction she had come. Empress moved past the archer and followed her, her long legs easily keeping pace.

Damaris glanced at her. "You can't be seen with me. If Galatea finds out that you told me, she'll kill you."

"She'll likely kill me before this is over anyway," Empress muttered. "Don't worry. I don't intend to be seen arriving with you. But two can play at this game, you know. I'm of more use to you if I stay near Galatea and learn her plans."

The Flame Guardian did not ask what had led to her change of heart and Empress slowed then, allowing the unicorn to continue on without her, hoping that she would arrive in time to save her Gate, but inwardly wondering how even she would fare against two Guardians and the wind spirit.

***

Damaris raced through the forest, back the way she'd come, hooves tearing up the pathway beneath her, mind reeling from what Empress had told her. She and Felix had just been at her Gate and they had seen no sign of anyone else, as expected. And now Galatea and Imhotep were on their way at this very moment.

Imhotep. Once more, Damaris wondered how he could do something like this. Didn't he realize that this would only end in disaster for him? How could he ally himself with someone like Galatea?

Empress had been right; she barely knew Imhotep, not in any way that mattered, and she had no idea the things he was capable of. The fact that he was her counterpart mattered not. She would kill him just the same, if it came to that.

An unseen force surged through the trees, slamming into her as if she had run into a brick wall, throwing her from her feet. Damaris gasped as she hit the ground, dazed. She shook her head as she scrambled up, confusion and horror warring within her.

But overpowering both was a different emotion altogether, clawing to the surface as the rage at what had just happened engulfed her. She had been too late to reach her Gate and far enough away that the blast hadn't killed her. But Galatea and Imhotep would still be there and she charged forward, moving even faster now if that were possible.

The two of them were just leaving the copse of trees when she arrived. It wasn't much of a copse anymore now, most of the trees having been flattened. A flash of fear appeared briefly in Galatea's eyes before it was quickly masked, replaced with satisfaction. Imhotep remained as impassive as ever.

Damaris snarled at him, keeping a rein on her temper with difficulty. She wanted nothing more than to leap at him and tear out his throat, but she wanted to hear an explanation from his lips first. "How could you?"

Imhotep's façade cracked, revealing a trace of the anger that must lurk beneath the surface. "What loyalty do I owe Wysteria, when all it has ever done is neglect me? Why should I have to live on Earth, my life wasting away, protecting a Gate, waiting for the day death will claim me, and then I can be replaced—when I could live here and never die?"

If he wished to never die, he should have picked the other side, Damaris thought, because she was about to put an end to his ambition. Like her, he was immune to fire, so she would have to come up with another creative end for him.

Her fangs, perhaps, would do nicely.

With a snarl, Damaris lunged at him. The wind rose up, pushing against her so strongly, she stopped in her tracks, unable to move forward. Dust began swirling around Galatea and Imhotep, concealing them from view.

The wind died suddenly, as quick as it had come, the dust blowing outward. Damaris blinked, choking on it, as it stung her eyes. When at last she could see again, she was alone. There was no sign of Galatea or Imhotep.

She let out a seething growl, slamming her hooves down. Flames sprang up beneath her with a roar before vanishing. What cowards they were, the both of them, for refusing to stand and fight. They had no sense of honor, but then, she'd already known that.

Of course they wouldn't want to stay and risk a fight with her, knowing how angry she already was. Why would they bother, when they could simply leave her to survey the destruction of her Gate, alone with the knowledge of her failure?

Damaris was suddenly glad that she had sent Felix away as she stepped into the fallen grove of trees. She wouldn't have wanted him to see this.

Along with the toppled trees, the grass had withered and all the silver roses that she had always found so lovely were dead, shriveled and dried as if they had gone too long without water.

The gravestones had been shattered into pieces, like the ones in the cemetery at the Ice Gate on Earth. The gravestones of Felix's parents were gone, no sign that they had ever been there. It was almost as if she had failed them a second time. She had failed to protect them while they were alive and now she hadn't even been able to protect their resting place.

But at least the earth beneath them was solid, undisturbed. Galatea had not attempted to raise the dead buried here, for which Damaris was immeasurably grateful. Her legs felt weak at the sight.

She raised her head to look at her Gate. The iron was warped and jagged as if a great force had plowed directly through it. The two stone angels on either side of it had not escaped harm either. One was missing entirely, the other decapitated, one wing shorn off and the other half gone.

The destruction of a Gate reminded her of a tornado. It was impossible to predict the exact course of wreckage, no explanation as to why one thing might be obliterated and something else mere feet away strangely untouched.

But there was no doubt that it was destruction all the same.

Damaris had always been relatively free to go about her business, knowing that her Gate was safe because very few people knew of its location. She had been a fool to bring Imhotep here, she saw that now, but there had been no other way and at the time, she had assumed that his loyalties were the same as they had seemingly always been.

That, too, had been a mistake. The Guardians were supposed to be sworn to protect their Gates, queen and country. But Galatea was proof enough that not every Guardian felt that way. Damaris had taken Imhotep's loyalty for granted, assuming he was on their side simply because he was a Guardian like her.

The people looked to the Guardians to protect them. They could, after all, control more than one element, where ordinary elementalists were restricted to just one. A Guardian would always be more powerful and the queen's subjects looked to the Guardians to keep them safe.

That was the trouble with betrayal. It never came from someone you suspected.

Damaris sighed. She needed to tell Lylla what had happened.

She glanced at her Gate one last time, an emptiness yawning open inside of her. She hadn't always been a Guardian of a Gate, but she'd always been a Guardian, even before they had such a name. The Flame Gate had been under her protection for so long, she had forgotten what it felt like to be without it.

Her identity suddenly seemed uncertain, her confidence in herself shaken in a way it had never been before. Who was she if not a Guardian of this Gate?

A Guardian of the realm, now. You have to help protect the others and make sure this doesn't happen again.

There were only two Gates left.

Dimly, Damaris imagined what the destruction of her Gate must look like on Earth. The Great Pyramid would have been severely damaged if not outright destroyed. The radiating blast might have leveled the Great Sphinx as well. Monuments that had stood for centuries, only to fall now to such an inglorious end.

Damaris turned, shaking the thought away and headed for the palace at a run, as if she could outrun her failure and escape the devastation behind her.

But the images stayed with her all the way there.

***

That morning, as the rain poured down, Sara returned to Wysteria. The previous evening, after her conversation with Lylla had concluded, she had briefly crossed back over to Earth.

She hadn't wanted to leave, even for a moment, but she needed to talk to Nadia. She didn't dare go home, afraid of finding her dad there. One day she would have to face him, if fate arranged it so, but she was not looking forward to the confrontation.

Sara and Nadia sat on the back porch of Nadia's house, sipping homemade lemonade, as Sara told her friend what had happened to Hank. Unsurprisingly, Nadia had already heard about it, but she didn't know the truth of what had really happened.

"It's the talk of the town," she remarked. Unfortunately, Felix, Wanderer and Damaris had all been seen that day, their presences remarked upon, along with the fact that they had taken Hank's body with them, disappearing as though into thin air.

Sara flinched as she heard that part. The two worlds had collided in the worst way possible.

"It's because of the war, isn't it?" Nadia asked. "What happened to Hank."

"Yes." Sara told her what had really happened and then brought up the painful subject of what had happened with her dad that day. The things he had said—she practically had his words memorized by now, the way they kept going around in her head—and what she had done in response.

"You were right," she added. "I'm an adult and I can make my own decisions, but I feel terrible about it."

"I don't see what you could have done differently," Nadia said, ever the supporting friend. "Nothing about this whole thing is great."

You could say that again. "Well, anyway, I knew I had to tell you. You don't mind if I spend the night here, do you? I can't bear the idea of going home. I just can't face my dad right now. Not after that."

"Of course. You know you can stay here whenever you like."

The next morning, Sara returned to the gas station, the only Gate remaining that connected her two worlds. This time, Nadia went with her.

At this hour, there was no one around. The gas station had been shut down, the convenience store closed. There was no reason for anyone to come here now. Caution tape ringed the building, a tarp having been stretched over the gaping section in the roof.

The broken windows were boarded up, barring entry, but Sara had carefully dislodged one from the inside when she had crossed over the previous evening. To any onlooker, it appeared secure enough, but one wiggle and Sara was in, ducking through the broken window and into the store interior.

Sara wondered what would happen to the building. Would it be condemned? Would someone buy it and tear the building down or would they repair it?

Nadia followed as Sara approached the bathroom, which had escaped unscathed.

"This is the Gate?" Nadia whispered, even though there was no need. "Doesn't look like much. No offense."

Sara raised one hand, closing her eyes to help her concentrate. Hank was no longer here to help her open the Gate if she needed assistance. Wanderer had let her through yesterday. The only way through now was to open the Gate herself—and her magic would have to comply for that.

But it had complied when she had shown her magic to Nadia and Max. Maybe it would do so now.

The Gate resisted her and she pushed harder, sweat breaking out over her forehead, her hand trembling as though she were pushing against an immoveable object. And then something broke free, a dam giving way. There was a brief flash of light and the hole opened in the wall.

Sara gasped, both from relief and the effort it had taken. *I did it.* Her magic hadn't failed her. She stepped forward, glancing over her shoulder at her friend, wishing Nadia could come with her. "Thank you."

Nadia waved her hand. "It's nothing."

"It's not nothing," Sara insisted, coming back and throwing her arms around her. "You're the best friend I could ask for. Better than I deserve."

"I'll remember you said that, next time I need something from you," Nadia said, her tone light, teasing, no doubt embarrassed by the praise. "Now go on. I can find my way out of here. Go save the world."

Sara did as instructed—though saving the world might be a bit much to ask for—and crossed over, closing the Gate behind her, which was much easier to do.

Wanderer was nowhere to be seen this morning, probably in the small cottage that stood beside the Gate, nearly completely covered in ivy. Sara didn't blame her if she had retreated indoors. Though it had been sunny on Earth when she left, rain poured down here.

Great. She'd be soaked through by the time she reached the palace. The soldiers that had once again been posted to the Gate looked as miserable as she suddenly felt. Due to the attack, there weren't as many of them as before, but they couldn't simply leave the Gate unguarded.

Sara began the trek through the forest to the palace. True to her prediction, she was completely drenched by the time she arrived, changing into a dry set of clothes in her room before joining Serai in the healer's quarters.

Serai had run out of silver rose petal, used to dull pain, no doubt used up by the soldiers injured in the attack on the Lightning Gate. Other herbs had also been depleted or nearly so and the healer informed Sara they would need to venture out into the forest and gather more.

Luckily, the rain did not last long and had stopped completely by the time they set out, each with a basket on one arm. The forest air was crisp and cool after the rain, moisture shimmering on the leaves and blades of grass. She could hear birds chirping but couldn't see them. A sense of peace descended on her and she found it hard to believe, in this moment, that a war still raged outside.

Sara still hadn't mastered the anatomy tome she'd been given, but the head healer wasted no time in pointing out which herbs were worth their weight in gold and which to avoid at all costs.

The silver roses were easy to spot, their petals glimmering slightly in the weak light. They had thorns like most roses and so Sara was mindful not to prick herself. Hardy plants, the petals could be plucked off without damaging the plant itself. They would simply grow back as though nothing had happened.

Sara didn't know how long they had been working together in peaceful silence when a deep *boom* resounded through the forest. It wasn't very loud, far in the distance, but there had been no mistaking it.

She looked up, meeting the healer's gaze. "What was that?"

The two of them listened but the sound did not come again and eventually they went back to work. Sara's basket was half full when she next glanced up at the head healer. Serai's basket wasn't yet full either. The patch that Sara had been working on was picked over now and she moved on, searching for more flowers and finding none.

Frowning, she walked further into the shadows of the forest, stopping as she nearly ran into an enormous briar, the thorns as thick as her torso and long as her forearm.

She hadn't realized how close they'd wandered to the Briarwood. She turned to Serai, who had followed at a distance. "Should we turn back?"

The elf's lips pursed. "The Briarwood is one of the best places to find silver roses. It should be fine, but let's not go too far."

They continued onward and true to the healer's word, the roses began appearing almost at once. The birds had stopped singing here and Sara shivered even though it wasn't cold, uncomfortably aware of how close they were to the swamp.

She'd never laid eyes on the ruins of Malenwar, but she'd heard stories. It was here Galatea had retreated to last year, here she had made her home. She might even be there now…

Here the sorceress had wanted to bring Sara, sending one of her disguised lackeys to kidnap her, all in a bid to get the Echo Stone from her.

Sara shivered again. She had no Echo Stone to give now.

"Sara!"

She whirled around to see Serai behind her, green eyes wide, staring at something past her. Sara turned back around to see what the elf was looking at just as a fire wolf burst out of the brush, charging at her.

A scream slipped past her lips as she remembered the last time she had been chased by wolves through the forest. Her magic had revealed itself then, but she didn't believe it would come to her aid now. Felix and Lylla had come looking for her then, but now it was just her and Serai alone in the forest.

She turned and ran, her fist clenching the handle of her basket. Serai fled as well, her long green dress whipping around her legs. Sara glanced over her shoulder to see that three more wolves had joined the first and worst of all— she recognized one of them.

Venryk had confronted her on Earth the night she had been brought to Wysteria and she would never forget the wolf's leonine build, muscles rippling beneath the thick crimson fur or the icy eyes.

Sara had caught up to Serai now, but the wolves were rapidly gaining. There was no point in trying to fight them; Serai's magic was for healing only.

"A tree," the healer gasped. "We need to climb a tree."

"Won't they just burn it down?"

"What other choice is there?" Serai snapped, her fear making her angry. "You want to stop and fight them?"

Serai had a point. She skidded to a halt in front of a tree with a fork in the trunk low enough to climb. Sara helped give her a boost, the desert elf nimbly clambering up, out of harm's way.

Sara had never been good at climbing trees. She turned to see how much time she had left and realized the answer was none. The wolves had reached her, encircling the trunk. Her heart leapt to her throat and she backed away. If she turned to climb now, they would be on her in seconds, dragging her back down.

Running or fighting. It was a lost cause either way and that left only one choice. If she were going to die, she would rather do so having put up a fight. Perhaps, if nothing else, she could frighten them off. They knew she was a Light Guardian after all.

Clenching her teeth, Sara waved a hand forward, praying that her magic would respond. The hair on her arms stood up, her skin tingling and heating all at once as the power coursed through her.

A flare of light appeared, blinding in its intensity, gone as quickly as it had appeared. Venryk yelped, shaking his head as if to clear it. Sara extended her arms out on either side of her, sending beams of light at two of the wolves. Before they even realized what was happening, the light had struck them and they cried out as the smell of singed flesh filled the air.

Sara whirled on the last wolf and summoned another illumination, her adrenaline surging. She didn't think. To do so would be to freeze and that would mean death. She had to kill her attackers before they killed her or someone else.

The beam of light tore through the wolf's chest, leaving a gaping hole and it collapsed upon the ground, fur smoking, without so much as a sound.

That left only Venryk and she couldn't kill him. That privilege belonged to Felix. The wolf bared his teeth at her, having cleared his vision. With one last glare, he turned and darted back into the bushes, out of sight.

Sara gasped, sinking back against the tree trunk, shaking as the full realization of what she'd done hit her. She'd just killed three wolves and fended off a fourth all on her own. She stared down at her hands. Her magic had once again responded when it mattered most. Dimly, she noticed that the birds had begun trilling again.

Leaves rustled above her as Serai clambered down, taking in the dead wolves around them. "That was incredible. You were just like Lylla. Are you sure you want to be a healer?"

"I can be both," Sara said numbly, barely registering the words. Lylla was both herself.

The question was, would her magic aid her in training or would it once again disappoint? It seemed to obey her commands when it was do or die, which Sara was thankful for, but found frustrating all the same.

"We'd better get back, before they come with more."

Sara picked up her basket, which she had dropped at her feet. "I'm afraid I lost all my petals." They must have fallen out when she had run.

Serai waved it away. "You more than made up for it."

***

Venryk returned to the swamp alone. The three wolves Galatea had sent with him were nowhere to be found.

"What happened?" Galatea demanded. "Where are the others?"

"Dead," the wolf said flatly.

"At least tell me you managed to kill the girl."

Venryk shook his head, long fangs glinting in the dim light. "We were no match for her magic."

Galatea hissed. Yet another setback.

Even though she had succeeded in destroying the Flame Gate, a feat which she was quite proud of, she hadn't anticipated on being confronted by Damaris.

If the girl was able to use her magic to such a degree, Galatea would have to take care of it herself. It would be easy enough.

Thus far, they'd heard little of the other Lightbringer and seen even less. But she couldn't allow another light attribute—and a Guardian at that—to join the fray. Inexperienced or not, it was too dangerous.

She snapped her fingers at a group of mountain dragons sitting nearby. "You. With me."

****

Upon returning to the palace, Sara excused herself from healer duties for the day and sought out Lylla, explaining that she'd like to try combat training instead.

"Healing not working out?" the queen asked as they walked out into the pasture behind the palace.

"I don't know. I haven't really healed anything yet." Briefly, Sara related what had happened in the forest, Lylla's expression darkening as she did so. "But I was able to fend them off."

"Show me."

The training dummies still stood where they always were. This was it. The moment to find out if her magic had really returned or if it stubbornly refused. Sara raised one hand, trying to imagine that the dummies were fire wolves, closing in and eager for blood.

No sooner had she thought it than the light flared, coming to life. It ripped through the chest of one dummy, leaving behind a smoking hole.

It was nothing compared to what she was capable of doing, given more time to master her element, but it was more than what she had been able to do ever since losing the Echo Stone.

Lylla nodded. "Impressive."

"Why now?" Sara asked, turning to her. "Why does my magic work all of a sudden?"

"I don't know. Magic is very responsive to emotion. Perhaps there was something holding you back, something that you needed to work through."

Then what had changed? Her grief had reappeared after Colin and Hank had died, dredging up all the unhealed pain. Talking about it had helped. Was that what had done it? She had expected to be over the hurt by now, but had instead come to realize and accept that you never really got over it. You simply had to accept it and move on with your life, the way the person you loved would have wanted you to.

Whether that was the reason or something else was responsible, Sara was just glad to have finally made some progress.

After the training session was over, Sara went to find Felix, who had been posted to the Lightning Gate again. By then, the day was nearly over, slipping away before she knew it, the sun sinking lower in the sky.

Lylla offered to come with her, no doubt thinking of the earlier fire wolf attack and not wanting to let Sara go alone. When Sara insisted she would be fine, the queen merely remarked that it would be good to be seen at the camp, making the rounds and inquiring after the soldiers there.

Sara had no complaint with that, glad of the company.

She had barely greeted Felix when he said, "Did you hear about the Flame Gate?"

"What?" Sara asked, her elation at her magic draining away, replaced by the heavy weight of dread. "No, what happened?"

"It's gone. Destroyed this morning."

Sara thought back to the noise she had heard earlier that morning in the forest with Serai. Could that have been it? Had she heard the Flame Gate's destruction and not realized?

"I was there shortly before it happened." He shook his head. "It's crazy to think about." There was sadness in his gaze.

"What is it?"

"Nothing important."

Sara didn't believe him but sensed that now was not the time to press. Instead she told him about the fire wolf attack.

He frowned as he listened. "This is what I was afraid of," he muttered. "There's nothing to keep Venryk from targeting you."

"But I fended him off," Sara argued, thinking back to what her dad had said about it being too dangerous to return to Wysteria.

This was the first time since last summer that she had personally been attacked. It was unnerving, but perhaps not as much as it should have been. Was her father right? Was it too dangerous? She had told him that she could take care of herself. It hadn't been true then, but perhaps it was now.

"I know," Felix said, breaking into her thoughts. "But there might be more of them next time. What if there's too many for you? You could have been killed."

"But I wasn't."

"I know," he repeated, drawing her close. "And I'm glad. I'm just…scared."

Briefly, she wondered if he was perhaps jealous of how efficiently she had dealt with Venryk. She could have killed the wolf if she wanted to, but she hadn't, knowing what it would mean if she did. Was Felix jealous of her powers as a Guardian, wishing he had that level of magic with which to deal with Venryk?

She didn't think so, but she would understand if it were true.

Behind her, someone cried out a warning and a moment later, an ear-splitting roar filled the air. Sara flinched back away from Felix, a shadow falling over them, illuminated by the dying sun. Air buffeted her face as the dragon's black wings beat above them.

It let out another screech and swooped down toward them, black claws extended.

"Run!" Felix cried, pushing her out of the way. "Get to the Gate!"

In the blink of an eye, he'd nocked an arrow and fired it at the dragon. It lodged in the creature's thick white fur. The dragon growled and dove at him. Felix flattened himself on the ground, the creature whizzing harmlessly past, the force of the air pulling at his hair and clothes.

Sara glanced over her shoulder to see more dragons, some in the air, and others on the ground, charging in her direction. More shouts rang out around the camp as the alarm went up that they were under attack.

The dragon Felix had shot kept coming, nearly upon her. Sara's foot snagged on a tree root and she cried out as she fell, catching herself on her hands and knees. The dragon's claws narrowly missed her, passing by just overhead, and she realized that if she hadn't tripped—

Best not think about that.

Gasping, she scrambled to her feet and ran for the Gate, visible just ahead. Wanderer called to her as she summoned lightning, striking the nearest dragons and knocking them from the air.

Get to the Gate, Felix had said, and she knew what he was thinking. If she crossed over, she would be safe. The dragons couldn't reach her there. But she could fight! Her magic would obey her now. Sara hesitated, debating whether to listen to her instinct or Felix.

And then, materializing out of the darkness as though she'd teleported there, Galatea was suddenly to Sara's right, stalking toward her, Shadowblade in hand.

Fear clawed its way up Sara's throat. She might be able to fight, but her magic was no match for the sorceress's.

A flash of light lit up the dusk as the Gate opened. "Go through!" Wanderer cried. "Now!"

Was this to be it? The moment the Lightning Gate finally fell? She would be trapped on the other side, unable to easily get back. Only three Gates—no, two, Sara quickly corrected herself, with the loss of the Flame Gate. Only two Gates remained. If the Lightning Gate fell, she would not only be cut off, all her friends here would die.

She couldn't leave them. Her eyes latched onto Galatea, still advancing, and instinct took over. She turned and pelted for the Gate with all the speed she could muster.

And then she was through, stumbling from the transition, but managing to stay on her feet. She reached the loose board in one of the windows and paused, panting. She could hear her heartbeat in her ears as she glanced back toward the bathroom.

The hole in the wall had closed behind her, but instead of the bathroom being empty, Galatea was there, making her way toward her. A man was with her—Imhotep, the traitorous human Flame Guardian.

Sara's eyes widened in horror. *Oh, God.* Why were they here? Why weren't they focused on the Gate? They had followed her through and onto Earth. She was trapped here with the sorceress and nowhere to go.

Run, she thought to herself, at the same time, thinking, *You can't lead her home.*

Even her own home was off-limits to her now.

Sara yanked the board back, nearly tripping in her haste as she ducked out of the window, dashing into the parking lot. Galatea followed, pace unhurried. Sara was halfway across the parking lot when the sorceress sent the first tendril of darkness spiraling after her. Gasping, Sara summoned an illumination, canceling the darkness out.

But she couldn't keep this up forever. Galatea was far more powerful and even if their attributes canceled each other out, the sorceress still had the wind spirit.

Running was pointless. All that was left was to hide.

But hiding behind or inside of something wasn't good enough. The sorceress would see where she went. *Think!*

It was hard to think, her heart beating so hard Sara feared it would simply stop, the stress too much for it. She suddenly remembered one of the training sessions she had done with Lylla, before her magic had decided to comply. It was the defensive maneuver, turning yourself invisible.

She'd never succeeded in doing it to her whole body. If it worked, she might be able to circle back around and reach the Gate, crossing over to safety. With the sun going down and less light reflecting off of her, she just might have a chance.

Sara looked down at her body, taking note of the way the light reflected off of her and bent it, forcing it to reflect as it would if she wasn't there. Galatea halted, a look of confusion coming over her.

Sara crouched down as slowly as she dared, hoping to present a smaller target. Galatea still stood between her and the Gate. She reconsidered her plan, not daring to take a step. If she did, the air would shimmer and with Galatea paying such close attention, alert for the slightest movement, it would give her away. She wasn't sure how good her invisibility even was; she only knew it had worked because of Galatea's expression. But if the sorceress got closer, or if Sara moved, the illusion might shatter.

Hardly daring to breathe, Sara watched motionless as Galatea and Imhotep slowly stepped forward, the sorceress's gaze darting around.

"Where did she go?" Imhotep asked.

Galatea ignored him. "I know you're here," she called. "Come out. Don't be shy."

Terrified is more like it.

Galatea summoned more darkness, the mist wrapping around her forearm. She flung it casually outward. It traveled some distance and then evaporated. Sara tensed. What would happen if one of those tendrils struck her? Was she in more danger standing still or daring to move? She could be hit either way.

Helpless, feeling like a mouse already caught in a trap, Sara remained unmoving as more darkness was sent out, seeking her. It was a test of will for her not to move. Every time one got close, it was all she could do not to cry out and scramble away.

She looked back at the store, wondering if no one else had seen Galatea come through. Where was Wanderer? Why wasn't anyone coming to help her?

Another beam of darkness speared outward, heading straight for her. Crouched down as she was, there was no time to move. Sara gasped as it struck her, knocking her onto her back. Cold stabbed her in the chest, where the darkness had struck, but it didn't seem to spread and Sara hoped that was a good sign.

Her concentration broken, her invisibility vanished, leaving her exposed. Imhotep raised a hand and a ring of fire sprang up around Sara, surrounding her. Galatea covered the distance between them in a few quick strides, the fire parting to let her through, and came to stand over her.

Sara stared up into her dead black eyes, thinking that this was the last thing she would ever see. This was how she would die. Her father would be devastated when her body was found here, in the middle of the parking lot.

"There you are," the sorceress murmured, raising her Shadowblade above her head.

Sara closed her eyes as Galatea brought the blade down. There was a cry of warning and a *whoosh* as the fire went out.

A metallic *clang* rang out and Sara's eyes snapped open to see Lylla standing over her, holding the white sword that had blocked the killing blow.

"Get to the Gate, Sara," the queen said, voice unnervingly calm.

Sara backed away from the crossed blades, scrambled up and ran. She could hear steel ringing out as more strikes were exchanged and parried. Her steps slowed. How could she leave Lylla to face Galatea and Imhotep alone? She was sure the queen was more than up to the task, her magic the perfect counterpart to Galatea's. But there was still the wind spirit and the Flame Guardian.

What if she needs my help? If she could distract Galatea somehow, it might give Lylla an opportunity to finish her and then all this madness would be over.

Sara ducked behind the dumpster in the parking lot and watched as the two fought, moving so fast, it was hard to follow what was happening. Light flashed as Lylla summoned her magic, absorbed quickly by Galatea's own.

Imhotep came to Galatea's aid, summoning his flames. A shield of light appeared around the queen, absorbing the incoming attacks until it exploded outward, throwing Imhotep back.

And then Lylla disappeared. Galatea whirled, futilely searching. A moment later, Lylla had returned, only there were several copies of her, surrounding Galatea. Sara let out a gasp. The queen was using her ability to reflect light to create the illusion that she was everywhere at once.

The illusions sprang forward, moving as one, so quickly that they were a blur as the air distorted around them. Galatea and Imhotep cut down illusion after illusion but they merely reformed and scattered around the parking lot as though taunting the Guardians. They had failed to locate which one was the real Lylla and not a mere reflection. Sara herself had even lost track of where the queen really stood.

Suddenly there was a blur behind Imhotep as Lylla's invisibility dropped. Sara stared in astonishment at the queen's ability, the power and sheer mastery of her element on display. She had turned herself invisible and snuck up behind Imhotep while her illusions provided a distraction.

Sara could only hope to one day be so adept as she watched Lylla plunge Pharus through Imhotep's back.

His mouth opened in a silent cry and he slumped to the ground. Lylla resumed her invisibility. Galatea whirled and saw her ally lying lifeless on the asphalt, blood pooling beneath him. Azuma reared up behind her.

Sara refused to take her eyes off Lylla, tracking the slight blur she could see now that she knew where to look. Lylla was trying to sneak up behind Galatea the same way she had Imhotep and Sara silently urged her on.

She could do it and then this would be over. Her breath caught; in that moment, she could believe Lylla invincible.

She watched the air shimmer as the white sword swung toward Galatea's neck. The wind spirit roared a warning and the sorceress spun around, bringing her Shadowblade up to block. The impact of the two blades meeting rang out across the parking lot, white sparks flying from Pharus.

Sara could have cursed. *Damn that wind spirit!*

Lylla spun away, disengaging before Galatea could. In the same moment she turned invisible, she created another clone in the exact location she'd been just a moment before. The transition was seamless, so smooth Galatea didn't realize it had happened.

Her sword sliced through the illusion and it vanished. The sorceress let out a cry of frustration.

She lunged for the nearest illusion, cutting it down with her sword. One by one they vanished, only to crop up elsewhere. Galatea didn't have time to chase down the real Lylla.

It was a game that could go on for eternity until she weakened—and then Lylla would strike again.

There was no way Galatea could win, Sara realized. Lylla would simply wait her out or the sorceress would be forced to flee.

As she watched, the wind spirit rose higher above his mistress, feathered wings stretching wide.

The air seemed to be sucked from her lungs, as first the wind pulled one way and then blasted outward. The dumpster Sara crouched behind blew over and she threw herself to the side to avoid being crushed by it. The wind slammed into the illusions, all at once, shattering them and the real Lylla, who had once again crept behind Galatea, was thrown to the ground by the force, her invisibility failing as her concentration faltered.

Galatea didn't give her a chance to regain her footing, plunging the Shadowblade down.

Sara screamed, but there was no sound that could be heard over the wind.

Her ears popped and suddenly there was a third person present as Damaris, in unicorn form, wreathed in flames, lunged at Galatea. The sorceress danced away, cloaking herself in darkness. She vanished, having gotten what she wanted.

Damaris whirled, looking around vainly for the sorceress, but she'd gone. The Guardian's eyes were blazing a bright, pure red. Sara could no longer see the amber sclera.

"Coward!" the Flame Guardian roared, her voice echoing down the street, ricocheting off the buildings.

The rage in her voice rang in Sara's ears long after the sound had faded. She huddled behind the overturned dumpster, afraid to move.

***

Damaris extinguished her flames and assumed her human form. If Galatea came back and dared show herself, she was dead.

She knelt down beside Lylla, a pool of blood already gathering beneath her on the pavement, staining her white and yellow gown. Her breathing was labored, but her eyes were clear. In the darkness, she still gave off a slight golden aura.

"Ris," she whispered.

"Don't speak," Damaris ordered, lifting one hand above her.

It won't work, a niggling doubt hissed in the back of her mind, chased away instantly by the next thought. *I have to try.*

Lylla snatched her wrist with surprising strength. "What are you doing?"

"I'm going to heal you." She knew the legend they had discussed at the meeting the day Hank had died was true, but whether it would work for her was another matter entirely. There was only one way to find out.

Lylla shook her head vehemently. "No. You can't."

"They need you," Damaris insisted. They were running out of time. Soon the darkness would have spread too far and deep for the wound to be healed.

"I can try," a tentative voice spoke up behind Damaris's shoulder.

She turned to see Sara standing there. A light attribute could heal darkness. "Try."

She knelt beside Damaris, extending one hand. Light flared from her palm and fingertips, but as they watched, the wound did not heal or close. At last, exhausted from the effort, Sara let her arm drop uselessly to her side.

"It's not working!" she wailed.

"Then it falls to me," Damaris said grimly.

"No," Lylla said again. "They need you, Ris. It may not work. Even if you survive, without your magic…" She grimaced, breaking off. "You're all they have. They need you."

There has to be another way, Damaris wanted to scream in frustration. She knew the tradition as well as anyone. If the reigning monarch died without an heir, the crown passed to the most powerful Guardian, and with her Gate having been destroyed and no longer a responsibility, she was the perfect candidate. She wouldn't have to worry about protecting a Gate that no longer existed.

She would have to do something far harder—protect an entire realm and its people.

I can't do this! We need you. Don't leave us.

"Promise me," Lylla gasped.

The words tore through her to the core. They were the exact words Bella had spoken to Damaris as she lay dying, torn apart by fire wolves, and Damaris, helpless to do anything, had swallowed back her tears and made the vow she may not be able to keep. Was this to be yet another promise she may not be able to honor?

Would she be doomed to fail in this endeavor as well?

She swallowed, forcing the tears back by sheer will, her throat aching with the effort. She grasped Lylla's hand, colder than it should have been. "I swear it," she ground out through clenched teeth. "I will destroy Galatea for this."

Lylla nodded. "Stop her, Flameseeker."

"I'll stop her. I promise."

Lylla's eyes went to Sara, who already had tears streaming down her cheeks. The queen reached out to touch her as a mother would a child. "Don't lose hope." Her voice was barely audible. "So long as you have hope, I will always be with you."

She closed her eyes, body relaxing and then she was gone. Her expression was one of peace. If not for the wound, Damaris would have believed her asleep.

The lights that always shimmered in her hair had gone out. That one small detail was what nearly sent Damaris over the edge.

I was too late. I should have come sooner. I should have stopped Galatea from escaping. I should have stopped her before that. I should have healed Lylla anyway, despite her wishes. All of this flashed through her mind, but she couldn't speak them aloud. Her role had changed now.

She didn't know how long the two of them had knelt there before one of them spoke.

"We should go." Sara's voice sounded more like a whimper as she struggled to get the words out. "Before someone sees us."

Damaris knew she was right, but how could she face the others and tell them what had happened? Was this how Lylla had felt when her parents had died in the Exodus, leaving her the inexperienced young leader of a scattered world?

You promised you would do this. Even if it was the hardest thing she had ever done, she would do it. For her.

"You're right." Damaris gently picked up Lylla's body, surprisingly light. So fragile.

Sara bent down and retrieved the sword, still pulsing its white glow. Wordlessly, they made their way to the Lightning Gate. Damaris glanced at Imhotep's body as she passed, jaw clenching as she set it aflame, incinerating the evidence.

At least Lylla killed the bastard.

Wanderer opened her mouth to say something the moment they crossed back over, the camp behind her a frenzy of chaos still scrambling to make sense of the attack. She froze, face blanching at the sight. She covered her mouth, falling to her knees.

Damaris did not bother saying anything. Words could wait.

***

Pharus felt heavy in Sara's hands. It was a sword that belonged to another, a sword she never should have had to hold.

She searched the crowd of soldiers gathered until she found Felix. His lips were parted, eyes wide with horror. Her breathing came in quick, ragged gasps, but it was never enough. She couldn't get enough air. Darkness began to creep in at the edges of her vision, heart stuttering in her chest. She was going to pass out—

And then he was there, wrapping his arms around her, something solid and real anchoring her. She didn't know what happened, but the next thing she knew, he was leading her up the palace steps with no knowledge of how she'd gotten there.

He led her inside, through the palace corridors, to the heavy wooden door that marked the entrance to the room that had quickly become both of their favorites.

The palace library was full of books and paintings, statues, weapons, tapestries, and other curiosities. A giant tree stood in the middle of the room, its branches extending up to the second floor and to the ceiling above. Steps embedded into its trunk led up to the second balcony. As always, small golden orbs of light hung in the room, giving it a warm glow.

Tonight, they seemed somehow diminished.

They reached the window seat, but neither one sat down. Felix turned her toward him, gently gripping her arms. Behind him, through the glass, the courtyard was visible, and beyond, the cliffs and the Green Sea, moonlight reflecting off the waves. Sara barely noticed its beauty. Dimly, she was aware that she still clutched Pharus.

"Galatea came back through while you were still over there," Felix murmured. His voice trembled slightly and Sara didn't know how he managed not to shatter into a million pieces. He reached up, brushing a strand of hair out of her face. "What happened?"

The sorceress must have gone straight for the Gate after she'd run from Damaris.

Sara opened her mouth to answer, but no sound came, as though her throat refused to work. She was shaking, tears running over freely. She couldn't see.

"Hey." Felix's voice was gentle, his touch even more so as he brushed the tears from her cheeks. "Look at me. Breathe."

She did, forcing herself to meet his dark green eyes and not look away. In a flat voice, she managed to tell him what had happened, feeling all the while as if she were hearing someone else speak.

"I tried to heal her, Felix," she said, feeling hysteria and panic rise up within her all over again. "I tried but I couldn't!"

"I know."

"It's my fault! It's all my fault. She crossed over to save me and I couldn't—"

The words simply would not come after that, refusing to slip through her choking breaths.

Felix's arms went around her, pulling her to him and she pressed her face against his chest as the sobs took her, pouring out her grief and fury at the futility of her magic. Just when she thought she'd gotten it to obey her, or at the very least that it responded to her in critical moments, it let her down when it mattered most, failing the person who had always believed in her.

She had thought Lylla invincible. She'd been so certain that she would win and that she was about to watch her cut Galatea down and put an end to this nightmare. And then Galatea had summoned the wind spirit that had taken so many lives and would likely take many more.

And the nightmare continued. One she couldn't wake up from.

She clung to Felix like a life raft. She must have set Pharus down, her fists gripping the material of his shirt. At some point, they must have sank down onto the window seat, legs no longer able to support them. Sara felt Felix's body shuddering against hers as he wept with her, sharing in the pain, his composure at last giving way.

The grief she had thought she had come to terms with had been ripped open, the wound raw and bleeding. It would never scar, never heal.

The next thing Sara knew, tepid daylight was streaming through the window at her back. Felix was turned sideways on the window seat, one leg propped up and the other dangling over the edge. Sara was curled up beside him, still in his arms, head lying on his chest. He was still asleep and she didn't have the heart to wake him.

Consciousness would return soon enough and with it, the pain.

Sara found herself wondering what her dad would have to say if he knew how close she'd come to dying last night in that parking lot. Quickly, she pushed the thought away. It brought her no peace and there was no point in thinking about it now.

She had made her decision. Whatever the risks, whatever the cost, there was no chance she could go back now, even if she had wanted to.

Not after last night.

19

Damaris sequestered herself in the upper most room of the palace. The queen's quarters. It felt wrong being there without Lylla. Everywhere she looked, she was reminded of her, knowing she would never set foot in this room again.

Half of the back wall was open to the elements, letting in a warm breeze which stirred the windchimes hanging from the ceiling. There were bookshelves lining one wall, with a desk and colorful drapes, reminiscent of the desert, hung above her head. A fountain bubbled quietly in one corner, a small stone basin set into the floor catching the overflow of water. The walls were decorated with paintings of various landscapes and a harp stood in another corner.

This was Lylla's room, not hers. It would never be hers. But it was private and that was all that mattered right now. Damaris knew she should be out there, reassuring people and trying to offer comfort in some way. It was what Lylla would have done. But she couldn't bring herself to do it. Not yet.

For now, she could still be just a Guardian, until the coronation ceremony was complete. That would finalize everything and then there really would be no going back.

She sighed, feeling a sudden anger surge through her, startling in its intensity. She hadn't felt such impotent rage since the night Felix's parents had been killed. She had failed them as certainly as she had failed Lylla.

Damaris had been too late to save Bella and William, too late to save Hank or the Professor, and now too late to save Lylla. *How many more will I fail to save?*

Damn Galatea. I will destroy her. I will reduce her to ash.

Damaris flexed her fingers, curling them into a fist and then relaxing over and over again, focusing on the movement. She would have to get used to being in human form. As queen, she would be expected to maintain it.

She had often wondered what Galatea had seen in Jack, what had tempted her to cross over to Earth in the first place. Galatea hadn't been alive during the Exodus. Born decades later, she had only ever been in Wysteria, never having been to Earth and Damaris could only assume that had fed her curiosity.

The sorceress had heard stories, no doubt, of how the humans had turned against the elementalists, both fearing their magic and wanting it for themselves. The human Guardians they had managed to turn had imbued swords with elements, infusing the weapons with power, just as Galatea had done with her Shadowblade. The humans had used the weapons, turning the elementalists' own magic against them, forcing them to flee to Wysteria and close the Gates, posting Guardians to ensure that the two worlds did not interact.

Perhaps Galatea had wondered how much Earth may have changed after so much time had passed? Maybe she had wondered if all humans were so hateful and violent. And when she had met Jack, she realized that they were not. So why wouldn't they be allowed into Wysteria? Why should they be viewed as outcasts, somehow less worthy?

It was easy to see how she could have rationalized it. But that didn't excuse what she had done and her selfish, destructive decisions made it all the worse.

A knock sounded on the door. Damaris wanted to tell whoever it was to go away, but she couldn't. She owed them something.

"Come."

She glanced over her shoulder as the door eased open and Cassius stepped in. He took in the room and the fact that she was there alone.

"So it's true?"

"It's true."

He closed the door behind him. "Did she say anything?"

Damaris didn't answer for a moment. She had to keep a tight rein on her emotions, no matter the cost. "She made her intentions clear."

"So you're to be queen, then." He didn't sound angry at all, where once he would have.

Their elements were opposites and they had always disliked each other. Damaris had long suspected Cassius to be jealous of the freedom she had and the fact that she was more powerful. But that had been before the Battle of Malenwar, where his sister had been killed, reanimated, and turned against him.

Despite their differences, Damaris couldn't let him be killed and so she had intervened, saving his life. His attitude toward her, while not exactly friendly, had been decidedly improved ever since.

"God, Cassius." Damaris whirled to face him.

So much for keeping her emotions in check, but she couldn't ignore the helplessness welling up inside her. She needed to tell someone and he would have to do. She wished Kadir were here. He would have known exactly what to do and say. But he was dead, like so many others.

"What do I do? What do I tell these people? I'm not a leader, Cassius, I'm a Guardian. I'm a soldier, not a general. I follow orders, I don't give them."

"But you could and there's the difference. You're the only one of us who can do this. You have more experience than anyone else on this entire island. You've been in wars, seen empires rise and fall. You know about strategy." Cassius shook his head. "Galatea made a big mistake, doing what she did. And she's about to realize it. You're a dangerous enemy to have—far more than Lylla."

That much was perhaps true.

She sighed again, turning away. Some of the people who now fell under her command had never known a Wysteria without Lylla. "How can I take her place?"

"You can't. You can only be yourself. They'll follow you, if you lead them."

"I was going to heal her and she told me not to. Why didn't I? Why did I listen to her? It would have worked. I could have done it!"

His dark blue robes rustled as he stepped forward, laying a hand on her shoulder. A comradely gesture. She turned to him. Leave it to the Water Guardian to understand her best.

"She must have known what she was doing," he said softly. When Damaris didn't reply, he added, "The funeral preparations are already underway. You need to get ready."

Ordinarily, the coronation and ascension of the next monarch would wait until the proper mourning period was observed. But in a time of war, they couldn't afford to wait.

Damaris looked up into Cassius's amber eyes and spoke the two words she never uttered.

"Help me."

***

The crowds that turned out for the funeral were massive, the news having traveled far and wide. Sara stuck close to Felix for fear of being lost or crushed in the crowd. Lylla had been laid out on a stone slab in the middle of the pasture so that everyone could see their beloved queen.

Her turquoise hair was loose, curling slightly, and she wore a golden gown, the color of her element. There was no sign of the hideous wound. Her arms were clasped over her stomach, her body surrounded by flowers. Mourners approached to touch her, whisper a few last words, and move on. Some simply were overcome by grief and couldn't bear to approach.

Nearly overwhelming Sara's own grief was a crushing sense of guilt. She had been there. She'd had the chance to heal the queen and she had failed. Her training as a healer had been useless. She couldn't remember how to knit sinew back together and no herbs would be of use.

She was a Light Guardian, the only one with the element to heal a wound caused by darkness. Had Lylla been disappointed with her, in her last moments, or had she not found it surprising? Sara wasn't sure which would hurt more.

But worse still, Lylla's death was her fault as surely as Professor Lawrence's had been. Galatea had been after her and Lylla had come to save her. *I always need to be saved.* If she hadn't run, if she had only tried to fight the dragons on the Wysterian side... If she hadn't crossed over at all, then Wanderer and the gathered soldiers could have helped.

This would never have happened.

Felix found her as the funeral was beginning to wind down. Sara had retreated back into the palace, in the sitting room, on the couch with her legs tucked up beside her.

He held a plate with a few pieces of bread on it, covered in some sort of jam. "Here. I didn't want to bring you anything too heavy, but you need to eat. Starving yourself won't help. Trust me."

Sara didn't want to take it, even though she was hungry, but she took it to please him, nibbling on a piece of toast. It was quite good, but to her, it tasted like ash. It reminded her of the breakfasts she had shared with him, Colin, and Lylla over the past year.

She put the toast down. "I'm sorry."

"For what?"

She looked up at him. "How can you not blame me? What happened is my fault."

"Sara, we've been through this. There was nothing you could have done. It's not your fault. If I'm angry with anyone, it's Galatea. If you want to blame someone for what happened, blame her, not yourself." He sat down beside her. "One thing I've learned is that you can blame someone else for what happens to you, or you can get over it and move on. Galatea blames others for what happened to her and look where we are."

Sara thought back to Lylla's last words, directed at her. *Don't lose hope. So long as you have hope, I will always be with you.*

She had known that Sara would struggle and had offered encouragement for when she could no longer be there. *Don't lose hope.*

Sara clung to those three simple words and refused to let go.

***

Damaris saw to the burning herself, after the last of the mourners had filed away. It was quick, instantaneous, as she poured all the heat into her flames that she could. She forced herself to watch as the ash scattered in the wind, feeling suddenly cold. The sun had not appeared at all that day, as though it refused to shine now that its queen was gone.

Wanderer helped Damaris prepare for the coronation ceremony. She had attended Lylla's, all those centuries ago, and she could barely remember what it had been like. Each ruler dressed in colors that symbolized their element. Wanderer selected a crimson dress, long and flowing, in a halter top style, with off-the-shoulder sleeves and gold embroidery, along with the gold collar necklace Damaris had worn at the festival.

She undid Damaris's two signature braids for the ceremony, pinning her hair up instead, stepped back and surveyed her work. "You look beautiful. You've got this."

Damaris looked at her. She didn't feel beautiful or powerful. She didn't feel like a queen. "I can't do this, Wanderer. I can't lead these people."

Funny now that she thought about it, but she could remember Lylla expressing much the same sentiment to her, facing her own coronation, all those years ago.

"Yes, you can. I was there the night Khae was destroyed and I saw the way you took command."

"That was different. They needed someone to step up and there was no one else to do it."

"Exactly. They needed you then and they need you now," Wanderer said solemnly. "More than ever."

Damaris knew that she was right. She couldn't put this off forever and she certainly couldn't run away, no matter how fearful she was inwardly. What Cassius had said was true; she had fought in wars, so why was this the thing that scared her most?

There was nothing left to do but wait until the steward came to fetch her. Cassius had agreed to perform the ceremony for her and she followed her escort out onto the balcony in the front of the palace, her eyes briefly skimming the massive crowd gathered below. They had come for the funeral and stayed for the coronation.

Damaris steeled herself, aware that they were all looking at her, and turned to face Cassius. She repeated after him, taking the oath to defend her people and this realm, to put their needs before her own, to be loyal, benevolent, and wise until her reign may come to an end. It reminded her of the oath she had sworn the day she had become Guardian of the Flame Gate.

Only now it was not just a Gate she was protecting.

Cassius turned, addressing the crowd as he placed the crown, gold and silver, inlaid with multicolored jewels to represent all of the elements, atop her head. "I give you Queen Damaris the Flameseeker." He turned, looking her in the eye. "Long may you reign."

The crowd took up the chant as Damaris stepped forward, to the edge of the balcony, and gazed at them all, chest heaving, the words ringing in her ears.

"Long may you reign!"

20

Felix opened the door to Lylla's quarters without knocking. The queen had never minded, but she was no longer here. He didn't think Damaris would mind, either, if she was even in. He would have to get used to the idea of thinking of Damaris as queen and not the Flame Guardian.

She looked up as he entered, still in the crimson dress she had worn for the ceremony earlier. The crown was gone and she was in the process of returning her hair to her two signature braids. Her human form was yet another thing he would have to get used to.

She said nothing, knowing that he would speak when he wanted to, though she could probably guess the reason he had come. He sighed and sank down into the chair by the desk.

Felix glanced over his shoulder, out the window at the Glowing Gate beyond that marked the entrance to the palace grounds. Throughout his entire life, it had always glowed a mixture of rainbow hues, like light shining through a prism, which had made sense given Lylla's attribute.

But now, it glowed a mixture of crimsons and scarlets, oranges and yellows, giving it the appearance of silent, flickering flames. It reflected the new queen's element now. In his head, he could imagine hearing it roar, but of course, it wasn't truly on fire and so made no sound.

He ran his hands over his face, feeling the stubble along his jaw. He'd gotten little sleep last night, eventually dozing off beside Sara, but it wasn't enough. Felix felt exhausted, completely scoured out by his emotions. It felt like he couldn't draw enough air into his lungs, no matter how deeply he breathed.

He had never known a Wysteria without Lylla. In his mind, perhaps he had come to equate her with Wysteria itself. How could there be one without the other?

Damaris had rescued him from the fire wolves, but it had been Lylla that had taken him in and given him a home at the palace. She had taken in Colin as well, another orphan, and by doing so, gave them both a home and a companion. She had always been there, offering advice when asked, calming him when he was younger and woke up terrified and screaming from the nightmares, singing him back to sleep.

That had stopped as he grew older and could handle things himself, but she was always there. She had tried to heal his scars after Venryk had attacked him, to no avail. When faced with a death sentence, knowing his time was limited unless he could kill the wolf, she had helped him face that.

And now she was gone and Damaris was queen.

Damaris was a lot of things. She was the Flame Guardian and his protector and friend, a fierce fighter and a dangerous enemy, but Felix wasn't sure he could think of her as a queen. He wouldn't say as much out loud, of course. She needed support and he would give it.

"Do you still want to be a Shadow?" Damaris asked, turning to face him. "I'll understand if you don't."

A Shadow. Felix hadn't even thought of that. He and Colin had both been Lylla's Shadows, so named because they seemed to follow her like her own shadow. Officially, they were supposed to be her personal guards and protect her, but they had both known that she was far more powerful than either of them. And so it had been more of a status symbol than anything, but Felix had been honored that she had chosen him all the same.

She was dead now and there was no need. The idea of becoming Damaris's Shadow, of guarding her, was absurd and yet what else was there for him to do? It was all he'd ever known, for so long.

"I will," he replied. "If you'll have me."

Damaris nodded curtly. She headed for the door, pausing on her way out to lay a hand on his shoulder. And then she was gone, leaving him with the ghosts.

***

Part of being a leader was diplomacy and public relations, which Damaris hated. She'd rather be out on the battlefield, facing down an enemy. At least then, things were clear. She knew who the enemy was and what she had to do to remedy the problem. And she was good at it, unlike this.

Still, duty compelled her to pay a visit to the refugees from Khae. They were from the desert, after all, and would support her. Undoubtedly, Lylla had checked up on them from time to time, to see that all of their needs were seen to, but Damaris had been too busy to have done so.

The eldest elves had been given rooms in the palace, but there were too many to possibly fit all of them inside and so the rest had pitched tents in the pasture, within the palace grounds. Sheba, being their leader, had elected to stay with those living in the tents.

Sheba came out to greet her, nodding respectfully. "Your Majesty."

Damaris had never understood why Lylla had disliked being addressed so formally. In her mind, it merely made sense. You had to be addressed with some level of respect or how else could you expect them to respect your authority?

But she understood it now. It was so formal and distant in its way. It made obvious a clear gulf between her and Sheba that made Damaris feel rather distant and alone. She wasn't the Flame Guardian anymore. She was "Your Majesty."

It was all she could do not to ask Sheba to call her by her name. That could be dealt with later. "How are you and the others? Do you have everything you need?"

Sheba nodded. "Aside from a permanent home."

Damaris somehow felt as though she'd made a mistake already. What an indelicate question. She wasn't used to feeling so self-conscious, her usual confidence having abandoned her.

She took a deep breath, pushing the doubts away. "Will you rebuild after all of this is over? I hope you will."

"Yes. We will rebuild Khae and make the city even larger and more beautiful than before."

"I'm happy to hear it. And I will offer any assistance I can." She would personally help them rebuild the city they both loved, when the time came.

"Thank you, Your Majesty. I look forward to it."

Damaris looked closely at Sheba. There were dark circles beneath her eyes and she looked haggard, the strain of assuming leadership after Kadir's death and then what had happened to her people weighing heavily on her.

Damaris felt sorry for her. She had never particularly liked Sheba, always having viewed the girl as irresponsible and a bit immature. She'd had the burden of leadership thrust upon her quite suddenly, much as Damaris had now, and that was something they shared. Sheba had done admirably, all things considered.

"You've done well," she murmured. "Kadir would be proud."

For a moment, Sheba's façade faltered and Damaris glimpsed the pain that lingered just beneath the surface. The chieftess's eyes filled with tears and something else—pride.

"Thank you," Sheba whispered and Damaris knew she had said the right thing. "He was a great man."

She spent a little longer with the refugees, walking among them and taking time to speak to some of them the way she thought Lylla would have done.

At last, exhausted from the effort it had taken, she turned away to see Wanderer approaching her.

"What are you doing here?" She'd have thought the Lightning Guardian would have returned to her Gate by now, following the ceremony.

"I wanted to know what we do now," Wanderer explained. "What's our next move?"

Damaris hadn't even thought that far ahead. She couldn't continue doing what she had been before. Tracking Galatea down was pointless. One thing she was certain of was that the sorceress wouldn't fight fair and it was too risky. Even if she believed she was powerful enough to take Galatea, there was still Azuma.

If she fell, who would take her place? She didn't think the people could take losing two queens in such rapid succession. They had been devastated by Lylla's loss, but they hadn't given up hope. It reminded her of Lylla's last words. *Don't lose hope.*

They hadn't given up hope because of who Damaris was. They believed that she could win and they would follow her into battle because of it.

She took a deep breath, walking back toward the palace. Wanderer fell into step beside her. "There are only two Gates left. That narrows down Galatea's options. She'll have to come for them. We don't know which one she'll strike first, but I can guess."

"Cassius's," Wanderer guessed.

"Yes, I think she'll come for the Water Gate first. She's already attacked the Lightning Gate several times and failed to destroy it."

"So what do we do?"

"We take all of our forces and split them between the two. Set up encampments. Larger than before. And then we wait until she arrives and when she does, we finish this, one way or another. I'll go to Cassius's Gate with him and Sara will go to yours."

It made for an even number of Guardians at each. It was still shocking to think that now there were so few.

Wanderer nodded. "Then there's something you need to see."

Surprised, Damaris followed as Wanderer took the lead, heading back toward the palace. As they walked, Damaris turned to her and asked, "How are you holding up?"

There had been little time to check up on the Lightning Guardian since Hank's death, but she had been there when it had happened and knew how hard Wanderer had taken it, even if she showed no outward sign of it now.

Wanderer sighed. "I miss him," she said simply. "But I can focus on how I feel after we've won this war."

They entered the palace and took one of the staircases down, into the armory, where the army's armor and weapons were stored. They would need to be distributed soon.

Torches guttered on the walls, casting flickering shadows. Wanderer ignored all the weapons, from short swords to broad, maces and shields, lines of bows and quivers stuffed with arrows. There were rows upon rows of pieces of armor, breastplates, greaves, pauldrons, and bracers, all made of silver, which would burn Galatea if she came into contact with them, since she had given herself over to dark magic.

There were even armor pieces to fit unicorns and horses, but Wanderer led her past them all, to the very end of the long corridor, where an enormous wardrobe stood. Without preamble, Wanderer pulled the doors open.

Damaris stared back at herself, reflected too many times to count. It took her a moment to realize what she was looking at. A set of armor colored silver and gold, plated with countless mirrors.

She knew without asking that the armor had belonged to Lylla. The mirrors were perfect for her element. They were disorienting enough on their own, reflecting the enemy's own appearance back at them, but in the blazing sunlight, they would be blinding. If there had been any lingering doubt as to who the armor was for, the helm would have given it away, with long, sharp points arrayed along the crown as if rays of sunlight.

"I can't take this," Damaris said. It felt wrong, the idea of donning Lylla's armor that had so clearly been made for her. "It wouldn't be right. Besides, it wouldn't fit."

But it did give her an idea.

***

Sara mounted the stairs to Lylla's quarters, wondering why Damaris had summoned her. She wanted nothing more than to go back to bed and stay there, the way she had when Professor Lawrence had been killed. It had taken her months to snap herself out of that funk, but they didn't have months now. She clung to Lylla's final words, repeating them often to herself. It seemed to be the only thing that kept her going.

She knocked and pushed the door open when told to enter. Damaris had changed out of her crimson dress and back into the armor Sara had only seen her wear once. It had been during a training exercise, when Damaris had taught her how to use fire as a secondary element. That had been when Sara still had the Echo Stone and she hadn't attempted such a thing since.

The ensemble consisted of a crimson tunic and skirt, short in the front and long in the back, with gold embroidery along the edge, and black leggings. Golden greaves covered her legs up to mid-thigh—the knee part separate so it could bend—gauntlets protected her arms and pauldrons shielded her shoulders. The armored gloves covering her fingers ended in sharp claws.

The expression on the new queen's face was severe, shaking Sara out of her gloom. Lylla may be gone, but they weren't out of danger yet. They still had a sorceress to deal with.

"I have something for you," Damaris said, turning to the desk. She picked up the glowing white sword and offered it to Sara.

Pharus. Sara hadn't seen it since the night she'd set it down in the library. She'd completely forgotten about it since, but someone must have fetched it.

"I can't take this," she said. It was Lylla's sword.

"I think Lylla would have wanted you to have it. It will complement your attribute."

Slowly, Sara reached out and picked up the sword. It was heavy, but surprisingly lighter than one would expect for a blade of that length.

"Thank you," she said numbly, holding it up and looking at it, letting the white glow wash over her.

"You'll need to be fitted for some armor if you're going to the Lightning Gate."

Sara lowered the sword. "What do you mean?"

"I'm splitting our forces," Damaris explained, "between the Water and Lightning Gates. I'm assigning you to the Lightning Gate with Wanderer. I don't know which Gate Galatea will strike first, or when, but my money is on the Water Gate. I'll do my best to stop her there, but if we fail, it falls to your group."

Sara hesitated. Wasn't this what she had always wanted? Not only being accepted as one of them, but standing by their side as a true Guardian would, no matter the threat faced?

But her magic had failed to heal Lylla and there was no reason to think it wouldn't fail again. There was no reason to trust it, not anymore.

As if sensing her hesitation, Damaris added, "You don't have to do this. But you're the last light attribute we have. It's your duty to stand against the darkness."

Sara swallowed her shame and asked the question she was dreading. "Are you sure you want me at the Lightning Gate? I don't know if my magic can be relied upon."

It had been cooperating lately, but that had been before... Her grief had held her back. She'd made peace with that and her magic had responded, but now, her grief had returned anew. She hadn't tried to use magic since, but she wasn't confident it would work.

Part of her was too scared to try. She couldn't face the disappointment again.

"You are a Guardian, Sara. You deserve to be here as much as any of us," Damaris replied and then added, more softly, "I once struggled with my magic the way you do."

Sara looked at Damaris in surprise. It was hard to imagine someone so powerful ever struggling the way she did. "How did you get over it?"

"This likely isn't the answer you want, but your magic will be there when you need it most."

But what if it doesn't work? It already had failed her when she needed it most. If that hadn't been her moment of need, what would be? "How will I know when I need it most?"

"You'll know."

***

Felix was in the library, sketching to try and keep his mind occupied, when Sara found him. He didn't like being idle; having something to keep his hands busy seemed to help keep his thoughts from straying into whatever direction he wished to avoid.

"Damaris wants to see you," Sara informed him.

Setting his sketchbook aside, he rose and returned to the queen's quarters at the top of the palace. Damaris had changed out of her red dress and into battle armor.

Without mincing words, she told him of her plan to protect the two remaining Gates. "If you've no objection, I'd like to send you back to the Lightning Gate with Sara and Wanderer."

Felix felt himself frown, his thoughts turning back to Hank, Colin, and Lylla. That Gate had seen much sorrow recently, but it still stood. In that, they hadn't failed.

"I have no objection," he told her.

Damaris nodded. "Then you'll need to take this with you."

She lifted a large bundle from where it lay atop the desk, revealing a bow. It didn't look like much on the surface; there was nothing remarkable about it, no little details such as the changes he'd made to his bow, to make it his own.

But he accepted it from Damaris all the same, wondering why she was giving this to him when he already had one.

The moment his fingertips touched the bow, lifting it from her hands, the shaft began to glow a gentle, pulsing white—just like Pharus always did. Warmth spread from his hands throughout the rest of his body, reminiscent of the feeling of sunlight on his skin.

He could feel the power of the magic humming through the bow—through him—and he sucked in a breath.

"Lylla made that for you," Damaris told him. "She knew she might not always be here and so she had it imbued beforehand, should anything happen."

Felix stared at the bow, remarkably light in his hand, with a sense of awe. It was imbued with Lylla's own magic. She had saved a piece of herself and thought of him, wanting him to have it. It even somehow felt like her, reminded him of her, to hold it.

It was a weapon that was steadfast, solid, trustworthy— just as she had been. A sense of peace washed over him at the knowledge that he carried a piece of her magic with him. In that moment, she was right there in the room with him.

"Thank you," he whispered, finding himself choked up a bit. The words were directed toward Damaris but they were meant for *her* as well.

He blinked, finding tears had clouded his vision, touched that she had thought of him in such a way.

Even now, Lylla was looking out for him.

***

Empress glared at Galatea in the dim light of the swamp. The sorceress had been smug ever since returning from the attack on the girl and the Lightning Gate. Empress herself had not participated, but some of her fellow dragons had, acting as a distraction and allowing Galatea to slip through the Gate after the girl.

Galatea had told them that she merely wanted the girl, but she had boasted of what had really happened upon her return and it made Empress's blood boil. Not only had the dragons been used, but they'd been deceived as well.

"You've doomed us all," she growled, no longer able to hide her disgust and dissent.

Galatea scoffed. "You're a fool."

"You're the fool. At least Lylla could be reasoned with. You knew who they would appoint in her place and yet you did it anyway. Damaris won't reason with you. She'll kill you as soon as look at you."

"Damaris has always been arrogant and that will be her downfall. She can no longer afford to hunt us down, going where she wishes, when she wishes, and so we don't have to worry about dealing with that nuisance anymore."

"Your own arrogance will be your downfall. I warned you that this could only ever end in your own destruction but you refuse to believe me. By killing Lylla, you haven't broken their will. You've only strengthened it."

Galatea turned as Empress hopped lithely down from her perch atop one of the ruined buildings, taking a step toward her. She was no longer afraid of the danger. They couldn't afford to sit idly by and be dictated by Galatea's whims. She had forsaken reason long before now.

She should have seen it for what it was the moment Galatea had believed herself powerful enough to subjugate a wind spirit.

Empress could feel other dragons at her back, sense their growing resentment. "You can do what you want," she spat. "But you'll do it without us."

There, at last, she was making a stand. Would that she'd found the courage to do so before now. But the choice had been made. Whatever happened now, at last her conscience was clear.

Galatea raised her eyebrows. "You think I'll just let you walk away?"

"No," Empress said levelly. "I don't."

The dragons behind her sprang forward, claws outstretched, while Empress sent forth a jet of blue flame. Galatea had already summoned her darkness and behind her, Empress saw the wind spirit rise.

21

The rest of the day was spent mobilizing the armies that would travel to the Water and Lightning Gates. Sara packed everything she would need for the duration into saddlebags, reminded of the way she had done so before heading to the desert. It seemed so long ago, but it wasn't really. So much had changed in so little time.

By the time she was done, her horse was laden with the weight of her belongings and the armor she was bringing. Lylla's sword was strapped to her side, its weight familiar and comfortable. It made her feel closer to her mentor somehow and proud that Lylla would have wanted her to have the weapon.

Her horse walked beside Felix's as they accompanied the other soldiers back to the Lightning Gate. Some had remained, unable to attend the funeral or coronation ceremony. Someone had to be on duty at the Gates at all times.

The forest closed in around them, the trees offering protection and shelter. Sara found comfort in their presence. They stopped and pitched their tents near the Gate, Felix helping her after finishing his.

Sara was reminded of the time her family had gone camping in the summer, before her mom had gotten sick. They had always used a camper and not a tent, so she had no idea what she was doing, and even if she did, Wysteria's tents were very different.

They were much larger, for one thing, tall enough to stand upright within. They were white and golden, matching the armor she had been given. Lylla's colors. It saddened her to see, but at the same time, there was something poetic about it. She may be gone, but her soldiers were still fighting bravely on, beneath her colors.

Lylla had died unafraid of the future. She hadn't worried that they would somehow fail to stop Galatea. Sara wished she could have that level of confidence.

Once her tent was raised, she stepped inside and hung her hammock, supported by the tent's sturdy structure. She arranged her few belongings and then stepped outside, breathing in the smell of wood smoke.

Fires and braziers had already been set around the camp, weapons being sharpened and armor fitted. Her own armor had been quickly adjusted before leaving the palace grounds.

A slight breeze rustled through the forest, stirring the flags atop the tents. Felix stepped out of his tent, next to hers. He was dressed in the same black leather tunic and pants as usual, fingerless gloves extending up his forearms.

He fingered the sword sheathed at his side. "Care for some practice?"

Sara looked around. Some of the other soldiers were already sparring, trading blows in preparation for the oncoming battle. With any amount of luck, Galatea would strike the Water Gate first, Damaris's forces would stop her, and there would be no need for the army amassed at the Lightning Gate. With any amount of luck, they would be unnecessary, merely being overly cautious.

But Sara knew better than to assume. If luck were on their side, they wouldn't be here.

She had sparred with Felix and Colin countless times over the summer and though she could best Felix if she were clever, she had never beaten Colin. And they had never dueled with real swords before, but always wooden ones. There were no wooden practice swords to be found here, that would only leave bruises instead of lacerations.

She hesitated. "With real swords?" She knew he wouldn't hurt her, but accidents did happen.

"I've done it before." Mischief sparkled in his eyes. "I'll go easy on you, if you like."

Sara smiled. "Not a chance." If she was going to fight in a real battle, she needed all the preparation she could get and that meant making training as realistic as possible.

Besides, if something did go wrong, she could always go to one of the healing stations that were being set up and have one of the healers see to it.

She unsheathed Pharus, the white glow flaring, feeling its weight in her hands as Felix did the same. Even in the daylight, the sword gave off its faint white glow, the entire blade white from end to end. Felix's blade was ordinary silver, but he had a longer reach than she did. His tunic was sleeveless and she glanced at his bare biceps, knowing from experience that she couldn't defeat him using strength. She had to be swift and clever.

Still, she could count on the fingers of one hand the number of times she had succeeded. They circled each other, waiting to see who would strike first. In the end, it was Felix who became impatient. Sara easily parried the blow, the force of the two blades meeting vibrating up her arms.

A crowd gathered to watch as they continued to trade blows, wanting to see the Light Guardian and the Shadow duel, but it was clear that Sara was on the defensive from the start. Felix wasn't as quick as her, but he was much stronger. It was all she could do to keep him from knocking her sword aside, leaving her exposed and vulnerable.

The muscles in her arms tired, her grip weakening until at last Felix tried to use his sword to shove hers aside. Sara pushed back. Light flared where the two blades met, a wave of light suddenly arcing outward. Felix was blown off his feet from the force, tossed several feet through the air.

"Oh my God!" Sara cried as he hit the ground with a muffled grunt.

She lowered the blade and hurried over to him. "Are you okay?"

He picked himself up off the ground, brushing hair damp with sweat from his brow, and grinned at her. "That was awesome."

Sara blinked in surprise.

"Valiant effort, Lightbringer!" Wanderer called out. She had been watching from a distance, remaining near the Gate.

Lightbringer. "That's Lylla's title," Sara said, returning Pharus to its scabbard.

"You may as well have it," Felix replied. "You're the only Lightbringer now. Speaking of which," he lowered his voice, "have you tried using magic lately? Other than just now?" He nodded at Pharus.

Sara shook her head, glancing down at the sword at her side. "Not since…"

Not since that awful night. The magic within the sword had flared just now, but Sara hadn't made it do that. At least, she didn't think so. Certainly, she hadn't expected it.

"Give it a try."

Sara knew she would need it. She couldn't rely on her swordsmanship. It was decent, but it wasn't good enough. And she knew her smaller size would always put her at a disadvantage against a larger opponent. She had seen Galatea only a few times, but knew that the sorceress was as tall as Felix, if not slightly taller. All it would take was one nick from the Shadowblade and it would all be over.

She closed her eyes—even though she knew she would need to keep them open in a fight—reaching deep down to grasp her magic.

It didn't come. She tried in vain to bring it to the surface, to force it to obey, the way she had been able to a short time ago.

No. Nothing.

The brief rush she had felt when wielding Pharus was gone. At last, frustrated, and without even a glow to show for it, she lowered her hands in defeat, feeling more exhausted than she had at the end of the sparring session.

"It'll come," she said, seeing Felix's concerned expression, though she felt she was trying to convince herself more than him.

Damaris said it will come when I need it. A training session hardly counted as needing it. The Flame Guardian must know what she was talking about. Sara would have to trust her.

"Ah, well," Felix said, sounding forcefully cheerful for her sake. "The magic may not have responded, but Pharus did."

Sara considered the sword once more, very much aware that it was not her magic within, but Lylla's. Lylla, who was gone now, yet somehow still with them.

She looked up at him. "I wonder how long the charge will last?"

Felix didn't have an answer for that.

Sara didn't attempt to use magic the rest of the day, not wanting to think about it. She helped make dinner and then, as day slipped into night and the stars began to come out, went over and joined Felix, sitting against a tree trunk.

He put an arm around her and she leaned her head on his shoulder, staring up at the sky, more visible now than it should have been through the canopy of trees. Many of their leaves had been ripped off the first time Galatea had attacked the Gate, thanks to the wind spirit's gale.

She sighed. How was she supposed to face Azuma? Crossing blades with Galatea was terrifying enough, highly inadvisable, but still possible. But a wind spirit?

Sara wondered what her dad was doing at that very moment, wishing she could tell him somehow that she was all right. He'd probably been freaking out ever since she had left and hadn't come back, not knowing if she was dead or not, or if she would ever return. If he would ever see her again.

Tears pricked the corner of her eyes at the thought. They might never see each other again. If she died defending the Gate, never getting to apologize. How could she do that to him? She had to survive, no matter what. It would be too cruel for him to lose her, too, after her mom.

She focused on what she could see of the stars to distract herself. She had once searched for familiar constellations, wondering if the stars in the Wysterian night sky were the same as back home. Try as she might, she hadn't found anything familiar and so she had concluded that they were different.

Different, but still beautiful.

Felix pressed a kiss to the top of her head. "What are you thinking about?"

"Death," Sara answered honestly, knowing it was hardly surprising given what they were facing. Nothing was certain.

It seemed stupid suddenly to mention to someone who had been facing down death for as many years as he had.

She shifted slightly. "Do you think Venryk will come?"

"Yes. I've thought of little else."

Sara hoped Galatea wouldn't strike at night, though she was in no hurry to retreat to her tent and hammock. Would sleep come at all? She wondered what they were doing at the other Gate. Were they, too, enjoying the current respite, the calm before the storm?

Or right now, at this very moment, were they already fighting for their lives?

***

Damaris stood at the edge of the cliffs, where the grasslands ended and the Green Sea began, the moonlight glimmering on the water's surface. Wind blew off the water, stirring her mane and tail. Now that she was here, she intended to remain in her true form. She could fight in her human form, but as a unicorn, she had more power and speed, a greater size advantage.

The border of the Enchanted Forest stood in the distance, behind her, the trees dark silhouettes just visible in the darkness. If Galatea attacked, she would come from that direction. The flat grasslands offered nowhere to hide, no chance of an ambush, the grass rolling like waves in the wind.

Snatches of song drifted on the breeze. There was no point in trying to hide their presence, with the fires and tents clearly visible, and so there was no need to be silent.

Damaris's ears perked at the sound of footsteps treading softly on the grass. She turned to see Cassius making his way toward her.

"We have company," he murmured, nodding out toward the open fields.

Damaris squinted, making out the forms of large, winged creatures approaching on foot. *The mountain dragons.* "What are they doing here?" Empress had told her that they would remain with Galatea for the time being, maintaining the charade.

"Do you want me to see what they want?"

"No. I'll go." She wanted to reach them before they got too close to the camp. She still did not trust the dragons completely, despite the fact that Empress had told her about the attack on her Gate.

The warning had still come too late and part of her couldn't help but wonder if Empress had done that on purpose so that Damaris would be unable to arrive in time, while making a convincing argument that Empress had reconsidered her loyalties.

If this was a trap or a distraction, anyone that might be waiting behind the dragons would have to get past her in order to reach the Gate.

As she drew closer to them, she could see the leader was limping, putting as little weight on one of her hind legs as possible. The crystals on her headdress were glowing a soft blue, marking her as leader. *Empress.*

Though the dragons were taller, Empress's head was bowed, looking Damaris in the eye, the dragon's wings hanging loosely at her sides.

Empress stopped before her. "Your Majesty. I heard the news."

"What are you doing here?" Damaris demanded.

"I come once more to give you a warning. Galatea's coming. She's on her way here as we speak."

22

"Why should I trust you?" Damaris asked.

Empress waved one of her wings at the dragons gathered behind her. "As you can see, we're not with her anymore. I made a point of telling her so, and she didn't appreciate it. We're the few that made it out. We'll fight beside you, if you'll let us."

Damaris frowned, debating within herself. Empress had ordered her soldiers to attack her in the swamp. Apparently, she had made quite the impression, proving to the dragon she could win, in order for her to switch sides and present herself here now.

But at the same time, she knew better than to trust the dragon. She was slippery as an eel at the best of times, always having only her own interests in mind. There was no way to prove that the warning about the Flame Gate hadn't been done only because it was somehow in Empress's best interests.

She jerked her head back at the camp behind them. "Fall in. Try anything and I'll kill you where you stand—and I won't make it quick."

Empress nodded, falling into step beside her with her limping gait.

"When will she arrive and how many should we be expecting?"

"She's already left," Empress answered. "Her forces are on foot. Anytime between now and dawn is the best estimate I can give you. She's bringing everything she's got—undead, fire wolves, and of course, that wind spirit."

Quite the force, then. "Have one of the healers see to that." Damaris nodded to the dragon's injured leg and then went her separate way, joining Cassius at the Gate.

He nodded to the dragons. "What did they want?"

"To fight with us. Galatea's coming, with all her soldiers in tow. They could arrive at any moment so be alert. Spread the word. I want our troops armed."

The two of them dispersed throughout the camp, giving the order for the soldiers to arm themselves if they hadn't already. The camp became a flurry of activity as they rushed to obey.

The task finally done, an eerie silence settled over the camp, the wind whispering through the grass the only sound. It had picked up slightly, the Green Sea growing restless. In the distance, dark clouds gathered over the sea and heat lightning flashed.

Damaris turned to face the Enchanted Forest in the distance, knowing that Galatea would have to come from that direction and would be easily visible across the open grasslands. Despite Empress's prediction that Galatea could arrive at dawn, Damaris knew the sorceress would be loath to miss the opportunity that darkness provided.

There was nothing left to do but wait. A feeling of unease had descended over the camp, growing more intense the more time went on and Galatea failed to appear. The soldiers were becoming restless and Damaris didn't blame them.

What if Empress had been lying? Had she been wrong to trust her? Was what she said nothing more than a distraction, while Galatea attacked and decimated their forces at the Lightning Gate?

She moved over to where Empress was waiting, surrounded by her remaining soldiers. There were only a few dozen dragons left.

"What does she want?" Damaris asked softly as she reached them. "Other than destroying the Gates? Did she confide in you?"

Empress shifted her weight. "She claims she wants to take something from each of the people she blames for Jack's death, the way they took something from her. I'd watch my back if I were you. Given what you did to Jack last time, I'm sure she's got something special planned for you."

"I hope so," Damaris growled. *Let her come. I'll end her.*

She could feel her magic stirring beneath the surface, smoldering rage ready to spring to life at a moment's notice. This was what her magic was made for, to ravage and destroy, and she was all too eager to give it what it wanted when it came to Galatea.

"Looks like you'll get your wish," Empress murmured, blue eyes staring out across the grasslands. "She's here."

The dragon's eyesight was better and it took a few minutes before Damaris could see that she was right, just making out the dark figures moving across the grass. Difficult to make out in the darkness, but there. Their exact numbers were hard to estimate from this distance, but she could see enough to know that they would be in for a fight.

Doesn't matter.

She could destroy a great number of them, but she would have to be careful with her magic. If she risked using too much, too soon, then there would be nothing left should she need it later. But if she found herself face to face with Galatea, there would be no holding back.

The soldiers in the camp had noticed Galatea's army approaching and were muttering nervously to themselves. Armor clinked as weight was shifted. They were facing down a dangerous foe, knowing that some of them, or possibly all of them, might not live to see the dawn.

Damaris sighed. She needed to reassure them, or failing that, to inspire them.

"Mount up and form ranks!" she shouted and the soldiers scrambled to assemble.

Once they had gathered, she strode out along the front line.

"Stand your ground, warriors," she called, raising her voice so that it carried. "I know you're afraid, but after today, there will be nothing more to fear. Today, we put an end to this madness. Today, we avenge our fallen. Today, Galatea pays for every life she has taken. Duty unto death! For the Lightbringer!"

"For the Lightbringer!"

She reared and turned back around to face Galatea's oncoming army. They were much closer now than before, not quite reaching the middle of the grasslands. Damaris intended to reach them before they got there. Keep them as far back from the Gate as possible.

Though they could use his skills in a fight, Damaris had instructed Cassius to remain by the Gate itself. If anyone happened to get through, it fell to him, and the rest of the soldiers who hung back, to dispatch them swiftly. The rest of them would do everything in their power to ensure no one passed.

Damaris reared again, the signal to charge, and sprang forward. She could hear the thundering of hundreds of hooves as her army leapt to follow her. Thunder crashed behind them as the storm neared. And then all sound seemed to fade away and all Damaris could hear was the wind rushing past her ears and her heart hammering as reality settled in and fear threatened to take hold for a moment.

The fear burned away in the face of her anger. She did not fear death or pain. There was only one thing she feared, and as long as he was at the Lightning Gate and Galatea's forces were here, he was safe.

Time seemed to slow as the two sides drew closer to each other. Lightning lit up the grasslands and Damaris could just make out the glowing green eyes of the undead and the individual flaming pelts of the fire wolves, but not the person she sought. In a few more strides, a matter of seconds, they would be upon each other.

She conjured a wall of flame that sprang up between the two sides just as they collided. The smell of searing flesh filled the air as the undead walked into the flames. The fire wolves passed harmlessly through it, as did Damaris and her allies, for she commanded the flames not to harm them.

Damaris let out a battle cry, her fangs exposed, and then the sound was drowned out by a crash as the two armies collided. She lowered her head, leading with her long, spiraling horn, impaling a fire wolf.

Around her, the battlefield descended into chaos, filled with writhing bodies, a good number having already fallen in the initial clash. The sound was utterly deafening with the wind, thunder, snarls, roars, and cries of pain or rage.

One of the undead lunged at Damaris and she summoned fire directly beneath it, surging up into the air, white-hot. The undead creature shrieked as it was incinerated, its form destroyed.

The unicorn threw herself back into the fray, searching for Galatea and not finding her. But she must be here, for whenever one of Damaris's allies fell, their eyes shone green almost instantly and they staggered back up, reanimated and now on the opposite side of the fight.

Damaris focused on the undead, which were the greatest threat. Only her soldiers that could wield fire stood a chance against them and unless they were destroyed completely, the undead would simply rise again and keep fighting.

Empress was also targeting the reanimated soldiers, blasting torrents of blue flame at them.

Damaris blinked as the skies opened up above them, the rain coming down in sheets, weighing down her mane. Impatiently, she shook it out of her eyes, but visibility had greatly diminished. The ground quickly turned slippery and treacherous underfoot, with a mixture of rain, mud, and things Damaris knew better than to dwell on.

The wind strengthened, becoming a gale, howling. Through the lashing rain, Damaris could see the form of Azuma rise up, over the Green Sea, enormous white wings beating the air. *Where the hell was Galatea?*

Suddenly, as if conjured by her thoughts, the sorceress stood before her. Damaris blinked, rain running down her face, hardly recognizing the elf. Galatea had shed her usual black dress for one made of black chainmail, which Damaris could only assume she had found hidden somewhere in Malenwar among the relics. Her long black hair hung in a thin braid, neatly keeping it out of the way, and her Shadowblade was gripped in her right hand.

With a wicked sense of satisfaction, Damaris's eyes raked over the burn scars she had given Galatea last summer, on full display.

"You look surprised to see me," Galatea jeered, slashing at her once with the sword.

Damaris reared back, feeling the rage she had kept such a tight leash on race through her blood. She released her magic, flames springing up at the sorceress's feet, spiraling up to engulf her. But as soon as they appeared, they were snuffed out by the wind spirit, as easily as blowing out a candle.

"After all these years, you still haven't learned any new tricks." Galatea waved her hand and Damaris gasped as she was nearly blown off her feet by a sudden, concentrated gust of wind.

She staggered back from the elf, realizing that what they had all feared had come to pass. The sorceress had mastered her control over Azuma. Even though he was out over the ocean, behind the Gate, Galatea could still call upon his power as if it were entirely her own.

"Why don't you just lay down and give up?" Galatea asked, striding forward.

Damaris bared her teeth. "*Never.*"

If she couldn't use her fire against Galatea, she would have to overpower her. She lunged at the sorceress, slashing with her horn, but instead of dancing back, the elf repelled her with another blast of air. It was as if an invisible barrier surrounded Galatea, preventing Damaris from reaching her at every turn.

She was really fighting Azuma through Galatea, the sorceress acting as the conduit for his power. She had never faced someone with such mastery over their element as the wind spirit had, ancient and primal.

Damaris could feel herself tiring from the constant barrage of attacks and she wondered if Galatea felt at all winded, and how much longer she could maintain her level of defense. If she felt the effects, the sorceress gave no sign of it and Damaris refused to either.

Each time Galatea summoned darkness, Damaris seared it away, the two of them making no progress whatsoever. At least she was keeping Galatea occupied, preventing her from reaching the Gate or harming anyone else.

"Give it up, Flame Guardian," Galatea hissed.

Damaris snarled in response. Every failure added to her fury, strengthening her magic until it threatened to burn out of control. Her attacks were wilder now, more reckless, but she had to stop this witch before she could destroy the Gate. She had failed to kill Galatea in the past, but she would not fail now.

The elf raised one hand toward the sky. A single bolt of lightning arced down, striking Damaris, who screamed and fell to her knees. Clenching her teeth against the pain, she pushed herself up, but froze as cries reached her ears, carried on the wind.

Cries coming from the Gate.

She whirled around, dashing back toward the Water Gate. The wind spirit was in a frenzy, lashing his wings, churning up the sea. Tidal waves were surging toward the shore, each larger than the last, until they became high enough that they would crest the cliffside.

Cassius stood faithfully by his Gate, arms outstretched to try and exert control over his element and stop the wave before it reached them. The wind was whipping his long black hair, robes billowing like sails.

Damaris couldn't tell if he was making any progress, but even if he was, it would be too late. He couldn't hold back the wave alone—not without help.

She skidded to a halt and nearly slipped on the wet grass. The clouds were swirling above them and in the first rays of dawn, she could make out the funnel that dipped toward the ground. The twister swept across the ground, tossing the soldiers that had tried to make it back to the Gate into the air like ragdolls, their limp bodies crashing back down to earth.

Damaris's eyes widened in horror. The wave had nearly reached the cliffside. If it crashed into the Gate, the results would be catastrophic. Quickly, she shifted into her human form and thrust a hand out toward the oncoming wave.

Water had never been her specialty, the opposite of her element, but there was still a way her power could help and she lent it to Cassius now.

The water slammed into the cliffside rather than the Gate, surging upward, hissing as some of it turned to steam, seared away by her flames.

Cassius vanished from view beneath the remaining water. She called out to him, but there was no way he could hear her from such a distance.

Heedless of her own safety, Damaris charged forward, waiting for the ground to shake, for the radiating blast to throw her back. For an explosion that never came. Through the lashing rain, she could see the Gate still stood and let out a cry of relief.

But while the Gate stood, its Guardian did not. Cassius lay sprawled at the foot of the Water Gate, robes blown out behind him, hair sodden.

No…no. She would not lose him, too, this elf she had once despised and now considered a friend. Damaris knelt beside him, hands roaming his body, searching for anything broken.

"Cassius!" She reached out, touching his face. His skin was cold, but his eyes flickered open. "Oh, thank God. Cassius, are you hurt?"

For a moment, she feared he had simply expended too much magic trying to keep the wave at bay.

Then he coughed, sitting up slightly, brushing hair out of his face. "I've felt better." His hands were shaking, likely from a mixture of cold and the amount of energy he'd used.

"Don't push yourself," Damaris instructed. *Any more than you already have.* She reached out, taking both his hands in hers, an orange glow appearing as she poured warmth back into them.

"It's so quiet," Cassius whispered, his voice sounding suddenly loud.

Damaris looked up. The wind spirit had vanished, and with it, the wind had ceased its howling. The rain still poured. Damaris scanned the battlefield, at the soldiers that had been killed, first by the cyclone and then by the wave. There were far too many littering the ground, only adding to Galatea's numbers as they slowly rose.

Galatea. Where was she?

She watched as the undead rose, tensing, expecting them to advance on the Gate, but instead, they turned and began shambling off in the direction of the forest.

What on earth...

"She's gone," Cassius murmured. "She's heading to the other Gate."

Damaris scrambled to her feet, shifting back into her true form. "*Retreat!*" she heard herself roar. "Move, now! To the Lightning Gate!"

The others had no idea that Galatea was coming. They needed to be warned. Damaris sent a column of flame shooting straight up into the air, surging to a height even above the trees. Those gathered at the Lightning Gate might misinterpret the signal, believing the Water Gate to have fallen, but at least then they would be prepared.

As she ran with the remainder of her forces, she told herself that their losses didn't matter in terms of a victory. She had been forced to divide her forces between the two Gates, while Galatea had attacked with all of hers.

Now the tables would turn. Once their armies were united at the Lightning Gate, they would be a force to reckon with. Galatea would not find victory so easy. Damaris just hoped that her other army was ready, because the fight for Wysteria was coming to them.

And even though they had lost many soldiers at the Water Gate, it still stood, which was a victory in and of itself. But there was still one more Gate that needed defending and they weren't out of danger yet.

They would make their last stand at the Lightning Gate.

23

A rumble of thunder in the distance woke Sara as she lay in her hammock, listening. It was still dark inside her tent, but she could see light beginning to bloom behind the walls and knew the sun was rising. Outside, she could hear footsteps as people ran back and forth, a low constant murmur hanging over the camp. Something was wrong.

Throwing the blankets off, Sara sat up in her hammock, preparing to climb out, when the tent flaps parted and Felix poked his head in.

"The signal's gone up. The Water Gate must have fallen."

He ducked back out and Sara threw herself out of the hammock, now wide awake, fear engulfing her, thick and clawing. She hastily changed out of her nightgown and threw her black training uniform on. With deft fingers, she quickly tamed her hair into a braid and stepped outside.

The other soldiers hurried to prepare themselves for the battle that was coming, strapping on armor and weapons and hastily dousing the campfires. Sara shivered. There was a stiff breeze and it was decidedly chillier than it had been.

Lightning flashed in the distance, the roiling dark clouds visible through the forest canopy.

She had been confident that Damaris's forces would stop Galatea, but they hadn't. The Water Gate had fallen and now Galatea was coming here. The one thing she had hoped would never happen was now coming to pass. What if they, too, failed? There would be no Gates left.

"Felix," she called, spotting him. He was standing outside his own tent, strapping on his daggers. "Can you help me with my armor?"

There was no chance she could strap it all on by herself and they needed to hurry. For a moment, she saw her own fear reflected in his green eyes and then, in a few quick strides, he had crossed over to her. Taking ahold of her arm, he led her back into her tent.

Sara snatched up the breastplate and slipped it over her head. He fastened the straps she couldn't reach and then moved on to the next piece of armor until there was nothing left. Greaves, pauldrons, gauntlets, breastplate, they were all there. Sara had ignored the helm, fearing she wouldn't be able to see out of it.

She turned to him. "Are you not going to wear armor?"

He was dressed in his leather tunic and dark trousers, but in the space where sleeves should have been, she could see chainmail. Silver greaves protected his shins and he wore a jaw guard that extended from his chin along his jawline and behind his head to shield the back of his neck. But other than that, he wore no heavy armor. Sara only hoped it was enough.

"I need the freedom of movement," he replied, flashing her a quick smile. "Don't worry. I don't plan on getting close to anyone." As an archer, his best advantage was to stay as far back as possible.

He held out Pharus to her and the moment of levity vanished.

"I can't believe they lost the Water Gate," she whispered as she strapped the sword at her waist.

"I can't either."

The armor and sword together were heavy, but they didn't restrict her movement too badly. She wasn't sure she could run away if she had to, but at least with the armor protecting her, hopefully she wouldn't have to run.

"Thank you for helping me. We should get out there."

Felix lingered, pursing his lips. "Are you sure you want to do this?"

She hesitated. "What do you mean?"

He stepped closer. "I know you said you weren't leaving, and I respect your decision. But this is your last chance to go through the Gate. If Galatea destroys it…"

"If Galatea destroys it, then we're all dead and it hardly matters anymore."

"Well, when you put it that way…"

"It's my decision to make, Felix. I'm not leaving you here to fight alone."

"I know." He reached out, taking her hands in his. "I just want you to be safe."

"We're not losing this Gate," she said firmly, with more confidence than she felt.

"No. Not this one." He pressed a chaste kiss to her lips. "We'll look out for each other."

Sara nodded. For a moment, she could almost believe that they were the only two people in the world and that they weren't about to risk their lives.

"Stay by the Gate," he whispered, the words nearly drown out by the clamor outside.

Felix reached up to brush a stray strand of hair out of her face, tucking it behind her ear. He quickly stepped past her, slipping through the tent flaps and into the forest. Sara followed.

Damaris and the first of her troops had arrived. Sara tried not to think about the glaring fact that there seemed to be far fewer soldiers with her than she would have thought.

She took a deep breath, glancing at the Lightning Gate. Wanderer caught her gaze and nodded. Felix mounted Tempest, hooking one foot in the stirrup and swinging up into the saddle. With a quiver full of arrows and his longbow on his back, a sword at his side, and his various daggers, he looked dangerous. Lethal.

A drop of rain landed on Sara's cheek and she brushed it away. The wind was strengthening, heralding the approach of the wind spirit. Without warning, Azuma descended upon the forest, shrieking in rage. Each beat of his large wings caused the storm to intensify, tearing at what remained of the canopy, snatching the leaves away.

Felix gave his horse a nudge with his heels and the steed lunged forward into the crowd. The majority of the soldiers left this part of the camp, vanishing into the forest, hoping to block Galatea's path to the Gate. The swirling wind carried sounds of conflict that could have been miles away for all Sara knew.

Flashes of light lit up the dark corners of the Enchanted Forest. Thunder crashed, competing with the explosions of fire. The ground beneath her feet shook slightly, but so far, no one had approached the Gate.

Sara clenched and unclenched her hands nervously, finally drawing her sword. Nervous as she was, part of her would rather have been out there, fighting with the others. At least then she wouldn't have to stay in one place, wondering if Galatea was coming for her at any given moment.

***

Tempest snorted, tossing his head. The stallion didn't like the close, narrowed quarters the forest presented and neither did Felix. The underbrush offered too many places for an enemy to hide, waiting for an ambush, and the trees obstacles that one had to maneuver around constantly.

His old bow had been useless against the undead, but light was one of the few elements that could destroy them and so he raised the bow Lylla had enchanted and fired at the nearest one. The arrow flew straight and true, a beam of light itself, searing a hole through the undead as it struck.

Felix felt a thrill of exhilaration go through him. He was wielding Lylla's magic through the weapon she had given him. Never in his life had he held so much power and it felt at once foreign and familiar.

He took careful aim at any fire wolves he saw, easy targets due to their dark red fur. With the wind blowing so hard, he couldn't use his control over air to ensure that the arrows flew straight and sure, always finding their mark, and he missed a few times.

With every wolf that fell, Felix scanned the trees for any sign of the one he wanted most, but to no avail. His scars weren't burning, which told him Venryk wasn't nearby. But surely the wolf must be searching for him as well?

Something about this encounter felt different, as if he knew that neither of them would ever get another chance.

Despite the thick clouds obscuring the sun, the forest was lit up by the fires that raged throughout, roaring as they spiraled up the trees, fed by the howling wind. It was Damaris's doing, no doubt, to help cull the undead. Once she set something on fire and then let go of her own control over it, it would catch and burn like a normal fire, as long as it had something for fuel. But that also meant that if it was no longer under her control, it would burn like any other fire and he made sure to steer clear of it.

Felix tried not to pay much attention to the faces of the undead, but it was hard not to notice that some of them were his fellow soldiers, having been struck down at the Water Gate and reanimated. Tempest trampled and lashed out at any that got too close with his sharp hooves. As long as Felix stayed in the saddle, out of their reach, and had arrows in his quiver, they posed little threat.

The rain was coming down steadily now, the chill stinging his skin and making it hard to see. He had run out of arrows and drawn his sword when a burning, stinging pain lanced up the side of his face. He hissed in surprise, wheeling Tempest around and desperately searching.

Venryk was here.

Tempest screamed a warning, but he had seen the wolf too late. Venryk sprang, knocking Felix from the saddle. He gasped as he hit the ground, fighting for air. His sword had been knocked from his grasp and there was no time to find it.

Venryk circled a few feet away, teeth bared, long fangs protruding from his mouth. There was a wicked gleam in his ice blue eyes as his fur caught fire, the unnaturally dark red flames flickering. The same fire that had consumed Felix's home and family.

"I've waited years for this moment," he growled, not giving Felix enough time to recover.

The wolf sprang, jaws open wide. Heart leaping to his throat, Felix only had time to remember what Damaris had told him during their training session, where she had transformed herself into a wolf. Summoning his magic, he extinguished Venryk's flames so he wouldn't get burned.

The wolf stood over him, lunging for his throat. Felix raised his arm to block and Venryk's jaws clamped down.

The last time, the force of Venryk's bite had broken his arm, but Felix had learned from that mistake. He winced at the pressure from the wolf's jaws, but the silver bracers on his forearms held firm.

He yanked one of his curved daggers out of his belt and plunged it into the side of the wolf's neck. Venryk yelped, releasing him, and in the split second before he could strike again, Felix pressed his open palm against the wolf's chest and sent him flying backward with a concentrated blast of air.

Venryk scrambled to his feet, shaking his head, the hilt of Felix's dagger still protruding from his neck. Blood trickled onto his fur, but the wolf's coat was thick enough that the wound wasn't serious.

"Not bad," the fire wolf growled, catching fire once more. "But you'll have to do better than that, boy."

He charged. Felix slashed at him with another dagger, but the wolf veered to the side, raking his long black claws down Felix's thigh, above the bracer on his shin. Felix cried out as the beast's claws ripped through the material of his trousers and into the flesh beneath. He could feel warm blood trickling down his leg, but there was no time to check the severity of the wound.

Felix clenched his teeth as he spied his fallen sword among the grass, as lightning reflected off the blade, winking up at him. He threw his dagger at Venryk and made a mad dash for the sword. The dagger missed, blown off course by the wind, but it was enough to delay him.

With a snarl, Venryk sprang, landing on Felix's back, the air once more forced from his lungs as he landed on his stomach, pinned beneath the wolf's weight. He stretched out his fingers for the hilt of the sword, just out of reach.

He hissed in a breath as he felt the tips of Venryk's claws tearing through his tunic, trying to slip through the small links in the chainmail underneath. The wolf's jaws clamped down on the back of his neck, meeting the armored neck guard.

Letting out a cry of frustration, Felix knocked the wolf off of him with another blast of air. He pushed himself forward, fingers latching around the sword. He scrambled to his feet in time to see Venryk charging for another attack, his eyes alight with fury and murderous intent.

He waited, blade lowered as though in defeat, until Venryk sprang. Felix whipped the sword up and through the air, the silver blade slicing through the thick fur and sinking into Venryk's neck.

A high-pitched yelp rang out, quickly cut off, as the wolf's head severed from his body. Venryk's momentum carried his body forward, crashing into Felix once more, but when they hit the ground, the wolf did not move. Felix placed his palms against Venryk's shoulders, pushing him off and sat up, panting.

The severed head lay at his feet.

As his adrenaline began to fade, the pain surfaced from the beating he'd taken. Beneath the chainmail, his body was likely riddled with bruises, but it didn't matter.

He had won.

Felix stared at Venryk's lifeless body and stood slowly, letting the rain run down his face, the full realization of what he'd done dawning on him.

He had killed Venryk. He had broken the curse. He was free.

Hardly daring to believe it, he reached up with one hand to touch the left side of his face. His fingers met with smooth skin. The jagged, raised flesh of his scars were gone. The darkness no longer lurked within.

"Such a waste."

Felix whirled, the sound of the voice chilling him more than the rain ever could. Galatea stood behind him, Shadowblade gripped in one hand.

There was no time to move. She lifted the sword and thrust it forward. Agony speared through him and he let out a strangled gasp, eyes widening as he stared down at the Shadowblade protruding from his stomach.

Galatea yanked the sword back, the blade sliding free with a sickening wet sound, slicked red. Felix met Galatea's gaze for a moment and then the world seemed to tilt beneath him and he fell, barely registering the impact.

Galatea's cold black eyes lingered on him for a moment and then she walked away, leaving him lying on the ground beside Venryk's body, staring up at the sky as rain continued to fall, landing on his skin.

Felix gasped, each breath harder to draw than the last. He pressed one hand to the wound, his own blood warm against his clammy skin, but knew there was no point.

He could only delay the inevitable. If blood loss didn't kill him, the darkness coursing through his veins would. He could feel the icy chill in his bones now, through the pain, as his life ebbed away.

Galatea's words echoed in his mind. *Such a waste.* She was right. What a waste to have come so far, to have finally triumphed over Venryk and broken the curse, only to die now. The darkness would kill him after all. Felix felt like letting out a sob at the cruelty and pointlessness of it all, but couldn't find the strength to do so.

Dimly, he thought he heard someone calling his name and thought of Sara. He had let her down, and despite his best intentions, would only end up hurting her anyway.

I'm sorry, he thought as his eyes closed.

***

Stay by the Gate, Felix had told her. Sara found herself running forward, away from the Gate, as Galatea approached, the blood boiling in her veins.

She had seen what the sorceress had done. She had watched Felix defeat Venryk and had been about to rush over to him, knowing how elated he must have felt at finally breaking the curse. Sara had seen Galatea approach out of the corner of her eye and had screamed Felix's name in warning, but the wind had snatched it away.

She was too far away to reach them in time and had frozen, staring in horror, as the sorceress plunged the Shadowblade into Felix, leaving him for dead, knowing he would succumb to the darkness. And then she had turned toward Sara and the Gate.

A quick glance confirmed that Wanderer was nowhere in sight. Sara didn't know where the Lightning Guardian had gotten to, but it was just her standing between Galatea and the Gate.

Just her and Lylla's sword.

She gripped Pharus and stood firm, adopting one of the stances she had been taught, fury coursing through her veins and tears threatening to blur her vision.

Galatea smirked. "If the Lightbringer herself was no match for me, girl, what makes you think you are?"

She swung her sword and Sara easily moved to block it, white sparks flying with a hiss as the two blades connected, darkness and light warring with each other.

I am the only one standing between her and this Gate. I am the only light attribute left. I'm the only one who can heal Felix. But for that, she would need to get rid of the sorceress who stood in her way.

Sara reached for her magic, feeling for it. *Come on.* Damaris had said that it would come when she needed it.

If ever she had needed magic in her life, it was now more than ever.

I am the only one who can do this.

Galatea had stabbed Felix and he would die if she didn't do something. Galatea had killed Professor Lawrence and Hank and Colin. She had killed Lylla and Sara had been powerless to do anything to save any of them. But not this time.

This time, Galatea would *pay.*

Fire surged through Sara's blood as her magic broke to the surface. She gasped, staring down at her hands. The veins beneath her skin were lit gold, extending upward. Galatea hesitated, taking a step back, eyes wide, as if realizing her mistake.

At last her magic had finally, fully awakened. With Pharus in her hand, Sara could feel it coursing through her, hot and swift and *powerful.* Despite the heat on her skin, chills went through her, the hair on her arms standing up.

Sara stared at Galatea, the face of her enemy, and was not afraid. "*I* am the Lightbringer now."

Sara swung Pharus in an arc, a wave of light surging toward Galatea. She barely managed to deflect it with her blade. Sara strode forward and brought the sword down, the reverberation rattling up her arms as the two swords connected.

The fury fully on her now, Sara relentlessly barraged the sorceress with illumination after illumination, steel ringing as Pharus crashed into the Shadowblade over and over again. It was all Galatea could do to fend her off, absorbing the attacks with the darkness she summoned.

She blocked again with her Shadowblade. The darkness that swirled near the base of the blade flickered and vanished. Galatea stared at it in disbelief. It had absorbed so much light that the darkness she had charged the blade with had been overwhelmed. No longer holding a charge, it was once more an ordinary sword.

Pharus glowed as bright and pure as ever. With a cry, Sara swung again. This time, the white blade sliced cleanly through the Shadowblade, breaking it in half.

Hissing between her teeth, Galatea turned and fled, vanishing into the shadows of the forest. Sara let her go, shaking from the adrenaline coursing through her. The glow in her veins faded and she sheathed her sword. Her braid felt heavy, weighed down by the rain. Exhaustion threatened to creep in, but she shoved it away and ran to Felix's side.

She fell to her knees beside him. "Felix?"

She could tell he was still alive from the rattling sound of his breathing and his eyes fluttered open, dimly focusing on her. His naturally fair skin was far paler than she'd ever seen, almost completely white, making the freckles on his face stand out starkly. His leather tunic was stained crimson, the Shadowblade having plunged straight through the chainmail beneath.

He had one hand pressed against his stomach in an attempt to try and staunch the bleeding, blood seeping through his fingers. His trousers also had been ripped, revealing a bleeding wound beneath on his thigh.

Sara took a deep breath. "It's not that bad."

He gave her a small, knowing smile. "You were brilliant out there. You should have seen yourself. Even your eyes were glowing." He coughed, a bloody froth appearing on his lips.

"Don't talk," Sara ordered, seeing how difficult it was for him.

She could well imagine how terrifying she must have looked. Sara stared down at his face, the skin perfectly smooth where once there had been scars. She had never known him without the scars, but now she was seeing him free of the curse.

She reached out, her fingertips brushing against his cheek.

"I love you," he murmured. "I should have told you that sooner."

Sara steeled herself for what she was about to do. She was more terrified of this than of facing Galatea on her own. What if she didn't have enough magic left? What if she had used it all on Galatea? What if it refused to come at all, as it had for so long?

She shoved the doubts away. There was no time for that. If she was going to do this, she had to do it now, before it was too late.

Gently, she took Felix's hand and moved it away from the wound, trying not to flinch at the sight. Her heart was racing in her chest as she tried to remember what she had learned about anatomy from Serai. She had to remember how organs, flesh and sinew knit together normally or she would be unable to fuse them back together.

I can't do this.

I have to do this.

Lylla wasn't here anymore. She was the only light attribute who could save him.

She could not fail.

"What are you doing?" Felix asked, his voice so faint it was merely a whisper.

She met his gaze. "I'm going to heal you." She pressed her hand to the open wound, ignoring the blood and whatever else she touched there, and reached for her magic.

***

Small fires burned along the forest floor, the larger blazes having been extinguished by the rain. The grass was scorched and the ground singed so black it would probably never grow back, where an abrupt explosion of flame had incinerated one of the undead. Damaris stood there, panting, looking at the charred forest around her. Leaves had been stripped by the wind, which still howled, and some of the trees had been uprooted.

She had avoided the fire wolves, for obvious reasons, leaving them for others, but throughout the fight, she had kept an eye out for familiar crimson hair among the crowd. Even as queen, with her duty now to protect all of her people as much as possible, she still had a promise to keep.

The Gate still stood when she went to check on it, but there were no soldiers standing guard around it and she had no idea what had become of Wanderer. Damaris broke through the trees, scanning the area, her eyes falling upon two figures laying on the ground not far from the base of the Gate. She felt her muscles lock, frozen in horror.

She recognized Sara, kneeling beside Felix, who was pale and motionless.

Damaris took a step forward.

"Going somewhere?" a familiar voice taunted.

Damaris whirled to see Galatea standing behind her. There was no sign of her Shadowblade, but both hands were free to help her cast magic.

When Damaris spoke, her voice came out far lower than she had expected, with only the slightest tremble to it. *"What have you done?"*

"What have I done?" Galatea asked, her voice rising, slightly hysterical. "This is what *you* have done, Damaris, what you reaped for taking Jack from me, ensuring I can never again bring him back. So I took someone from you. It's only fair."

A familiar feeling stole over Damaris, igniting her blood like liquid fire as warmth flickered over her skin. The cold and the rain did not matter. Heat flooded her, a fiery rage kindling to life, a fury so intense that she had last felt one night, standing over a little boy, as the smoldering ruins of a village burned around her.

She didn't know what she intended to say to Galatea, if anything, but all that came out was a roar of fury. This time, she didn't bother trying to control her emotions. They were more than a fuel to her fire now. They begged to be released, to be given control, and she let them, releasing the tenuous hold she had left. Her vision became bathed completely in red, her eyes glowing solid scarlet, and she saw a flicker of fear cross Galatea's features.

She was a fire wind, the flames themselves, and she exploded.

The Flame Guardian lunged forward, her lips peeled back over her fangs, feeling flames burst to life over her coat.

The forest shook and reverberated with the explosions of the fire she summoned, sending everything she had at Galatea, her only intention to burn and destroy until there was nothing left.

The sorceress sprang back, calling upon the darkness to create a shield in front of her. The flames crashed against the barrier and though it held for now, Galatea was being forced back, away from the Gate and away from Felix and Sara.

Galatea called upon the wind spirit for aid and Azuma descended below the forest canopy, coming to hover just above his mistress. The dragon beat his wings, lashing Damaris with wind, but neither it, nor the rain, could extinguish her fire now.

The wind spirit's protection prevented Damaris from reaching Galatea, but even though they couldn't harm each other, it felt good to be able to lash out. To watch the flames flicker and dance, and Azuma's futile attempts to put them out.

At last, the flames burst against the shield one last time. It flickered and went out. Galatea did not conjure another one, unable to summon the energy. Baring her teeth, Damaris closed in for the kill, but she never got the chance.

Azuma threw back his head and shrieked. Lightning arced down from the sky, reflecting off his golden scales, as he rose higher into the air, pumping his wings. The gray sky was lit up almost constantly as more streaks of lightning shot across it. The wind died suddenly, cutting out, only to begin again, swirling around Galatea's legs.

Galatea raised her arms in front of her face to shield herself from the wind, her braid whipping around her head wildly. Azuma flexed his silver claws, gazing down as darkness continued to leak from his golden glowing eyes. He looked down at the sorceress trapped within the vortex of swirling air.

Then the wind spirit folded his wings and plummeted down toward her, jaws spread wide.

Sand began to spin around Galatea, lashing at her, becoming thicker as more and more was conjured, swirling up around her, until it had hidden her from view as the wind spirit dove. Damaris could not see the sorceress within, but a scream rang out above the wind.

Damaris flinched as blood splattered her.

A moment later, the wind dispersed, the whirlwind evaporating like a sigh, leaves settling back to the ground. Galatea and Azuma were gone. All that remained of the sorceress were bones, stripped bare of flesh and sinew and even armor. The sand had stripped it all away, leaving only bone behind.

A single, unenchanted, broken sword lay beside the bones in the pile of sand.

The few leaves that remained on the branches overhead rustled gently as a brief breeze stirred them, the forest seeming to sigh in relief.

The lightning flashing overhead had ceased. A final rumble of thunder sounded. The rain, which had been pouring nonstop, slowed to a gentle trickle.

Around her, soldiers wrestled with the remnants of Galatea's army, now made up of only fire wolves, but they were already being pushed back, further from the Gate. The undead had collapsed, the life leeching out of them now that the one who had brought them to life was dead herself.

The sounds of conflict faded away, a heavy silence hanging over the forest.

Damaris looked down at the pile of bones, her rage fading. The wind spirit had made the sorceress powerful indeed. But even she did not have the strength to keep a hold on that power for so long. Galatea had gone beyond her limit, trying to use more magic than she was able and it had killed her.

Azuma had seized his chance and broken free.

She should have known better than to think she could control the wind. It was a fitting end.

It was over. They had protected the Gates, but at what cost?

With a heavy heart, Damaris turned back toward where Felix lay.

***

Sara closed her eyes and felt her magic respond the moment she reached for it. Light flared beneath her fingers and rose up around her until she and Felix were both surrounded by its radiance. He had fallen unconscious, but as long as he wasn't dead, there was still hope. Sara winced as excruciating pain ripped through her as her magic was torn away, every nerve ending on fire. But she did not cry out or stop the spell.

The pain was intense, far worse than anything she had ever experienced before. It was as if her very essence was being pulled from her and Sara had a fleeting thought that this might kill her.

She gritted her teeth and reached out, gripping Pharus. The steel was hard beneath her fingers, anchoring her, the sword lending its power to her own.

And then it was done, the light flaring beneath her hand in a blinding glow and vanishing completely.

Sara collapsed to the ground beside Felix, the edges of her vision turning dark.

But she was alive. When her vision cleared and she sat up, she saw Damaris standing beside them, peering down anxiously at Felix. The unicorn's white coat was spattered with blood.

Felix did not move. He remained motionless, still pale as death. There was no longer any sign of the blood or his wounds. Sara felt for a pulse, her own heart seizing as she felt nothing.

For a second, she feared that the spell hadn't worked. That even after all that, she still wasn't strong enough and that she had paid a high price for ultimately nothing.

And then she felt his pulse beneath her fingers, strong and steady. She jumped, startled, as he suddenly gasped in a deep breath of air, his back arching, green eyes flying open.

Felix glanced around, looking bewildered. "What happened?"

"I healed you," Sara murmured, hardly daring to believe that it had worked herself.

He sat up slightly, looking down at where the wound had been. There was no sign it had ever been there at all. Not even a scar.

Realization dawned in his eyes. "You—you didn't. Tell me you didn't give up your magic for me…"

Sara felt for her magic. In the past, it had always been there, but reluctant, fighting her all the way. Recently, it had nearly surged to the surface, eager to be used. But in every case, she had sensed it there. Now she felt nothing at all.

It truly was gone.

She had known the cost and the risks, but still, the knowledge saddened her. She had given it up for something far more important, but she would still miss what had become a part of her. What had always, in a way, been a part of her, even when she hadn't known it.

"Why?" Felix whispered, seeing her expression.

She looked at him and hot tears suddenly burned her eyes, the mingled fear and relief too much to contain. He had nearly died and she'd thought she had lost him. But he was here. Whole. Alive.

"Because I love you." She threw her arms around him in a hug, knocking him backward in surprise, her emotions overwhelming her. She had been so afraid that he would die, despite her best efforts. He leaned back, supporting himself on his forearms. "I thought you were going to die," she murmured, releasing him. "I had to do something. What good is having all this power if you can't use it to save the ones you love?"

And then she was leaning in close, pressing her lips to his. Sara felt Felix tense at first, out of surprise, but then he relaxed, melting against her, kissing her back. His lips were warm and the whiskers on his chin tickled her gently. Sara kissed him as if she were suffocating and he was a breath of fresh air, not caring if anyone saw them.

At some point, Damaris wandered away, giving them privacy. Sara pulled back, leaning her forehead against Felix's, feeling the solidity of his body against hers, the way he smelled of leather and horses and the woods. His warmth and steadiness, the heartbeat she could feel beneath her hand on his chest. She reached out, touching his face where the scars once were.

She could think about the loss of her magic later and what she planned to do now without it. For now, she wanted to enjoy this moment.

Alive. They were both alive.

And the Gate still stood.

24

They later learned that the Water Gate hadn't been destroyed after all, which only added to the overall sense of relief. The immediate aftermath of the battle was to get the wounded healed first. Sara helped those she could, tying bandages and helping escort them to a healer, but once she handed them off to Serai or her assistants, she had to step back and admit there was nothing else for her to do.

Her training to be a healer had paid off when she needed it most, but there was no longer a need for it now. She watched Serai work, the knowledge bittersweet.

The once-beautiful Enchanted Forest was now singed, the trees leafless and a great many of them toppled over. But in the darkness, the plants that remained still glowed with bioluminescent light and the small floating orbs of light still hung in the air.

Damaris assured them that the forest would recover in time. The final two Gates hadn't been destroyed and that was what mattered or the story would have been very different. And as for the Gates that had been lost, perhaps they, too, would one day recover.

Iceland remained much the same as always, as did the desert. They were already inhospitable lands even before the destruction of their Gates. Even Malenwar wasn't a lost cause. As devastating as the destruction of the city had been, it had only fallen a little over fifty years ago. In the grand scheme of things, that wasn't all that long ago—even though it very much felt like it to Sara.

A memorial service was held for those who had valiantly given their lives in defense of Wysteria. To Damaris's relief, Cassius made a full recovery, his strength slowly returning and with it, his magic.

The last of Galatea's wolves had been dealt with. Such creatures had never been meant to dwell in Wysteria and for the first time in so long, they were once more free of them. Azuma hadn't been seen since, having vanished after Galatea's death.

Damaris approached Sheba afterward, wanting to know her opinion. Had the wind spirit faded from their realm as his siblings had so long ago, after being subjugated by Rehan?

Sheba didn't think so. "I think he's returned to the desert. But until we see him, we'll never know. After all the destruction Galatea caused through him, he might have left this realm, but I hope not."

Damaris hoped not as well. Azuma was a part of the desert culture and to lose part of that, after everything else that had been lost, would be a shame.

"He was fighting her the entire time," Sheba added. "He let her think, for a while, that she had complete control over him, biding his time. And then when she overextended herself, he saw his chance and took it."

"A fitting end," Damaris agreed. "Undone by her own arrogance."

Damaris nodded to Sheba and then moved on. Empress was sitting not far away, with the handful of dragons that had survived. Out of all of them, leave it to Empress to somehow make it out alive.

Empress shifted uncomfortably as Damaris approached. "Have we redeemed ourselves to your satisfaction?"

Damaris wasn't sure the dragons would ever truly redeem themselves. She couldn't forget the fact that they refused to pick a side and then when they had, they had chosen Galatea. They had attacked her in the swamp and acted as a distraction for Galatea, ultimately allowing the sorceress to kill Lylla.

No, she wasn't sure she could ever forgive them for that. Lylla would have found it in her heart to forgive and so Damaris supposed she should try. Even if she managed it, she could never forget what they'd done. They were wily and not to be trusted and it would be well to remember that.

"As well as could be expected," she said grudgingly. "What will you do now?"

Empress exhaled in relief. "Return to Iceland, I expect. With the greatest respect, I want nothing more to do with any of you for a long while. This peace was hard-won. We should enjoy it."

Damaris inclined her head. "Then I bid you farewell for the time being."

Personally, she was pleased to see the dragons go. They would have much to answer for if the war hadn't cost them so much already. Their numbers had been decimated and now there were only a few of them left. It would take them a long time to recover, and on top of the civil war that had ravaged their population previously, Damaris supposed that was punishment enough.

"But Empress," she added as the dragon began to walk away.

Empress paused, glancing over her shoulder, long neck curved.

"I won't be so lenient next time."

She wasn't above showing mercy, but she wouldn't allow the dragons to play them all for fools again. And Empress knew it.

"May there never be a next time."

***

Felix found Sara sitting in the back garden where he had first confessed his feelings to her. In the two days that had passed since the battle, she had seemed to avoid the others. She never shied away from his presence, but he could tell she had wanted some time alone to gather her thoughts.

He couldn't blame her. What do you even say to someone who gave up the entirety of their power to save you, knowing you owed them your life and the cost they had paid?

It was strange, knowing he could look at himself in the mirror now and not have to worry about flinching at what he saw there. The skin where the scars had been was smooth, with no sign that they had ever been there at all. Venryk's mark on him had truly been erased. The weight that he hadn't even known he carried around with him was gone too, his steps lighter.

Felix approached warily, sitting on the stone bench beside her, the wisteria surrounding them. He wasn't sure what to say to her, their relationship suddenly feeling uncertain. She had said that she loved him, that was true, but there was no getting around the debt he owed her.

"How do you feel?" he ventured.

She shrugged. "Still trying to get used to it."

Felix had no idea what it was like to be a Guardian. He had only ever been able to control one element, but that magic had been with him since birth, a part of him even when he couldn't use it. He had no idea what it must be like to have no magic at all, especially in her case, having had it once.

"I'm sorry," he said.

Sara turned to him. "For what?"

"You were a Light Guardian. You had the potential to become more powerful than anyone else, once you'd mastered all the secondary elements. And you gave that up for me."

She frowned. "I wanted to. You didn't make me."

"I know. But the fact remains that you saved my life and there's no way I can ever repay you."

"You don't have to. The fact that you're here, alive, is all I want." She reached out, touching the place where the scars had been. "My magic was given to me for a reason. I didn't know what that reason was, but it all led to that moment, for that purpose."

***

Sara knew in her bones that she was right. Her magic had fought her at nearly every step of the way, only to come to her aid when she needed it most. At the end, there had been no resistance, as if her magic had been given to her for that very reason.

She looked at Felix, taking in his appearance. She had never thought him unattractive, even with the scars marring his features, but with them gone, he was very much an elf, with flawless skin and a strong, chiseled jawline.

She felt her face heat as she took him in, the crimson hair, long, curved ears, deep emerald green eyes, and the freckles that danced across his cheeks and the bridge of his nose.

He was studying her in much the same way. "What are you going to do now?" he whispered.

Sara sighed. She hadn't thought about the future when she had acted. She had thought about only one thing and that was to save him. Even as she knew the cost in the back of her mind, she hadn't truly considered it.

"I don't know."

She had planned to train to become a Guardian and be assigned to Professor Lawrence's Gate because she had believed that was what he would have wanted and because she felt partially responsible for his death.

After Lawrence's Gate had been destroyed, she had taken on healing, but both paths were denied to her now. Without her magic, she could neither heal nor protect a Gate. Her dad had asked her what she wanted to do with her life and she'd thought she had her answer. All of her carefully laid plans had crumbled to pieces.

She could always do as her father suggested and go to college, maybe for photography, maybe to become a professor herself. Lylla had helped her come to terms with her grief and accept the reality of her mother's loss. That didn't mean it hurt any less, but she felt that she could finally try and pick up a camera again.

That had been the thing that they enjoyed most together, but after her mom died, Sara had lost all passion and desire for it. Instead of bringing joy, it only served to remind her of everything she had lost and would never get back.

But Lylla had made her see it in a different way. Her mother would have wanted her to pursue photography and make something of it. She wouldn't have wanted her to give up and now, Sara saw it not as something that reminded her of the pain, but of the joy they had shared together and a way to honor her mother's memory.

She spoke the idea aloud. "Maybe I'll take up photography again."

Felix put his arm around her. "You have time to think about it. You don't have to decide right now. But whatever you do, you know you'll have my full support."

Gosh, what had she ever done to deserve him? Sara leaned into him, grateful that she had sacrificed her magic. She refused to lose him, too. What good would her magic have done if she had lost another person that she loved? What comfort or joy would it have brought?

Some of her happiness dimmed as she thought of the bigger, more immediate problem facing her. With the war over, the Gates safe, and Galatea gone, there was nothing to stop her from returning home. She wasn't needed in Wysteria the way she had been.

But that would mean facing her dad and the thought made her feel physically ill.

"What?" Felix asked, sensing her mood.

Sara sighed, laying a hand on his knee. "What am I gonna tell my dad?"

Felix had been there during that last confrontation and so she didn't have to explain what she meant to him.

"The truth."

As if it were that simple. "What if he…what if he doesn't want to see me again?"

"Sara, your dad only acted out of love for you. He'll probably just be relieved you're alive. You'll have to face him eventually. He deserves to know."

"I wish I felt braver."

Felix chuckled. "I think you're plenty brave enough. You didn't see what I saw. A girl, standing alone, surrounded by glowing light, holding a white sword, facing down a sorceress."

Sara made a face. "That was easy compared to facing my dad."

Felix laughed and Sara felt warmth spread through her. She loved making him laugh. And maybe he had a point. Surely facing Galatea was the harder of the two.

Thinking of the two sides of her life caused another doubt to creep in. "Can we still be together?" she asked suddenly. "I'm not a Guardian anymore. You're an elf and I'm a human."

A human with no magic. A human who wasn't allowed in Wysteria. Would she have to choose between both of her lives, as her dad had said she would? Now that her role in all this was finished, would she have to leave Wysteria behind?

Would she have to leave him behind? Surely not after everything...

"Of course we can. You *were* a Guardian, after all. It's not like you never were. You'll have to ask Damaris, but I can't see why she wouldn't be okay with it. If she's not, I'll have a talk with her." He leaned his chin against her forehead. "You belong here, Sara. And we deserve a little happiness, don't you think?"

"Yes," Sara whispered. "Yes, we do."

She would talk to Damaris, but there was something else she needed to do first.

***

Felix opened the door to the queen's chambers and stepped inside. "You wanted to see me?"

Damaris had returned to her human form, but instead of a dress, she wore a crimson halter top, black pants, and sandals.

"I wanted to tell you that when I saw what Galatea had done, I wanted to heal you myself. I would have, if Sara hadn't gotten there first. I didn't want to break my promise to your mother…"

She was willing to forsake all of her magic for you. The idea of the most powerful Guardian to ever live giving up her power was almost too much to fathom. Not only was the most powerful Guardian willing to sacrifice her power to save him, the one with the potential to become the most powerful had also been willing—more than willing.

Felix felt overwhelmed, knowing that he meant so much to two different people. He couldn't remember ever feeling more loved than he did in that moment.

"You never did," he told her, "break your promise. I think it worked out better this way. Who would have taken over as leader if you had given up all your magic?"

Damaris looked away. "I've no idea. In that moment, I didn't really care. But yes, perhaps it's better this way. I shall have to thank her." She turned back to face him. "But what I really wanted to say was that I'm proud of you. You're free of the curse and you did it without me."

Felix felt himself flush with pride at her praise. "Thank you."

"You've proven what I've known all along. You're hardly the small boy I rescued all those years ago. You've become a man. You don't need me to look out for you anymore."

The words made him feel a mixture of both pride and regret. Their relationship was different now. It had changed and would never again be what it once was.

Much like Wysteria itself.

***

Mayfair appeared much as it always had when Sara crossed back over onto Earth. The gas station was still just as damaged, no one having bothered to make any substantial repairs. On the other side of the Gates, so much had changed while the townspeople here remained oblivious, going about their daily lives.

She had brought Pharus with her. The sword still hummed with magic, seemingly no different from the moment it had been given to her. She marveled silently at the sheer power it contained. Though her own magic was gone, the magic it contained would allow her to open the Gates and pass through without any assistance.

Sara sighed and began the walk home, clutching the sword for courage. She wasn't sure if she would find her dad at home or if he had decided to continue working as a way to distract himself. Come to that, she couldn't even remember what day it was. Was it one of his days off? She couldn't look at her phone and check; she had left it behind in the house before she had left, being unable to use it in Wysteria.

The door was unlocked when she turned the knob and she had her answer. It wouldn't be unlocked if he were away. Taking in a deep breath, heart thrumming in her chest, she opened the door and stepped inside the living room.

Her dad was sitting on the couch, but he rose to his feet as she entered. For a moment, they stared at each other, as if he hardly dared to believe she was really there. Sara felt like she should say something, but where to begin? An apology, probably, but her throat wouldn't work.

And then he was crossing the room, throwing his arms around her and pulling her close, the strength of his grip nearly crushing.

Sara tensed in shock and finally found her voice. "Y— you're not mad?"

Her dad released her and stepped back, looking her over, hands on her shoulders. "Of course I'm mad, but you're here! This whole time, I didn't know if you were alive or dead, if you were coming back, or if I'd ever see you again. You have no idea how worried I was!"

"I'm sorry," she murmured, feeling a pang of guilt. "I'm all right. I'm not hurt. And you don't have to worry anymore. The danger's over. Galatea's dead."

Setting Pharus aside, she sat down on the couch beside him as she explained why she hadn't come back—how Lylla had saved her and then been killed in the process. He stiffened as she described how close she had come to being killed but she knew she could leave nothing out. Felix was right; he deserved the truth. He deserved to know what had happened and why she had done what she had, and for that, she had to tell him everything.

She told him how Damaris had been appointed queen and both Gates nearly destroyed before the end, how Galatea had been killed by the wind spirit she had tried to tame, and ended with her giving up her magic to save Felix's life.

Sara had been unsure at first whether to tell him about the loss of her magic, worried he might see that as reason not to return to Wysteria, even though the danger had passed. But in the end, she told him because she had thought her future lay in becoming a Guardian and protecting one of the Gates, as Professor Lawrence had. Without magic, that path was no longer available to her and she would need to think of a different plan.

Her father was silent for a long time, digesting what she had said. When he spoke, his words surprised her. "Your mother would be proud of you," he said softly. "You're so much like her, you know."

Sara swallowed, her throat suddenly tight.

"I'd like to still go back," she murmured. "But I think you're right about college."

An idea was forming, which would allow her to tread both paths, as she had once considered. But she would have to ask Damaris first whether or not it would be allowed. The gas station still marked the location of the Lightning Gate, which still stood. She was no longer a Guardian and so the task of protecting it couldn't fall to her, and yet, there was no one else on this side who could do it.

Convincing the queen was one thing. Convincing her father was another.

Her dad sighed. "I'm glad to hear it. What did you have in mind?"

But Sara hesitated. "Are you still mad?"

"No. Everything's forgiven. But I'm afraid you are very much grounded."

***

Sara returned to Wysteria the next morning, with Pharus's assistance. She hadn't intended to go so early, but she found she couldn't wait any longer.

Yesterday evening, after the talk with her father had ended, she had visited Nadia and Max, who were both relieved to see her. Nadia had shrieked upon seeing her and wrapped her in a tight hug. They, too, hadn't known whether she was alive or dead on the other side or what might be happening.

Sara assured them she was fine and that the danger was over. They no longer had to worry about the town being destroyed. She even brought Pharus to show them, knowing Max would geek out over the sword.

"You *fought* with this?" Nadia asked, eyes goggling. "It's so heavy."

"Badass," Max said, nodding approvingly.

After the sword was put away, she shared with them her plans to go to college and Nadia was ecstatic.

"It'll be just like old times!" she exclaimed. "The three of us, all going together."

In such a small town, there was only one real choice to make when it came to colleges and that was the one in the next town over, where Professor Lawrence had taught.

Though they would all be studying different things—and Sara wasn't decided yet—Nadia was right that they would get to see each other. Sara had worried that their paths were diverging, taking the three of them in different directions. But that had been when she was still a Guardian, the path laid out before her very different from theirs.

The time may still come when they would all go their separate ways. Life had a funny way of doing that. But for now, Sara would enjoy it for what it was. Life was too short to do anything less.

"Oh," Nadia added. "You've simply *got* to introduce me to this boyfriend of yours. A guy worth giving up magic for?" She fanned her face dramatically. "Talk about romantic."

Sara hit her on the arm, blushing to the roots of her hair, but she promised she'd see what she could do.

Damaris was in her quarters when Sara arrived. The interior of the room that had once belonged to Lylla had been unchanged in appearance. The décor didn't really suit the Flame Guardian at all, but Sara wasn't sure what would, and she supposed Damaris had wanted to keep it the same to honor the one who had come before.

"Am I interrupting anything?" Sara asked as she entered. The queen was alone in the room and didn't appear busy.

"No. I was just enjoying a moment of solitude before I go out. It gets to you after a while and you need time to yourself."

Sara understood that and thought she would have felt much the same way if she were in Damaris's place.

"Was there something I could help you with?" Damaris prompted. "Or were you just hoping to talk? I'm not exactly known for my conversation skills, but I can try."

The queen smiled and Sara smiled back, clasping her hands in front of her, rubbing the skin of her wrist with her fingers. "I was just wondering if I would be allowed to stay in Wysteria, since I don't have magic anymore."

Damaris tilted her head. "And why wouldn't you be?"

"Well...I'm not a Guardian anymore. I'm just an ordinary human again."

The corner of Damaris's red lips turned up in a smile. "Sara, you never were nor ever will be just an ordinary human. Once a Guardian, always a Guardian. You fought beside us against Galatea, willing to give up your life and your magic for others. You're one of us and you always will be."

Sara felt her eyes water unexpectedly. "Thank you."

"However, since you no longer possess magic, I'm afraid your goal of being assigned to one of the Gates is no longer possible. Not that we have many Gates left to choose from anyway. I'm curious what you intend to do now."

"I was thinking more along the lines of honorary Guardianship," Sara replied and she told Damaris her plans.

***

Sara stood staring at the gas station convenience store. A tarp still stretched over the roof where it needed to be repaired. She felt a pang of sadness knowing that she would

335

never again come here and visit with Hank. It seemed wrong to think of it without him, to think of it as anything other than a gas station.

To think of it as being *hers*.

But when she looked at the building, she could imagine what the little house she planned to build would look like, the photography studio attached to it. The building had already been sold and a company was due at the end of the week to demolish the damaged gas station store. Damaris had assured her that the Gate would be unharmed by this, the wall of the building merely a physical representation of the invisible portal that existed between the worlds, and as long as Sara knew where it was, she was free to cross over.

Her dad had taken a lot of persuasion, but in the end, he'd agreed to help her buy the property.

It wouldn't be easy, but she would make it work.

And it would be all the more special knowing that, hidden within, was the Gate that started it all.

This was the Gate where it had all begun, over a year ago, and it seemed fitting that this was where Galatea's plans had all come to an end.

A lot of lives had been lost in the process. From the moment Galatea had returned after fifty years, Wysteria hadn't been the same and neither were its people. Even now, things were not the way they had once been. But they had emerged victorious and perhaps some good had come out of it after all.

Sara liked to think so. She liked to think that those who had been lost were smiling now, proud of what had been accomplished, and cheering them on even now. They had stood firm in the face of seemingly impossible odds and emerged victorious.

Don't lose hope, Lylla had said. And they hadn't.

"It will be beautiful. I can't wait to see it."

Sara turned to see Felix, standing behind her. Summer was rapidly drawing to an end and soon, she would be starting classes and they would have far less time together.

"I wish you didn't have to go," he said, as if reading her thoughts. "I wish you could stay longer. But I understand your decision and I'm glad your father approved."

"Getting him to agree to buy the place was the hardest part," Sara laughed. "I'll miss you, too. But I won't be staying on campus. I'll be commuting and that means I can come through the Gate whenever I have time."

"I'll hold you to that," he said, coming up behind her and putting his arms around her.

The two of them stood there for a moment, dreaming of what the future would be, and then he murmured, "I should get back."

"Yeah." She pulled away and turned to look up at him.

Felix reached out, hands encircling her waist, and leaned down, pressing his lips to hers. He purposely stalled a little—kissing her far longer than he needed to—and Sara let him.

"I'll see you later," he murmured when the kiss had ended. "I love you."

"I love you, too," she replied, reluctantly releasing him.

The last thing she saw was him glancing back over his shoulder for one more look, the afternoon sun landing on his crimson hair and turning it scarlet in places.

And then he stepped through the Gate and was gone.

Thank you for reading!

Thirteen years ago, I decided that my dream was to become a published author. I have since achieved that dream, but an author is nothing without their readers. So thank you, reader, for giving this book a chance.

If you enjoyed this book, it would mean the world to me if you would consider leaving a review. Reviews are essential for authors. They help our books get seen, they help our books get promoted, and they can be the difference between whether or not another reader decides to take a chance on a book.

While it may sound cheesy, you are literally helping make my dream come true. So thank you again for your support and happy reading!

ACKNOWLEDGEMENTS

Though writing is often a solitary endeavor, oftentimes there is a veritable small army behind the scenes, that help turn a story into a book. That is once again the case here.

Firstly, thank you to my mom, for believing in me, encouraging me, and reading this book who knows how many times. This won't be the first or the last time I say this, but I love you and your support means the world to me.

Thank you to Maw Maw, for also giving encouragement and love (even though I know you're waiting for those mysteries!). You, too, have probably read each of my stories too many times to count.

Thank you to Coco, whose artwork once again graces the cover of this book. You brought my girl, Damaris, to life in a way I never could have imagined and that exceeded all expectations.

Thank you to Rena for the cover design. I'm so grateful there are people like you out there, willing to help Indie authors bring their projects to life. I look forward to working with you in the future.

Thank you to Leah, Susan, Livie, Kelli, and Galen for your gracious help with both of these books. I am immensely grateful and humbled that you took time out of your busy days to step into Wysteria.

Thanks must also be extended to you, reader, for giving these books a chance. I am so touched by the support these two books have received and the love you have shown to my story, my world, and my characters. I look forward to being able to introduce you to many more along the way and to welcoming all the new readers I have yet to meet.

And once again, all glory to God, for giving me the ability to tell this story, the opportunity to share it with the world, and the stubbornness to see it through.

ABOUT THE AUTHOR

Rachel Terry grew up in a small town where nothing much ever happened, dreaming of grand adventures and far-away places, which she found between the pages of books. When not writing, she can be found reading, making YouTube videos, gaming with friends, or indulging in her love of history. She currently resides in the Midwest with her family and a cat named Crinkles.

Visit her online at: rachel-terry.com

YouTube: RachelTerryAuthor

Instagram: rterrywriter

Facebook: rachelterryauthor

LIGHTBRINGER

LIGHTBRINGER
The Guardians Duology Book 1

When an old wrong leads to war, one girl finds herself in
the middle of it all.